I0536741

Cardinal Points

Edge of Empire Series
World Turned Upside Down

Dory Codington

Dory's Historicals Press
doryshistoricals.com

Copyright © 2015 Dory Codington

ISBN: 978-0-9963226-1-4

Library of Congress Control Number: 2015915674

Published by DorysHistoricals Press, Newton, MA 02458

DorysHistoricals Press 2015

Second Edition

For My Sister

&

Those who won and those who lost

the American Revolution

Chapter 1

Jason gazed at the steeples and masts through the telescope. The watch in the rigging had spotted the town an hour ago, but he always looked for that first glimpse of land through his own tools. He had found rooms in the town the year before and was pleased to be returning. In front of him was a town of churches and ships, and of crooked streets that couldn't keep a name for more than a block at a time. It jutted into the harbor, connected to land by a spit so narrow that any storm or high tide made it another island in the island-dotted sea. And Jason understood the men and women who lived there. As in any port, the sea was the reason for their town, and for most employment within the town. Good years led to success, as more men were needed to build ships, man the ships and make sails, ropes and tar. Bad years led to failure; being out of work was a constant possibility and worry. Through good times and bad, however, the sea and the harbor were constants in their lives – as regular, and as important, as the four cardinal points on a seaman's compass.

Boston was built on its three tall hills – the 'tre mountain' that gave the land its first name, Tremont, one that only a few streets would retain. By the eighteenth century, as Boston passed its hundredth birthday, the town had become a center for trade. And by 1773 it was the busiest port in the English world west of Wales. Its origins explained the steeples, and deep roots of Puritanism and the Glorious Revolution ran through even the maritime/mercantile culture that had superceded them. Kings and Parliaments had spent a century ignoring Bostonians' striving for separation that began when James II's governor, Edmund Andros, was chased out of town by an angry mob, back in 1688. At each event or riot, Parliament had sent troops to control the town. Sometimes that had worked, but when they opened fire on March 5, 1770 it was a disaster, if not an actual massacre. But what everyone could agree on was that Parliament had no idea what to do about Boston.

Now, Jason was sailing into a town that was once again angry at limits that Parliament had placed on trade. Previous restrictions had been bad enough, having confined trade to British ports, which only encouraged smuggling throughout the empire. But although most of the taxes specified in the Townsend Act had been removed, the new limits, suggested by the East India Trading Company and imposed by its shareholders in Parliament, involved picking favored sellers from a list of merchants who were connected to the current governor by blood and friendship. Even Governor Hutchinson knew that other merchants would be angry enough to incite the famous Boston mobs, but with Parliament and the East India Company putting pressure on him to get the greatest profit for the company, the man felt trapped.

Jason left the *Chardon* anchored off Windmill Point to await the customs officials, and rowed himself to shore. He had sailed on the *Chardon* as first mate for three years, but he was leaving that security behind. She belonged to FitzSimmon Shipping, an enterprise created by his older brothers, Stephen and Thomas, the second and third sons of the Duke and Duchess of Chardon, the family home.

With the end of that contract, Jason realized that he had no roots in the world. Without the *Chardon*, the only home he could claim were two rented rooms in a small house on Beech Street. He had chosen Boston because the town offered opportunities not attached to family or loyalty. He loved his brothers, but was rankled that they had not promoted him. Moving on without them seemed to be the only option. He'd reached the conclusion that there was no reason to stand on ceremony waiting for their largesse. If his brothers were taking their time getting him a ship, and its captaincy, he was determined to learn what he could from every mariner willing to teach him.

His status as the son of aristocrats gave him cold comfort. There is nothing so superfluous as the fourth son of a duke. Jason had felt expendable for all of the fourteen years he had lived at home with his large family. Not unloved – his mother Elizabeth loved every one of her many children. She nursed each one herself, and saw to their educations and their happiness. But rules must be obeyed, and tradition dictated that only Robert, the eldest son, could inherit. Tradition also dictated that a second son had value as the spare; at least till the first married and spawned healthy sons. That was something Robert and his wife had done as easily as his parents, and while they were still quite young. That same tradition also ruled that daughters needed dowries to get them properly launched in life, and younger sons fended for themselves. The Navy, Army, law or the ministry were all acceptable options, but he had followed a rebel uncle to sea as a merchant seaman.

Worried that his younger brothers would feel the crisis as keenly as he did, Jason had attempted to instill a sense of worth, and a spirit of creativity and adventure, into them, as well as the need for a profession. Jason was pleased that John and William had never suffered through the crises that he had endured before leaving home completely. The next brother, John had chosen the Army, and an unusual hobby of designing ships Like himself, he must have yearned for the sea, at least occasionally. Now John was in the infantry – last heard, he was in the 23rd Regiment of Foot, and Jason had no idea where in the empire he was stationed. William, the sixth boy and youngest, was at university and happily accepting his life as a scholar. Anne and Janet, his younger sisters, were lively and beautiful, at least to a doting brother. He assumed that with their charm and large dowries, they would easily marry well.

Jason walked from the harbor up Summer Street to Orange, Newbury, or whatever they were calling Boston's long street these days. Solid earth under his feet lifted his spirits, as did the freedom of owning nothing but his skills and his tools. As well, he felt fortunate to have a meeting with a Boston merchant in need of a navigator, scheduled first thing this morning. Matthew Goodiel was rumored to be one of the best, and richest. Jason had high hopes.

Oona hid her packages and climbed the stairs to watch the ships come in with the tide. It was a twice daily ritual, the shallow waters keeping ships in channels at anything but the highest tides. It wasn't often that she allowed herself the luxury of communing with the grasshopper weathervane on the top of Boston's most famous market. But this morning the light was extraordinary, with just the right amount of warm air creating a mist and fog that swirled around the docks. The tip of Faneuil Hall was her favorite place, and the weathervane her most constant friend. She took her collapsible telescope from her pocket and peered over the walls of the tower at the ships sailing toward the town.

She wasn't sure if she had ever watched the fishing fleet in her childhood, but since arriving in Boston at ten, she had watched ships arrive and leave whenever she had the chance. She didn't know what had possessed her to put her spyglass in her pocket before she left for her errands. Maybe the day had just called to her. She watched for a while, mesmerized by the steady motion of the sailing ships. Then, realizing that she would be late to buy eggs at Mary Channing's if she did not hurry, she fairly flew down the stairs, grabbed her things and headed back to Fort Hill and home.

Jason stepped onto the busy street. He turned left toward Fort Hill and was startled by the clot of icy mud that hit him in the chest. It seemed too early in the day to be startled. He jumped out of the way and ducked behind a brick wall. He was fortunate that there was no hard projectile like a rock or ice ball involved. It was rumored that Boston's mobs were famous for the use of such things. He was not injured and did not even feel targeted, since no one knew him or cared about his comings or goings. But he could not help being curious, since such things did not often fly through the air on their own.

He plopped on the hard ground and waited a moment to gather his wits. It had been a short and productive morning talking shipping and navigation with the man he hoped would be his new employer. Matthew Goodiel was a merchant with a reputation for paying good money to build, staff, and maintain fast ships. Just the sort of man Jason would pick for his next master, if Mr. Goodiel chose him.

He rose onto his heels, staying just out of sight, in shadow and behind the low brick wall of the garden. He peeked over the wall and off to his left, on Oliver Street, was a group of young people singling out one young woman. They were yelling and throwing things at her, among them clots of mud and dirty melting snow. The girl was staying well away from the worst of it, but burdened with a bundle and heavy skirts she held one-handed away from the muddy street, plenty of the projectiles were hitting the blue silk – covering the gown with a gray-brown dusting.

The girl was young and pretty, certainly no more than twenty, and the same age as her assailants. Her long dark hair had escaped cap, hood and pins. It was dancing loose in the wind, down her back and around her face. From his spot, Jason could not see her clearly, but he got a strong impression of clear pale skin and bright blue eyes. He stood to get a better look, but the whole crowd had moved past him, up the hill. He stared after them, not sure what he had just witnessed. Not only was he now terribly curious about Boston's famous street mobs, but he sincerely hoped that in the near future he would have a chance to see if the quick glimpses of her extraordinary beauty would be proven correct.

Oona's early morning had left her time to collect the eggs on the way back home. Now she was tired and ready for her breakfast and a cup of coffee, if Mrs. Prince had any left in the pot. She trudged up Oliver Street, with her packages of fresh bread, cheese for lunch, a half a dozen eggs, and the same number of lemons. Just below her house she heard an unpleasantly familiar voice call out to her.

"Oona?" Lawrence called. "You're wearing that pretty blue gown again! Why don't you wear homespun and support the agreement?"

"Lawrence!" Oona put her bundles down and spread out her cloak, rolling the food into the thick wool as she spoke. "I get Mrs. Goodiel's castoffs for free, and you want me to spend my pennies on homespun? You're daft." She picked up her bundle of food and cloak, and started to run.

It was very cold, and she wanted to put her cloak back on, but she had had this conversation with her peers before, and she knew what to expect next. She wanted to get into Cook's warm kitchen quickly, so she picked up her pace. She was almost faster than the ignorant fools chasing her and throwing mud at her.

Being poor themselves, they should have understood her dilemma, but they were so convinced they were right about not wearing taxed silks and lace that they lost sight of her situation. Didn't they understand that she hadn't coin for new, whether it was homespun or imported? Her gowns were reworked; years-old and free to her. Not that the lot of foolish howlers cared.

Her mistress, Anne Goodiel, might treat her like an overworked servant, but she wanted Oona to wear pretty gowns, even while doing dirty chores. It was a point of pride with her that she gave her servant the outmoded gowns to make over. She liked to show off Oona's skill with a needle. After all, Oona had trained with the best dressmaker in town, and it had long been part of her chores to make simple gowns for her mistress and her two daughters. Oona liked fine clothes and had no shame in her skills at remaking a well-designed gown. At least she had liked it until her friends started throwing mud and clots of dirt at her.

Oona turned to the mob of screaming friends, still below her on the hill. She lifted her chin to stare them down and giving them an open grin as she escaped into the safety of the walled kitchen garden. She shook off the dust and realized that the damage was not so bad, and there was no need to change out of the blue jacquard. Luckily, the patterned weave hid whatever mud remained, and all she'd intended to do after breakfast was dust the shelves on the first floor and sit and read her new book, and then learn to use her new octant – two things she had actually wanted, and that she had bought with her few saved pennies.

Jason spent his day resting and enjoying a day off. After dinner at a public house on Essex Street, he walked back to the center of town. There, the mood was charged, as though there was lightning flashing in the air, although there was no storm. Curious at the large crowds, he followed a mass of people to the square in front of the large brick church on the corner of Milk Street. The crowd had moved into the square from a meeting at Faneuil Hall, and now gathered in front of the Old South Meeting House. It was enormous, large enough so that it contained nearly every adult in the town. It was also very quiet. Every man, woman, and young person who had not been lucky enough to get a seat inside on this cold damp night stood at the big windows, straining to hear the speeches. Occasionally the voices inside would make a point or call for a vote, then loud "huzzahs!" and "fies!" would pour from the windows.

It was a typical December night on the New England coast. Jason pulled his collar closer, but didn't mind. Coming from the north of England, he sort of liked it, but others found the freezing drizzle, constant rain, snow, cold and fog to be unpleasant. He shuffled his feet when the crowd moved, and listened. The arguments had been going on all week, and the crowds were here because of a shipment of East India Company tea – that small leaf, from a small plant, grown very far away, taxed by Parliament, and desired by nearly everyone. And held for ransom, it seemed, on three ships, the *Dartmouth*, the *Eleanor* and the *Beaver* – ships docked, but not yet passed by the customs men.

The three were loaded with legal tea, and their large cargo was ready to offload. The owners, who well understood the mood of the town, were prepared to sell cheap, just to maintain order, and give Parliament their bitty tax. But the mood of the town said that the ships should sail away with their cargo untouched.

The arguments in the Meeting House had to be finished this night because the ships had been docked for weeks, and tomorrow the customs men could legally seize the tea and sell it in the shops. What those same customs men did not know was that among Jason's possessions on the *Chardon,* anchored just off Windmill Point, was a lovely little cargo of tea from Holland. Of course, his was not legal tea, smuggled as it was, and then seized as a prize from a French merchantman.

So, as far as the East India Company and their cronies were concerned, his tea, nicely hidden in wine casks, was to rot onboard. The only way he would be allowed to bring his tea into town was to smuggle it in on a dark night. Now, the governor, with his stubborn insistence that the captains of the three tea ships not return to London with their cargo, had made the town too "hot" to sell any tea, even good quality Chinese tea, carefully smuggled.

It was unlike Jason to stand and listen to political discussions. Generally, he did not concern himself with Parliament and their doings. His brothers did that for him. He hadn't heard from either of them in a while, and there wasn't time at the present to get their intellectual, reasoned, Parliamentarian reading on the situation concerning the Boston tea. Governor Hutchinson was about to make his decision, and no doubt it would be to land the tea. The governor knew the mood of the town, but Thomas Hutchinson had never listened to the desires of his fellows, and he was not starting now.

It seemed odd, and yet not, to find himself outside

Old South, with the young men of Boston. He had been a sailor since he was fourteen, and maybe he had always wanted to defy authority and carefully, methodically, throw cargo off a ship into a harbor. Bostonians' natural aversion to taxes and restraint of trade might be giving him a unique chance to fulfill that dream, and take part in what was sure to become an important moment in history, something rare in any life.

Jason knew he could not open his mouth to speak. He occasionally was able to sound like a lowly seaman, but he could never sound American. The handicap had never bothered him, and the last times he had stayed in Boston, it had not mattered. But tonight he might sound like a spy, and he was not in the mood to follow the tea into the cold, wet harbor.

After word came from the governor to land the tea, the crowd broke up. Slowly, small groups moved into taverns and parlors around the plaza. He found himself with a group walking up School Street to the *Cromwell's Head Tavern*. There, a dark-haired girl, her own hat low on her head almost hiding her face, was distributing feathers and applying black war paint and burnt cork patches to disguise the participants.

The girl stuck a feather into his knit cap and drew some dark lines on his face. Until that moment, Jason had not been sure if he would accompany the men down to the harbor. He ran his fingers over the feather. "Miss," he asked, "I hate to whine, but do you have a longer turkey feather?" The girl pulled out his feather, grabbed a longer, more colorful one from the table, and replaced it. "Oh, thank you, Miss. If I am to commit treason, I believe it had best be done with aplomb." He spoke low so that only she could hear. "You agree, of course?"

She nodded quickly, and offered a quick grin in

assent. She seemed such a pleasant person, smiling at the men and laughing with the other girls, all very secretive, quiet with a low joy. Then, suddenly, she put her hands on his shoulders, leaned back, and looked up to inspect her work. Jason knew that revelry was probably inappropriate, but she was so pretty, and he had been at sea an awful long time. So, he put his hands on her waist in response to hers on his shoulders, and lifted her up – his arms outstretched – and kissed her. It was a quick public kiss, but it seemed to startle her above proportion.

She opened her eyes wide and looked stunned, but not unhappy. He put her down very gently, back on the floor of the small tavern. He stepped back and looked down to smile at his pretty helper. At the same moment he got an elbow in the side, while someone from the other side shouted at him: "No one kisses Oona!" That was foolish; she was a beautiful girl, and beautiful girls deserved to be kissed – especially this one. Her eyes, lit by the dim candlelight, sparkled back at him in shades of blue and violet.

Oona. Feeling distracted from that simple touch, he wondered where such a beauty hid herself so as never to be kissed. He had never seen eyes so nearly the shade of violets and sapphires. If the crowd had not been so restless, angry, and ready to head down to the harbor, he might have stayed and talked to her. He took an extra moment to stare back as the crowd moved off. If the rest of her matched her face and eyes, she was probably married or promised. He swore off pretty violet-eyed ladies, and headed down to the harbor with the moving crowd. He moved into the dark December night, but he imagined the girl in the tavern applying war paint and pushing feathers into the cap of the next lucky man.

Oona had her own ideas about freedom, both her own and America's. Years of servitude in a town yearning for its right to independent self-government had made her think long and hard about the words used around her. The minister at New South preached that children and servants should be grateful for their status, and for their parents and masters who cared for them. Yet, at the same time, those same ministers preached in favor of non-importation, and refusal to purchase Britain's taxed goods, and for America's right to representation in the Houses of Parliament.

"No taxation without representation," Mr. Otis had said in court and at meetings. She had heard men call out those words as they drank toasts at the *King's Mount Tavern*. And those same words reverberated through the town meetings, and meetings of the body, to which even she had a right to come and listen. Other words crept in, too. Samuel Adams, never shy about how he felt, called for total freedom from Britain, and complete separation from the crown.

Oona had thought that freedom from servitude sounded like a good idea. Tonight, she had been willing to participate in an event that would anger the governor and Parliament, and might well cause them to act against the town. She understood that sometimes action was so important that the consequences needed to be endured.

She had run away once when she was twelve. The beating she received when she was found had not been that bad. It was probably worth those few hours of freedom. Those hours had been sweet, but she had also been scared. She'd had nowhere *to* run, no family to return to – none that she knew of, and certainly none in America. So, all in all, she had been relieved to be sent back. It was good to be safe.

She decided that afternoon, nearly eight years ago,

that freedom and independence were things best dealt with when they presented themselves for real, not in a child's fantasy. She'd put away her rebellious spirit, and pushed down all attempts at self-discovery. She was a servant, indentured for ten years, and until those ten years were over, she would not try to discover what it meant to be Oona in the world. Instead, she studied and learned what she needed to do in order to survive until her indenture ended on May 25, 1774. And what she needed to do most of all was to let nothing, and no one, prolong her length of service.

She had researched it when she was fifteen. At the time, she had been staying in the town of Milton with her mistress, Anne Goodiel, and her daughters. Elisha Appleton, Anne's brother-in-law, was an attorney who seemed kind and sympathetic. At breakfast one morning, she summoned the nerve to ask him about herself.

"Mr. Appleton?" Oona carried a coffee pot in one hand and hot water for the tea service in the other, "would you like more coffee, tea?"

"No, thank you, Oona. Girl," – he spoke kindly, but was curious since she seemed to want to ask him something – "did you want to talk to me?"

"Yes sir, I did, if you don't mind."

"No, not at all. Put down the hot pots, and speak with me for a moment."

Oona sat at the edge of the chair offered. "Mr. Appleton, you know I'm indentured?"

"Yes, 'till you are twenty. It's a long indenture, but that is common where a child is involved. The law prefers not to have young people on their own before adulthood."

"I see. Does an indenture sometimes go longer?" That question was one she had wanted to ask, ever since she was old enough to understand her status.

"There are a few things that prolong an indenture." He rose from the table and moved out of the room, motioning for her to follow him. He went up the stairs to his study, opened a large book and read for a minute. "Assuming the servant has obeyed his or her master and completed the tasks set before her, there is not much a master can do to make the indenture longer. Not without having complained to the courts about a runaway or slothful servant throughout the years. Not at the end of the indenture. And then at completion, the master owes the servant something to help start a new life. But that is not always adhered to, especially with girls. Many times it is easier to get her married off. Not during the indenture, mind you, but right at the end. It's fairly common that if the girl finds someone she'd like to marry, and the master can pretend not to approve of the marriage, he can avoid her freedom dues.

"Things you should know, now that you are becoming a young lady." He read on, deadly serious. "A servant, male or female, may not legally marry without permission, and if a female servant becomes pregnant, any *time* she misses from her work due to the pregnancy, birth or childcare, has to be made up at the end of the indenture." He looked up and smiled kindly into the young girl's eyes. "So my advice Oona, because you are going to be a very pretty girl" – she blushed but he went on – "would be to be very careful not to fall in love, or into any charmer's bed. Twenty will come soon enough, soon enough for love and marriage."

Elisha Appleton had meant that as kindly advice. She was sure he hadn't meant that she hide behind a mask of placid acceptance, but that was what she had learned to do, what she had decided to do. Not only did she not show the world much of herself, she rarely met that person herself, finding it easier to be the friendly servant who didn't kiss handsome men or ever play at love.

She'd promised herself she would try to learn to be Oona when she was free to be her real self, at the end of this indenture that had run through all her years in Boston. Strange how the town's move toward ending its role as servant to an empire not of its choice should trigger memories of her own awkward movement toward freedom. Oona moved away from the crowds and walked toward her room on the cold top floor of the Goodiels's house, thinking of freedom and lost identity and wondering what role that kiss had in bringing them back.

Hundreds may have gathered in the square, but the public arguments that had gone on for three days had been made by men of substance, mostly voters. The speakers may have included a few who were either too young or too poor to be eligible to vote, but in any case, they were all men of reason, and important in their circles. This action at the harbor, the destruction of the tea, on the other hand, was to be undertaken by the anonymous mob.

Anonymity was important. Boston's important men needed to be seen in public as their proxies acted. They sat together, clothed in fine suits, back at the meeting house and in parlors, while others, dressed like wild-men, committed treason. Not that some of the speakers wouldn't enjoy their moment at the wharf, but Adams, Hancock, Young and Warren, if searched for in the early hours of December seventeenth, would be found safely, and legally, on higher ground.

Jason followed the crowd from Orange Street down the hill to the harbor. As he got near, the tiny sliver of a new moon became visible. It was just rising from the harbor, creating a weak light that reflected in the ocean from the dark sky. Around him were men disguised with paint, tar and burnt cork on their faces, wearing blankets and feathers – men who had left sail lofts, taverns, and back rooms all over town, and headed to Griffin's Wharf.

Around him, he saw servants and masters, merchants, sailmakers, sailors and caulkers, all prepared to board and destroy; all nameless, and all sworn to secrecy. The group at the wharf numbered just over one hundred, far fewer than the thousand Mohawks whose war cries the attendees inside Old South described.

At the wharf, they split up and moved in near silence onto the *Dartmouth,* the *Beaver* and the *Eleanor*, the three ships laden with the East India Company tea. Their voices were muffled in the mist and by the sounds of the harbor. As it was, no words were needed as experienced men climbed into the holds and handed and hoisted up the tea crates. On deck, the crates were broken open with axes, and then the contents were lifted and thrown into the dark water, followed by the now empty crates.

The men of the busy port were familiar with ships and cargoes. They moved efficiently, destroying nothing but the tea crates and the tea, carefully leaving all other cargo, and the ships themselves, intact. A few men stuffed tea into their pockets, only to be rebuffed for theft, or tossed into the cold harbor along with the bobbing crates.

When at last the final four-hundred-pound chest was hauled to the deck, the ropes and tackle used to pull them up stored neatly away, the decks swept clear of all rubble, and the last of the tea thrown overboard to join the rest, shouts of "Boston harbor – a teapot tonight!" echoed into the chill mist. Silently, the participants and their observers disappeared into the cold, dark night.

Like the others, Jason moved away from the still silence that now hung over Griffin's Wharf. He started toward his rooms on Beech Street, but veered off to Bass's Wharf to find some turpentine at the ropewalk. He sat on the edge of the wooden wharf, his legs dangling over the side, and used a handkerchief covered in the solvent to wipe the bootblack and paint from his face. Then, he hid the rag in the sand under the pilings, and completed the short distance to his rooms. He pulled the feather from his cap, but instead of throwing it high, into the brisk wind that was blowing off the harbor, he put it in his pocket, a strange souvenir from a fateful night, given to him by that beautiful bar-girl with the dark hair and the lovely violet eyes.

Oona washed and changed into her warm bright red nightrail. She climbed into her small bed, blew out her candle and stared into the dark. Her memories came to greet her as they did most nights, and suddenly she recognized the brown-haired, golden-eyed man who had so surprisingly kissed her. Of course, in her memory he was still an impish fourteen year old ship's boy, who was working very hard to cheer up the weeping ten year old.

She supposed she had changed a lot since she was that weeping child, so it was only fair that the handsome brown-eyed man in the tavern be allowed to age his ten years as well. From what she had seen, the changes had all been for the good. She was used to the men who worked on ships and docks. Jason seemed to have acquired the calm authority of many of the captains and mates, without the gruffness and audacious self-importance that often accompanied that authority.

It was a good thing that the men believed that "no one" should kiss Oona. She had held to that since she had become a woman. She did not own her time, and that edict had simplified her life. Preventing men from assuming a pretty servant was theirs for the taking with a simple flash of coin, or invitation to a good dinner, had kept her safe. But as she stared into the dark, she had to admit she had not minded that kiss from a grown-up Jason FitzSimmon. She had not minded it at all.

She stared at the ceiling, too excited to sleep. Certainly, tossing perfectly good tea into the harbor was going to have major repercussions. Her master, Matthew Goodiel, would not have condoned such hoolliganery, but even he had been angry at not being one of the consignees appointed to sell the tea in his shop. She tried to make herself consider what the destruction of the tea would mean for Boston once Parliament found out, but her mind kept sliding back to Jason.

She hadn't meant to look so hard, but when he turned away she did. He was wearing a workman's leather pants and singlet under his greatcoat. The skins hugged his body, showing wide shoulders, strong arms, and a narrow waist. His arms were tanned, probably from months in the warm sun, and she guessed that the rest of him was equally sun-kissed. No one needed to tell her how men on ships dressed, or undressed, on hot, sunny afternoons.

The deep brown of the skins he wore reflected in his dark eyes. She remembered those eyes. She could always conjure them in the lonely dark. Memories of them smiling at her had eased her fears and aching heart during the long, scary nights of her early years with the Goodiels. She would have recognized them anywhere, even in a dark tavern with a feather in a knit cap and black paint on his outrageously handsome face. At first glance his eyes looked dark brown, but the dark was shot through with green and even amber. His hair was like his eyes – they looked plain brown at first, but years of sun and sea had streaked the thick, dark hair with golds and reds. The years seemed to have brought him to a competent and secure manhood, as she supposed they had brought her to an uncertain womanhood.

Jason had radiated the same comforting energy, even in that brief encounter in the large, excited group. His energy said he was a man who was capable of jumping up and doing anything – anything, like controlling a ship in a fierce gale, or smiling at and kissing the untouchable but pretty bar wench. He had joy in his face and laugh lines that deepened when he smiled. He must still smile often. The years had not been too unkind to Jason. Oona wished she could smile more often, but it was obvious that life did not bring luck to everyone. She pulled her blankets higher against the bitter cold of the attic, and drifted off to dream of sun-warmed seas and smiling sailors with brown eyes shot through with gold and green.

Jason rushed the final steps to his rooms in Mrs. Channing's house, anxious to get out of the chill. His landlady did not know he was back yet, but like most renters in harbor towns, she and her son had learned to be heavy sleepers. The house was a rectangle, with a front door that marked the line of symmetry. It was in the modern style, with two chimneys standing sentry above the slanted roof. There was a low fence around the front, and a brick path that led to the front door and around the house to the kitchen door. Like many houses in the town, it was a wooden structure. Only the fieldstone foundation showed any obeisance to the town laws about building with brick or stone to prevent fire.

Jason walked silently to the back door of the small house on Beech Street. He remembered carefully not wake the chickens, who were very much alive and restless as he followed the path past their coop. The little house was well maintained, even when Mr. Channing was at sea. It had a tidy vegetable and herb garden, dormant and dead now in the early winter cold. He unlocked the kitchen door, quietly turning and locking the door behind him. He had heard there were towns where doors could be left unlocked, but the Channings had impressed on him that this was not one of them.

In the kitchen, he took off his boots and carried them in his hands up the narrow back stairs. Mrs. Channing, or her son, had left a small fire in the hearth, and the fading coals still gave the room a tiny bit of warmth. He washed and climbed into bed.

Tired as he was, sleep was elusive, and he spent a minute watching the clouds out the window and thinking of the extraordinary night. He had had these rooms with Mrs. Channing since the spring a year ago. He was glad. It was so nice to come back to a place he recognized instead of a heartless inn of the sort that would accept sailors. He liked Boston; it might be small, but the harbor was deep and the port had become one of the busiest in the empire. Like many merchants and traders, based in London or here in the Colonies, his brothers used the port for their North American trade. Now he was back, without their knowledge or approval, hoping for work with one of the Boston men.

He hoped his second meeting with Matthew Goodiel would be as successful as the first. It was scheduled for the morning, but the town would be in an uproar and there was no telling. He forced optimism over the melancholy that had been his unnatural companion during the past few weeks, and reminded himself that Goodiel seemed to be a good man. He was a successful merchant with a warehouse on Long Wharf, a fine house on Oliver Street, and a store on Cornhill. The man was known to pay well, and he was adamantly against using his ships as slavers.

Jason wasn't sure that his feelings were particularly strong in regards to human bondage. That was an issue of great importance for his mother, the Duchess Elizabeth. He had come to believe that carrying humans as cargo was wrong. But servitude and bondage just seemed to be the way the world worked, and unlike other members of his family, he didn't spend much time worrying over it. It seemed to be another of those Parliamentarian issues best left to his passionate mother and his political brothers.

In fact, the events of tonight would probably illustrate one of Mother's Parliamentary arguments that he'd listened to last time he was home. During that visit, his mother had been lecturing her eldest sons, both members of that honorable body, that they should pay close attention to the condition of the American colonies and the arguments coming from them. Jason wasn't sure how strongly he believed the arguments that the Americans were making about their supposed servile status in regard to colonialism. He really couldn't equate the thriving Atlantic seaboard with the starvation of the Bengalis in India, as one pamphleteer had. On the other hand, he had to agree that the East India Company had taken its cozy relationship with Parliament to an unpleasant extreme.

Only time's passage would show if the colonists' decision to ban the importation and sale of certain taxed goods would influence merchants and buyers enough to change British policies, just as only time would show Parliament's reaction to tonight's destruction. It was one thing to decide not to buy or drink the "evil brew," or even to pressure one's neighbors to refrain from buying and drinking it. It would no doubt prove to be quite another to have destroyed an entire shipment of tea. No, Jason corrected himself, three entire shipments of tea.

Those non-importation agreements enacted by the colonists in response to limitations of trade, and the taxes imposed by the Navigation and Townsend Acts, might not have changed British government policies, but they had made smuggling cheap goods from non-British ports a way of life for ships and merchants in Britain and in her colonies. Of course, the British Navy's attempts to rein in the smuggling had, in turn, made life at sea more colorful. Just before he fell asleep, he decided they all deserved to have the tea thrown overboard.

Oona shook herself awake, ignoring the bone-tired weariness as she had so many mornings. The sun had not even made an attempt to emerge in the cold dark of the late December morning, but Oona knew from long experience that it was time to start the day. She pulled on thick stockings, wool petticoats, working stays and yesterday's gown, and shoved her feet into fur-lined clogs. She thought she might as well wear it for dusting – the dress already needed a good-cleaning since Lawrence and his crew had decorated it with dust and mud. Like this one, her gowns were too fine for a workday in winter, but a heavy wool shawl, petticoats and a big work apron would suffice until she could get the fires going.

Mrs. Prince, the household cook, and the closest thing Oona had to family, had already arrived and gotten the kitchen fires started. They nodded "good morning" silently. Each had already focused on her tasks. There was a pile of kindling and light logs stacked by the door. Oona filled her sling and went to work. As always, she carried warm water and vinegar in a small bucket so that as the kindling caught, she could wipe the delft tiles that decorated the hearths in the finer bedrooms and parlors. She had learned through grungy experience that the weak solution cleaned a day's smoke without too much work or vinegary smell. She didn't linger in the bedrooms – she didn't like to be asked to help find a chamber pot or hook a gown, if anyone should wake before she slipped out.

The family Oona had lived with and served, the Goodiels, were as simple as their wealth and stature in the community would tolerate. If left to Matthew, no one would get a morning fire unless one lit it oneself. But his young wife, Anne, had been raised in more opulent settings, and insisted on warm rooms and pretty gowns, even on her young servant. Their daughters – Matthew's first wife had produced three sons who were now grown and in school near their mother's family in New York – were charming and lovely, and well on their way to being spoiled by their doting mother, or so Matthew complained when he thought no one was listening. Oona agreed with him, but she had helped raise Mary and Wilhelmina, Willie for short, and they were clever children. Oona had a growing faith in their ability to withstand their mother's fussing and fuming, even though they were still very young.

The girls had a governess who acted as their nursemaid and helped them get ready, so Oona quietly set the fires in the nursery room fireplaces and retreated. She knew they had a long day of visiting ahead, so she built their fires a little bigger than usual to help them rise faster. Then she took her little bucket and the last of her twigs to the main parlor.

It was there she lingered over the blue and white tiles that surrounded the large fireplace. She understood they were from Holland and were a mark of wealth when displayed in America. To her, though, they were windows into another world. Each showed a different scene: windmills, boats on calm waters, people doing ordinary things, and children playing. Her favorite was of a boy fishing with a pole and string; his small boat was nearby, its sail furled around the small mast. Across the water was a large house, surrounded by fields and gardens. The artist had created a sunny blue day by drawing big fluffy clouds in the sky. She did not know why she lost herself so much in this one tile, but she noticed that it was a bit cleaner than the others, as she wiped it while musing over it most mornings.

There is no way, after a late night, to be prepared for a bantam's crow at first light. Jason pulled his pillow over his head for a few extra minutes and gave in to the inevitable and opened one eye when little Georgie Channing came in with firewood. The child set the fire in the small fireplace, waved good-morning to Jason, and left. He pulled the pillow off his head, and let the invading warmth convince him to rise. The window in the small bedroom faced northeast by his compass, and the only natural light was the weak, cold light of the early winter dawn.

He took the chill off the wash water, leaving it on the hearth for a few minutes, and wondered again how the town was going to react to the events of the night before. He supposed the town knew all about it already, but official word of the misbehavior would be sent to Britain from Governor Hutchinson, and then Parliament would send its response, probably by summer. By then, he considered, as he scraped four days growth from his face, he would be long gone, hopefully sailing as navigator and mate on one of Matthew Goodiel's three-rigged merchantmen.

Clean and shorn, he dressed in his cleanest clothes for his meeting with Goodiel. Cleanest did not mean finest, but he had been at sea for nearly a year. It would have to be enough to be clean and be dressed in a clean white linen shirt and clean wool breeches, even if he wore a tan fisherman's sweater instead of a waistcoat and coat. Of course, if he had any interest in giving orders while on dry land he might acquire a valet, but, by and large, that seemed like nonsense.

Goodiel had hinted at the meeting yesterday that he had new charts of the Caribbean. He said that word was that Jason was a master navigator. He very much wanted Jason's opinion of the charts. If this morning's second meeting went well, Jason would be obliged to check them before he sailed, and then edit them during the planned voyage to the West Indies and the Mediterranean. Goodiel said he had enough staff to worry over the lumber, wood staves, dried cod, rice, and rum – he wanted a seasoned navigator to fix his charts, and whose only concern was time, longitude, latitude, and weather. The prospect of being chosen for such an opportunity was overwhelming, especially after being taken for granted by his brothers. It was nice that someone had a good word for him and told Goodiel about his skills. The charts, once returned to Matthew Goodiel, would be published and sold. To a navigator, a trip like this was life's blood.

Downstairs in the kitchen, he took the time to exchange pleasantries with the Channings, but not breakfast. He left by the back door and headed northeast toward Mr. Rowe's Wharf.

On his way he walked over to Windmill Point to check on the *Chardon*'s dinghy. The small boat didn't seem to be in anyone's way, so he continued along Sea Street, skirting the wharves until he arrived at Matthew Goodiel's warehouse. It was a long, strong building constructed of the white and gray granite quarried nearby in Braintree. Unlike so many of Boston's buildings, it had withstood the economic vagaries that found buildings, built during good times, ignored and allowed to deteriorate as business dried up or the navigation taxes increased.

The wharf was bustling on this cold morning, and Jason stood a minute to admire the bustle. He relished watching a thriving harbor, even when he was only a visitor. This early in the day, the night's catch was just coming in. Fish sellers and merchants were lined up, haggling over shiploads of cod, haddock, mackerel, halibut, small shark and the shellfish: oysters, clams, mussels, and even that common trash-fish, lobster. Sea gulls flew overhead, suspended in the sharp wind, waiting to grab what they could as men cut and threw away heads and tails.

The wonderful smells of cold salt air blended with those of the fresh catch. He inhaled deeply, pulling the chill fresh air deep into his lungs. Jason knew he was in the right place at the right time. There was nothing so right as a harbor at work, and he found, as he usually did, that he was content to be a small part of it.

Looking around, he found the door to Goodiel's establishment, and went in to find the master. By process of elimination, Jason found someone who seemed to know what he was doing. Needing to interrupt the foreman in the busy place for as brief a time as necessary, he asked where he might find Mr. Goodiel.

"At his warm breakfast, like as not." The man laughed as he answered. "No harm in joking, the man knows he can't wake on time when his woman's away. Just climb the hill to Oliver Street." He pointed due west from the warehouse. "It's the newer brick one at the top of the hill. He has most of his charts there, likes to look them over, bit of a navigator himself, as I'm sure he'll tell you." With that, the man went back to his work and Jason turned west, away from the water, to Oliver Street.

The mist and fog were colder than the night before, as though there was a notch that some weather-god could turn to bring deep winter one tic closer. Jason had opened his greatcoat in the windless building, and hadn't thought about it as he headed away from the water, the cold wind at his back. Then, at the top of the small hill, he was met by even colder winds howling off the marshes and rivers from the north and west. No wonder these New Englanders were so willing to face the sea, he thought to himself as he climbed Fort Hill. Weather on shipboard was nearly no worse than on this spit of land.

Chapter 2

*H*e was let into the house by the front door and left to wait for Matthew Goodiel. "FitzSimmon!" the man said coming into view. Jason nodded in greeting. "Good to see you again. Had breakfast yet? I was just sitting down. Wife and children left at dawn, ungodly hour to eat." Goodiel lead the way into a small dining room just off the kitchen, and motioned for Jason to sit. Goodiel, who looked like the prosperous merchant he was, went to the door and spoke to the cook on the other side of the wall. Minutes later, carafes of coffee and chocolate, plates of eggs, toasted bread, and slices of fruits and nuts were placed in front of them. Goodiel started right in eating and Jason joined him, amazed that he had not realized how hungry he was. As they finished, Goodiel stood and motioned for Jason to follow him into the hall.

"FitzSimmon, I have to head out for the day. I'm sure you understand; the town is in a bit of an uproar this morning. Bit of trouble at the harbor last night, as I'm sure you've heard. But of course work continues. If you need me, I will be at Faneuil Hall and at my warehouse." He finished speaking, but Jason was quite sure he mumbled something about being glad he was not one of the consignees.

Gathering his speed, he started again, "I've left the

charts on my desk for you to peruse. You'll let me know if they look good?" He nodded in anticipation of good news. "If it's going well, plan on taking all the time you need – the day if you like. Mrs. Goodiel and our daughters went to Milton to see her sister, so the house should be quiet. Ask the girl for anything you need, lunch, tea. Though she probably won't serve you tea, she does make something palatable. Takes this tea thing seriously – most of the young people do. I'm just hoping the store and house make it through intact. That, young man, is as political as I get. But I will tell you, because I see in you a serious young man, I am relieved that I was not one of the consignees. I was angry about that, let me tell you, we all were. But FitzSimmon, I don't need to tell you what a relief that's turning out to be." The man took a warm greatcoat and tricorn from a rack in the hall and let himself out.

It was interesting that even wealthy Matthew Goodiel was not one of the consignees. That was something Jason had not been aware of. So, most of the merchants in the town had not been allowed to sell that tea. That must have angered even those who had not had previous interests in choosing a side. Jason wanted to say that he understood how a man might not want to pick a side, but it seemed unlikely that anyone with any money or power would be able to stay quiet for long.

He went back into the breakfast room and poured himself another cup of Goodiel's good coffee, poured in cream, and carried it into the man's small work room at the back of the house. The room jutted into the garden. It was no doubt pleasant in the summer, but now it threatened to be quite chilly. Happily, there was a welcoming fire laid and ready to light. Jason set the flame to kindling and in a few minutes he was nearly too warm.

An empty house has a special feel, and Jason was almost sure that he must be alone in the house. He opened the doors to the main room, and was hit by a rush of cool air. It was a delightful change to the overheated little room. He left the door open, settled in to drinking his coffee, and gave Goodiel's new charts a good hard look. There seemed to be no reason not to put his feet on the extra chair, so he pulled off his new landlubber boots and rested his heels on the seat. He had purchased the boots in Philadelphia – they were shiny and very beautifully made, but he wasn't convinced the bootmaker had understood that he needed to be able to walk.

Jason wiggled his toes as he settled into the charts. He opened his case and pulled out older charts, a ruler, a compass and a magnifying glass. Situated with tools and good coffee, he set to work.

The sun had passed its weak December apex as Jason reached for the cold coffee cup and looked up to relax his eyes and stretch his back from sitting so long. He gazed into, and across, the long expanse of the large parlor, where his eye was caught by the maid dusting shelves. Goodiel seemed to be a collector, and the shelves presented many interesting things for one to view. He indulged himself, however, watching the maid's shapely back and graceful movements as she dusted and arranged Goodiel's trophies. Mesmerized by her rhythmic work after staring so long at the charts, he watched as the maid climbed onto a stool to dust the top shelves. She was nearly finished, with only a large Chinese vase on the far right yet undusted; too big, Jason thought, to be up so high. As the girl reached to replace the now dusted vase, the stool began to totter.

Jason had a quick flash of girl, vase, and stool all broken and crying on the floor. In moments he was around the desk and running the length of the room. He reached out to catch her, just as the stool toppled over. He may have held the pleasant rescuee a second too long, struck as he was by her clear blue-violet eyes and the soft, womanly body in his arms. Carefully and somewhat reluctantly, he placed the pretty maid back on her feet. He smiled good morning and forced himself to turn away and go politely back to his work. Something in her demeanor caused him to turn back to her. She looked upset. Jason guessed it was her near disaster with the valuable vase. Suddenly the maid gave a half jump, uttered something that sounded like an "eek," stared at him hard, thrust the large Chinese vase into his hands, and ran from the room.

Oona turned and stared at her rescuer. He had crossed the floor in almost perfect silence. Like Jason, she had thought she was alone in the house. The visitor had worked so quietly, she had not noticed him in the small room Mr. Goodiel used for his office. When Goodiel was home, he was always bellowing for more coffee or singing sea chanteys. The silence had falsely assured her that she was alone.

She was glad not to be sweeping up the pieces of the vase she was still holding. But she hadn't wanted anyone to see her in yesterday's dusty blue gown, certainly not Jason FitzSimmon. She pushed the vase at him, squeaked what she hoped was a polite but small "thank you," and ran mute from the room.

Jason considered the fine vase in his hands, as he watched the back of the girl in retreat. He remembered that blue silk from that interesting chase he had witnessed, and though he had lost his sight from all the close work he had been doing, he was positive the pretty maid was the dark-haired beauty who had stuck a feather in his hat at the *Cromwell's Head* late last evening.

Curious, he found the kitchen and asked the cook to send someone in with lunch or tea or whatever time it was. Then he went back to that big, open parlor. Using his sleeve, he wiped a last bit of invisible dust from the vase, then reached up and placed it neatly on the top shelf where, he trusted, it belonged. Smiling at the myriad possibilities offered by an afternoon alone in a house with a comely housemaid, he went back into Goodiel's pleasant chart room, hoping that the meal would be delivered by the pretty girl.

"Oona. Silly girl! Why are you hiding in the corner?" Mrs. Prince, the cook, admonished her.

"I'm not ready."

"Darling, men don't recognize little girls they met when they were fourteen. You can tell him another time. Just feed him. All men want food."

As she spoke, Mrs. Prince was placing dishes of food on a tray, a pot of dandelion and mint tea, and thin ginger crisps for dessert. It was only as she was carrying the tray into the office that Oona noticed that there was enough food for two, subtly arranged by Mrs. Prince. Oona put it down on a nearby table and marched back to the kitchen. She stood at the door, glaring at Mrs. Prince until the lady looked up from the broadside she was reading.

"You! You expect me to eat in there, with him?"

"Yes. How often are we alone in the house, girl? There are few days like this when I have so little to do. Tomorrow night they are having a dinner party; today I want to keep my feet up. Take the time and talk to the young man. Have fun. Act like a young lady, not the servant you pretend to be."

"I'm not pretending. I've been their maid since I was ten. I have months to go."

"I know dear, but it's not your choice and it will end. You need to practice chatting with nice young men. Don't you want to spend some time with a pleasant young man?" Oona could not explain that no, she did not want to chat, did not want to meet young men. As pleasant as this one or that one might be, she did not want to find one she liked, not until her servitude was over. Then, she would learn to understand herself as a free woman. She could not tell Mrs. Prince that she saw her life as frozen until next May, when, on her twentieth birthday she was free to do all the things young girls did, like talk to nice young men.

"Oh well, not everything works on a schedule." Oona grabbed a few more ginger crisps and put them in her pocket.

Jason looked up and watched Oona walk toward him into the little room. She put down her tray and spread dishes on the side table. He cleared the charts and his tools off the big desk, and put them against the wall where nothing would get spilled on or lost. Oona served cold meats, bread and roasted vegetables onto plates and put them on the desk. Jason poured tea; he sniffed at the herbal mixture and decided it wouldn't kill either of them. He sat back in his chair and enjoyed the food while watching the pretty maid. He wanted to be polite, but she was so nice to look at.

Yes, she was definitely the Oona from the tavern, the girl who wasn't supposed to be kissed. And yes, she was indeed the speedy wench who so delightfully kicked up her heels and outran the mob that had tried to dirty the lovely blue gown. She had put that same gown on this morning, he observed – very frugal, to dust the shelves in a slightly muddied gown instead of washing two.

Oona ate without looking up, keeping one hand clenched in her lap. Jason wondered why she was nervous. She had given as good as she got to her compatriots on the street, she had sassed and laughed with dozens at the tavern, but here in her own house she was keeping her eyes down, her breath coming in shallow gulps, forcing her luscious breasts against her stays. She had taken off whatever fichu or shawl she normally wore with such a low-cut gown, probably when she started to dust the shelves. He wouldn't mention it. The view was too pleasant. Jason knew it was vastly inappropriate to notice his new master's maid, but she was lovely. She was also shivering, making her breasts stiff and the slight shadow of her nipples show through the fine fabric.

He forgave himself for staring. He was a sailor, after all, and he had been away at sea for many months. That he was a gentleman could be secondary to the need of the first, but he couldn't ignore her discomfort. She really did look cold, but was frozen in place from more than the chill air. He looked beyond the doors and spotted a knit wrap. He strode over to it and brought it back, laying it gently over her shoulders, touching her bare skin ever so slightly as he pulled away. He felt her shiver slightly. He hoped it was from more than the cold.

Oona felt a tingle as Jason placed her shawl on her shoulders. It wasn't from the cold. She sensed that it would take very little to let the real Jason into her heart. Her dreams of him had been so real for most of her life that in mere minutes he might be able to undo all the careful barriers and vows she had made regarding men. And really, she internally stamped her foot, she did not know the real Jason, not at all. But here he was. It did not matter if she knew him or had imagined him. The fates truly moved in mysterious ways.

Jason finished his plate of food. She seemed to be done, too, so he pushed away from the desk just a bit and put his napkin on the desk. He looked up and grinned at her. "Hello, I'm Jason FitzSimmon, navigator and, I hope, mate on Goodiel's ship. Now it's your turn. You can speak?"

Oona laughed. "Yes, I speak. I'm sorry." She held out her hand, "I'm Oona. A household maid; sometime cook, nanny, gardener. Occasionally I write a poem."

"May I see one sometime?" he took her hand. It was warm and strong, Not the hand of a fine miss, but one that could sew a button or rub tired muscles at the end of a long day. He held it just a second too long, lifted it to his lips and whispered a kiss over her knuckles.

Oona started. No one had ever even tried to kiss her hand. "What? Oh a poem? Maybe. I am very shy about them."

Oona looked shocked, Jason had to admit he liked the way teasing and flirting made her cheeks turn pink and those violet eyes glisten." Fair enough. Keep your secrets. I keep a journal, but I wouldn't let just anyone read it." He picked up the tea pot and refilled their cups. They each sipped, comfortable with not speaking.

Oona enjoyed the companionable silence. She might have felt exposed, a sensation she rarely experienced because she never let anyone inside her carefully manicured barriers. But Jason seemed so pleasant and easy going. Not wanting anything more than what the moment presented, she forced herself to relax and to eat a ginger crisp and sip the tea. If she let herself remember, to think of who the man sitting right across the desk from her was, she might faint. This wasn't just any beautiful, golden streaked, brown eyed, smiling, teasing man having lunch with her – it was Jason, defeater of monsters and tamer of nightmares. And he was magnificent.

He wore only a simple knitted sweater over a linen shirt. It revealed a true shape most men would envy. Oh, and she knew enough of the world to know that most girls would cry foul that he was sitting here with a merchant's maid. His shoulders were wide, his waist narrow, his chest and arms were nicely shaped; he was clearly very strong.

His hair was a bit longer than was fashionable and tied into a queue with a leather band. His skin was dark from long voyages in the hot southern sun. Oona wondered how far that dark color went below that white shirt. He hadn't worn a waistcoat or coat. Only that tan wool sweater he was taking off and casually draping over his chair. Oona swallowed and tried not to stare, but the cabled yarns of the sweater and the smell of thick wool triggered a memory, long forgotten, of men hauling fish at a rocky shore. She hadn't thought of her Irish childhood in years. Strange, how memory worked.

Jason did not notice being watched. His head was down and absorbed in a ginger crisp, carefully not looking at her. Oona stared openly. She knew she was being rude or at the least very forward. But it was extraordinary that he was here. She stared even harder as she noticed his left ear. Men wore earrings, but Jason's was unusual. And beautiful.

Made by an artisan – no, an artist. It had inlaid pearls and small rubies in the gold band and a hanging cabochon ruby. It was unusual for a man to wear something so bold. In fact it was stunning. This might be the boy of memory, but Jason as a man was someone who lived just slightly beyond the proper borders of her world. Maybe he was someone who could show her how to live there, too.

She had the strongest urge to touch that earring, to feel the stones as the metal turned in her fingers. Oona wanted to try so many things. She bit into another ginger biscuit, reminding herself that she could try all the things that had come rushing into her mind after her indenture ended on May twenty-sixth, but not before.

She forced herself to sit straight, as a proper young lady should. Although she was a servant in their household, the Goodiels had made sure that Oona had been educated as a proper Boston young lady ought. There was one thing she had always wanted to learn, to ask every sailor and captain who had visited the house ever since she was a child. Of course it had been impossible that she do so, and Mr. Goodiel was not the sort of master a young female servant could speak to casually. She took a deep breath, knowing that Jason might be her last hope. She sat up, eager and ready to ask him how a crew found its way over the ocean. She knew that it would have to be Jason who showed her or there would never be another chance.

Oona looked up, "Mr. FitzSimmon?"

He cocked an eyebrow at her. "Jason, please." It would never do to be formal with such a beauty.

She took a deep breath to calm her nerves. "Jason. I know this will sound odd, and I'm sure you'll think it's a terrible imposition." She swallowed and started over. " But, please, would you show me how to read a chart?" She rushed on gaining energy and speed now that she'd started. "Jason, I know you are busy, Mr. Goodiel has all sorts of work he needs you to do . . . but if you have a minute, I have always wanted to learn how a navigator plans a voyage using the divider and course protractor."

Jason was surprised to hear her string so many words together at once. And the question surprised him as well. Divider and course protractor? How completely unexpected, and although he could think of more pleasant ways to spend the afternoon with the pretty maid, he had no good reason not to show her. "Why not!" He motioned for her to clear the dishes off the desk as he rose to get out of her way and retrieve some charts from the back. "Oona, you know no one has ever asked me to teach this, not even my brothers, and they own the ship I've been navigating." He realized he was excited to explain the basics of navigation. "Of course, I'll show you whatever we have time for."

Oona stacked dishes and cups back onto the tray, and carried them off to the kitchen. She left the remains of lunch on the work table and tiptoed out, careful not to wake the napping cook. She hurried back to the little room, anxious to start her lessons. Jason had put a log on the fire. He closed the windowed doors behind her as she entered. She dropped her shawl on the chair, pushed up her sleeves, and sat to the charts Jason had laid out for her on the desk. She felt his energy and smelled his scent as he arranged the tools she would finally learn to use. He smelled of the sea air and dark spice from a cologne or soap he must use. She was aware of him with every breath, and she was excited – thrilled that, at last, the indecipherable would be made clear. She was not sure if it truly was the opportunity to learn that set her heart pounding so loudly she was sure Jason would hear. It might have been the strange clenching in her stomach when he looked her way. She steeled herself to pay close attention to the lesson. As she did so, she could not help but be aware of her teacher as she looked at ruler, compass and chart.

Jason sat next to Oona at the desk, tools of his trade before them. He couldn't stop himself from letting his mind drift, supposing that there were warmer ways to amuse a pretty girl on a chilly afternoon. But if learning to read a nautical chart was someone's life desire, he would do nothing to get in the way of that dream. He opened a chart of Boston Harbor that had been prepared about one year before. He sharpened a quill so Oona could take notes.

Oona had never studied in such elegance before. She sat at her master's desk, in his chair with his charts laid out before her. If Matthew Goodiel came home to see this, he might merely lift an eye, as Jason had done when she used his surname, or he could beat her for being uppity and foolish. She had never even thought of sitting here before, but Jason had motioned for her to sit, so she sat. And here was Goodiel's new first mate, sitting on the stool next to her.

"I'm sure you know that a chart is a map of a waterway," Jason began, hoping he would not tire his student. "The chart, though, does not show landmarks such as Beacon Hill, but rather depths, obstacles, lights, and land masses that are important to the ship. It must be obvious, but can never be stated enough, that any ship must stay in a channel wide and deep enough to accommodate it. Massachusetts has many shoals, and although there is a deep channel into Boston Harbor, there are many traps hidden among the islands."

Jason went on with the lesson, eventually showing Oona how he charted a course from one place to another using his tools. He had her find a safe route from Salem into Boston for a ship the size of the *Chardon,* and then for a ship of the line of the British Navy. It was interesting to watch the wonder and excitement with which she tackled the project. Jason sat to the side and watched her concentrate on the charts, impressed with how quickly she caught on, her obvious enthusiasm, and the quality of the work. He quietly left the room to collect some more tea from the kitchen, waving hello to the resting cook as he poured his own hot water into the pot.

"Thank you for waking me, young man. I would have thought Oona would have come in and kicked me back to life by now." Mrs. Prince got up, repinned her graying black hair, and stretched her back, looking spritely and ready for work. "Leave some of Oona's tea for me, will you? I am trying to get used to life without good bohea." The cook gave him a nod and a knowing look as she waved him off. He poured her a cup of the herbal concoction, and went back to Oona, to see how she was doing with her charts.

Oona looked up, pleased with her day's work. She smiled at Jason as he set down the tea things. As they waited for the herbs to steep, Jason looked over her finished project. He made a few suggestions and showed her one or two things she had missed, but overall she had done a fine job, and they were both pleased. Sadly aware they were finished, Oona cleared away the charts. Her scribbled notes she folded and put deep in her pocket.

She did not want the pleasant afternoon to end. She had felt free from her role as servant. This was an indulgence she rarely allowed herself, and not since she had finished her schooling. She sipped her tea slowly, trying to prolong the sense of refuge that spending these hours with Jason had afforded. She stretched and looked up. Catching his eye, she quickly turned away, but not before a another shiver caught her. She carefully lowered her cup back onto its saucer, trying not to let Jason see the trembling in her hands.

Jason did not miss Oona's reaction when she caught his eye. He had been feeling an excitement between them from the first. He wondered how long the Goodiels would stay out, and what their feelings might be about the first mate ravaging the housemaid. It sounded like a tawdry novel to him, but he could see the advantages of the plot. It looked like she was not simply going to fall into his arms, so he closed the book on that idea, and returned to the day as it was presenting itself. Maybe it was true that nobody kissed Oona.

They finished their tea, and by the time Jason picked up the cups and saucers to stack them on the tray, the light was nearly gone. Oona stood and pushed Matthew Goodiel's chair back under his desk. She lit the lamp and then excused herself to light the lanthorns at the door. Jason walked through the dining room to carry the tray back to the kitchen. He felt eyes on his back as he heard the front door click when Oona came back into the house.

Jason walked back into the office they had been using for the afternoon. The fire was low, but wall sconces and lamps held the room in their glow. Oona held his coat and hat in hand. He could not help but notice that although he had watched her balance hot tea things on a tray, and she had no trouble lighting the indoor and outdoor lights, her hands trembled as she held his coat to him. He was intrigued. Most girls in service were not so naive as to be moved by the close proximity of a young man. He had already convinced himself that she wanted no part of his flirting. They had sat next to each other for hours, and she had been far more interested in the charts than in him.

Jason did not have the arrogance to think her sweet nervous trembling was specific to him. But whatever the cause, he accepted it, for he found her lovely. She had barely noticed that her long, thick dark hair had escaped pins and cap and had fallen down her back in graceful waves as she worked over the charts. Now she stood there waiting for him to take his coat and leave. He knew he should just go, but the air of exhilaration and success hung in the room, along with deep overtones of so much undone and unsaid. He should at least compliment her on her first attempts with the navigation tools and chart.

Were her nerves a sign of her attraction to him? No man in his right mind wouldn't be attracted to her. But what if the story he'd heard last night at the tavern was true, and "no one kisses Oona?" Maybe her reaction to him was special. Jason liked a challenge, and he never denied a lady – after all, he had just spent the day teaching this unusual housemaid about navigation. Was he to deny her pleasure? He realized it was worth possible rejection to feel her lush body against his and taste those lips, just once. He caught her bright violet eyes with his, holding her still with his gaze. He threw his coat over an empty chair.

Oona had been elbow to elbow with Jason all afternoon, and he'd been a perfect gentleman. In fact, he was much more refined and kind than any gentleman she had ever met. Now, Oona felt Jason's golden-brown eyes hold her still. She might have used the word freeze if there were not so much heat coursing through her body. She could feel his desire as strongly as if he already held her in his arms. She wanted to feel the strength of those arms holding her soft body against his lean hard one. She nearly swooned as her legs weakened, waiting for Jason to touch her.

Jason had been trying to move very slowly; not act like the lunatic that was itching to come out. His desire was nearly raging mad as he looked into her beautiful eyes and over her lush, tempting body. He imagined pushing her onto that big shiny desk, lifting her skirts and taking her long and hard. He wondered if the girl had any idea what a delicious morsel she was. He moved behind her at the desk and let his face fall into her hair. He was struck with the combination of lemons and rosemary that lingered in the dark waves. He ran his fingers through her dark loose hair, while he reined in his roaming imagination.

Oona knew that she ought to move to the front door and politely see Jason out. She thought about moving as

Jason stepped behind her and gently trapped her between himself and the large table they had been using for their work. She felt Jason breathe into her neck and hair as he put his hands on her waist and drew her back against him. Slowly he blew warm air onto her. She felt her body respond and she lost the ability to think. She let her head fall forward giving him her neck as his long, strong body moved around hers. Then his hands were in her hair, massaging her scalp and running his fingers through the loosened curls. She let her head fall back onto his chest, boneless with sensation.

Jason moved his hands from hair to her waist for a moment, holding her to him while he breathed in her scent. Slowly he moved his hands over her torso and very gently cupped her breasts. Oona let out a quiet sigh as she leaned back into him, trustingly, letting him catch her in his arms.

Jason felt her resistance go, as her body melted into his. He found her simple trust stimulating beyond measure. He turned her slowly, pulling her close. He wrapped her fully in his arms, and looked deeply into her beautiful eyes. He put his mouth to hers, anxious to meld more fully with the graceful maid. He leaned to her and gently brushed her lips with his, as prelude of what was to come. And wonder, Oona lifted her mouth to his, willing finally to open herself to a real kiss. It was at that moment the sound of a key in the lock and voices at the front door jolted them out of their moment.

Jason pushed Oona away and helped her regain her balance. Just as quickly, he jumped and grabbed his coat and cap from the chair. He opened the doors and pushed Oona into the hall and away from him. He followed slowly so it would seem as though they were coming from two directions. In seconds, Oona had pushed all that amazing hair into a mopcap, and turned to the front door to welcome the Goodiels. Jason went quickly past and waited at the kitchen door, knowing she would be there soon to resume her role as household maid. In what felt like an eternity but was really mere minutes, she came by him. Jason turned and grabbed her fiercely but not roughly, pulling her into his arms. He put his mouth to her ear whispering as fiercely as that touch, "Oona, you entrance me." It was all he said, but his grip on her arm and warm breath on her neck spoke of much more. Oona heard the door open and close as Jason FitzSimmon moved out into the early December dark. She leaned against the closed door, letting her mind replay those words over and over.

Chapter 3

Jason walked over Anne Street to Fish Street, past Mr. Hancock's Wharf and north to the *Salutation Tavern*. There he settled in for the evening, exchanging stories with other seamen and shipwrights till it was late. He made his way to his rooms in the cold dark, grateful to find his bed, but tired as he was, sleep was hard to come by. Visions and memories of the dark-haired Oona, and the extraordinary hours they had spent together pouring over charts, had him intrigued, and almost surprised at himself.

Jason considered himself a man of the world. He had no lack of women interested in bedding him. Some insisted it was his brown eyes, others his blond streaked hair. But he never sought out the lonely wives, the sweet widows or the young wives married to older noblemen – so available in every port, in every city he visited. He enjoyed nearly all women – their attitudes, their clothes, or the lack thereof. He did not consider himself a rake. He remembered his various lovers with fondness, not passion. He had fancied himself in love a time or two, but no woman, young or old, had ever kept him up at night, not when she wasn't in his bed!

There was something about this Oona, something almost mysterious. She held back her secrets as well as her kisses. He wondered, if she did not kiss, was the beauteous maid virginal as well? Her silence, and the questions that formed around her life with the Goodiels, intrigued him. How was she so well educated and well spoken? Wanting to learn navigation of all things – she had yet to explain these things to him, but he'd spoken the truth to her. He was entranced. He tossed and turned, dreaming, when he finally slept, of running his hands and lips through dark hair and over luscious curves.

The rooster woke him again at dawn. He was tired and his head felt fuzzy. He climbed out of his bed, washed in almost icy cold water and dressed. When he felt presentable, he set off to find breakfast and start the process of ending his tenure on the *Chardon*.

Mary Channing stopped him with an offer of eggs and potatoes which he could not refuse.

"Mrs. Channing, do you know the Goodiels's girl, Oona?"

"Yes, she has been with them for years, but we haven't spoken very much beyond pleasantries and egg orders. I don't see her out with the other young people very often. She keeps to herself, and of course she is younger than my daughter, and much older than Georgie here."

"So, as far as you know she doesn't have a beau? She's of an age."

Mary looked knowingly at the young man. "Not that I know of, Jason. She is very close to the Goodiels, but I don't know what the relationship is, always thought they might be relatives. Anne might have plans for the girl. I'm afraid you are going to have to ask her. No one else is going to know."

Jason finished eating, and thanked his landlady for

the meal. By the time he had grabbed his hat and coat and walked down along the docks, he had nearly convinced himself that Oona would never be interested in a mere ship's mate and navigator. He was not a good prospect – often away, gone to sea for months, sometimes years at a time. He would probably never be rich. She might be a maid, but with her stunning beauty and intelligence, Oona should only consider men who had their lives ordered, men with money and status – in other words, men who were not him. He found the thought as dull and depressing as the gray December sky reflected in the choppy water of the gray harbor.

He slapped himself. An afternoon dalliance with a pretty maid should not be worrying him so. It was only that he had no idea of how to proceed. And he wanted to proceed, very, very badly. If only the Goodiels had been a few moments later. Or maybe a few hours later. He was sure he had nearly tasted heaven.

It was past time to move his things off the *Chardon* and into his room at the Channing house on Beech Street. It had been a legitimate voyage, shipping goods from London to the Carolinas and up to Massachusetts Bay, but sometimes extra profit just presented itself in the form of a misplaced French Brigand. Privateering, the approved looting for national rather than personal gain, was occasionally profitable and sometimes problematical. Jason had taken his share of their captured bounty in the Dutch tea they had found aboard the French ship whose captain had not recognized their right to share the seas. Other fellows had taken silks and cottons, or pots and pans. Now he had a bounty worth a fortune, but one that he could not sell anywhere in Atlantic North America. He would not even try.

The small gain was not worth the pain and worry of getting tarred and feathered as a traitor to the cause by the Patriots, or hanged by royal authority as a smuggler or pirate. It would have to be hidden, and stay hidden, until something in the town of Boston changed, and changed dramatically.

He had a meeting with the *Chardon's* Captain Dick, to discuss getting his wine casks full of the bohea off the ship before its inspection by the custom's officers and its formal docking. Luckily the harbor was still in a chaotic state from the events of two nights before. The harbormaster and all customs officials were very busy trying to explain away the tea's destruction. In other words, they were working hard trying to keep their jobs. Chances were, after the destruction of the tea, and the latest small pox scare, they would not find time to inspect the *Chardon* for days yet.

He paid sailors he had sailed with for years to help row the casks to the dock and cart them to Beech Street. He would not ask any locals; it was a risk he would not impose on any but long-term friends, friends who were scheduled to sail away and not look back.

It took the whole morning, but finally the casks were unloaded, and the wrapped tea safely stored under the floorboards in his bedroom. No one was home to watch the men's work, but if she had been, Mary Channing, daughter and wife of sailors, would have seen nothing.

Saturday was Oona's day off. She woke early and lay in bed, enjoying the moments of silence that the time to herself allowed. Then she dressed and left the house. Experience had taught her that if she tried to spend her allotted free time at home, someone always needed her to help with something. She crossed the street and cut through a yard to arrive at the Hubbards's kitchen door.

"Oona, sit and eat. Sukey is running late and you look like you could use some food." Mrs. Hubbard was a kindly, plump woman. Sukey was her youngest, and the only child still at home. "Sukey!" She called up the stairs, "Oona is here already – get moving." She turned to her daughter's friend. "So, Oona what are you shopping for this morning? Sukey tells me that you need fabric for a new gown."

"I don't know about that, Mrs. Hubbard. You know Anne Goodiel gives me all her castaways, and with a little work most look as good as new. I thought I might try to find a hat." Oona knew what Jan Hubbard was alluding to, but refused to give in to the mob, whether in the guise of her best friend or of her best friend's mother.

In a little while, the women were ready to run their errands. Sukey was due at the dressmaker's for a fitting of her new gown. Oona was happy to go along to advise and encourage, just as long as Sukey refrained from dictating to her.

"Do you think Caleb will propose?" Oona asked Sukey as she pulled her cloak back over her shoulders.

"He'd better, especially in that new gown. I think I look fabulous."

'Of course you do, dear, and Caleb would be a fool not to, but he shouldn't need you to wear a new gown. In fact he shouldn't even notice the gown."

"Oh, he'd better notice," Sukey replied in mock teasing, as the young women walked out to the street to wait for Mrs. Hubbard, who was behind, talking to the seamstress.

"So, Oona, what sort of hat are you looking for?" Jan Hubbard was not the sort of woman to forget about a shopping mission.

"Actually, I thought about a sharp lady's tricorn,

something with flair." Oona lifted her chin as if to illustrate the wearing of such a hat.

"Now, normally I would not recommend such a hat to a girl your age, but your circumstances are not the usual." The matron nodded her head in approval. "Yes, I do believe such a statement is exactly what you need. Something that says to the world that you may be alone and without family to protect you, but you are not without personal strength and zest." Oona's jaw dropped in surprise at such words, but she followed Sukey's mother into a hat shop that neither of the young women had noticed before.

"Oona! Do you have the money for a place like this? I think my mother might have overstepped."

"Sukey, shhh. It's fine. I was planning on a new octant, but it can wait."

"You and your instruments. I swear, Mr. Crowninshield would close shop without you spending all your money there, every week since I met you, which is nearly all your life."

"It has only been nine years, and it certainly hasn't been all my money."

"Nine and one half years, and it's certainly well nearly all your money. I don't know how you can work at that terrible pub every week."

"I like it. It is more fun than I can have in the staid south side of town, and I get good tips."

"Mother is coming. Don't remind her about the *Mount*; she pretends she knows nothing about what you do on Friday nights."

Mrs. Hubbard came over with the proprietress, who ushered Oona to a mirror. She had already selected various styles of the hat Oona had described to her, and in no time, the four women had chosen a midnight blue wool, edged in silver trim and augmented with a long pale blue feather. Oona loved it, and happily paid, but she knew that in Boston, the winds and her circumstance would prevent the decorative feather from gracing the hat. She waved good-bye to the Hubbards after that and went off on her own.

She headed east, back to Kilby and King Streets near the harbor. There on the corner, with waves lapping nearby, was her favorite shop, run by her friend Thomas Crowninshield. It was from this shop that Mr. Crowninshield sold nautical charts and navigation instruments. She had wandered into the *Points East* when she was ten and had barely been in Boston a month. She had brought her favorite thing, a small hand-held compass, and asked Mr. Crowninshield to show her other instruments used by seamen. He had tried to convince her that her pennies were better spent elsewhere, but she had insisted. And now, not only did she have a collection of nautical instruments any sea captain would be proud of, she also had a dear friend in Mr. Crowninshield.

He looked up as the ship's bell on the door announced her entrance. "Oona, my dear, what a delight to see you on such a dreary December day. Is that a new hat?"

"Yes, I'm afraid I was talked into buying it instead of completing the purchase of my octant. I want to give a few coins toward it, and I will have the rest next week."

He knew better than to discourage his unusual costumer. So, he took the coins and marked the transaction in an enormous log book, the kind used by some mates for their ship's log. They chatted of the doings in town and the various Christmas activities that a young woman like Oona should be attending.

"I don't know, Mr. Crowninshield. It really is Anne Goodiel's decision. They are having a party with dancing.

She might have me join, or maybe just stay with the little girls while their nanny dances. I don't know."

"I understand, Oona, but by this time next year you must make your own decisions – which parties to attend, and when to stay in. I'm just an old man, but I have raised a daughter and I have a few daughters-in-law. I think you should practice choosing, even if you can't follow through with the choice. It will make going easier."

"Mr. Crowninshield, thank you, that is a very good idea, I will try it." Oona had spent her young life veering away from having to make choices. It seemed like too much bother to decide things when those decisions were so easily overruled. Since she'd been young, even before her years in Boston, none of her choices mattered. She supposed it was that way with most children. For her, the indenture had compounded the frustration. But twice this day, adults had told her she had strength and – what had Mrs. Hubbard called it? "Zest." Maybe it was time to at least make some practice choices and pretend she was strong. It was a lot to think about, and Oona was slow moving up the hill to the Goodiels's house.

Oona walked into a house in the midst of an ordered chaos. The preparations for the dinner party planned for the following day were in full swing. Smells of succulent meats and spicy treats came from the kitchen. The fresh, distinctive smell of pine and fir wafted from the front hall where Mary and Willie, the Goodiel girls, were dancing around watching their father's men bring greens into the dining room and put them on the long table. Oona went into the conservatory to collect her knife and some twine. She sent Mary, the eldest of the little ones, to Cook to see if she had a few old pots for the greens. In a few minutes, they met up around the table,

Mary carrying one small pot, followed by the two day maids, who carried in many more. Oona asked them to put the pots on the floor and assessed the branches strewn along the length of the table, waiting to be arranged.

The greens were fresh and varied. The men had left early for a boat ride to the Goodiel farm on Spectacle Island. They had brought back pine boughs, fir tips and cones, white cypress, juniper with its distinctive blue berries, holly branches full of red berries, and long vines of ivy.

"Oona?" Willie, the younger girl, called at her as she cast aside her cloak and hat, "Mother brought in candles too, see?" She pointed to the cabinet on the side where a drawer was open showing a number of beautiful bayberry candles. As these were the most expensive and elegant candles available, Oona realized that this was to be a very elegant event indeed. She sat with Mary and Willie and showed them how to place the greens, making the old bowls festive.

Oona sat her charges at the table, books under them to raise them high enough to work. She praised their efforts and, when pine and fir needles pricked their little fingers, kissed their ouches. The girls worked hard, and the three workers, helped by the extra hands of the kitchen maids, succeeded in transforming the staid, fashionable Goodiel residence on Boston's Fort Hill into a glorious Christmas set. When every bough and cone had been used, and every surface covered with festive greens, she sent the girls up to their nurse and Suzie and Darcie home.

Finally alone, Oona walked through the empty parlors thinking about her long and special day; of Sukey's gown and her new hat, and of the new octant she would own next Saturday and the sextant she would get as soon as they were shipped from London to Boston. But mostly she thought about what Jan Hubbard and Thomas Crowninshield had said, each in his and her own way, about her strengths and abilities, and how she must soon be ready to find her own path. The house echoed around her in a quiet Christmas way, and she sent a prayer to any Christmas angel who might be listening to a servant girl, that whatever bramble-strewn path she chose be the right one. She knew she shouldn't, but she added a small prayer that Jason somehow be a part of that journey.

Christmas was not openly or joyously celebrated in Boston in 1773. The holiday had been banned as pagan by the Puritans, and then discouraged by subsequent generations. Cotton Mather, minister of Boston's Second Church, proclaimed that the celebration of Christ's birth should be considered daily rather than as part of a solstice ritual. But, by the latter half of the eighteenth century, as the larger American towns had become more English in ritual and domestic possessions, even Bostonians began to embrace English traditions. Christmas rituals, such as gatherings of friends and family, and decorated houses with greens from the forest and glowing candles, became acceptable.

The Goodiels, like most of their class, found ways to enjoy the darkest days of the year with friends and family, good food and warm drink. If that gathering was also a way to show those people how prosperous a year they had had, it was all for the better. Anne Goodiel was proud to belong to the Church of England and worship at the King's Chapel on School Street, but Matthew was equally proud of his Puritan heritage. They found a compromise in having their Christmas party the week before the holiday. They would spend the actual day in church, and at home with close family.

The greens and candles were Anne's idea, but without Oona's skill and vague happy memories of the bright windows and parlors of her childhood, Anne's dreams would not have come to life. She had asked Matthew to have his workers collect greens from the island farm, but even she was amazed at the transformation she witnessed Sunday morning when she went down to inspect the parlors. Already the furniture had been taken out or pushed to the walls, and the rugs removed for dancing, for her friends and neighbors loved to dance. It was never publically done – in Virginia maybe, but never in Boston. There were no prohibitions, however, against such things at a private party, so Anne had hired a trio of musicians who would arrive for an early dinner.

Anne trudged up the hill toward church, and reminded herself to thank Oona for doing such a good job with the greens, and to make sure the girl dressed to dance at the party. It would have to wait, because Oona preferred the Puritan service at the New South Meeting House to the servants' pews at Kings Chapel. Her daughters caught up with her on their walk, and she turned to concentrate on their words. "Mommy, did you see what Oona and us did with the branches?"

"That's 'Oona and we' did, dear. And I think 'boughs' is a nicer word than 'branches,' don't you?"

"Yes, Mama." Mary, silenced by her mother's corrections, jabbed her sister in the side and started to run as the girls raced up the hill to church.

Oona sat in a public pew in the small wooden church. Her mind wandered from the minister's words, and she stared out the clear windows at the clear winter light. It always served to clear whatever confusion she suffered in her life. But this morning her mind was full of other things. Oona shivered against the cold, glad of hot coals in her small foot warmer.

She continued her prayers begun the evening before, asking for guidance on the new path she would have to follow. As the minister talked of things that meant little to her, she found her mind wandering and she began to think about Jason FitzSimmon. Not all her musings were pleasant, and she kept asking herself why Jason, son of a duke, with a title and a family that would catch any American heiress, would waste his time with a maid who had nothing. Of course he wouldn't. She had nothing to offer, no dowry, no family name, no family. What would he want from her but what every man wanted, and that she would not give him, even if that was what she wanted, too.

She stopped her wandering thoughts and pulled her mind back to the service just as it ended. She pulled on her cloak and grabbed her small brazier. Many people would return to the meeting house after lunch for an afternoon of prayer and instruction, but ministers understood that servants had obligations to their earthly mistresses and masters. So when the minister wished them a good meal, Oona thanked him and made her way back over the hill.

New South's service was longer than what the Goodiels attended at King's Chapel, so she hurried home and went right to work in the kitchen, helping Mrs. Prince knead pastry dough for the fancy dinner that evening.

That was where Anne found her an hour later. "Oona, when you are done here, could you mind the girls? They need to dress for the party and so do you. Nanny has the night off. Suzie and Darcie are here, so don't worry about being needed to serve. I think you should wear the red. I haven't seen it, but if you've finished it, I believe the color should suit you." The woman rushed on, not leaving Oona space to agree, comment, or disagree. Anne Goodiel called back at her " . . . and, Oona? I need you to come to church with us next weekend. It's Christmas, and I think the household should be seen together."

Finally given a chance to speak, Oona muttered a "yes, Ma'am." She went up to the girls' room, where she found nurse putting on her cloak and hood, getting ready to leave. The children curtseyed to her as she left.

Oona dressed Mary and Willie and sent them off to help Darcie, and to tell Suzie to come upstairs to help her dress. She went up to her room to find the red gown Anne Goodiel had requested she wear. Originally, it had been a deep red augmented with the rust-colored trim that would bring out Anne Goodiel's red highlights. It was a lovely, light wool, made in a split skirt and split sleeves with the dark rust silk used for the petticoat and undersleeves. Oona's re-creation of it was more daring. She had closed the split skirt and removed the silk in the sleeve, replacing it with a white, ethereal lace. She had changed the neckline, too, lowering it and changing the bodice, so that with the proper stays, her breasts were pushed right to the edge of the top of the bodice, waiting to spill over. She was tempted to hide her neckline under a warm shawl or fichu, but she knew that was just cowardice, and she had vowed to be brave on her new path.

Jason approached the well-lit house with some anxiety. He had attended a service at the Christ Church in the North End that morning. It was a church whose architecture appealed to seamen, since it was built by shipwrights as an upside-down ship. He liked its tall steeple and the clear windows that let in the cold early winter light. It was generally expected that everyone would go to one church or another on a Sunday morning, but that seriousness ended at lunch, and he'd spent the early afternoon with friends, eating good food and listening to tales.

Although he had gone to sea before his fifteenth birthday, spending another Christmas away from his family left Jason feeling very far from home. He would like nothing more than to find a way to create a home, somewhere in the world, but an evening spent among Boston's elite merchant class did not feel like the best way to realize his dream.

A knock with the fox-head brought immediate attention, with little Willie doing the honors, overseen by her sister Mary. The little girls looked up at Jason and, not recognizing him, ran for their mother. Anne Goodiel returned a moment later with her small daughters in tow and took his coat to hang. She offered the rest room, a small room off the main hall he had noticed on an earlier visit. There were guests there, fixing their clothing and applying powder to hair and face. But, since he had traveled no more than three blocks from his home to the Goodiels's dinner party, he thanked her and shook his head "no."

Anne chased her daughters toward the young maid who came to collect them, and showed him into the great room. There were tables covered with cheeses, fruits and bowls of various flavors of punch, and everywhere boughs and hangings of pine and fir. Jason thanked his hostess, and helped himself to food and drink.

He realized that he was the stranger in the midst of merchants, captains, their wives and their families. These men and women had known each other their whole lives, grown up together, married into each other's families and gone into business together. He thought he might know a few of the men who sailed for Matthew Goodiel on other ships, but they were probably at sea, or home with their own families.

The crowd was relaxed, even boisterous. Talk often veered to the tea's destruction only a few days before. Curiosity, but not real worry as to what Parliament's reaction would be, ran high. Jason assumed by the talk that most of the Goodiels's guests were loyalists, with the caveat that they be left alone to earn their fortunes. Jason sympathized with that attitude; it was one he had always harbored toward his aristocratic and autocratic family and, secretly, toward the monarchy as well.

There were people dancing. Jason watched a set and realized that although he had not set foot at any sort of assembly or party for many years, he remembered most of the dances. He turned to a group of young ladies waiting to be asked to dance. He had seen these same girls with their parents only minutes before. Now they had coalesced into a giggling group, leaving their mamas and papas on the other side of the room, but it was obvious they were the daughters of merchant and ship-owning families. Jason asked one young lady to dance. She smiled a polite yes, and he escorted her into their place in line. The dance was a reel, and although some couples danced far better, and some far worse, Jason enjoyed moving around the floor with his partner.

He tried to push away the thoughts of Oona and the day they had spent pouring over charts in these very rooms, but he could not help looking to see if she were serving punch or dancing with one of the men. It was toward the end of the first set that he noticed a group of young children dancing and being instructed patiently by Oona and one of the other girls. The children were doing a good job of keeping up with their teachers, and the whole group was obviously having fun. He could not help but be envious of the children who had the undivided attention of the pretty maid. But it was not his place to abandon the young ladies who expected Goodiel's new mate to partner them in the coming dances.

Oona lifted her head from teaching little Jimmy Russell the steps to a gavotte. As she looked across the hall, she recognized many of the guests and felt comfortable. She had spent the day rehearsing her new outlook. It was good, she thought, to understand the world in which she lived, even if one did not quite fit in, yet.

Scanning the small crowd, she spotted Jason. He was dancing with a very pretty girl, Cordelia Bonnel, a rich captain's daughter. Oona knew her and their household. She was precisely the sort of young woman Jason should marry. Her father had the connections that would aid Jason in his work, and her dowry would propel him forward. In no time he would be the captain of a fine vessel himself. She swallowed her sorrow, and worked at being delighted for him.

She turned back to her small charges, but after the next dance they were ushered off to an early dinner, then games and sleep in the nursery while their parents ate and danced. Anne Goodiel had asked Oona to attend the party as a member of the household, so as much as she might want to, she could not go off and hide with the children. She got herself something to eat and drink and set to watching the dancers for a while. She didn't know if she was delighted for herself or disappointed for Jason as he walked away from the charming Cordelia. The girl made no effort to tie him into another dance. In fact, she barely looked back and walked away, not looking at all smitten or wistful. She watched as he next asked Natalie Rowe to dance. Her cousins were the powerful merchant Rowes. Her father was a lawyer. Another good match for him. Natalie was pretty and lively. She smiled and flirted with Jason as they danced. The reel was not one in which partners spent much time together, and both Jason and Natalie seemed to smile and flirt with all their partners equally. Oona fixed the girl with Jason in her imagination. She remembered that she was a skilled artist and a good musician. She would make a fine wife; her connections and money would help Jason in untold ways. Oona scolded herself that Jason would be happy with these girls or others just like them.

She watched as he took his farewell from Natalie just as he had Cordelia. He kissed the girl's knuckles very politely, and he smiled pleasantly but blandly into his partner's eyes. Oona watched Jason's eyes as he moved from one dance partner to the other. Yes, he'd gazed appreciatively, and smiled gently into their eyes. His eyes lacked intensity. She was sure she would have noticed that yellow-eyed glow his eyes had when he looked at her – the gleam that she could only describe as wolfish. She smiled a self-satisfied smile, and hummed silently as the small orchestra began their next piece.

Oona was asked to dance by a merchant's son, nephew of Dr. Church. Peter Church was a well known dandy and man about town. He was also a fantastic dancer. They spun around the floor, always ending where they should, Peter's skill making her feel lovely and light. Oona smiled her thanks as Peter leaned over to kiss her hand. He stared into her eyes just a second too long. Oona felt uncomfortable and turned away to stifle a nervous giggle. There was something odd about the man. On the dance floor he was tremendously skilled, but off, he was like a fish out of water. Maybe – Oona held up a linen handkerchief to hide her smiling lips – his natural domain was the dance floor, just as a fish's was the ocean. In seconds, another young man asked her to dance. And she left Peter Church, and images of his floundering on dry land, behind.

Jason watched Oona laughing and swirling with the eligible young men of Boston. These really were the men she should hope for. As the Goodiels seemed to be sponsoring her, maybe this evening was her entré of sorts. He fisted his hands in frustration, knowing he would never be considered eligible. Certainly he had his youth and lack of funds working against him. He stood in the shadows and watched Oona fly around the floor. As the set ended, he saw Anne Goodiel hurry over to speak to her young charge.

Oona thanked her latest partner and leaned against a tall chair for support as she caught her breath. She was having a very good time. She was surprised that Mrs. Goodiel had asked her to attend. She had the thought that maybe now, with her indenture nearly ended, her mistress wanted to secure her entre into local society. Oona hadn't considered that she ever would, but this evening was an unexpected treat.

"Oona! Could you see to a small problem we have at the punch bowl?"

"A problem at the punch bowl?" She followed Anne's gaze to the other side of the room and a large puddle of punch spreading on the floor.

"Yes, Ma'am," Oona muttered dutifully, her lovely bubble bursting just as she was so enjoying the evening.

She had stashed a bucket and rags behind the cloth that covered the punch table. She had also pointed out the location of the cleaning supplies to the staff who were hired to work the party, so it had not been necessary to ask her to deal with the sticky floor. Oona understood Anne's message very clearly, as she got on her hands and knees in her fine red wool gown to mop up the spill. She just didn't understand why the woman wanted her at the party after the children had left. Oona wished she could wipe so hard a hole would open in the wooden floor and she could fall into it.

Jason was shocked and disgusted as he watched Anne Goodiel send Oona to mop up a spill at the punch table. He hastened over to that table, striking up conversations with the gentlemen and ladies in the area. He hoped to be so distracting they did not notice the dark-haired girl in the beautiful red gown mopping the floor. As he heard her shove the bucket and rags back under the table, he turned to offer his hand and help her rise.

"Miss Oona, may I have this next dance?" Jason spoke in his most elegant tones, thinking his oldest brother, the duke in training, had nothing on him at this moment.

"Oh yes, that would be lovely." Oona was only barely aware of Anne Goodiel glaring at her from nearby, as she put her cold, slightly damp hand into Jason's warm, safe one. She looked into those brown, wolfish eyes with their intense light. She felt a tingle of something more than simple pleasure as he tightened his grip ever so slightly, and lifted her up – as if out of a deep court curtsey.

Time stopped. Jason whirled her into the dance. Oona paid no attention to her feet, which instinctively followed Jason's every step. Instead, she looked into his deep brown eyes. Those canine streaks that had been lacking as he danced with the merchants' daughters had reappeared, and her heartbeat sped up more than the jig's speed required. She recognized the signals of a man's interest, but Jason's fascination exceeded that. She understood that she was being hunted. She also knew that she should drop her gaze coquettishly as other girls would. She couldn't; instead, she continued to accept his direct gaze. She held her chin high as that same gaze moved approvingly over her body and gown.

As the dance ended, she curtseyed to him as he bowed. She watched the dancers move off to the dinner room. No one bothered looking in her direction. She took a moment to catch her breath before politely thanking Jason and moving away. He made no move to leave her side; instead he seemed to be scanning the room, seeking something. He turned back to her and smiled, and she smiled back, in what she hoped was an appropriately genteel way. She took a step away, as if to do something elsewhere. Jason touched her arm to stop her from going. They stood together, each looking out into the room as though they were each looking to move on. Oona felt Jason's hand on her back. He moved his fingers slowly and teasingly up back to play with the soft hairs at the base of her neck. He had angled them so that his arm and her back were successfully out of the view of anyone still in the room.

Before that dance with Oona, Jason had had enough of the Goodiels's party. He could not leave early. His new post on Goodiel's ship, and a long-ingrained politeness, prevented him from grabbing his coat and storming out of the house, but he could not dance with any more town lovelies. It was just as well Mrs. Goodiel had tried to humiliate her pretty maid before the crowd. It had distracted him, given him something to do.

He whispered something in her ear, then he moved off toward the dinner room with the rest of the stragglers. Oona walked the room, looking for broken glass and tipping candlesticks. She kept busy with the normal mess left behind by a successful party. The bayberry candles she had helped Mary and Willie put around the room had burned to stubs, and many were already out. The dancing was over and the musicians had gone home, so there was no need to find replacements. Oona cleaned up the stubs, putting them aside for the candlemaker to reuse. Then she gazed about, simply enjoying the quiet and privacy of the darkened, empty room.

In a few minutes she stepped behind the heavy winter drapes into the cold, bowed window. She summoned her courage, telling herself that this was a necessary step in becoming her new self, but a part of her knew that she was simply giving into delightful temptation. Footsteps sounded in the empty room and came toward her hiding place. She felt the shiver of something she barely recognized as excitement, from her toes to her chin. She moved back into the darkest shadows of the alcove and looked down. Black shiny boots stood still, just on the other side of the heavy drapes. In one step they were through.

Oona stared at the shiny leather, and then slowly moved her eyes from the fine boots up to the face of the man who had suggested their meeting. As her eyes found Jason's, she didn't know if she was delighted to see her new friend, or frightened by the look of conquest in his eyes. She was just realizing that the smart thing would be to push herself away from him and flee upstairs to the lonely safety of her cold room on the third floor. But instead, she pushed herself closer to him. Almost without movement he gently compelled them into the deepest shadows of the alcove and out of the direct draft of the cold glass. He leaned into her, pulling her to him at the same time. He very gently brushed her lips with one hand, while the other wound escaped tendrils of soft dark hair around his fingers at the back of her neck. As he feathered her lips, he traced her delicious neckline slowly with one finger, not upsetting the elegant gown or its wearer.

He kissed her gently, deepening it and holding her close but not intimately, while waiting for her response – positive or negative.

Oona lifted her hand to Jason's shoulder, feeling the soft wool of his jacket. She turned her mouth to his, opening her lips to his gentle query. She felt herself pulled into the safety of Jason's arms and the warmth of his wide chest, drawn to him as the needle in her compass turned to north. She felt her constant loneliness fall away, sure that she would never be herself again.

The kiss she had waited for was more than she could have imagined. It tugged at her soul, and she opened herself to the gentle sensations Jason was weaving through her body. He teased her mouth open, touching her cheek with a finger and tracing her lips gently with his tongue. Oona relaxed in Jason's arms. She opened her mouth to his and slowly responded, her tongue finding his and drinking him as he tasted and teased her. She felt her legs get wobbly and a yearning began deep in her body; she would have liked to sit before her legs gave out.

As Jason's hands roamed over her breasts and touched her back and hips, Oona found the sensations overwhelming and wonderful. So this was what the whores at the *King's Mount* went on about – what she had been warned to avoid all her life. Acting only on instinct, she let her head fall back, opening her neck to his touches, and he kissed and nipped at her neck, cheeks, eyes, and lips, feathering touches that teased and aroused. Gently, he ran a finger over her soft breasts, the pale skin of straining mounds peeping from the fashionable neckline of her beautiful gown. He put his mouth on one, then the other, planting gentle kisses, only inches from where he would have suckled and continued her journey to rapture.

He left her clothes and body intact, even as he cursed himself for another opportunity lost. This time she was his, willingly, with no discernable interruptions. But the girl was so vulnerable, she should be given time to understand the passion he knew was part of her, heard in her breathing, felt in the quickening of her heartbeat under those delightful breasts, and saw in the sweet pink she turned whenever he touched her. A cold floor was a poor substitute for a soft bed in a warm room. He squirmed slightly, trying to stifle his raging cock, telling himself they would soon explore this more fully. Now all that mattered was that she wanted him and was wonderfully responsive to the gentlest touch, and he could barely wait till their next meeting.

"Oona," Jason whispered in her ear. "Oh, my sweet lady." He took her hands in his and kissed one and then the other. He turned as if to leave She put a hand on his arm to stop him before he slipped away. He turned in question and she slowly put his hand on her cheek and nuzzled into this warm palm, placing a kiss on the center and closing his fingers over it. Then she let him leave, following herself a few minutes later.

His mind full of Oona, he headed away from her so as not to cause talk. Her scent lingered in his mind, and he could feel the heated kiss stored in the palm of his hand. Right now he needed to put some distance between them or he was likely to take her on the parlor floor. As he opened the door to leave through a half empty room, he heard footsteps and turned back. Oona was trimming candles and fixing greens that had been knocked askew by the dancers. She looked up and nodded at him. Her smile, meant for him alone, was far from the shy glance he'd seen a few minutes before. No, it was as bold an invitation as he had ever been given.

Oona walked the dance floor, using a snifter and trimmer to tend to the remaining candles. She knew that she didn't want Jason to find someone who could help him in his profession. She didn't want him to marry into a family that his own would be proud of. She wanted him to hunt her. To tease and thrill her. To make her legs weak and her toes curl. She wanted him to finish whatever it was that they had started behind the draperies in the little alcove.

Oona heard Suzie quietly calling her.

"Oona, Mrs. Goodiel is looking for you, she is near the kitchens."

"Okay, Suzie, I'll be right there." She walked to the kitchens feeling like a new person, brave, strong – branded.

Jason put just enough food on his plate to look like he had already eaten a portion of it. He poured himself a glass of wine and watched out of the corner of his eye as Oona moved past the dining room toward the kitchen. She was as lovely from a distance as she was soft and willing in his arms. That gown was stunning, and to think she had probably designed it herself from a castaway! He remembered how the bodice had felt as his hands circled her small waist, pushing her breasts into tempting mounds. He was almost hard again just watching her elegant back. He let his mind roam over their stolen minutes together. He nodded in blank agreement at his dinner partners' chatter.

Jason wasn't sure what happened during the rest of the evening. He vaguely remembered the dinner, the cards and the brandy, but all he could think of were Oona's amethyst eyes, and her soft skin, and her heavenly curves. Even through layers of clothing she entranced him. Oh, he could wait till fall when Goodiel's new ship, the *Catherine,* returned to port – he could, but he'd rather not. Rather not wait for soft September breezes to play with her hair, tearing it from its pins and leaving it free – free for his hands and his lips. He'd start now, and after this voyage, he would spend time in Boston really getting to know her. He would spend time pleasuring her as she deserved to be pleasured. Yes, even as he was talking to the charming matron to his left and the charming young thing to his right, he was dreaming of those amethyst eyes.

"Oona, you know Mr. Church? He has asked that I introduce him to you." Anne Goodiel caught her in the servant's hall near the kitchen. She was standing with Peter Church, a man who showed symptoms of good living, and wore clothes even the most fashionable man might find a trifle over the top.

Oona curtsied. "Yes, we had a dance," she schooled her expression, trying not to recall the man as a flounder gasping for air, "and I believe we have met at King's Chapel." Of course, Peter Church would never attend any but the highest church services. "How do you do, Mr. Church? What can I do to help you?" She noticed, too late, the sharp edge to her voice.

"Bold, ain't she? Doesn't waste time on banalities, I see." Peter Church spoke to Anne Goodiel, ignoring Oona.

Oona jumped in, feeling like there was a part of the story she had missed. "Yes, Mr. Church, I try to be forthright and honest. Is there some way I can help you?"

"Perhaps, my dear. Yes, perhaps." His eyes ran over her body, lingering uncomfortably on her breasts. Again he turned to Anne Goodiel. "Ma'am I will arrive here on my way to church Sunday morning. I will accompany the girl, then we will speak again. I should return to my table. I believe your fine dinner may be getting cold in my absence." He nodded his head to the women and turned to return to the dining room. Oona looked at Anne Goodiel for an explanation, but she was afraid she understood perfectly well.

Peter Church was one of the richest men in town. He did not dabble in any sort of trade himself, but he had the good sense to have had fabulously rich relatives on both sides of his family. Other family members continued to work hard and maintain a high level of economic success, and Peter continued to benefit from their hard work. Peter's reputation needed repair. Everyone knew it. From the highest representative of the King, to a merchant's indentured servant on Fort Hill, and most folks in between, all understood that Peter had spent too many years drinking and engaging in loud and infamous debauchery. His associates were of his ilk, and he had a suspect friendship with a certain young man from whom he rarely separated. In short, Peter Church needed to marry.

No woman of standing would agree to such an obviously irregular arrangement. Peter could find some young girl whose father was down on his luck, but it might be easier to negotiate with the mistress of the delectable Oona. She wouldn't be surprised if she learned that Anne Goodiel had offered to sell her for a portion of the indenture.

Well, she knew the law, and she would call the magistrates if Anne or Matthew Goodiel tried to force her into a marriage. She had not protected herself, or allowed Anne to insist on her purity, just so she could enter into a false marriage with a known dandy. Impossible!

She steeled herself. She must behave perfectly, and refuse all offers politely. She curtsied quickly to Anne and retreated into the kitchen to visit with Mrs. Prince.

Toward the end of the evening, Jason was taking his farewells. He was speaking with Anne Goodiel, thanking her for inviting him, when Matthew found them and reminded him that the *Catherine* was to sail on Thursday the thirtieth, at the high tide. They would load the goods beginning the week prior. The crew should be on board by afternoon of the twenty-ninth.

Jason wished he could say good-bye to Oona. It felt wrong to leave her home without a word. After he'd completed his leave-taking, he circled the house back to the kitchen garden. Suzie and Darcie were in the small yard, throwing scraps on the heap for the pig man. He walked into the light of the lanthorn. The girls started and then giggled, but ran in to get Oona when he asked.

Through the stillness of the cold night, he heard other guests call goodnights to the Goodiels. He heard voices and tired children awakened just enough to be carried or climb into carriages homeward bound. He heard the sounds of horses and carriage wheels, saw the steam from the animals' noses in the cold night, and then quiet settled. He imagined Mr. and Mrs. Goodiel gathering their things and heading upstairs where warm water miraculously waited for them in clean pitchers, and clean sheets were pulled back so that hot bedwarmers wouldn't burn their toes.

Soon, Oona came outside. Suzie and Darcie left at the same time, waving goodnights as they made their way up the hill toward home. Oona turned to the shadows, rubbing her arms for warmth. Jason pulled her into his fur-lined cloak and took her into his arms. They did not speak, but hungrily found each other's mouth. Oona pulled away and cupped Jason's face in her hands, drinking in his features.

"I have to get in before Matthew checks the doors. Go home, stay warm." She kissed his cheek and ran lightly back through the kitchen door.

"Goodnight, Oona." Jason called softly to the night.

Behind the garden wall, hidden in the darkness, Jason listened to Oona lock the planked wooden door. He imagined her climbing the plain, narrow stairs to the third floor. He hoped the attic room wasn't too cold. He hoped she had a warm nightgown, and that she had remembered to bring herself warm wash water and hot coals for her own bed-warmer. He would hate for her to have cold feet.

He had never bothered with such domestic thoughts before, not even for his own comfort. It was strange where a mind would wander, given a chance. His own existence might feel inconsequential to him, and be of little consequence to others, but he would strew rose petals in Oona's path if he could.

Oona ran the bed-warmer through the sheets. She had brought up flat flannel-wrapped rocks, warmed at the kitchen hearth. They were her favorite trick for heating cold feet, learned from stories told by trappers and soldiers who traveled through the winter woods. She pulled her warm night rail over her head, and undressed inside the overlarge garment, letting her evening clothes fall to the floor. The wool flannel gown was her other great winter trick. She had made it of fabric meant for baby blankets. It certainly wasn't thin or homespun, and the red she had chosen to dye it was not humble.

She picked up the lovely red gown, and put it in the clothes press. Her other clothes she ignored on the floor till morning. She blew out her candle, and crawled into her cozy bed, an island of safety and warmth in a cold room and a colder world. Or that was how she had always perceived it. Tonight, though, there seemed to be a ray of warm sunshine penetrating the dark. She had always imagined, always prayed, that someone, somewhere was thinking fond thoughts of her, wishing her well. Now, she was confident that was true.

She knew that men admired her. They always had, but that had never made her confident. Instead, it had frightened her. But Jason's desire was different. Maybe she was different. Jason wanted her, he had left no doubt, but it did not frighten her. Instead, it gave her confidence. She laughed out loud in the dark room. It was unique, this feeling, this having someone thinking good thoughts about her. In fact, it was better than her most elaborate daydreams. She had never imagined, for instance, that knowing someone was thinking of her would set her breasts tingling or start an odd craving that seemed to radiate upward into her belly from between her legs. No, she would never have imagined that, nor would she want to stop it.

Chapter 4

A few days later, Jason's friends found him to inform him that a celebration was in order. It seemed that freeing himself from the *Chardon* and signing onto the *Catherine* was worth a night out. They were right. Circumstance now dictated that he was a free man, ready to rise or fall, and eat or starve, as the fates would decide. To celebrate the changes, he went with friends to the *King's Mount*. The *Mount* was on the wrong side of Cambridge Street, just a block up the hill. The tavern sign showed a red-faced fellow with an ill-fitting crown, looking backward astride an enormous black horse. The king held a huge flagon of ale in his hand as he giddily attempted not to fall from his mount. Jason found the sign put him in a fine mood for an evening of drinking with his fellows.

The tavern was dark, with smokey wall lanterns and small candles on the tables providing the only light. There was a fire in the back of the room, the kitchen and kegs in the front. The crowded room was smoky and hot, and the crowd was loud. Dark ale was poured by Goody Brackett, a woman of indeterminate age, and brought by two bar wenches who were kept busy serving the large crowd.

Jason relaxed with his first beer and contemplated the clams and brown bread that decorated his plate. He looked around the smoky room, letting the boisterous chatter of his fellow drinkers swirl around him like the smoke. He was neither happy nor sad, just a bit thoughtful about new directions in his life. He sensed that too much of Goody Brackett's ale might well lead the evening to a maudlin end. So he limited his drinking to match his dinner. He wasn't bored, the patrons were a jolly bunch, and the drink was good.

As the evening wore on the crowd shifted, some people came in and some left. Jason's instincts were that he should leave with the dinner crowd. Knowing he had nowhere to go, he settled with another flagon of the thick dark ale. He was jostled from his revery as the men at his table rose to make room for a newcomer. She looked a few years older than Jason and his friends, but she might not have been. She wore a fashionable gown, in an unfashionably daring and revealing style. Her hair, on closer inspection, was a well-kept wig of a slightly unnatural color. She made no attempt to hide the fact that she belonged to that guild of women known from Lisbon to London, and from New York to Newcastle, as the hardest working whores of the Atlantic world, Boston's finest. Jason rose with the rest of the table and she climbed over him to sit comfortably between himself and Kevin Babcock.

She looked around the table till she had caught everyone's eye. "Hello gentlemen, I'm Belle. Shawht for Isabelle. My mothah cleehly imagined great things fa me."

It was clear from the tone of her speech that she had given the talk many times before. A few of the men, including Jason, cringed at her obvious Yankee whine, hideously broad "a"'s and dropped "er"'s. But Kevin, to Jason's left, had better manners or a tin ear, and spoke for all of them.

"Well hello, Madame. Welcome, make yourself comfortable. I am Kevin and on your other side is Jason." He continued with the other introductions, pointing around the table and politely introducing Belle to each of the men. The group engaged the woman in conversation, hearing the story of her life from farm to city. Belle, a natural storyteller, was a regular at the *King's Mount*, plying her trade from there and nearby. After telling her story, Belle turned to the group and asked a question.

"Gents, I ask this every week and no one can give me an ansah that I like. So this week I inquire of you: why does that pretty dahk hayahd gal werhk heah when she don't get no big tips?'"

Jason turned to Kevin on Belle's other side. "Translate please Kev, I'm lost."

Kevin spoke in a stage whisper: "She said, 'why does that pretty dark haired girl work here when she doesn't get the tips?'"

"Oh, why is that, Belle?"

"I'm not going to tell you. First you have to figgah out why she don't get no tips."

The table all turned to watch the barmaids deliver the drinks. The blonde teased and pushed teasingly at most of the men she served. She happily allowed them to grope her breasts over her bodice, and cheerfully accepted the bills and coins stuffed between her ample breasts. The dark-haired girl was equally teasing; in fact, she was downright sassy. She served her patrons with a smile and a quick wit, pushing them away if any tried to grab or grope. She did it all with humor and a tempting smile, but her tips were meaner and she pushed her money into her apron pocket herself.

Oona never minded making less in tips than Nan. Nan was a few years older. She was married to a sailor whom she adored, and loved to flirt. No one took her flirting particularly seriously, and when someone did, it didn't take more than a word or two to convince him otherwise. Whatever words Nan used left everyone happy, and the tips continued to be pushed into her bodice.

Oona knew she could sass with the best bar wench in Boston. But she was happier at her tavern job if her patrons kept their hands and lips to themselves. She was good at playfully pushing customers away, and the bit of money she put aside each week was more than the Goodiels would give her. Those coins paid for her treats and her collection of nautical instruments. Right now, there was a brand-new rosewood and ebony sextant expected to arrive at Mr. Crowninshield's shop any day from London. She was pleased that she would have one of the first sextants in North America. Meanwhile, there was an octant three-quarters paid for.

Oona knew that she would once again be part of Belle's storytelling. It happened whenever the woman had a good crowd of young men listening to her. Tonight she had a nice group. Nan had served them twice, and once the man at the end had gone up to Goody for a round. Belle was in her element, but the story was always the same. Belle would call Oona over and have one of the men try to pay her the way the regulars paid Nan. It wouldn't work; it never did, and Belle knew it wouldn't work tonight.

"Okay boys, one of you has to try to pay the dahk hayahd girl the way they do the blonde. You," she nudged Jason, "change sides with that fellow and try to get her to kiss you. There is a standing bet in the pub that you won't. But if you do, at least half the men in here will pay a crown."

"What do I owe if I fail?"

"Don't think anyone has ever paid up on that, most everyone fails, so it amounts to nothing."

Jason tried not to cringe at Belle's voice. He moved into the assigned seat without enthusiasm, ready to be rejected by the tavern-wench. He was already drunker than he liked, and would rather be making his way back to his bed than playing tavern games with the aging whore. But it would be bad sport to leave after she had chosen him for the game. So he turned around for the first time all evening to cast an eye on his prey.

Oona filled a tray with fresh tankards and carried them over to Belle's table. It seemed the man with his back to her was the designated payee for the night's ritual. She was four or five steps away from the table when the man turned to look at his victim. She almost stumbled, and would have spilled the ale, but Jason jumped up to help her with the heavy tray. She got the drinks safely onto the table and distributed them, just as Jason pushed half the money he held into her apron pocket. Someone on the other side of the room shouted something about that not being good enough.

Abruptly she was on Jason's lap. How had he done that? His brown eyes danced flames warmer than the fire in the hearth. He shot a silent challenge at her, somehow assuring her that she would be safe. He smiled just slightly and put his mouth to hers. Her first instinct was to stop him as she had stopped all the others. They had barely kissed, even in private, even in lonely dark corners; this was so public. But her hands found his hair; it felt so thick that she ran her hands through it, pulling him to her instead of pushing him away.

Jason wanted to deepen the kiss, to pull his beauty

tightly into his arms, and show the crowd that she had waited for *this* kiss – his kiss. But he would not humiliate her or skew the bet. It was better if the revelers believed she was rewarding him for his kindness when he helped her with the tray, or maybe his lovely brown eyes. He pushed her away, subtly, so it would not be noticed, not even by Belle, and whispered into her ear.

"Oona, slap me." Her eyes flew open as she swallowed her laughter. She nodded understanding and slapped him across his face. Her eyes told him she didn't mean it.

Oona turned to the crowd in the *King's Mount*. She put her hands on her hips and patted the money in her pocket. She looked over her audience, their mouths agape, looks of shock on their faces. "Well, that was nice, but if any one of you" – she moved her finger and pointed to patrons sitting around the tables – "tries to duplicate it, I'll pour cold ale on your balls." She squeezed Jason's hand behind her skirts while the crowd clapped approval. She took the rest of the tip money and placed it between her breasts, ever so deeply into her bodice. She walked away from the table and out into the tavern kitchen, swinging her hips as she went. Once she was out of the room, the crowd howled, and coins and bills started piling up in front of Jason. He shrugged his shoulders at Belle. The older woman was clearly impressed.

Jason bought a round for the house, and even helped Nan and Goody Brackett serve. Then he pushed the winnings into his sack, waved to the happy crowd, and left the *King's Mount*. In the alley just outside the tavern, he heard footsteps matching his, and turned. Oona was tucked into a warm cloak, waiting for him. He started to speak, but she put a finger against his lips to shush him. Jason tilted his head in inquiry. His question was answered as Oona pulled his face to hers and put her lips on his.

This time Jason pulled her close and deepened the kiss, letting his tongue tease open her willing lips and meet her tongue in her mouth. She tasted heavenly, of apples and cinnamon, with a hint of the ale she had been serving all evening. He was sure he was less fresh, but he was so mindless with her closeness, her smell, her taste, that he made no effort to spare her. His hands pulled her to him inside their warm cloaks. He ran his hands over her back, pulling her closer, feeling her breasts, soft against his hard body. He moved to touch her, wishing there was somewhere more friendly than a dark alley on Mount Whoredom, as the hill was called. He cupped her breast in his hand, making circles around a stiff nipple as they kissed in the dark night.

This was so much more interesting than kissing in the hidden corners in the Goodiel mansion. This wasn't the shy, well-behaved servant who worked for the staid, wealthy merchant on Fort Hill. This was an earthy, sexual woman who could handle a crowd of drunken sailors with the twitch of her hip or a look. That was it – he was beyond entranced, he was ensorceled.

"Jason, I need to go back." She pushed her hair back into its pins, and ran her hands over her skirts. In seconds, she was as neat as if a lady's maid had spent an hour fixing her hair and gown.

"Meet me." Jason leaning against a wall, gasped.

"I am free all day tomorrow. They give me the day to myself when they visit family. They will be back in the evening. I must be back for a late dinner, but I have all day. Do you know the grasshopper weathervane on the Hall? I'll be there at seven tomorrow morning."

Jason nodded mutely. "Don't you need to sleep?" It

seemed to take a great effort to speak.

"I have to wake to help with master's breakfast. I'll be there. I think I should talk to you."

Jason's body didn't want to speak or listen. There were so many better things to do. The bulge in his pants was making that painfully clear. But he would meet her as she suggested. He grabbed her hand as she turned to go back into the tavern. He kissed the back of her hand slowly and deliberately, then turned it over, breathing hot air onto her palm as he kissed it and closed her fist over the kiss. Then he watched her go through the door.

Jason turned north and walked down the hill and toward the river. He watched the tide come in over the back bay. The moon was just rising over the harbor on his right. He listened to the raucous voices of people leaving the taverns and heading home, walking south at a leisurely pace, maybe hoping to catch a glimpse of Oona as she walked home to Oliver Street. The town wasn't yet empty. The watchman spied the late goers with a discerning eye, checking for anyone who might be ready to cause trouble, or who was so drunk he would be better off spending a night in the guard house. But he did not hurry anyone along. The watch did not need to urge speed. The cold air and a settling frost took care of that.

Rubbing his hands together for warmth, Jason thought of Oona's hands. They were not the hands of a lady of leisure. They were strong, and used to hard work, as her legs must be – he remembered that he saw her outrun her tormentors just the other day. He felt heat course through his body, as he considered those strong hands holding him and those strong legs wrapped around his hips, pulling him into her. He was glad, he thought, for the cold night. Without the frost, he might not have made it home.

She was not a lady as he knew them, but she behaved like no servant or bar wench he had ever met. He barely noticed a brewer's wagon rolling by with Oona as a passenger. She waved and called out something that was lost in the rattle of the empty beer barrels hitting against each other, proclaiming by their emptiness the quality and success of his product. With a quiet shout and a friendly wave he pushed his mule on. Jason waved goodnight and continued his walk toward home. He had high hopes for their meeting in the morning.

The brewer let Oona off on Orange Street near Oliver. She waved her thanks, and man and mule rattled on south. She was grateful for the ride; she would never have been able to keep her job at the *King's Mount* if Mr. Brackett, Goody's brother, did not give her a lift on work nights. If she were any later, she would find the kitchen door barred, and she could expect to spend the night in the cold shed.

She leaned back against the garden wall, letting the memories of the unusual night move over her. She might have stayed there half the night reliving the evening and Jason's kiss, but her reverie was cut short before the night's chill could invade.

"Oona? Are you out here, girl?" It was Matthew Goodiel's voice. "Oona, I'm ready to bar the door. Come in now or you're going to have to wake mistress to let you in."

"I'm here, sir, just clearing my head and lungs from the smoky tavern. I'll be right in." She turned her smile on the master of the house, her white teeth picking up the stray light from the door lantern.

"So, Oona, how was your evening at *King's Mount*?"

Matthew Goodiel asked as he barred the door against the night. He always seemed ready to ask for more from her. Luckily, he never had.

"Better than most, Sir, thank you for asking." She patted her pocket where a roll of bills sat, and gracefully avoided his kindly hug. She smiled tiredly, and let herself up the back stairs, relieved that the door to the kitchen closed behind her and did not reopen, leaving her truly alone.

The door had never reopened, but she always worried that it might. Matthew had never concerned himself with her raising or training, having been gone most of her younger years. Unlike his wife, Anne, he did not see himself as Oona's parent. Oona knew she would feel safer if he saw himself as her father, and since he did not, she had another reason to wish this servitude over and herself out of the Goodiels's house.

She thought about Matthew Goodiel. He had never frightened her. But he was not a man used to servants, and did not ignore her as most people did. There was a kindness in that, but it sometimes made her uncomfortable. Matthew and his first wife had three sons, each just a bit older than Oona. She had been fortunate to share their tutor when she was young. It was unusual for a girl to have that chance, but the Goodiels hadn't wanted to pay for the Dame's school when there was already a tutor in the house, and they had agreed that she should at least be literate.

She never discovered if the young man resented the little girl's intrusion into his scholars' schoolroom, but she remembered working hard so as not to disappoint Mr. Ellis. He had not been cruel, saving his stick for boys who teased, rather than for the girl who sat there confused and scared. He had made sure she mastered her reading before writing, her arithmetic before astronomy, even if it meant the boys fidgeted between their Greek translations.

In earlier years, Oona had dreamed that one of the young Goodiels would fall madly in love with her and insist his parents end her indenture. But as gentle as they were with her, they went off to New York City to King's College and had barely been back. Probably three grown men had little interest in Matthew's young wife and two noisy half sisters. Those little girls had been hers to help care for since their births. She could not recall the brothers' faces, nor had she favored one over the other two. Life was funny sometimes. She had never forgotten Jason's smile or his eyes from that long-ago ship.

Chapter 5

*J*ason woke at dawn on Saturday morning, excited to spend the day with Oona and help her spend money she did not yet know she had. He lay on his back enjoying the fantasy of a willing, wanton Oona sharing this bed. The rooster was not the only male up and celebrating this morning. He shook himself out of his fantasy, not wanting little Georgie to find him in this state. He jumped out of bed before the boy appeared to make his fire. He was more excited to be out at a winter dawn than he could remember being.

He washed, dressed in plain, warm clothes, and ate the orange he had stored on the windowsill. Then he grabbed his heavy wool greatcoat, knit cap and leather tricorn, ready to face the day, and feeling ridiculously like a school boy. He headed to Dock Square and Faneuil Hall, with its golden grasshopper weathervane.

Dock Square was the central market of Boston. Owned by the town, Faneuil Hall was not only the marketplace for goods of all sorts, from books to fine foods, but also the upper hall was used by the town for its public meetings. It was here that the non-importation meetings that led to the tea's destruction had been started. Jason thought the arguments of those three days would echo through Boston's streets for centuries to come, especially if war was the outcome.

The brick building, painted an odd shade of ochre, was named by Peter Faneuil, the town's richest merchant and benefactor, when it was completed in 1742. Unfortunately Peter, who was a bit wild and unloved by the town's elite, died before he could enjoy watching his neighbors' reaction to the name he'd chosen for their grandest public building. One could only imagine him as the golden grasshopper looking down on the hard working ants scurrying through his marketplace.

No sign of Peter's ghost was visible this morning. Goods were moving into Peter Faneuil's Hall from the busy docks, in wheelbarrows and carts loaded with barrels and crates of grains, flours, fruits, nuts, molasses, and cured meats. Jason walked closer, and saw the goods displayed on overloaded pushcarts and stalls inside and around the building. Every door and shutter was open to shoppers even in the cold morning, and the cries of mongers and merchants filled the air.

The cold night had left frost and a thin layer of ice at the edges of the harbor. The day promised to be clear and chilly, with Boston's typical wind from the east off the cold water. Jason grabbed at his hat against a gust, and listened to a bookseller's directions to the tower. He found the door as directed and started to climb. At the top, he looked down at the marketplace. It looked crowded and busy. Jason had been in the world of trade and shipping most of his life. He could tell from a quick glance that there were items missing. The repeal of the Townsend Act, the act of Parliament that had taxed most everything sold in the colonies, might have opened up trade, but goods of British manufacture were still not for sale. There was pressure on merchants and customers not to sell or buy British-made merchandise. At the same time, towns were lowering and removing taxes on American-made items, and even sheep were exempt from the head tax in an attempt to create an American wool industry. Sadly, the new manufacture could not keep up with demand, and the lack of goods was apparent.

Merchants could supplement with British goods, but they feared the loss of trade that would come with crossing the powerful men who controlled the Sons of Liberty and the Boston Committee of Correspondence. The richest and most famous merchant in town, John Hancock, was well-known for having a fully stocked store and selling only goods that were legal under the agreements. Of course, many of his goods were successfully smuggled into Boston, past the Customs officials.

Jason opened the door to the tower platform. It was enclosed so that workmen could not fall. Of course, no effort had been made to protect visitors from the wind. He saw her hair before he saw the rest of her. She wore a dark blue tricorn with a frivolous feather, pulled down low so it could not blow away in the wind, and a man's dark blue wool greatcoat. He corrected himself. The coat must be a boy's coat. It fit her perfectly. He wondered briefly where she had gotten boys' clothes, but let the thought fly. Most women would have looked coarse or mean wearing men's clothes atop a bright blue and white gown, but with her dancing locks, the look was startlingly feminine.

Jason watched as Oona laughed into the wind as it whipped her hair. The combination of her unusual clothing and her black hair dancing in the gusts compelled him to her. He walked over unseen, smiled, lifted her chin with a gloved hand, put his mouth on hers and pulled her into his arms. He took a deep breath and spoke without thinking as he sighed. "Good morning, my enchantress."

The sun had almost completed its reluctant rising. It floated white in the icy mist of the harbor. The morning light bathed the marketplace. The couple watched as light animated the place with buyers and sellers coming to life with the light. They moved apart naturally Oona took Jason's hand and led them out of the windy tower and down the stairs.

Jason was almost sorry to leave the shiny gold grasshopper, the only witness to their morning kiss. But he sensed that he should let this day unfold as it would. Down below they found warmth at the chestnut roaster's cart. They huddled at the fire, letting the heat cure their chilled bodies. Jason bought them a bag of roasted chestnuts, the roaster's first of the day. He fed her a few, teasing her mouth with his fingers in the public marketplace. They found a hiding place behind some crates, and fixed windblown hair and clothing. Oona had gotten her hat just so when Jason lifted it, put one finger under her chin and kissed her. It was an act of spontaneity that took Oona by delighted surprise; she stood on tiptoe and kissed him back. Caught in her gaze, his eyes turned dark and he pulled her to him, covering her mouth with his. Jason felt Oona shudder in his arms. This time, he was fairly certain it was not the cold.

As they walked the market, looking in the pushcarts and stalls, Jason wanted to ask about Oona's life at the Goodiels's, but he schooled his curiosity. "How is it," Jason asked, seeking a mundane topic, "that you look completely groomed and lovely and I continue to look a fright?"

"That, sir is because, although I am as windblown as yourself, men think a woman's deshabille is attractive, but do not desire the effect for themselves." Oona's voice was teasing and happy. She had unwittingly answered one question. So this was how she managed her friends as they chased her up the hill on Oliver Street. Even in adversity and chaos, wind tangling wild hair or dodging mud clots, Oona always found a morsel of joy.

Jason swallowed hard, trying to keep his voice light. "You should take that as a compliment, Oona. I mean it, you look not only presentable, but really lovely."

"My new hat! Jason, you noticed! Thank you, it cost me an octant. And Tommy's coat." She twirled, modeling the boy's coat in an unlikely manner. "Thomas Goodiel, Matthew's youngest. He outgrew it of course, and Anne put it in a pile to give to the church. I'd always liked the coat, so I'm afraid I took it for myself instead of giving it to the more deserving." She emphasized the word "more." "I wear it for cold weather errands and such; when today turned up so cold and windy, I saw nothing to be gained by wearing a cloak. I hope you don't mind being seen with a woman in a man's coat."

"Mind?" Jason answered by narrowing his eyes and giving her a look of pure, flaming desire that, without words, spoke of getting her out of her coat, and everything else. He took a breath and mentally shook himself. "Oona, you said something odd – how does a hat cost an octant?"

Oona had felt the wolf's eyes bore into her. Her body clenched and she felt warm in the deepest parts of her body. She was suddenly in no mood to banter. She squeaked, "Jason, it's a long story, breakfast!" She took his hand – this time, neither of them wore gloves – and she was keenly aware of his warm hand in hers. She led them to a small bakery just north of the main market. The shop smelled wonderfully of hot coffee, sweet rolls and fresh bread. They climbed onto low stools and settled their food onto an overturned barrel.

"Did you know that New England is famous for its

barrels?" Jason asked, struck by a need to begin again, just to make conversation.

"No, Jason, I didn't, though I have always seen many barrels. Tell me, why are ours famous?" Oona put her elbows on the barrel, pantomiming great expectation.

Jason assumed the pose of a schoolmaster, "Barrels, you see, Oona, use the same wood and techniques as shipbuilding, on a much smaller and simpler scale, of course. The leftover wood in the shipyard makes excellent barrels. Strong and waterproof – the best trees make the best ships and barrels. So I have been told by my American friends. The Brits might disagree about the ships, but the barrels even they will concede."

"I see." She grinned with pleasure and picked out the pecans of her sweet roll, keeping her eyes glued to him.

They finished eating in a pleasant silence. He motioned for more coffee, and sat back wondering if she would tell part of her story.

"Oona. How does a hat cost an octant?"

"Simply, that I bought the hat with money I'd saved for an octant. But you can't ask me why I wanted an octant."

"Fine. Then I have another question – why were those young men and women chasing you up Oliver Street and throwing clots of dirt at you?"

"You saw that? I didn't see you."

"I was behind the brick wall. I'd just left my first meeting with Goodiel."

"Oh." Oona paused as if wondering how much background to go into. "Lawrence and his stupid friends have a game, or they think it is a game. They try to dirty my gowns so I cannot wear them."

Jason wondered just who Lawrence was. "Why do they play this game? I don't understand." This was a strange story indeed.

"They want me to wear homespun or American-made cloth. You see, Anne Goodiel gives me her old gowns, like the red from the party." Jason nodded, understanding that much. "She has some of the nicest clothes in Boston. Fabrics from London, Madrid and Paris, made by dressmakers who keep up with the latest styles, or try hard to. I've learned to make them over to my liking in fit and style.

"Lawrence and the other apprentices tease me for wearing lovely gowns and rich fabrics. They do not care that the gowns are hand-me-downs from Anne Goodiel, and that I worked hard at a modiste's to learn to sew – Saturdays for two years. They care only that the fabrics are from Europe and are not plain homespun. So even though homespun would be more costly, they try to make me spend money on local goods by destroying my gowns. They daren't rip or discolor else Anne Goodiel would have the watch on them."

"You held them off – do you really care what they think?"

"I shouldn't care about Lawrence and his brothers, but I do care about the non-importation agreements. If I could, I would have a gown or two made from fabrics spun and woven in America."

"Then that will be our mission for today. We will spend the day looking for the prettiest and finest homespun Boston has to offer."

"Jason, I don't have the money for 'prettiest and finest' and neither do you. You've just signed on with Goodiel. He's not paid you yet." Oona nearly stamped her foot and might have, except she found that the floor was covered with straw to keep down the mud, and it muffled any sort of good foot stomp.

"Faith, Oona, I have a bit of a tale to tell you about

last night." He opened the saddlebag he had been carrying and let her look at the coin and paper money that nearly filled the sac.

"I think I'd best be hearing that tale." Oona sounded so old world that Jason wanted to laugh. He did not know if she understood that an Irish brogue had briefly appeared, but he found it endearing. He wanted to hug her. There had been a nurse to his younger siblings who had sounded precisely like that. Meghan was her name, and she always brought him sweets. He picked Oona's hand from their little table and gave it a squeeze. He turned it and brought it to his lips for a kiss. She felt that warmth again, but she ignored it and settled, waiting for his story.

"Well, it started with Belle." Jason did not want to be the villain in his own tale, so he felt it was important to lay the blame elsewhere right from the start. Oona knew the beginning of a good yarn when she heard it. She sat back on the little stool to enjoy it.

"Belle, as you probably know, has a running game to get someone to successfully kiss you at the *Mount*. The regulars all know about it, and every week they wait to see what sucker will end up getting slapped. I was happily drinking, letting the other fellows flirt with the blonde bar maid. Belle was starting her story about 'why don't the dark-haired girl get any tips?' Oona, it wasn't till I saw that the 'dark haired' girl was you that I decided to earn you some money. I was sorry I took advantage until the coin and specie got thrown on the table. I want you to have all of it. Or, if you like, we can spend like kings today.

"So that was the howling and screeching I heard! I did wonder." Oona might have been embarrassed. But, even more, she was delighted at having so much ready cash to spend. "Finish your coffee, Jason – we have places to shop and specie to spend."

First, they walked to the shops on Long Wharf for new stays and shifts. Oona even bought a few that required a lady's maid to do the backs. Normally she wouldn't have thought of bringing a man along on such a trip, but Sukey would have asked too many questions about the money, and would never have believed the simple answer. Anyway, Jason was a good companion, and he carried all the parcels. She found she was enjoying herself as she never had.

At the dressmaker's, they found a new homespun gown of a delightful dark green that someone had forgotten to pay for and collect. The modiste also had yards of fabric in from local weavers. Oona bought enough to sew her own. They looked at new hats, but Oona liked the one she had gotten with the Hubbards, and Jason didn't want a new one. Oona ordered one for him anyway, to be delivered to his rooms. In turn, Jason made Oona buy two pairs of new boots; warm ones lined in fur, and a fancy green pair that would look wonderful with her new gown.

She noticed that they carried on a single conversation; it seemed to stop at shop doors and resume on the street when they exited. "Anne expects me to buy *some* of my own things, with the money I earn at the *Mount*. She is disappointed when I don't. Doesn't like it that I save so often. I wonder what she will say when she notices so many new things." Oona mused. She did not mention that she spent her savings in other ways.

Oona argued with herself about going to *Points East* with Jason. She was feeling very comfortable, almost too comfortable. She sensed there was danger in that comfort. Did she dare let Jason see her interest in all things nautical? She shrugged her shoulders; she wanted that octant more than she cared about Jason's curiosity.

Oona had gotten quiet as they headed toward his rooms along the harbor on Kilby Street. She stopped at a little shop and turned as if to go in. She hesitated, shrugged, and pushed open the door. Jason followed, curious.

Points East, said the compass on the door. Jason had shopped in many similar shops, in London, Bristol, Plymouth and now interestingly, and unexpectedly, in Boston. He stood in the corner. His eyes toured the room as he admired the man's stock.

Oona handed Jason all the parcels to watch, and walked up to the bearded man at a cluttered desk. He looked up, recognized her and smiled his welcome.

"Oona, my dear, are you here for your octant? It's just over here." He walked to a long cabinet built into the wall, and unlocked a door with a key from his pocket. He handed Oona a triangular box of polished rosewood. They walked back to his desk, where Oona carefully put the box in front of the man. They put their heads together in quiet discussion.

It was clear that man and girl had performed this ritual before. She had been interested in learning to read the nautical charts that afternoon at the Goodiels's. Perhaps she also used nautical instruments. Jason wondered how many of the fine tools she had used her meager funds to procure, and why.

The shelves of the store were covered with tools and boxes showing shiny brass dials and polished wood bodies. There were telescopes, round and octagonal, some long and others quite short. There were octants of many varieties out and on display. Oona's box was a similar shape. Jason made the connection. The hat "cost her an octant." Of course, he almost hit his head in discovery. She was not able to pay for it, or finish paying for it, until today.

Leaving her to her privacy, he pushed their packages under a table and moved to look at the watches. Longitude was a problem even with the best equipment, but worse with a watch that had begun to lose time. He supposed it was too much salt, or too many months at sea – anyway, it was time for a new one. It would be great if the man had the chronometers he had been reading about. Probably not. They had not even been for sale in London last time he was there.

Looking for an available clerk, he spotted Oona again. This was a delight, as so many of Oona's little surprises were. Had he expected to spend part of this day with Oona here in a nautical goods shop? The answer to that was an obvious "no," yet here they were. A clerk walked over and helped him chose a watch worthy of a navigator. He was pleased. He paid for his purchase and trod carefully through crowded aisles to the front of the shop.

"Thank you, Mr. Crowninshield," Oona was handing the man some cash. The bearded man put the box aside.

Oona felt Jason move next to her. Her instinct was to push him away, not let him into this secret world of hers. But she had brought him here, so some part of her wanted him to know. "Oona" – he didn't whisper, but spoke so quietly only she could hear – "you must use our ill-gotten wealth." She jumped at the words, but nodded. Jason peered into Crowninshield's large ledger, reading the numbers upside-down from his side of the desk. He handed the man the remainder, bowing slightly at the fellow's knowing and approving smile. Oona didn't notice the men's shared look. She waved good-day to Mr. Crowninshield and led Jason out of the store.

"Oona, let me carry that, it's heavy. I'll trade you for

something light and bulky." Jason wanted to be helpful, but he was terribly curious about her reasons for the purchase. He wondered if Mr. Crowninshield knew why she was a regular customer at his shop. They seemed to be well-known to one another.

"No thank you, Jason, the box is not too heavy. I can carry it. Yes, I bought an octant, but I won't tell you why and you must promise you won't ask."

"I promise," he replied. Everyone deserved his, or her, secrets. "Perhaps one day you will trust me."

She smiled. "I've waited a long time for this octant. I have another, but this is more accurate. Next, I am purchasing a sextant. They are not here yet, and Mr. Crowninshield will not let me pay ahead, but he promises they will be here soon. The sextant can take altitudes at night, but you know that, don't you?" Jason had never seen Oona so excited before. But she halted midstream when she realized her enthusiasm might be interpreted as foolish, since this was a subject Jason understood so much better than she. Jason said nothing, but he thought his mouth might be hanging open in awe.

Again, he pushed himself out of stunned silence, realizing they were at the house."Let's go in and get warm. Michael Channing is in port and the family has gone visiting for a few days. I'll show you to my rooms, and if you feed the fire and make tea, I'll bring back lunch. I won't be gone but a few minutes." He kissed the top of her head, and before she could tell him that she would just leave a few things behind and go on back to Oliver Street, he was gone.

Oona knew she should leave, however tempting Jason's hearth and a warm lunch sounded. She stared at the door as Jason left, considering her choice. Just last week she had resolved to make choices that would please her. The

Channings were gone – more reason to run home – but on the other hand, there was no one to know she had been here. Lunch, warmth and an afternoon alone with Jason in his rooms offered risks, but she wanted, really wanted, to stay, like little Willie Goodiel wanting candy.

Oona blew on the coals and brought the fire to life. Waiting for the room to warm enough to shed her coat, she wandered through Jason's small space. Oona felt she was an expert on people's things, and the way they cared for them. His apartment was a large room with a half wall and a double door. When they were open, the room was quite large. The first room had the fire. There were a few cook pots at his hearth and, next to it, a wash stand and mirror. His shaving things, brush and comb, sat on the side of that. Oona was pleased that all his things were rinsed clean.

There was a thick rug in front of the fireplace, a nice place to sit and warm one's feet when the fire was big enough. Facing the hearth was a small couch, just big enough for a small person to nap, or for two people to sit. This little room was safe, friendly and warm. It was the sort of room any renter of furnished rooms might expect. It was the second room that drew her attention. That bed did not come with the furnishings provided by Mrs. Channing.

Oona had been around houses of the region's wealthy since she was ten. She had seen the best of what was made in America and England, many of them family heirlooms and antiques brought from Europe. She had never seen anything as elaborate or beautiful as the bed in Jason's bedroom. In fact, there was only room in there for the bed. It was set diagonally with only a few inches on either side for walking. The clothes press and chests were hidden behind the large headboard.

The bed was high and elaborately carved. There was

no room for its canopy. The foot and headboards were carved with crests and intertwining vines and flowers, the thick posts were carved with wheat shafts, and the same vine and flower motif circled the posts, reaching upward to the sun. Jason had no bed curtains hanging from it; Oona agreed that they would make the room too small. Of course, it might have nothing to do with size.

The door opened. "Oh, you noticed the bed." Jason asked blandly.

"Were you trying to hide it? I would have thought you'd do a better job." A sparkle of laughter glinted in her eye.

Oona had meant for Jason to find her sitting quietly in front of the fire warming her toes. But if she meant to be bold she might as well start. She ran to the door and helped Jason with his packages, laying them down on the carpet in front of the fire. She pulled the boiling water off the hearth. "Sit and get warm. Jason, do you have anything we can make into tea?"

Jason stood at the fire, his back to the room, warming his fingers. He turned, still not speaking, maybe suppressing laughter. He pointed to the other room. Then he dived under the bed. Jason was a big man and Oona couldn't help but be pleased he fit, but she had no idea what he was doing under there. He came out laughing, pushing something that looked like a tea crate.

"For shame, Jason! Shame!" She said laughing back at him. "Where on earth did you get that?"

"Dutch Antilles. Actually, I was trying to smuggle French tea into Boston the night of the destruction. I got the tea because of an interesting meeting with a French owned vessel. Her captain did not think we had the right to be on the sea. We proved him wrong, and I got the tea as booty.

The other fellows got pots, cloth, silverware, but I wanted the tea. In December of 1773, I wanted tea!" He groaned and she laughed. "Now, of course, I cannot sell it here. So, I am stuck with it. However, I have no guilt since I was working behind the back of the East India Company anyway. So I say we enjoy a cup."

"Yes, it will be so good to taste some again, though I think I might still prefer coffee. It has been years since the Goodiels had tea, even though they are nearly loyalists." She found a teapot, spooned the leaves into it, and let them steep. She wandered the room again, not sure where to be until Jason settled somewhere. Oona stopped in the bedroom, wondering where the tea had been hidden. She looked under the bed and saw the floorboards were up. Jason walked in, returned the tea crate and fixed the floor so that nothing showed. He rose and stood behind her, wrapping his arms around her and pulling her close. They stared together at the bed.

"Quite a bed, isn't it? It's old, from my mother's family; no one really knows who first owned it. Probably Scot – notice the Celtic motifs and the thistle. Mother shipped it last year when I took these rooms. She couldn't have, you know, if it had come from my father's side. But, she inherited it, so it is not entailed. I guess no one else in the family wanted it. I've always loved it, even when I was young and it was in the attic, unused and dusty. My mother noticed and remembered. So it was a kind wave across the ocean to her fourth son."

Oona heard the sadness in Jason's voice and wanted to ask about his family. Four sons – she wasn't sure what entail meant, but she wasn't ready to change the mood. "I see the Celtic knots and things. Hmm, your mother must trust you not to be in the habit of bedding stray ladies in your rooms. You know. . . ?" Little Jasons running around. She didn't say those last words, but even as she thought them, she felt a wave of desire flood her body, suddenly wanting all of those little Jasons herself, suddenly sure she would kill any other woman who thought of it. She swallowed hard. "Look at those wheat sheaves."

Jason chuckled. "Yes, I know. Does the wheat mean something?" He knew, of course. He had known since he had found the bed in the attic when he was nine years old. Later, he had understood the symbolism of the carvings, and his mother explained to him that tradition called for newlyweds to spend their wedding-night in this bed. The workmanship and delicacy of the carvings had moved him then, but he was coming to understand the magic in the carvings. He stared at the familiar piece, and saw a dream as real as life. It was of Oona as beautiful as today, but dressed like a comfortable, well-cared-for matron. She was surrounded by children, their children. They were laughing and jumping and throwing pillows on this beautiful, luxurious, over-sized bed. The image was so real it made his stomach clench and his loins harden. He blinked, and it was gone.

Oona looked at him as if she read his mind. She shoved him playfully, and went back to the fireplace and poured the tea.

She handed him his cup, and a slice of the meat pie he had brought back. "Jason, why do you sound so sad when you talk about home? Do you miss them?" Oona had been an observer of human relationships far more often than a participant in them. She could tell that whatever troubled Jason was more than homesickness.

She picked up her cup, and sipped and savored the rich flavor. She turned to look at Jason, ready to listen.

Neither of them had revealed very much about their lives. She knew that she had much to tell before the afternoon was spent, and suspected that Jason did as well. She settled onto the thick carpet, filled her plate, and looked at him expectantly.

"Oona, you might as well hear the truth from me – someone is bound to tell you. You know that my father is a Duke?" She nodded. "That's as well, but I am the fourth son, born into a world where the first is the heir and the second is the spare, as they so crudely put it. My oldest brother already has sons. The second one does, too, so in the world of the aristocracy into which I was born, I am superfluous and inconsequential, not only in my own generation, but in the next one as well."

Oona wanted to object – she almost spoke, telling him strenuously that he was not inconsequential or superfluous – but she stayed quiet and let him go on.

"I knew from the time I was little, that although I was loved – I have extraordinary parents – I simply was unnecessary to our place in the world, not important to the continuation of the duchy – that is, to the people of the town, the farms, the house, the region, or the county. I saw the worry my parents had if there was any bit of waywardness or illness in my sisters or my oldest brothers. But not the third, fourth, fifth, or sixth – Thomas, John, Jeremy or me – though I left home before Jeremy could get into any sort of trouble. No one ever worried about me if I got home late or even if I was gone for days. I recognized this early, and it hurt. I hope I've protected my two younger brothers from feeling the same way, but I am not sure.

"I shouldn't imply they didn't care. They did care, we were their children, but it was as though there were two sets. One belonged to posterity, to the past and the future:

the heir, Robert, and his offspring. The other was this big group, this big family where everyone loved and needed each other. But a few people belonged to both groups, and the rest of us did not.

Oona wanted to be surprised at Jason's family. She'd always hoped that children with parents and money were automatically happy. But even here on the coast of New England, removed from aristocracy and aristocratic rules, she understood that unhappiness came in many forms. She stayed quiet, hoping he would say more.

Jason went on speaking in the warm, safe room. He had pulled Oona's head onto his shoulder, his fingers at the nape of her neck, gently playing with her soft stray hairs. "My eldest brother will inherit the estate, a seat in Parliament – which he already attends – a house in London, and various other properties. My sisters have all had generous dowries arranged for them. Stephen, my second eldest brother, has money from my mother's family, from our grandmother's will. He was a mewling infant, but born while Grandmama was still alive. So, he was remembered in her will. He's an MP, Member of Parliament, and represents our county in the House of Commons.

"My brothers Stephen and Thomas, and our sister's husband, Nathan Gwynn, have gone into trade. Quite shocking on our side of the Atlantic, quite normal here. They own the FitzSimmon Shipping Company. I sailed for them before I signed on with Goodiel. I was on the *Chardon* for over three years."

They finished their tea and a bit of the pie. Oona curled her feet under her skirts and leaned closer into Jason. Conversation was easy in the warm room, and the early dark of the cloudy winter afternoon drew them together. Jason pulled the ribbon from Oona's braid and was gently undoing the plait as they talked. It was her time to talk, her turn to reveal something of the mystery that was Oona.

He was tempted to forgo the conversation, to simply pull her onto his lap, to carry her to his bed, and take her as long and powerfully as he could. He put his nose into her hair and let the enticing essence of lemon and rosemary, mingled with the feminine softness of hair and body, invade his senses. He yearned for her as he waited for her to speak – simply waited, not moving, and doing nothing but plying his fingers through her though her long, loose hair.

Oona stared into the fire as she spoke to the man she had curled into. She wasn't ready to tell what she knew of herself, to let go of Jason's story yet. "Jason, is it that your brothers, FitzSimmon Shipping, won't promote you because they don't have confidence in your ability to captain your own ship? Could they afford to offer you a captain's berth if they chose to? Can they afford to lose you to Goodiel?"

Jason was awestruck with Oona's questions. He'd not supposed that a servant, even in a large port town, would know enough of the world to understand how positions like captain's berths were doled out. He could never have imagined that this girl, without any training or family, would have insight into relationships as complicated with personality and economics as his were. Perhaps the ten years she had spent living with the Goodiels – years spent listening to the comings and goings of merchants and sailors on the edge of England's great empire – had given her quick, observant mind an education available to a very few.

His hand stilled in her hair, "I don't have an easy answer to that, Oona. I think I may be tired of working for them in a kind of expected anonymity. The brothers assume I will be good at what I do, so they see no reason to reward me. After all, they believe I work for God, the King, the

Empire, the firm, and the family, in that order.

"But I don't see that I do. I live here now, in America, in the Massachusetts Province. I like it here and intend to stay here and carve a life. There is nothing that pulls me back to England." He put his face into her hair now spread over his shoulder, and breathed in her scent. "I confess that I work for God. That seems natural, we all work for God; no sailor attempts the wrath of any deity."

Jason ran his fingers through that mass of hair and rubbed the head beneath. Oona shivered with pleasure and tilted her head closer to Jason's hand, responding deep within, but still listening carefully as he spoke. "I'd rather not think too much about the king and empire; nor do I want to be concerned with my brothers' firm. Rather, than work for the family in which I was raised, I would rather start a new family, my family."

His hand left her head and wandered down onto her long soft neck. He drew mindless circles on her shoulders, and across her back, teasing her senses and making her aware of his touch and her reaction to it. She forced herself back to his words, but he wasn't making it easy to listen.

"As to your question about their capital – I don't know how their holdings are. These are very uncertain times, but the *Chardon* was doing quite well when I sailed with her. My mistake was taking my bounty in tea instead of linens or lace."

Oona smiled in sympathy, knowing how hard it was going to be to convert bohea into ready cash.

Chapter 6

*J*ason leaned over and lifted Oona's hair and kissed her neck. He stood to work on the fire which had gotten low, taking a moment to turn and look back at the beautiful woman leaning against his couch, waiting for him. Her long hair was loose and delightfully disheveled, thanks to the wind and his fingers. Her lovely violet eyes were shielded as she fingered her skirts.

He needed to understand her, to know her before they moved on with this undeniable attraction. He could seduce her – they had fallen into a spell that wove around then whenever they were together. He could seduce her, but he would not hurt her.

Oona lifted her eyes and looked directly at Jason. He moved back to their spot on the floor and took her into his arms.

"Oona, tell me. You are not a Goodiel, not related to them. But you don't go home the way most servants do. Where is your family, who are you?"

Tears formed at the corners of Oona's eyes. He would take back the questions to let her avoid this pain. Maybe he should just gather her into his arms and finish what they had started days ago in Matthew's cozy map room. He pulled her close as she turned to him and opened her mouth to his. He hoped that Oona could gather comfort from his kiss. He moved to deepen it, but she pulled away. Abruptly, she started to cry. Jason held her tight against him and let her sob. She climbed into his lap, her arms clenching him as tightly as he had ever been held. He kept his hold secure, not letting her think for a moment he was ignoring her pain. It must be that she had not cried for a very long time. After a while he found a linen square and handed it to her. She wiped her eyes and blew her nose.

"Oona, I think you had better talk to me."

"Yes, I'm afraid you are right." Oona seemed resigned, just maybe slightly relieved to begin. "Jason, I don't go to visit my family, because I have no family. At least not in America, that I know of. I'm not a maid like you imagine." Jason felt Oona stiffen and pull away. He pulled her back, trying to offer some security. "I am an indentured servant. I have a ten-year indenture to the Goodiels that ends in May 1774, on my twentieth birthday."

There were such contracts in Britain, and he knew of passengers to America who paid off their passage with the traditional seven year indenture. "Oona, isn't being indentured to the Goodiels just the same as being their maid, except you can't leave for another job – the work is the same, yes?"

"Yes, but you see the restrictions and punishments are more severe. For instance, my master, or mistress as in my case, Anne, can forbid relations with men, and she has. She has made it very clear. At first, her strictness was to protect me. It began when I was twelve or thirteen. By then I had lived with the Goodiels for three years and knew all the apprentices and young servants on our side of town. We were all quite independent, living without parents and the like. Anne made sure I sat with her stepsons for lessons, and I already told you I sewed with Mrs. Anderson on Saturdays.

But afternoons, when lessons and chores were over, those who could would meet.

"Lawrence Morse was the butcher's apprentice on Orange Street. He comes from a big family. They're from the North End. He has two brothers. They were apprentices too, but not this far south.

Oona stopped, and with a new breath asked, "Jason, you know all the stories about maids, the shepherdess, or the milk maid who would lie with the good looking boys, or the serving girl who was easy?"

Jason nodded. He held her close, but did nothing to stop her from telling her tale.

"Well, Lawrence and his brothers knew all about serving girls. They just didn't know any out of storybooks – only me. Most girls in Boston live out – that means they live with their parents or other family, and work days. So the Morse boys did not see them as servants. Or maybe they did, but those girls were protected.

"I was a servant, and the Morses had a stubborn idea about what servant girls did. They told me over and over that they knew what 'servant girls were for'." Oona stopped speaking. She swallowed, shuddered and took a deep breath. Jason held very still. Without noticing, Oona had put her strong hand in his. He held it tightly, willing her the strength to continue.

"One day, Lawrence and his brothers chased me over Cornhill from Tremont. I was carrying bread home from the baker's. They cornered me and trapped me in a stall in the livery stable. They pulled at my ties till they loosened my bodice, all the while shouting 'show me, Oona, show me.' I don't know what would have happened, but Anne Goodiel found us, and beat those boys to within an inch of their lives.

"She didn't yell at me in public, kept absolutely silent, but when we got home she whipped me for letting them chase me, and locked me in my room. Later, when she came to let me out, she told me I was never to let a boy near me. I was to stay pure. She impressed on me that my purity was valuable. It was the only thing I owned that had any worth.

"The law is on her side, too. Fornication is punishable by whipping, twenty-one lashes. And if a female indentured servant gets pregnant, she may have to work a week or even a month for each day she misses her chores due to sickness, delivery, or care of the child. The master or mistress can legally be very strict, and enforce the edict that an indenture may not marry during the time of the contract.

"The law protects the servant, too. An indentured person cannot be forced to marry, but the master or mistress can induce or even force a man to marry their indentured girl and, if they time it right and she marries right at the end of her contract, the master avoids paying freedom dues to her. That's the specie or goods required by law to set up the indenture in his or her new life. I hadn't thought that Anne or Matthew had that in mind."

Jason gripped her hand. He wanted to cry in frustration himself, realizing that any hope he had of bedding Oona before he sailed had been effectively thwarted. He still thought he could seduce her, but he would regret that immediately. He must have looked sad, because Oona pulled out of his arms and turned to face him.

"Wait, Jason! Telling you this reminded me of something that happened at the party. Anne may be in negotiation to sell Peter Church the honor of marrying me. They approached me at the party, after I left you."

"Who is Peter Church?" Jason was ready to

challenge his rival. Though he could well understand the value of securing the rights to Oona, it seemed uncivilized to do it behind her back.

"She can't make me marry. The law protects the servant. But she can make me miserable if I don't do what she wants. Peter Church is a nice enough man. But he's never had any interest in girls. He shares his houses with a man, and likes to buy pretty things, clothes and jewelry and such. I'm afraid one of his relatives told him he needs a wife, and that Anne Goodiel told him that I was a pretty thing he could buy – from her. I will have to disabuse him of that idea. He won't care one way or the other, but if there is money involved, and I'd guess there is, Anne will be very, very angry.

Again, Jason wanted to take her into his arms and show her that not every man was a cad like Lawrence Morse or a fop like Peter Church. He had never desired a woman more than he did Oona. He felt so close to her and unexpectedly content with her in his rooms. The idea of a women's virginity having monetary worth seemed medieval to him. Maybe it mattered to people who lived in the world of the aristocracy, where bloodlines and succession must be ensured. There, the child's paternity was proven by the woman entering the marriage in a virginal condition. But what did it matter in the Goodiels's world?

He wanted to pull her into his arms. But the whole point of the long story was that he could not, and this was probably not the time to explain all the nice things they could do to each other that would not result in small membranes ripping or pregnancy. He was afraid that those would also be punishable by twenty-one lashes if Oona's mistress was a stickler for the letter of the law.

"Oona, what can I do to help you?"

"I don't know." Oona stared out the window at the gathering dark. "Would you kiss me, knowing that I can't...?"

Jason silently groaned with desire. He leaned into her, and planting a gentle but definitive kiss on her lips. He put out his hand for hers.

Oona put her hand in Jason's and was willingly pulled back onto his lap. She felt his hands moving in her hair, playing on her scalp, and the tightening of the muscles deep in her belly. His mouth owned hers. She opened to him and found that she searched his mouth with her tongue. Her hands found themselves loosening his hair and running her fingers through it. She forced her eyes open, as if these were the last things she would see on earth, and watched the fire catch and dance in the gold streaks of Jason's hair. She caught him looking at her, and his eyes flashed the yellow streaks of the hunting wolf.

Oona felt pulled into Jason's vortex. She whirled in sensation and building desire. She opened her mouth to his and melded her tongue with his, as he deepened the kiss. She was aware of movement, of Jason lifting her and moving her, still holding her close. She looked up into Jason's eyes and then under her back was the soft carpet. His hand traced her neck and over her taut nipples; she arched to him. He made no effort to untie her bodice or even reach below it. On the outside of all her layers his hands moved over her, raising goosebumps, causing her to quicken with desire.

She didn't know how long they kissed. She didn't understand what a kiss was, what a kiss could do, until then.

Jason was rock-hard. He had felt every one of Oona's sighs, her hands in his hair, on his chest and back, her body arched against him, her legs spreading below him, as though they were knife thrusts to his groin. He was in hell. He had never had a more pleasant afternoon.

The clock downstairs struck five. It was full dark, and they had been in Jason's rooms for hours. Oona thought she should jump up embarrassed and rush home, but she felt no such thing. She did not feel violated. She had Jason to thank for that. She was not satisfied either; no, there was tingling in every part of her that wanted completion, whatever that was. But she felt adored, safe and warm. She dozed those last few minutes with Jason's arm around her, her head pillowed on his chest.

She moved his hand slowly away, and quietly got up. She used the chamberpot behind the screen, not wanting to step into the cold yard just yet, and sat to brush her hair with Jason's hairbrush. Now, she thought, if I were the upstairs maid set to cleaning this room, these long dark hairs in my master's hair brush would certainly tell me what he did last night. When she was finished, she used a comb to clean the long hairs out of the brush, and threw the knot into the dying fire.

Jason woke as Oona stood, and the cold hit him where her head had been. He watched her move across the room and sit at his washstand. He lay on his back, hands beneath his head, and drank in the sight of Oona as she brushed knots out of long black waves. He didn't know if she saw him watching, for at that moment, he did not care. He had seen women do many things, some of them to him, but nothing was as charming or as intimate as watching Oona brush her hair.

Jason rose as Oona walked to the hearth with her loose hair. He would have stopped her, saved it in a silk bag, but that was maudlin, and too romantic for a plain old sailorman. He found his boots and pulled them onto his feet, and then knelt in front of Oona to tie her half boots.

"Jason!" Oona started to object to his waiting on her, but he silenced her with a look of command that said she must allow him to kneel before her and tie her boots. She bit her tongue. They walked up the hill in a comfortable silence. As they approached the kitchen door of the Goodiels's big house, Jason clasped Oona's fingers in his. He pulled her glove off her hand, lifted her fingers to his lips, and kissed each in turn. He ran his tongue over her little finger; he pulled it into his mouth with his lips teasing and sucking till he heard her gasp. He repeated that with each finger in turn till Oona was nearly jelly leaning against him in the kitchen garden.

"Oona," Jason spoke in a quiet breathy voice that made her clench in places of which she had only become aware that afternoon. "I promise you I will not compromise you, nor will I do anything that would risk either your reputation or a pregnancy. But Oona – I want you to know, deep in your most secret places, that when I find the right time and place, I will make you moan with pleasure. I will make that tiny gasp you just uttered seem pallid. And together we will make those nasty voices of the Morses and the preachy voice of your mistress disappear. And," he let the full force of his mischievous grin show, "it will be my pleasure to do it."

"Lets get your packages up to your room." He picked up the few he had put down to kiss Oona's fingers, and they waited for someone to let her in.

They brought all the bundles to Oona's small room in the attic. She had tried to prevent him from coming up, but he had laughed, asking her if she knew how a seaman lived shipboard. She had to agree her room could be no worse than that, so she let him follow her up. He'd left right away, after leaving bundles on the small, hard bed, and giving the bed a sort of yearning look that made her laugh. And before he'd left he had answered 'yes' to her request that he attend King's Chapel on Christmas morning. She turned and waved, as he motioned for her not to walk him back down the stairs.

Oona followed him a few minutes later to bolt the door against the night. She caught a glimpse of the lanthorn light in his eyes as he turned away from the house. She could have sworn she saw those amber streaks in his eyes, even in the dark night. It felt very good to be hunted by Jason FitzSimmon.

Chapter 7

Jason did not see Oona again before Christmas. He had a meeting with Matthew and wanted to find her at the Goodiels's, but when he arrived at the mansion the morning after their day together, he was told by Matthew Goodiel that he was being taken inland. Goodiel decided that Jason would accompany him as he met with vendors of pelts and lumber. For a sailor to be privy to the origins of the merchandise he normally saw only in barrels and crates was unusual, and showed enormous trust from the owner. He could not insult the man by turning him down. He caught only a glimpse of Oona at a window as he climbed into Matthew's well-appointed carriage.

Jason would have preferred to ride. The day was crisp and cold, and the ground was hard. In short, it was a perfect day for traveling. Most of his stays in Boston were so brief he had barely seen the interior. So it wasn't often he got to see the towns west of Boston. They rode south over the neck and headed north through Brookline, that small town situated on a series of marshes and rivers. Then they stayed on the improved turnpike until the Newtown. This far inland, the trees were noticeably taller, the forests deeper, and there were glimpses of wild animals like deer and wolves to be had out of the corner of an eye as they traveled.

Newtown was nestled into two curves of the river named after Charles I, who had granted the first Charter to the Colony. There was irony in that, Matthew explained, because the Puritans here in Massachusetts applauded the beheading of the King after he was convicted of treason. It was rumored that three of the judges who had presided at that trial had been hidden in New England. The regicides, as the judges were called, who had not fled across the Atlantic were hunted down and killed by officers of James II after the monarchy was restored. Jason had not been aware of the connections between the Old England and New.

They stopped at the falls on the Charles River. Here the river rushed through a narrow ten-foot drop to turn mill wheels. One of the sawmills powered by that water was working on a shipment of lumber for the *Catherine*. Jason took a moment to look into the dark shade of an ancient hemlock grove, deep green now in the cold of winter. He would have loved to take time to stand in the sheltered wood and enjoy the quiet trees with their feather-like needles and tiny cones. But he was on this journey to check on goods and shipments. He snapped himself out of his daydream and listened to Matthew negotiate with David Tyrie, the mill owner. He knew it was a kindness to be allowed to listen, but his mind kept wandering back to wishing a certain dark-haired girl were hiding in the hemlocks.

Finally, Mr. Tyrie directed them to a tavern run by his sister, a widow who had taken over the place since her husband's death eight years before in the French and Indian War. The road followed the river a few miles downstream to another falls, where there was an unexpectedly substantial stone tavern serving people from the growing towns. Jason was surprised to see that the tavern owner and assistant brewer, the widow, was hardly older than himself. A boy about eight rushed in with an armful of wood for the cookfire. If the woman was widowed in the last war, she must have married and had that child when she was nearly a child herself. It must have been a hard life. A memory stirred at the corner of his mind, but was knocked out by Matthew Goodiel asking what he would prefer for lunch.

At Bigelow's *Wheel and Hammer* tavern, named after the forge and smithy across the road, they met with the fur trader who had contracted with Goodiel for the sale of his pelts. They shared their meal, and then Matthew went out with him to inspect the furs and make arrangements for the skins to arrive in time for the launch. Jason stayed behind in the nearly empty tap room, nursing the good ale made by the young widow.

"You seem a bit done in by the merchant's chatter. You don't actually work with him, do you?" Nina sat at the table, her own tankard in hand.

"You're right, I don't, but how did you guess?" She really did look too young and too small to be running this tavern. She was thin, worn out by the look of her, but not if the spark in her eyes told the real story. She still maintained most of the beauty of her youth, but she really did need more help than the young boy could give.

"You keep trying to drift off into your thoughts, and Goodiel keeps asking your opinion. I've seen such often enough. We are at a major crossroads of river and road, in and out of Boston, so we get lots of working meetings, as well as travelers. Nina Bigelow." She held out a hand. Jason took it in his and shook it.

"Jason FitzSimmon. Nice to meet you, Mrs. Bigelow."

"Nina, please. I was married to John Bigelow for six days before he went off to York. He was killed, and I had Jack. I was sixteen. I never did feel like a missis. But I learned a skill and inherited a living and got a better name than the one I was born with – at least around here. And I would never have given up Jackie, though some in the family thought I should.

"Now tell me, Jason FitzSimmon, who are you thinking of when you drift away? There is a pleased smile that keeps floating over your face. Tell me. I feel the need of a happy story."

Jason looked in his tankard, and up at the pretty woman across from him. Perhaps sensing the story would be worth the price of a pint, she took both pewter cups and returned with them overflowing. A few hours later, Jason had heard the life story of Nina Tyrie Bigelow, and she had heard the past and future dreams of Jason Howe FitzSimmon. The sun was well past halfway to evening when Matthew finished with his meetings, and motioned to Jason that it was time to go.

"Jason, I wish you a fruitful voyage and a good life with your love." Jason had warned her that using Oona's name in front of Goodiel would be a problem.

"Thank you, Nina. I wish you prosperity and a grand love. Something that will surprise even you. Thank you for your hospitality and your fine food and drink." He kissed her fingers as a gentleman ought. She giggled and waved the carriage on its way.

They arrived late to a dark and shuttered house. Jason made his adieus to Matthew, as the older man opened the kitchen door and waved him inside.

"Nowhere to get food at this hour, I'll ring for the girl. She'll get us some cold meat and bread. Better than going hungry." He ushered Jason inside and closed the door against the cold night.

Oona heard the kitchen bell ring. She opened her door to listen and see what sort of emergency was worth waking for. She heard Matthew ask for her to come down and serve some food.

She shouted "yes, sir" just loud enough for whomever was in the kitchen to hear, but not loud enough to wake anyone on the other side of the house. She pushed her feet into fur-lined clogs and pulled a heavy wool shawl around her shoulders. She checked to make sure her hair was neat in a cap, and went down. In the kitchen she worked on the fire and reheated the stew the family had had for dinner, and cut meat and bread for the late diners. When it was ready, she carried the food into the small dining room Matthew preferred.

Jason sat at the table. He was deep in conversation with Matthew about the products and vendors they had met on their day's journey. Although he did not turn to address her, she could tell he was fully aware that it was she who had brought the food. Then he stared right into her eyes as he stood to take the tray from her and put it on the table between the men. A glint of a smile teased in his eyes traveled from head to feet, and he took in the red flannel nightrail and fur slippers. He let loose a smile and nodded with deep approval. Matthew was already busy with his dinner and paid no attention. Oona directed a flirtatious curtsey at Jason, told the men to leave the dishes till morning, and went back upstairs.

Red. Of course she slept in red. She had obviously developed a keen ability to rebel in ways that would cause no ripples or crosswinds to keep her from her destination – freedom. He ate in silence. The garment was an outrageous color, oversized and concealing, yet like the man's greatcoat, he found it enchanting. He nodded at Matthew in agreement, but offered little as the man droned on.

He wanted Oona, naked and willing, in his bed. He

understood that. But this need to hold and protect a woman against the cold and dark was new. He wondered, as he walked the short distance back to the Channings's house, what it was, this new feeling. There were those red roses being grown in a glass house just west of the neck. He had only days until the *Catherine* sailed. Those flowers might be a good place to start.

The next morning, a red rose was delivered to the Goodiels's kitchen by Georgie Channing. Friday, the boy brought a length of delicate Irish lace. Oona cut a small square from the corner of the lace and put it under the slender vase that held the red rose. Saturday, the day before Christmas, while Oona was out, a gown length of midnight blue patterned wool fabric was left inside the kitchen door. It was followed that afternoon by enough red silk for a fabulous and daring petticoat. Oona imagined embroidering red roses on the blue to match the underskirt and split sleeves for the gown she was going to make. Christmas interrupted the parade of gifts, but Oona had high hopes for the following week. Instead, on Christmas morning on her way to collect an armful of wood for the parlor fire, she found two packages – one was a warm fisherman's sweater, unusually small and finely knit. The other, with a note apologizing for the rush, was a warm cap to match.

She did not know if Jason preferred to see her in the fine gown, or in men's trousers with the sweater and cap, maybe out on the beach helping to pull in the night's catch. She had grown to understand that both of those women were part of her and, miraculously it seemed, so did he. She felt well-gifted.

Oona pulled the rose across her lips, smelling the fragrant flower, and imagined Jason's finger teasing them open to kiss. He had promised not to take advantage. Her body quivered.

Christmas day was dark. There was a storm threatening, but luckily for fine boots and best cloaks being walked through the streets of Boston, it was holding off. Oona had agreed to accompany the Goodiels, and to meet Peter Church, at King's Chapel. She filled the brasiers with hot coals. There was a large one that Matthew would carry to the Goodiels's pew, and another for her in the servant's. She went upstairs to dress. Even if Jason came, she could not sit with him, but she decided to dress as though she could. She dressed in the warm brocade she had altered for herself last winter. Its color could only be described as hyacinth. The dress would please Anne Goodiel, and make Jason smile. If Peter Church thought she was pretty, that would be his problem, not hers.

The little girls took turns carrying the small brazier up the hill. At the church, she settled the girls in the Goodiel family pew near the front. When the girls were tucked in with robes and the warmer opened, she turned to leave, to sit in the back.

"Oona," Anne Goodiel crooned. "Sit with the family, dear, Peter will be joining us in a few minutes. You look so lovely in my old blue."

"Thank you, Ma'am." Oona sat near the girls and decided to concentrate on the music and the sermon. Peter Church arrived after the minister began. The man had no embarrassment, and noisily found a spot on the far side of Matthew. His late arrival had made it impossible for him to sit next to her since the little girls had effectively sandwiched her between them. Oona was as pleased with the arrangement as she could be.

The service was lovely, and Oona enjoyed the music, incense and candles. The effect was so pleasing and so different from the Congregational church where she had chosen to worship. She scanned the pews, hoping to find Jason. He was sitting to her right and a row behind the Goodiels's pew. He was dressed in a most elegant coat, threads of a distinctly hyacinth color woven throughout. His hair was dark and shiny in a room of powder and white wigs. She caught his eye and saw a glimmer of humor in his as he viewed the similarity in their fine clothes. There was something more, even in the crowded church with rows of closed pews between them. She felt the protection he always offered.

As the congregation broke up, Peter Church took her arm. He asked general questions concerning the weather, the service and such topics. Oona answered politely, offering nothing much in return. They walked down the hill and into the Goodiels's front hall. He seemed to be waiting for something, or someone. Oona suspected it was Anne Goodiel. She was not there, and Peter had to talk to her directly.

He leaned a little too close, and he did not seem happy at all to be alone with her. Oona stepped back and looked at him. He must be nearly forty, slim and too well-dressed, even for Christmas. In all, he was not bad looking. He looked like he had been in a fight or two, with scars to show for it, although he did not look very strong.

He seemed to give up the wait. "Well, Oona, lets get to it, shall we? I am a wealthy man who has never had much interest in finding a bride. Mrs. Goodiel tells me she would like to have you happily situated before your indenture is over. So she and I thought that maybe you would like to come and live with me."

"As a servant? A bride? I don't understand."

"I guess it would be a little of both. You would be my wife in the eyes of the world, but I would not require regular wifely duties of you. I do need an heir to my considerable wealth but, you see, since I am not interested in such things, I would bother you very little."

Oona tried not to laugh. He spoke so seriously. He also checked the time on his pocket watch, and fixed the ruffles of his silk shirt. She could see that he really was not interested in her performing her wifely duties.

"But this would mean that I would never marry anyone else, isn't that correct?"

"I do hope for a long life. So yes, but there is a great deal of money involved." He looked a bit uncomfortable bringing up the money, but Oona was not at all surprised that Anne Goodiel had considered such an arrangement.

Oona knew there were things about her background that Anne had never told her. There had never been another indentured servant, man, woman, or child in the household. Her mistress probably begrudged the cost and bother of raising and training her, and it rankled. As though Oona's work in the house, the gardens, with the children, and in the kitchen had not paid her back ten-fold! There was probably one cash outlay that the woman would dearly love to get back. Oona took a deep breath and tried to let out all the anxiety she felt.

"You know, Mr. Church, my indenture ends in May of this coming year. I'm afraid this arrangement only benefits Mrs. Goodiel. And you must know, the magistrates frown on any sort of abuse of the indenture, either the law or the person. Mine ends on my next birthday, May the twenty-fifth. I intend to make sure that it does.

"Sir, I thank you for your generosity. I am sure you

meant only kindness, but a false marriage will not do." Oona shifted her weight between feet. "I have a thought on your situation, if I may?" She took his arm and pulled him further away from the gathering. She spoke close to his ear in a conspiratorial manner. "I suspect there is a slightly older woman among your crowd?"

"Ahuh." He nodded, assuming they had the same person in mind.

"Older, but not so old? Someone who could give you the heir you need?

Again he nodded, revealing nothing.

"Well, Peter" – she touched his arm flirtatiously – "if this woman is a widow who sometimes enjoys your amusements, don't you think she could be convinced, for a large amount of money and a lifetime of leisure, to marry you? Wouldn't that be ideal? So much better than burdening yourself with a blushing bride, who might expect attentions from her husband?"

Peter had been nodding in agreement to Oona's solution to his wifely problem. It must have felt a better fit to him than bringing home a beautiful innocent who might expect him to change. He thanked her most sincerely for her honesty, and left her to enjoy the luncheon.

After the guests had left, Oona changed from her hyacinth gown into warm, sensible clothes, and went for a short walk to clear her head. Peter Church had probably meant well. At least she would like to think he did, but she had made quiet inquiries as to his home and his friends; really, his home was no place for a woman who did not have similar debauched tendencies. She was glad she had suggested an alternative. Oona supposed Anne Goodiel was not going to be pleased, but it was time Oona made her future a priority. Anne should understand that.

Chapter 8

Oona had walked to the Common to watch the sun set over the marshes of the Back Bay. The walk back over Fort Hill was made treacherous and plodding by a harsh storm that started just as Oona turned toward home. She pushed back the hood of her cloak so she could see against the driving sleet. She was happy for the warm fisherman's cap and sweater Jason had left. The thick lanolin-soaked wool was warm and waterproof against the cold and wet. She lifted her face to the stinging ice and steadil-increasing wind, loving the howling wind and the energy of the storm. Hours later, alone in her room after the long day, she looked out the attic window. The wind had picked up and was roaring now. The reflected light from the thick clouds and white ground showed that ice had begun to stick and accumulate on every tree limb, roof, and mast.

The Nor'easter raged all night and all of the next day. It was Sunday, but no one ventured out for church. The ground was a solid sheet of ice, too treacherous for horses' hooves, or for a walker on anything but the most important errand. With each gust of wind, another heavy, ice-coated tree limb crashed to the ground, making the world even more treacherous. Someday, Oona thought while staring out the window, when the sun came out again, this dull gray world will be changed by the ice, snow and freezing rain into a shiny, sparkling otherworld.

And so it was Monday morning that people emerged from their hearths to get on with their week. Frozen mud and brick walks, coated with a day's worth of accumulated ice, greeted them. Oona, like other brave souls ready to face such a day, held tight to her stout walking stick as she maneuvered through town. Like everyone she stepped gingerly, but it was the sight overhead that captivated her. The clouds had cleared away for bright winter light that caught the ice on every surface and brought it to an unearthly life. Nothing looked as it had before. Things like tree limbs, window shutters, shop and tavern signs glittered in the bright light, moved unnaturally in the wind, broke loose from their anchors, and simply shattered when they hit the ground. As the morning progressed, and no heat could be coaxed from the sun to melt the layers of accumulated ice, a new wind arrived from the harsh north. Gusts from this frigid wind took the ice-covered trees and ships' masts and snapped them like twigs.

Oona headed home with bread, eggs and stew beef for dinner. She was pleased to have made it home and not slipped and fallen on Mrs. Channing's fresh eggs. Back in the warm kitchen on Oliver Street, she put down her bundles and pulled off her cloak and warm undergarments. "Mrs. Prince, it's bad down at the harbor. Masts broken, ships on their sides. I didn't see the *Catherine,* but I don't see how she could have come through with nothing damaged. Leastways, not completely. None of them did."

"Don't tell the master."

"Don't tell? Why not?"

"If he goes out now and gets hurt on a fall, mistress will blame you. I think she is quite angry enough over Peter Church."

"Really? Did something new happen?"

Mrs. Prince poured two cups of chocolate and sat Oona down for a chat. Nothing had happened. But there was no reason to upset Anne Goodiel, or make Matthew run out before the streets were cleared. The cook was absolutely right.

The harbor was a mess. Every launch was off schedule. Matthew Goodiel inspected his ships the next morning; there was no question that the *Catherine* needed to get to Windmill Point and Gibbon's Shipyard as soon as possible. Damage to the brig was extensive. Her main mast had become thickly coated with ice, and had snapped like a twig in the storm when the wind picked up. The decking was partially destroyed, as were the secondary masts. The smaller masts could be repaired, Mr. Eames was sure, but the main had to be replaced or the ship would be in danger during any storm at sea. Goodiel wouldn't mind a fresh coat of paint, but that would depend on the weather. Lucky for him, the shipyard had a mast the right size right at the site. Matthew knew he would pay dearly for that mast, and that someone's ship would be delayed for months because of his need. He had the coin, and what had to be done would be done.

The captain of the *Catherine* used the delay to visit his family in the Maine Territory, and planned on returning in a week or so. So the work of removing the stowed goods back into Matthew Goodiel's warehouse on Long Wharf, and seeing the ship safely to Gibbon's, south past the neck, fell to Jason, the first mate.

Jason spent the twenty-eighth of December supervising the moving of goods from the ship into the warehouse. Matthew spent the day making sure that his new merchandise did not get mixed with the goods rescued from the ship. The men worked all day and long into the night, moving crates and carefully labeling barrels. They were all understandably exhausted after moving the entire contents of the ship back to the warehouse over the icy, slushy streets. Jason planned on catching the morning tide to float the disabled *Catherine* down to the shipyard. Happily, the high tide was predicted for late morning, allowing the men a few good hours of sleep between days of hard work.

Before work started for the second day, Jason went down to Rowe's Wharf where the *Catherine* was waiting. He gave the watch a few minutes off to go get breakfast before he would be needed for the move. The empty ship was a sad place. Walking into the small room assigned to him, he packed his instruments and the clothes he had left onboard. When the morning watch returned, he carried his boxes back to his rooms. Reluctant to wake the men earlier than necessary, he made three trips from the harbor to Beech Street. By the time the tide was near high, he was back at the wharf with a dozen workmen, ready to tie the *Catherine* to tugs and dinghies and tow her south.

Towing a wreck was not a particularly onerous task. In theory, one righted the ship and moved her along, however possible. Getting her to the shipyard with no further damage was paramount. They had pumped out whatever rainwater the storm had left behind, and without her contents, and no ballast, she rode high in the water. That buoyancy made it easy to tow her over the shallows, but also increased the likelihood she would list and crack the secondary masts. They spent the better part of the afternoon moving her the single mile from wharf to shipyard, and securing her at the drydock.

Jason's men were not the only crew busy that

afternoon, and as the sun set the whole came together as a happy, thirsty group, ready for dinner and drink, a well deserved reward for a job well done. They toasted each other's work, some heroic, some comic, until no one escaped being as tipsy as the *Catherine* had been. At full darkness, Jason excused himself, begging exhaustion. The men nearly laughed him out of the tavern, and he headed back toward his rooms.

The night promised to be a cold one. Jason felt his fingers chill in his wet gloves. He'd have liked to cut across fields and yards to get out of the cold night, but with the dark came the thin coating of ice that made untrampled paths treacherous. He backtracked down the hill and headed south on Sea Street along the harbor. As he got close to Walner's Ropeworks, he heard angry voices interrupting the normal sounds of the docks. At first, the sounds were indistinguishable. It was not a calm night; the air was filled with the sounds and smells of sea, wind, ropes clanging against metal, and wood creaking against itself. He stopped and listened, hoping it was just revelers and that the sounds would fade away or turn into laughter. He was not so lucky.

Oona, like many townspeople, had gone to the harbor to watch the ships moved. It had been a busy day with lots of activity as ships were moved, docks and warehouses repaired, and attempts made to put the harbor right. As a member of Goodiel's household, she had been among the women who had brought hot drinks and chowder to the workmen. She was seeing to the last of the fires as the work was finished, and the men moved off to more substantial fare. She kicked at some coals with her toe, and poured the last of the coffee into a coarse, badly-glazed mug, taking a minute to herself before heading home. She looked out over the dark sea, enjoying the sounds and solitude, the end of a long day brought.

"Hello, Oona. Thought I might find you down here, always around when folks need help."

Oona recognized Lawrence's voice from the first whine. "Hello, Lawrence." Suddenly she was sorry for the solitude she had been relishing. She had a strong feeling that she should leave the spot, even if it meant coming back at dawn to finish her tasks. She stood and took a step toward the path. Lawrence grabbed her arm.

He pulled her against his powerful body. "You've missed me, I know you have." He put his mouth over hers and kissed her hard, forcing her lips apart and brutally forcing his tongue in her mouth. His breath was foul, he tasted horrid, and he smelled of rum. "I heard that Brit sailor had you up in his rooms last week." Lawrence hissed into her ear.

"Nonsense! Do you believe anything you hear? Lawrence Morse, let me go!" Oona pushed against him, but he tightened his grip, pulling her into a dark, unused shed.

She kicked his shin and ran, as for a moment it seemed he might let go. He grabbed her elbows and held her off the ground, where her kicks were harmless. "Lawrence, don't do this. Please let me go. We can talk about it when you haven't been drinking." Oona tried pleading with the stubborn man, knowing even as she tried, that it would do no good.

"Oona, do you think I'll just move aside and let some other man have you?" He put her down, but grabbed her wrists behind her back, forcing her into his arms. His grip was so strong she could not move her arms, nor break away. "You have been mine since we were kids; I won't let him."

Oona tried to scream, to push away, to trip him into

the icy water that lapped against a hole in the floor. But he covered her mouth with his, and holding her two hands in his one, forced her body hard against his. After a moment of trying to breathe with Lawrence's tongue in her mouth, she turned away and spit. He slapped her hard, forcing her head to turn. Oona took a deep breath and spoke as loudly and clearly as she could – she bellowed.

"Lawrence, if you think your cruelty has cemented me to you, you are deranged! Now, let me go!" She tried not to scream, because she knew muffled screams were often heard as lover's spats, or even the more intimate sounds, and judiciously ignored.

Lawrence growled "No!" at her. He half-carried and half-dragged her deeper into the shed.

She pulled away from him hard. Startled, he let go, but in a second he swung out to hit her. She fell to the ground and he grabbed her and carried her to a corner and threw her to the floor. She screamed, hoping to keep him away from her as she had so many times before. But he was so much bigger now, and there was no one here to stop him. Oona scrambled backwards and hid behind a barrel, knowing that even in the near full darkness, it would be only minutes before he would grab her and do what he intended. Her face stung where he had slapped her, and her heart was beating so loudly she was sure he could hear it.

"Oona," the man fairly sang her name, "I know you have always thought of me as someone you could love. Your mistress didn't understand that, but you never minded. You liked it when I looked at you and touched you. You liked it, didn't you? You've always been mine; even my brothers said so." He taunted, his voice slurred and loud.

"Lawrence, you are wrong! I never liked it! Never! You and your brothers scared me, and you are scaring me now. You don't want to scare me, do you?" She tried to remember where the door was. If only it wasn't on the other side of Lawrence! Oona tiptoed toward where she thought the door might be – the last thing she wanted was to fall into the cold water. "Lawrence, stop this, just let me go home."

Lawrence appeared out of the dark and loomed right in front of her. He grabbed for her bodice, pawing at her breasts beneath the layers. As he spoke, he snarled. "You don't have a home – remember, little servant girl Oona? You're a maid in a big house on the hill. Remember? Servant girls are fun, we told you that. How could you forget what we taught you, Oona? It's time you had a real man show you what we were talking about."

He caught her in his large hands. He threw her down onto some old rags and pushed up her skirts. He opened the buttons on his breeches and reared over her.

Oona closed her eyes and took a deep breath. She forced herself into consciousness and yelled "NO!" as loudly as she could. Then she collapsed, giving in to what was surely meant to be her fate. So much for her high plans to live by the choices she made.

"Shut it, ya bitch. You've been teasing me all your life." Lawrence hit Oona across the face, as he pushed into her. She felt herself tear and wanted to cry out, but she would not give Lawrence Morse the pleasure of knowing he had hurt her. He thrashed around for a few minutes, grinning down at her until he shuddered into her.

He pulled out and rolled off her. "That wasn't so bad, now, was it, Oona?" His whiny voice sneered in the dark. "He won't want you now, that fancy Brit. You'll have to be mine. hat there should be enough to chase away all your fancy men who only want a pure wench." He stood and stretched his legs "Dry your eyes girl, you got no reason to be crying. Give me a minute and we'll do it again."

A small flame hissed and lit at the other side of the small building, and Oona heard footsteps walking toward them. Her first thought was the fear that someone else had come to hurt her. But she forced her fear away and pushed at a crate. It toppled with a satisfying clatter. She wanted to shout "here!" but she didn't trust her dry throat to make more than a creak.

The candle seemed to move closer as the footsteps got louder. They were heading right toward them. Oona heard Jason call.

"Oona? I heard your voice. Are you here?"

"Yes." She tried not to let him hear the tears in her voice.

Jason felt, more than saw, a fist moving toward his head. He ducked, and the massive fist missed. Lawrence picked up a length of wood that was lying on the floor, and swung it at Jason's head. It made a weak contact on his right shoulder. Jason winced in pain, and moved over to catch his breath away from the small circle of light. As he came up, he swung at Lawrence – hard.

As Jason's fist hit him on the jaw, Lawrence dropped the wooded plank, stepped back and charged. He knocked Jason to the ground and jumped on top of him, punching his face and stomach. Oona heard Jason call out to her over the nauseating sounds of fists hitting flesh. "Oona, go home!" He heard her scramble for her things, then soft footsteps faded into the distance and out the door. With both feet, Jason kicked Lawrence off of him and got up. Lawrence sprang to his feet and grabbed for the length of wood that had fallen just out of reach. Jason jumped out of the way, just as the plank swung where his head had been.

"I assume you are Lawrence Morse?" He asked as he

moved out of sight to catch his breath.

"Yes, and you're the pain in the ass Brit who's been sniffin' around my girl."

"Your girl? That's how you treat your girl? Drag her into a filthy shed and try to rape her?"

"Try? Too late for you, she's ruined. Now I get to keep her."

"You are a twisted, disgusting man!" Jason roared as he ran at Lawrence so hard the man fell backward, and hit his head on the metal edge of a barrel. He stopped moving.

Jason checked his neck for a pulse. It was there, but weak. He dragged Lawrence by the ankles away from the hole in the floor. He found the man's flask and poured rum into his mouth and a drop or two on his shirt. He left the wretched ropework, figuring that if Lawrence woke up it would all be nothing but a drunk dream. And, if he never woke, it would look to anyone who found him that he drank himself into a stupor and died of the cold. Jason was hoping for the latter.

Jason reported to Matthew Goodiel first thing the next morning to tell him about the successful moving of his goods and ship the day before. The older man looked over a swollen cheek and slightly purple eye without saying a word. As before, he invited Jason to share his breakfast and they moved into the small dining room. Jason expected to see Oona as he had the previous week, but the cook herself came out, bringing rolls and eggs. The men spent the better part of the morning discussing routes and possible variations on the postponed voyage, seeing if it would be possible to make up time by choosing one port instead of another. After an hour, other merchants and sailors dropped by to exchange their own moving stories.

Occasionally, the men had heard loud voices coming from the back of the house, but the work and good-natured chatter had gone on. At one point, it got loud enough that Matthew had gone to tell whoever was shouting that it was disruptive. The voices had hushed, but still there was a shout or two that broke through the talk in the chart room. After the long meeting Jason excused himself, explaining that he had another engagement that afternoon.

He found his fur-lined cloak, and went to the kitchen. He had wanted to check on Oona first thing that morning, but they had agreed that it would not do Oona any good for them to broadcast their friendship. He had seen to the merchant first. Now, since the shouting had stopped, there had been silence in the house – no giggles from the schoolroom, no clatter of dishes, no quiet gossiping from the back hall. In fact, the house was so quiet, after all the chatter and shouting of the morning, that it seemed loud in its omission.

The Goodiel girls must have gone out visiting either with their mother or nurse. And Anne was most certainly out. Curious, he made his way to the kitchen to ask Oona's friend, Mrs. Prince, where he could find Oona in the quiet house, and inquire as to her well being.

"Girl looked fine. A bit tired, but then she got herself all worked up when the Mistress asked her if she had agreed to marry Peter Church. Said she wasn't in the mood to discuss it. I heard the mistress say she saw them go off together to talk at Christmas dinner. The girl said she talked to the men, and Peter and his friend Elias were sorry about her decision. But then Mrs. Goodiel looked beside herself."

"She must have been very angry that two men came here to judge her."

The cook looked up, slightly alarmed. "You can't

mean?"

"Knowing of Peter Church and Elias Glover, I'm afraid I do mean. Mrs. Goodiel was willing to overlook such potential debauchery?"

"Perhaps she doesn't know. I hope she didn't know." The cook looked ready to defend her friend from any and all insults to her integrity.

"So that was all the yelling this morning?"

"Mistress yelled at Oona that she was destroying her chances for a profitable marriage. She said she would give Oona some time to think it over. Oona laughed in her face and said that was never going to happen. Mistress got madder and louder till she locked Oona in the closet under the stairs.

"Where are Mrs. Goodiel and the girls?" Oh poor, poor Oona! Jason's heart sank with worry. Last night she endured Lawrence Morse, and this morning her mistress's anger. Jason went upstairs, prepared to sit outside the closet door. He would talk to Oona all afternoon if possible, tell her that she was as valuable and wonderful as she ever had been, convince her that Lawrence Morse, and hopefully Peter Church, would never bother her again.

And maybe if her could push himself to say the words – words he would rather whisper in her ear than through a locked door – he would tell her that if she would wait for him till the *Catherine* returned, he would care for her for her through a thousand lifetimes. But if it was such that he could only talk to Oona through solid wood, then he would do that. He got the direction from Mrs. Prince, and climbed the uncarpeted back stairs, relieved that Anne and her daughters planned to be gone all afternoon.

Jason looked at the door in the wall, and laughed out loud when he saw that in her tiff, Anne Goodiel had left the key in the lock. The closet was built in the space below the third floor stairs. Most likely it was tall enough for him to stand at the high end – probably not a bad place to spend an afternoon, especially if most days were spent in hard work. The key was right in front of him. The only thing better than spending the day talking to Oona through a door was holding Oona in his arms. He considered turning the key, and walking in on her, but decided against it. He went back down to the kitchen.

"Mrs. Prince, I've found that the key was left in the door. I would like to bring Oona some luncheon."

"Jason, you are a dear. Did anyone ever tell you?" The cook started bustling things onto a tray, and in what seemed like seconds, there was hot water and some of Oona's herbs steeping. Mrs. Prince spread a plate with grapes, cheeses and a loaf of bread she had just pulled from the oven. She handed Jason the tray and saw him up to the next floor.

"Thank you, Mrs. Prince, you are the dear."

"Jason FitzSimmon, just you take good care of that girl. She has had enough."

Jason nodded agreement. Enough of what? He knew the whole, but wasn't sure the kindly cook did. He hoped she did not.

He put the tray on the floor, tapped lightly and turned the key. The door opened to a very upright and startled Oona, blinking in the bright noonday light that poured through the open door. Jason picked up the tray and carried it into the closet. He closed and locked the door behind him, hanging the key on a nail on the doorframe. He put the tray of food down between them.

The closet was more of a storage room, with a few rays of light coming through the risers of the stairs above, and from around the slightly ill-fitting door. The room housed the unused carpets, carefully rolled and wrapped in muslin. When she saw her intruder, relief flooded her eyes. She blinked tears and forced a pale smile on her face.

Oona had been half asleep, after having a great cry at the unfairness of her life. She woke when she heard footsteps in the hall, and realized that she already recognized Jason's step, but was surprised that he walked past and disappeared down the kitchen stairs. When he returned and opened the door, she was unprepared for the look in his eyes. She expected concern and sympathy, or maybe revulsion over the events of the night before. What she saw was Jason the hunter. He looked at her with his wolf's eyes, desiring her and devouring her with his glance.

He pulled her into his lap when he saw how near tears she still was. "J-jason, I am so sorry. I should have run away when I saw him. And then, just now, I decided never to talk to men ever again, then you come in here all – all Jason. Not fair!" She sobbed louder and buried her head into his warm chest.

Jason chuckled. "Sweetheart, I know why you are crying, but why are you in a closet?"

Oona tried to stop crying. She sniffled a time or two and pulled a handkerchief from her pocket, wiped her eyes and blew her nose. "I told Anne Goodiel that I was not in the mood to talk, but that I would not marry Peter Church anyway. I almost blurted out that no decent woman would marry him, and that no decent mistress would suggest it, but I bit my tongue."

"I am very proud of you. " Jason attempted a bit of wry humor.

"For insisting that I would not marry that fop, or for governing my tongue?"

"Both. Let's eat lunch. You'll feel stronger."

He offered the plate of food and waited till Oona poured the tea. They ate in companionable silence. As Oona finished, she rose to her feet and, still hunched over, she walked to the door and unlocked it. "I'll be right back, prisoner's promise."

Jason finished his lunch, thinking how strange it would be to be sitting there alone when Anne Goodiel opened the door. But in a few minutes, he heard Oona's steps on the stairs from the third floor, then the door opened and she came in. Her hair was brushed and her face was scrubbed clear of tear trails. She looked resolutely better, and smelled of whatever heady scent she wore. It hung over her, gently mixing with the lemons and rosemary he always associated with her.

She settled down next to him, leaning against a roll of muslin-covered carpet. Jason spoke."How is it you always smell of lemons? "

Oona smiled at him."I wish it was because lemons are some exotic, sexual scent known only to women on America's north coast. But alas, I smell of lemons because I use lemon oil to polish the wood in the house. I've spent years perfecting my lemon oil recipe, Anne will be so angry that her furniture doesn't stay so pretty when I'm gone. I can use lemons because Matthew is so successful in Spain and the Carribean. They are plentiful in his kitchen."

"I approve of lemons; I love the smell. Mmm." He murmured as he leaned into her and breathed her scent deeply. She let her head fall onto his shoulder. "And rosemary?"

"The oil makes dark hair shiny. I learned it from Mrs. Prince when I was ten. I brush it in every week."

Jason ran his fingers gently over her neck and into

her hair. He smiled as she inhaled sharply. Slowly, he pulled the mop cap off her head. He put the small linen circle next to him on the floor, reached behind her, and unpinned the long plaits from her head. He ran his fingers through the long braids until her hair hung loose. He lifted her hair and buried his face in her thick dark mane. "Oh, Oona, I could get very used to doing this." He whispered to her ear.

Oona was passive as he played with her hair. Jason wondered if she was stricken with fear, or perhaps she was not ready for this and he should stop. "Oona, you know I promised I would never force myself on you. I absolutely refuse to take advantage of our friendship, nor would I compromise you. But I would love to give you some pleasure – to undo last night, at least a tiny bit."

Oona shuddered, but said nothing. There was very little light in the room, but Jason could sense her terror.

"Oona?" Jason moved into the darkest corner of the closet, away from the door. He opened one of the muslin covers and unrolled a few yards of carpet. He opened his fur cloak and placed it nearby. "If it would not frighten you, please let me chase away the nightmare and show you how much I value you. Let me hold you. If you feel brave, I would show you the pleasure you missed in last night's crass attack." He whispered to her with a broad smile that spoke of a lighthearted afternoon, so different from the gloom and dark anger she had experienced the night before. "And," he went on, "I promise I will make no move to slake my passion in you."

She seemed to be relaxing, so he went on. "Sweetheart, you know that I was happy to wait till you were free of the indenture. To wait until next fall. I had plans, then, to make your life heaven."

Oona did not speak or move. Jason did not want to

leave her so frightened. He continued to speak softly, hoping for a response "Oh, Oona my dearest, I would choose that your first time be in a rose-petal strewn bed, not an old boathouse, nor a closet filled with stored carpets, but life is odd sometime. But if you are willing, I'd love to give you some comfort and pleasure."

He had called her "dearest" and "sweetheart." She waited silently, thinking, listening to Jason's measured breathing and quiet speech from a few feet away, as he waited for her. Oona could tell Jason had not rehearsed this. He had probably been about to kiss her. She probably would have melted at his touch, as she had just a few days before. But things had changed, she had been changed. Could he really still want her?

She knew he would go no further if she said "no." He would stay away, far on the other carpet. Probably he would stay to keep her company till Anne released her. He would obediently discuss the nature of winter storms in New England or some other interesting, but neutral, topic.

But, if she said "no," would he think that she did not trust him? She suddenly realized that he needed her to trust his desire and his restraint. At the same time, she needed him to want her. And, she thought, as her mind started to wake up, she desired him. So if she refused him, denying what they both wanted, she would be the bitterest witch. She did trust him, and as afraid as she was, she wanted him to believe in her trust.

"Yes, Jason."

His sigh was audible as he moved slightly to make room for Oona on the rug, silently inviting her to join him.

Oona was pleased to see the hungry wolf in Jason's eyes. She trusted him not to violate her. But understanding and respecting the law did not lessen the intensity of his desire. She would be foolish if she believed his gentleness made him less of a hunter. Willingly, she crawled deeper into the closet and sat on her heels next to him. He took her small, cold hands in his warm ones. He rubbed his thumbs into her palms, then out along her fingers. He made no move to move closer or pull her to him, and yet Oona was sure she had.

Jason felt a barrier fall away. He hadn't known it was there until it wasn't. Oona's eyes darkened as he held her hands, twining her fingers through his. Her breath quickened and she made a slight forward motion with her body, as if the distance of a few inches between them was too much.

Jason caught her as the tension flew away. He pulled her into his lap and continued to fascinate her fingers. He pulled her right hand to his lips. He kissed each fingertip, then pulled her littlest finger into his mouth. He twirled his tongue around the finger, suckling on it as Oona's breathing deepened and quickened further.

Oona recognized this from the night of the party, but they had been outside in the cold, not warm and safe curled against Jason's solid body. Jason's suckling caused an oddly pleasant sensation deep in her belly, and a tightening in the sensitive places between her legs. As he moved to other fingers, she thought she would swoon.

"Oh, Oona, you taste so wonderful." Jason murmured into her mouth as he covered her mouth with his and kissed her fully. Oona welcomed him and intertwined her tongue with his, feeling the ridges of his teeth as he explored hers. She was really beginning to grasp the kissing thing, she thought, as Jason deepened the kiss until they breathed the same air. Thoughts fled.

He moved his hand off her back, and his fingers traced the line of her neck and collarbones, playing in circles on the soft skin in the valley between her luscious breasts. He put a thumb over her right breast and, on the fabric of the gown, made gentle circles over her nipple. In a few minutes, he moved to the other breast.

Oona thought she had come to understand kisses since her first kisses at the *Cromwell's Head,* the *King's Mount,* and the afternoon spent kissing in Jason's room. But those showy public displays and gentle affections were nothing at all compared with what she was experiencing now. Lost in sensation, she forgot how to tell up from down. But though she was floated out of space and time, she had never felt more alive. Parts of her, whose names she did not know, nor where they were located, were clenching and demanding a kind of attention that she did not understand.

Jason had not even attempted to remove any of her clothing – well, except that silly hat. As he started drawing lazy circles on Oona's nipples, she wished she could rip off her clothing herself. She felt hot, like she was on fire, and her clothes felt tight. She wore an old fashioned jacket, bodice, and skirt over stays and a simple shift. She had dressed for a day of cleaning the bedrooms and airing the sheets. She unpinned her jacket and pulled it off her arms. She untied the knot at the top of the laced bodice, and was about to loosen the laces when Jason stopped her.

"Let me." Jason loosened the laces of her bodice, pulling them apart bit by bit as he traced the growing opening with a finger. Oona gasped as he reached the top of her skirt. Then he grabbed the bottom hem and pulled her bodice over her head. "Easier to pull back over your head when the inevitable approaches." He kissed her gently on her lips, her nose, her eyelids and cheeks.

She smiled into his eyes, feeling a strange tension that, when coupled with his touch and look, made her feel loose and warm. Jason untied the bow of her shift and opened it to its full width, pushing down her stays. He pulled it over her shoulders, exposing her breasts and holding her arms still at her sides. He sat back on his haunches and stared. Oona would have liked to squirm away and cover herself with her hands, but they were fixed at her sides, held in place by thin wool.

She was as beautiful as he had dreamed her to be. Pale skin glowed in the half light, drifting through the spaces in the floorboards overhead. Full mounds crowned with pink nipples. They were rigid with her arousal. He gently cupped the fullness in his hands. He kissed the left, starting at the top of the breast, making teasing kisses and licks around the circle. He repeated this on the other breast before he bit the left nipple gently with a little nip before deeply suckling as he had her fingers.

Still resting on her knees, Oona swooned slightly toward him, feeling that she really couldn't hold herself up. A small murmur left her lips. Jason was careful not to duplicate Lawrence by having Oona on her back. He lay on his back and pulled her over him. She straddled him and he pushed her shift off her arms. It fell to her waist, and her arms were free. Before she could think of covering those lovely pink buds, he returned his lips to her breasts as his hands pulled her skirt up over her hips.

Oona found herself on top of Jason, being pleasured by the man beneath. It would be so easy to stop him, to roll off and reclaim her clothing. But the sensations were so lovely and the raw craving increased in that odd space above her legs. She didn't think she would stop him, or should stop him. Jason suckled her nipples as he moved his hands beneath the skirt on her legs. She felt him urge her legs apart and he touched her inner thighs, teasing her sensitive skin in the most delicious way.

Oona sensed that if she couldn't be very bold, she should switch places with Jason. She moved apart and stood up to untwist her skirts so they were less in the way. Then she lay back down on the carpet, next to Jason, facing him. Oona ran her hand through Jason's hair. The queue was already undone, but the thick, rich brown hair drew her fingers. He rose above her. Gently touching her hip, he covered her mouth with his in a now familiar, searing kiss.

Jason understood how difficult it was for Oona to change position and come to him. He was honored by that and humbled by her trust. Again, he pulled up her skirts while his teeth and lips teased at her breasts. His fingers gently stroked the smooth skin of her inner thighs and curled around the hair above.

Oona had two minds. A moment ago she could have rolled off of him and scuttled back to her corner. Now she had changed that, showing that she trusted him. She was aware in her own arousal that his clothes were all still on him. His gentle touch as he moved in her deepest place wove a magic of tension and desire. Then it changed. The urgent pain that had taunted at the edge of pleasure increased. She arched against him, needing him to fill her, knowing she was pleading for what he had promised he would not give. He increased the speed and pressure on her delicate places and she shattered, flying and floating, her pieces flying in a thousand directions into the thin air. For a moment she was lost, then she found herself grounded and safe, all her pieces gathered together and clutched tightly in Jason's arms.

Jason felt Oona's release, his own arousal made painful by her passion. But he delighted in her pleasure, especially so soon after that brutal encounter. He let his eyes wander over her as she fell into a sated sleep. She was beautiful – her hair fell over her shoulders and curled around her breasts. Her lips were curved into a small smile. She inhaled in her sleep, murmuring something unintelligible that ended with his name.

A strange need for passion and possession came over Jason. Oona responded to him – she had since that first kiss, but did she see his restraint as kindness, as he hoped? Had he inadvertently told her that he did not care? That he did not want her? That he might allow another to possess her? His schedule was fixed. He sailed with the *Catherine.* Would she take her new power and find another in his absence? The thought of that almost had him howling in anguish.

She was his. He growled deep in his chest wanting to take her, to possess her. His cock throbbed with need. But powerful as that urge was, the promise he had made to her was far more powerful. Jason pulled his cloak over her and leaned back against a rolled carpet to think. He pulled his eyes away from the sleeping woman, wondering if she understood what was now so clear to him, that she belonged to him. His to protect, his to defend, and in return she was his, Jason FitzSimmon's – not Lawrence Morse's or Peter Church's, and not the Goodiels's, though they might have a contract for her work.

He knew of only one way a man could truly claim a woman. The law of indenture said she could not marry. If they did, it would have to be a secret, not the sort of public ceremony of possession that would matter. How did a man claim a woman if he could not make a public pronouncement of his intent to marry her, offer for her to her guardians, and consummate that marriage in the traditional way? Certainly he would not take her with his body, the oldest and clearest act of ownership. Lawrence Morse, may he rot in hell, had forced himself on her to try just that. Jason had just spent a wondrous afternoon disproving the butcher's fallacy.

Oona woke herself and stretched, opening her arms wide and letting the warm cloak drop from her shoulders. That was the most relaxed sleep she had ever had. During the nap she had felt safe and cherished. It was a feeling she saw on others' faces – the small Goodiel children, Mrs. Prince when her husband came to walk her home – but she had thought never to feel that way herself. Increasingly, these last days she was coming to believe she might have that too. It was simply the way she felt whenever Jason was near.

She reached up to him. He had been staring into a beam of light, letting her sleep. She pulled him under the warm cloak. She kissed his eyelids, his nose, his swollen cheek, and wrapped her arms around him. She held him against herself. Jason pushed her hair away from her mouth and kissed her deeply and long. Oona broke the spell by pulling back and sitting up on her knees.

"Jason, take off your shirt, I want to feel your skin against mine."

Jason felt he should argue, that it would be too intimate. That it would take a dangerous step beyond simple pleasure. But he knew they had already moved way beyond mere pleasure. He pulled his shirt over his head and resumed the kiss, relishing the feeling of her breasts against the sensitive skin of his chest. His own arousal, which he had kept under tight control till now, was becoming insistent.

Jason moved his lips from her mouth over her body. He feathered kisses down her neck and to the soft, sweet mounds of her breasts. He suckled one than the other, biting and sucking insistently until her hips bucked and she moaned in response. He moved a finger between her legs and opened the petals of her moist warmth. She moaned again and started making pleading noises for him to finish her.

Jason growled with his own need. Carefully he pushed her skirts down, as Oona tried to fight him in her discomfort.

"Sweetheart, it will be better this way." Jason found the air to laugh gently as he reared over her. He was counting on the friction of his breeches and her beautiful body to release his own tension. The mess in his drawers he was something he could take care of at home.

Oona's body objected to Jason's abandoning her. She understood what he was doing, and why. But she was ready for him, she wanted him, and he had the audacity to stay sane while her body cried for the insanity that passion bred. In a few minutes, she felt his release. He pulled her into his arms, so that she could share the last tremors with him.

Oona stretched her needy body, pushing her breasts forward, reminding Jason that he had left her unsatisfied.

Jason watched appreciatively. He let his fingers trace the circumference of each nipple. Oona mewed and pushed herself at him. "Oh, would there be something I forgot, sweet miss?"

Oona felt needy and inarticulate. She would like to be able to answer that question, but there were no words in her head. She opened her legs to him as he moved her skirts aside and found the core of sensation. He let her moan and beg as he pulled his thumb away and almost touched her. She writhed, loving the gentle torture. Jason pushed her skirts up over her hips and moved down over her legs.

Oona jumped as she felt his mouth kiss where his thumb had been. He held her legs so she would not fight, and she allowed herself to fall into a molten pond of sensation. Again she flew and shattered, coming to rest in Jason's arms.

She relaxed as he pulled both arms around her, fixing her skirts for warmth as well as decorum. He lifted himself onto an elbow and looked at the lovely, sated woman lying content in his arms. He was overwhelmed again with the question of possession, an animal passion of which he was only dimly aware. He was afraid to ask permission – afraid that, in this age of reason, she might see his action as barbaric. She might refuse him.

Jason pulled the ruby earing from his left ear. He examined it, turning it in his hand as if he had never seen it before. He had acquired it five years before, on a journey he'd undertaken alone through the ancient Italian cities. In Florence he had met a jeweler, and in a moment of homesickness and rebellion he had ordered the family stones of rubies and pearls made into a man's single earing. The jeweler had added the cabochon ruby that hung from the ring for cost. Other sailors wore rings in their ears, but he hadn't met one with another that spoke of such workmanship or such quality jewels.

He reached behind him for his coat. He pulled the flask of clear rum from his pocket. Jason eased Oona onto her back, and allowed his animal compulsion to rule. Acting on instinct, rather then rational thought, he poured a bit of rum on the earring, letting it drip onto Oona's left breast. He rose onto his knees. He kissed her mouth and he moved away quickly. He did not know if there was protocol for an act of possession such as this but, in truth, explorers and conquerors never asked permission. Would they if they could?

Oona watched Jason, spellbound. She felt the cold of the rum wet her sensitive nipple and hot breast. She was curled, protected against Jason's warm body under the fur cloak when he rolled her onto her back. Jason looked different – slightly mad. His eyes were dark and glowing with amber streaks: The hunter claiming his prey.

A feminine instinct hidden deep within her responded to what she recognized as possession. She stayed still, captured. She held herself calm, breath moving slowly. She was at once the audience and the willing participant. Jason held his earing next to her body. It was a beautiful and valuable ruby, but more important, it was part of him, something everyone who knew him would recognize. She saw intention in his face; her body responded with desire. Pain was irrelevant. She wanted this. She wanted him. She stared at him, willing him to complete his task. She opened her arms, holding them away from her body in an act of willing surrender.

He kissed her right breast, and then set his gaze and full concentration on her left. He sat back on his haunches and held her left breast as steady as he could. He braced himself, ready to make the stab in one motion. Oona looked deep into Jason's gold streaked eyes. She breathed as he breathed, willing him to hurt her and claim her body, as Lawrence's act of force never could. She breathed in and exhaled as Jason pushed the gold ring through her breast and fixed the clasp. It hung just below the nipple, just in the areola, so stays would not irritate it, nor would a prying mistress notice the stone under a shift and stays.

She pulled him down to her, holding him very tight, as though she could never let him go, and knowing they would be a long time apart. "Thank you, Jason."

"I hope you don't mind. I didn't ask." Jason kissed her breast.

She whispered very softly in his ear. "I would have suggested it, if I had known as much." She looked at him, declaring her possession of him in return. He pulled the warm fur over them and they curled together. They may have slept, but soon Jason woke and noticed how far the slant of the rays of light coming into the closet had moved. They dressed. It was cold in the closet and, if they had to separate, warm clothes felt good. Oona pulled her shift up and tied the drawstring, feeling like a different person, powerful and ready to fight her battles again, but it was sad and cold to have to give up the warm feeling of Jason's skin against her own so soon.

Jason helped Oona stand, and pulled her garments up. He dropped her loosened corset and bodice over her head and pulled at the long tapes. He fluffed the hem of her skirt so she would look just as presentable as a servant who had spent the day locked in a cold closet would look. Oona helped Jason find his shirt and waistcoat. Soon he was ready to leave. He stood, key in hand.

"Oona, we should marry." Jason sounded very matter of fact.

Oona hoped this was not out of a sense of duty. "Jason, I can't, you don't have to, but are you proposing?" Words and thoughts jumbled together and out.

"I thought I had." He shook the cobwebs out of his head and started over. "Oona, I would like to marry you before I leave. There is no other protection with which I can leave you."

"But I explained, Jason, I can't marry without Anne's approval."

"Will your minister?"

"Reverend Peirce."

"Will Reverend Peirce marry us quietly without Anne's approval or knowledge? You needn't tell anyone until the indenture is finished. We will keep the marriage secret, but if you need help, the reverend will know. He can bring it to light to the magistrates, if you are threatened."

"He is very understanding. He might. I think he will understand. He and his wife have always been very sympathetic."

"I will speak to him tomorrow and see if he will read banns Thursday night and marry us on Sunday. Say yes."

"That is very quick for banns. I thought we needed a month and both our parishes."

"I have been at sea for years. If I had wives in twelve ports, banns would not help. I don't, by the way." He laughed, feeling like there might be something real he could do for this girl. "As for your parish, what could they know in thirty days they don't know about you yet?"

"Yes, let's speak to him tomorrow morning. He and Mrs. Peirce wake early, do you mind?"

This was such a huge kindness on Jason's part. Oona understood he had no compulsion to marry her. It did him no good to be married before he sailed. But what would not benefit him would protect her in so many ways. If Anne had another prospective groom lined up, he could be stopped. And if she was with child from Lawrence's attack, it would be Jason's in the eye of the law. Lawrence need never even think it was his. And she hummed, as she laced up her boot. It would make these last months go faster, knowing that Jason would come back for her.

Jason kissed the top of her head and wrapped his warm, fur-lined cloak around her shoulders.

"The sun is still up. Anne may be hours. Stay warm

and return it another time." Oona nodded. She stopped herself from rushing the door and dragging him back to her. Instead, she rolled the rugs and re-covered them with the muslin and listened to Jason quietly turning the key in the lock.

Chapter 9

*I*t took most of the morning, but Jason was pleased with his meeting with the Reverend Charles Peirce at the New South Meeting House. The minister was kind, and listened carefully to Jason's reasons for hurrying the banns and marriage. Reverend Peirce had known Oona since she had wandered into the plain, white wood church one day when she was thirteen. He agreed that Oona needed the protection that marriage would offer a lone woman. What he wanted to know from Jason was why, as a stranger in town, he was willing to take this extraordinary step.

"Sir, it may seem extraordinary to you, and I can't blame you. We both know that I have known Oona for only a few short weeks and that her time is heavily regimented. But more than my own life, if you will, I need to know she is safe, at least, in the ways that this marriage can keep her safe."

"Son, I understand you know the law surrounding her indenture, but I would expect you to keep your vows to Oona and God. Do you think you can do that?"

"Yes sir, I believe that will not be a problem." The problem, Jason thought on his short walk home, after he got the man's approval and that of his wife, would not be keeping marriage vows. In fact he would like nothing better than to consummate the marriage and be loyal to Oona for a lifetime. No, the problem was keeping his vow to her, that he respected the laws of indenture and would keep his hands and body off her. Yes, that was the problem vow. He didn't suppose that he needed to be in love, as the poets termed it. She was lovely and in need of a protector. Her master's family was no longer protecting her, now that Anne Goodiel was pursuing her own interests. So it fell to him. It was that simple.

The banns were read that Sunday morning. Oona and Jason stood up before the congregation and were smiled at and greeted kindly. If those few people, those who had come to church very early in the morning, including Jason's landlord and lady, thought it was odd that the wedding ceremony was scheduled only four days later, they made no comment. Rushed marriages were not unknown in the port town, where tradition and law were strict, and men had a habit of sailing away.

The following Thursday, Oona wore a blue split gown with a ruby-red silk petticoat. The sleeves were split as well, showing the same heavy red silk. There was white lace at the bodice, the cuffs and the hemline. Jason had no idea how Oona had found the time to construct such a garment from the fabric he had delivered only the week before, but he was no longer surprised by her tenacity and willingness to endure hard work.

Sukey Hubbard and Jason's friend, Kevin Babcock, stood up for them. They hugged and kissed, and looked shocked, but said nothing, when the wedding couple just walked away after the church service. Jason wore his finest suit. His silk waistcoat was embroidered with what Oona was sure were real ruby buttons. His breeches were light brown, and he wore a long velvet coat that matched the embroidery in the waistcoat. Later, Oona would say she remembered parts of the service such as his clothing – the velvet coat and the buttons. But she could not remember the minister's words or her response. One thing she did remember was that Jason did not take his eyes from hers, and those eyes had what was becoming a familiar glow. He escorted her from the church after, and placed a small ruby ring on her finger.

Outside, he explained that he understood that she could not wear the ring, but it was hers. Refusing to be sad at her short engagement, irregular marriage and a husband who was sailing within the fortnight, Oona laughed. She put the ring on a chain she wore on her neck, and tucked it deep into her bodice. Jason hoped it was tucked away safely, next to his earring.

He walked her back to the Goodiels's house, holding her hand tightly in his. They walked around to the back and into the kitchen garden. The paths were clear of snow, the piles growing weekly with continued winter weather. Jason felt as desolate as the garden, knowing that his bride would go back to a day of cleaning and waiting on the Goodiels, while she should have been enjoying her wedding breakfast and a wedding night in his arms. At the door he kissed her briefly, holding her tight against him. She returned his kiss; pulling back, she put her hand to his cheek. She left it there briefly and let it drop to her side before she turned to go indoors. Back on Beech Street, Mrs. Channing, a long-time member of the New South Meetinghouse, greeted him with a simple hello. She might be sad for Jason that he was coming home alone, but she was wise enough in the ways of her world not to need, or ask for, an explanation.

Jason knew that whatever unease or loneliness he

felt, it was worse for Oona. That didn't make him feel better, but it gave him a sense of purpose. He threw himself into work at the shipyard; he hoped his small contribution would help ready the *Catherine*. The sooner this voyage was begun, the sooner he would return.

Oona went back to her room, and took off the gown she had cut and sewn faster than she had ever made anything. The lovely lace was still loosely basted, a project to be finished in the future. She put on a plain, warm gown and resumed her place in the Goodiels's home. Her life did not change that afternoon in any noticeable way, but she felt as though she had shed the weight that had hung from her shoulders for most of her life. The tilt of her world had changed. She had a new life waiting for her as soon as she was able. She felt for the new ruby ring, nestled close to Jason's earring in her left breast.

It was after midnight when Oona, wrapped in Jason's warm fur lined cloak, stumbled the mile from Oliver to Beach Street. It had snowed again, and walking was slippery. Oona's feet went out from under her too many times to count as she pushed herself forward over bricks and frozen mud. She was wet and bone-chilled. The sky was that white gray that predicted more snow, and lit the night. The watch had seen her and asked where why she was out. She had been tempted to lie, but saw no reason not to explain that her mistress had beaten her and she was running to a friend's for the night. He had nodded sympathetically, then told her to move on and get off the streets.

He was right, and nothing could have made her happier than to be out of the cold. Oona hugged herself in the warm cloak – it smelled so much of Jason, but also of rum, lemon oil, rosemary and the undefinable odor of sex. It comforted her.

It was after lunch that Anne Goodiel told her that Peter Church had written to her. She ordered Oona to her boudoir and read his letter out loud,

"*Mrs. Goodiel, Since the pretty chit did not seem interested, I have decided to withdraw my offer. It seems that you misinformed me as to her willingness. I will not force a young girl into this unusual marriage. Please consider the matter closed.*"

"Oona," Anne Goodiel voice oozed with anger, "I think you made a terrible mistake. You did not spend enough time with Mr. Church. You saw him only at chapel and at the dinner. When you could have spent an entire day with him, you chose to spend the day away from your home. I am very angry." She picked up the strap and ordered Oona to pull down her gown and stays. Oona had received the strap before – all servants and children did, but she had never before seen Anne Goodiel this angry. As she leaned over the small stool that Anne had pushed to the end of a table, telling her to grab the table leg, Oona knew this was going to be worse, far worse than before.

She could have defended herself, telling her mistress that marriage to Peter Church was too unusual for a decent girl to consider, reminded her that her days off belonged to her, to go where she wanted and do what she wished – reminded her that any decision to marry was hers and not her mistress's, except that she must get permission. But she knew that Anne did not care about reason, law or tradition. She was angry because she had lost money on a sure bet, and it was Oona's fault.

She was sorry to bring Jason into her problems with

the Goodiels. Matthew Goodiel was his master, too. She would never want him to lose his berth on the *Catherine*. But she had nowhere else to go. She would rather have taken care of herself, but she was afraid that by morning, her back would be more than she could handle alone. Jason was truly the only one she could run to. He would also understand the betrayal she felt at Anne's wrath. The Goodiels had been her family for ten years, her only family in America.

Oona sat on the back step, feeling that perishing in the snow would be easier than knocking on the door. Her back ached, and she could feel welts start to rise and the drips of blood hardening on her back. She let her head fall against the door, hoping someone inside would hear.

"Oona, darling, come in out of the cold. Are you here to see Jason?" Mary Channing helped her inside and called to Jason from the bottom of his stair. "You don't look well dear, what is wrong?"

"My back." Oona tried hard not to cry out. As the kitchen warmth moved into her body, the pain was increasing. "Anne Goodiel was very angry." Oona just wanted to collapse into a chair, but was afraid of leaning against the chairback.

Mary helped her take off the cloak, and gasped at the open sores on Oona's bare skin that had been covered only with the cloak. "We better get you upstairs and take care of that back." She tried not to show her shock and worry. She kept her kindly smile glued to her face.

Jason stood on the bottom step. He had been about to step into the kitchen when Mary took off Oona's cloak and he saw Oona's back. The sight made him want to roar in fury but, pulling himself in order, he carefully picked Oona up into his arms and, careful not to touch the wounds on her back, carried her up to his room. "You said it was Anne?"

Oona nodded at him, nearly to weary to speak. "Why did she, was it our marriage?" Jason had a burst of fear that he could have brought this down on Oona.

"No, she does not know about us. This was over the failed Peter Church arrangement."

"Oh, my poor sweet." Jason said nothing more, but he had every intention of making sure the Goodiels would never touch their servant again.

He had been sitting in front of his fire, toasting his bride with a glass of French brandy, when he heard Oona in the kitchen. His reverie was so soothing and pleasant that his first thought was that she had found a way to come for a real wedding night.

Instead, he found himself with a bowl of warm water, soothing purple welts and softening dried blood off of his new bride's back. Mary had also brought up a soothing salve and a cup of laudanum to help her sleep through the first night. Then she left. "It's a good thing I saw you two married this morning, or this would be very irregular. As it is, if anyone asks I will say nothing until you give me permission." She leaned over and kissed Oona's cheek, an act of maternal comfort that brought her to tears.

Before the draught brought sleep, Oona wanted to talk. Jason found an old night shirt, warm, worn and very soft. Sitting on her knees, she held her hands up and he slipped it over her head. It was long enough to cover her legs. It was big and loose across her back.

Jason sat facing her. "Oona, can you tell me what happened?" He kept his voice under control, though he wanted to scream and rail at the Goodiels.

Oona sat on the bed with her legs crossed in front of her, like one of the Chinese idols Matthew had on a shelf in the chart room. Slowly and quietly, she related the story of

Anne yelling at her and ordering her into the small sitting room.

Here she was, warm and safe, her wounds cared for. Suddenly all the pain and fear hit her. She started to tremble. She had held back her tears as Anne Goodiel beat her, lashing at her with the belt, over and over. She had made herself stay quiet, bitting into the upholstered footstool as the urge to scream and plead for mercy nearly overcame her. She had not wanted to give Anne the satisfaction of her tears, and she did not want to show the utter dejection that she felt. No, she did not cry until Mary spoke kind words. Now she saw the worry in Jason's eyes – gentle and brown, wide with concern.

Oona sobbed. Her shoulders heaved, and the effort to breathe made her back ache. She let her head fall forward onto Jason. He wanted to put his arms around her. His natural instinct was to hold her tight and stop bad things from hurting her. She flinched when he touched her back. He swore and let her sob herself out, his hand in her hair, petting her gently as she cried. He really didn't need to hear about Anne's thwarted dreams of making a profit from Oona's marriage to the town dandy.

As the sobs stopped and Oona sat up and pulled away, Jason took her hands and stared into her eyes, waiting for her to finish her story. "Please talk to me, sweeting, please."

Oona didn't feel brave enough to tell Jason the whole story. But she knew she would if keeping silent might mean he could blame himself. "Jason, it was a perfectly normal day. I was happy, but I didn't tell anyone about our wedding. Instead, I held it to me like a precious secret. I ate early, with the girls, then I finished a few of my normal chores: laundry, dishes, nothing unusual. When the girls were ready, I brought them to their room and listened to them read for a few minutes. Anne came in, as she always does, and listened to their prayers. When she left the girls, she called me down from my room and met me in the hall where she was waiting. She said there was something she needed to ask me.

"She led the way down the hall to her rooms and sat me down on a little chair in her boudoir. She told me she had received a note from Peter Church, which arrived today. In the short letter, Mr. Church withdrew his offer for my hand in marriage, saying that he would not connive to put a young woman in an unusual marriage against her will. I have to say, I appreciate his decency." Oona smiled at the irony of that and went on. "She never asked me what I said to Mr. Church to discourage him. She had nothing she needed to ask me.

"While I was sitting there, she got up and got her strap. She has never beaten me for speaking my mind. Sometimes she says she has been disappointed in me, and then she talks me near to death, but not the strap. She has only used the strap on me if I'd done something very wrong, like when I was twelve and tried to run away, and the time she thought I wanted Lawrence and his brothers to look at my breasts.

"But tonight, I could tell she was oddly angry by the sound of her voice, so I didn't say anything at all. Then she had me loosen my gown off my back, told me to lean over her little footstool and grab hold of the table leg . . . ."

Jason felt his stomach turn as he listened to Oona. He nearly retched as she grabbed his arm with the tension of the beating. Again he wanted to hold her against the pain and injustice of Anne's wrath, but his anger was better saved till the morning. Oona needed sleep and a safe place to heal. He could make sure his small bedroom in Mary Channing's house was that place. He would make sure the Goodiels understood that.

Jason had been around the brutality of shipboard justice for years. He had seen men beaten for infractions and mauled in brawls. At times he had meted out that justice – he hoped it had been fairly. But he had never hurt a woman, and seeing Oona injured made him speechless with rage. He would near kill Anne Goodiel if he ever got the chance. By law he could do nothing to punish Anne Goodiel for what was her right to punish her servant. But they would understand that this was not to be repeated.

Now, the important thing was to make Oona comfortable. He held her arm and helped her to the chamber pot and then back into bed. He found pillows so she could sleep comfortably on her side, and when she started shivering with shock and cold, he climbed in with her for warmth. Worry kept him up, and the closeness of his new wife in his bed, her breasts pressed deliciously against his back, on this, their wedding night, led his imagination in licensed, but forbidden, directions.

That night Oona woke twice. The first time she was thirsty, groggy and confused. Jason got her a drink and put more of the cooling salve on her back. After tossing and turning in her hunt to find a comfortable position, she eventually fell back to sleep. As the clock struck two, Oona woke the second time, crying in feverish pain. Jason had no ideas except to give her another small dose of the opium, and hope the pain would recede by morning.

She was deeply asleep when the rooster woke Jason, and he dressed quickly to tell Mary Channing that Oona was feverish.

Mary looked at her tired tenant. "Jason, I think the

fever is only her body's way of chasing away the poisons made by the bruised skin. We'll just keep her back clean and watch for infection. But I think she'll heal given a little time. Did your marriage to her girl set Anne off?"

"She says not." Jason explained what had happened with as little detail as possible. He sat in the comfortable kitchen watching Mary Channing sort her eggs. "Mary, she will need to stay here until she is strong enough to go back."

"Of course. When will the *Catherine* sail?"

"I don't know exactly, probably next week. Maybe by then Oona will be well enough to go home.

"No."

"Excuse me?"

"I know Anne Goodiel's anger. We grew up together." Mary Channing poured a cup of something hot and sat to speak to Jason. "She doesn't mean to be, but sometimes it gets away from her and she explodes. It happened once when we were at school, at dame school at Mrs. Stevenson's. One of the girls stepped on a hair ribbon that matched her new gown, and Anne went after the girl with a horrible vengeance.

"Oona will stay here until she can move without any pain. If you sail before that, I will nurse her myself till she can fight back. I won't return an injured bird to a cat." She went back to her work, and Jason went upstairs to his room, feeling just a little less worried for his new wife.

Oona went in and out of the fevered sleep for three days. Mary sat with her and nursed her when Jason was out, and Jason spent the nights in an anxious worry, hoping that she would soon begin to recover in earnest.

Jason took out his instruments and checked their condition. This was something he did daily on shore and at sea. He set to polishing glass, brass and wood until each device gleamed, enjoying the careful work and the sounds of Oona's quiet sleeping, her fever having finally broken.

Oona woke feeling less feverish and more rested. Her surroundings startled her and she panicked. She steadied herself, remembering why she was lying in Jason's fantastic bed. Unfortunately, that meant remembering that her back was a sea of purple and red welts. She did not move, but watched from the bed as he worked on his instruments. She immediately recognized his skill with them, even as he simply cleaned and polished – a knowledgeable amateur marveling at a professional collection. Jason's competence pleased and reassured her. She watched for awhile, feeling strongly that she was in a safe and familiar place. This feeling was rare for her. Sometimes, she found that she felt safe and on course when she used or polished her own set of nautical tools. Contented, she soon she fell back into a more comfortable sleep.

Later in the morning, she woke again and was eating the toast and eggs that Mary Channing had brought up with the wash water, when Jason came in dressed for visiting. "Oona, I am going to the Goodiels's to tell them you are staying here with Mary and Michael until you are healed. If they want you back sooner, I will call for a doctor and a magistrate, but I won't push unless they're nasty." He leaned over and casually kissed her good-bye on her cheek. His fingers lingered just a moment in her hair, raising an awareness in places on her body that lacked bruises. She sighed, smiling up at him as he left.

Oona thought Jason's decision to tell the Goodiels that she was with the Channings was a good one. She agreed, as well, there really was no good reason to make her beating a public issue as long as it was not repeated. A part of her would love to drag her mistress in front of the court, but it wouldn't turn out in her favor. She would heal soon, and after that she would leave the Goodiels. That would be the best outcome.

No, the best outcome, she forced herself to admit, would be if Jason truly meant their marriage to be more than a way to protect her, if he really came back to her and claimed her as his wife. But if he did not want that, she would not bind him. Few knew about the marriage, and they would forget if necessary. She and Jason would take up the question when he returned from the *Catherine's* voyage. Autumn would come soon enough. She cried a few tears, feeling pain and frightening loneliness. She tried to find the place of safety she had felt earlier, watching Jason with his tools, but her back hurt too much. Finally she fell back into a painful, restless sleep.

Things were not the usual calm at the Goodiels's when Jason arrived. A footman was loading boxes into a carriage, the little girls were holding each other and crying, and Matthew was blustering about, directing people.

"Oh, FitzSimmon, good to see you here. Wife won't stop crying Oona's name – says she killed her or something – can't get a word of sense out of her. We're shipping her off to her sister's in Milton for a few days till I get the situation calmed down here. The girls and I will go with her now, and see that she is all right. Do you bring word of the *Catherine*?"

"No sir, Oona."

"You bring word of Oona?"

"Yes sir, I found to my surprise that she had come to Mary and Michael Channing's home a few nights ago for succor. She was badly beaten, and needs to stay put a few weeks. So Mrs. Channing tells me."

"Fine, very good in fact. You tell Mrs. Channing to tell Oona that she should heal up and come on home. We won't hold a grudge. The good Lord preaches forgiveness."

"You mean Oona did something to get so badly beaten?"

"Must have surely upset my wife to do it."

"Yes sir, I see, sir. I will deliver your message."

"FitzSimmon!?"

"Yes sir?"

"Need you to keep checking on the *Catherine*. When there is news send word to Milton – if I am not here, name is Appleton."

"Yes sir, have a good journey. I hope to have news by the end of the week."

"Excellent. Take what you need from the kitty at the warehouse to hurry the work along if you need it – eh, FitzSimmon?"

Jason left, feeling that there were too many places and too many people he needed to be. His responsibility to the ship meant that he needed to hurry the work along, sail out of the harbor, and begin the winter voyage that was already delayed. And his responsibility to Oona meant that he should stay in port as long as he could. Mary Channing would see to it she was better before she returned to the Goodiels. That at least calmed his mind.

He spent a few hours at the warehouse doing work for Goodiel, checking that the *Catherine*'s crew would still be available when needed, checking on replacements for the few men who had found other berths, and then seeing about the ship herself. Since all ships are *shes*, he mused as he walked back to Beach Street, he really was a lucky man to have the care of two beautiful but injured females.

It was late in the afternoon, the light already going, when he returned to his rooms. Oona was sitting upright in the bed, her back well away from the backboard and pillows, trying hard to look alive and awake. In her lap was a book, but it did not look like she had turned more than a page or two.

"Hello beautiful, how are you feeling?"

"Tired, but honestly better than I've been. Mary moved the couch next to the window and had me lie with my back in the sun. It was chilly, but I think it eases the pain. That's all I know, since I can't see behind me."

Jason walked behind her and untied the bow holding his backwards shirt together. He pushed it gently below the tender back and checked the bruising. The improvement was incremental, but even slight improvement was better than none, and, thank God, there was still no sign of infection. "Oona, it is indeed better." He forced a smile into his voice. "Soon you will walk and move your arms without pain."

"How did you know it hurts to move my arms or walk?"

"Shipboard justice." He sat on the edge of the bed and looked at her. She casually placed a hand on his knee.

"You?" Oona felt an aching concern for the young man he must have been when he was flayed.

"Of course. I have also meted it out and nursed men who have been whipped. Yours ranks with the most brutal. Anne would not last long outside the navy. A merchant captain restrains his punishment to keep the crew happy, and to prevent skipping out to another ship. Merchant seamen are too valuable to chase away. The navy – that is another story. Then shipboard justice meets military – there, Anne might find a place." Jason smiled, adding a rueful laugh.

Oona tried to laugh at the image of Anne Goodiel in a British naval uniform, but laughing hurt the muscles in her back. She picked up a pillow and hit Jason playfully with it.

"Ooo" – his playful noise turned into a moan and he jumped up and away from the bed, turning to look at Oona. She gulped when she caught the intense boring from his eyes. His deep and raw desire simmered just below, and was obvious from the tension in his hard body and the unmistakable bulge in his breeches. His eyes glowed with the yellow streaks that made her breathless and caused a deep longing to radiate from her center downward. She tingled.

Jason took a deep breath, but he did not take his eyes off his lovely quarry. He said nothing, but turned and walked out, returning to keep her company and warm the cold bed, many hours later.

As the door closed softly behind him, Oona shivered and pulled Jason's soft shirt up over her shoulders and tied it behind her neck. Jason's look had answered the question that had been rattling foolishly in her head. He had said nothing to her over these days, and he had made no move that would lead to a sexual encounter or even a touch, and yet she felt as though she had been stroked.

Jason woke as the clock struck two. Oona was curled into him. Her thick black hair was loose on the pillow, her luscious breasts pushed against his back as they had every night. Her arm was draped over him, holding him close to her. He sensed she was uncomfortable – healing wounds caused horrible itching and pain. He pulled the blankets tighter, careful to keep the weight on him and let them tent over her. In a few minutes, her discomfort eased and she relaxed. Being unable to roll onto her back, she did not turn away, but continued to hold Jason close. He reminded himself not to worry, that the short fevers and discomfort were symptoms of healing and nothing more. To punish himself for his discomfort, he lay awake imagining all the things he would do to her once they were together again without injury or indenture. So it was that during the long sleepless nights of Oona's healing, Jason lay awake, plotting afternoons and nighttimes of glorious, delicious, tantalizing revenge.

On the fifth day, Oona found she could move her arms waist high without wincing. It was a huge relief to feel better, and she took advantage of her strength to help Mary with some light housework. Later, after a short nap, she helped Jason pack the clothes and bedding he would bring on the voyage. While they had his things out, they packed away his winter things, like the fur cloak, that he would leave behind. She promised to lay fleabane in the box with the clothes when it flowered in the summer.

Jason's hard work was paying off. The ship was back at the wharf and the men were getting the goods stowed. Jason couldn't help the excitement he felt whenever he saw a ship being readied to take to the open seas, but he felt torn between Oona's care and his thirst for sailing away. He had come home ready to finish packing and leave. He tossed his coat and hat on a chair and gazed at her sleeping form, drinking in her curves as she slept in the pale light of a winter sunset. As usual, his body reacted to her lovely form, half naked in his old shirt. He adjusted his breeches and chastised himself to stop spying on her and behaving like a schoolboy. He closed the door behind him, making sure it closed with a loud click.

Now that she felt better, Oona tried to quicken the

healing. As Mary had taught her, she lay on pillows with her back exposed to the sunlight in the late afternoons. The rays from the sun heated Mary's salve and seemed to add extra healing properties. Usually she was dressed again by the time Jason returned from the *Catherine*. This afternoon, Oona woke when she heard the click of the door closing. She looked up, slowly tying the strings of the shirt closed behind her neck, holding her elbows at her side to avoid the inevitable pain that reaching behind herself caused. "Jason? I am up and nearly decent."

She heard the door open behind her. She recognized Jason's lighthearted voice. It worked to cover his worry. "Oona, you have been trapped up here for days. I leave in only a day or two. What can I do for you, now that you are feeling a tiny bit better?"

"I know it is too cold for a bath. But I would love one. I know I must smell from all my fevers."

Jason laughed. He knew how much healing wounds could itch. He understood Oona's desire to be clean. "Your wish is my command." He bowed out of the room. The continual cold limited the water at the wells and springs, but Mary Channing kept a good supply on hand for her family and tenant. Jason poured water from the boiling kettles and supplemented the buckets with cold water, until he had four wooden buckets of warm wash water. He carried them upstairs, two at a time, and set them next to the fire.

While Jason was downstairs, Oona remade the bed with the sheets she and Mary had hung that morning, and set the room to rights, pulling the small settee up to the fire, and putting her feet in a small flat washtub. In a few minutes, Jason returned, carrying a basket of soap and towels.

Jason had every intention of leaving the room, of letting Oona wash in peace without his greedy hands running over her wet soapy body. He knew Oona was just as frustrated, in part because she seemed to yearn for him as he did her, and in part because she harbored guilt for needing to refuse him. He should just walk out of the room and stop making her feel guilty. He should.

"Oona." Jason spoke before he could stop himself. "If I were reasonable, I would leave you the warm water, soap and towels. I know you can't reach your hair, and I would send Mary in to help you." He stopped her from saying anything; holding up a hand. "I should leave. And you want me to go because you think I'm angry that you can not have sex with me. Married even. You think I am angry because I want you and you accuse yourself of rejecting me.

"Oona, stop being angry at yourself. I may be frustrated. That is a physical thing. It will not kill me. I do not believe you have been rejecting me. Sit on the little stool near the fire with your hair over you face. Close your eyes. I don't want too much water falling over the few open wounds still on your back."

The next thing Oona knew, strong hands were working suds out of soap shavings and massaging warm water through her long thick hair. After an ecstasy that seemed far too short, Jason poured rinse water through her hair until it ran clear and clean. Then he surprised her by unveiling a lemon which he squeezed through her hair to help rinse the last of the soap. He massaged the juice through, rinsing one more time.

He took her comb and ran it through toweled hair until the knots were out, then he wrapped her hair in the towel and stepped back to examine his old shirt, now soaking wet and clinging to Oona's wet body. The water made the shirt nearly translucent. He shifted his feet, trying to find a stance where his arousal would not increase her feelings of guilt if she happened to look at him. He wanted to tell her how much he wanted her, tell her how amazingly beautiful she was, and how delighted he was that she was healing so well – so well, in fact, that she would be able to lie on her back very, very soon. He imagined her lying there, those pretty legs wrapped around his hips as he thrust deep into her. His momentary fantasy nearly had him swooning at her feet.

Sharply, he reminded himself that he had promised not to do anything of the sort. He desperately wanted her to know that he reveled in her, and did not blame her in any way for not becoming his wife in more than word. His body, however, was less reasonable and not schooled in modern contracts. The sight of a wet and nearly naked Oona had caused most of his blood to pool in a raging erection. He might try to hide that as he stood behind the towels piled on the stool, but he knew it was harder to hide his eyes, which flashed hard with desire. He felt like an oaf. How could he convince her he was not angry at their dilemma, when he was so aroused?

Oona looked a question at him. She wanted to believe that he did not resent her, that he could desire her without hating her for denying him. She untied the wet string that held the loose shirt up, and let it fall. She caught it and tossed it aside before it could land in the tub.

Oona closed her eyes as Jason washed her. She swam in the sensation of the warm cloth being moved over her body in the most sensuous circles and delicious diagonals. She wanted to look at Jason, to catch the passion and raw need in his eyes that she felt herself. But she dared not look up. She could not bear to let him see the same desire shine from her eyes, or the love she had borne him for ten years, that had sprouted and blossomed in these past weeks. She could not bear for him to see the tears in her eyes.

Jason did not see the tears that formed in her closed eyes. But he did not miss the small sighs of rapture as he washed her breasts, making small circles of lemon verbena soap suds from her neck to her feet. She tried to grab the cloth as he got to the hair on the front and between her legs, but he would not relinquish it. He did not do more than wash and rinse her most delicate parts, but every touch made her warmer, until she felt her body tighten and begin to yearn for him, and for release.

"Oona, if we do what our bodies are begging us to do, I will never forgive myself." Jason finished rinsing her. He handed her a towel for her legs and stomach while he gently cared for her still-sensitive back.

When she was dried, salve rubbed gently on her back, and wrapped in another of Jason's soft old shirts with warm socks on her feet, she lifted a hand to his cheek and held his face in her palm, memorizing the curve of his chin and the special light in his eyes. He leaned over and gently kissed her lips, stopping them both as each moved to deepen and prolong their kiss.

Oona sat before the fire and brushed her hair. When it was fully dry and braided, she lay on the bed. Lying on her stomach, she watched the dying flames over the footboard. Her body still tingled with the arousal that being bathed by Jason gave her, and she reveled in feeling so alive and clean in the fresh night shirt, on a clean, aired bed. She sighed.

She had tried to keep her eyes closed, to avoid seeing the pain of rejection on Jason's face. But just once she had peeked. Jason had not looked to be in pain, nor did he look sad. Now that she had a minute to think about what she had seen, he looked happy. Not just happy, positively joyous.

She had never met anyone so full of life, and – now that she could sit and think for a minute with a clear mind – so full of love. She understood now what made her willing to disregard the contract and take him fully; to become his wife in more than name. She loved not just the first Jason – the kind boy who had cheered her on a long ocean crossing – but Jason the man, who showed his love in nobility and restraint by not allowing her to throw away her goal.

The fire died to cinders, and by the time there was nothing left, Oona knew what she needed to do and say to Jason as soon as possible. She also needed to return a gift he had given her all those years ago. It was time to tell him they had met before.

She climbed into the clean bed, pulled up the warm blankets, which, she noted, hurt her back only slightly, and fell asleep. During the night, she thought she heard the voices of Michael Channing talking to Jason and a third man downstairs, but she was too tired to wake up. In the morning there was a note on her pillow.

My love, My dearest Oona,

I am sorry, but I cannot kiss you good-bye. Please consider yourself well kissed.

Oona licked her lips, taking a moment to imagine being well kissed.

Late last night Goodiel sent a man to tell me that the

Catherine will sail this afternoon, and I was expected before dawn to oversee the last of the goods and preparations for the voyage. It seems that the warming thaw of the last few days convinced the harbor master and Captain Powell that we should get the underway.

Darling, I will write as often as I am able. I miss you already and anticipate next autumn with great delight.

– Jason

Oona rolled onto her back and read the note in the morning light. It was still early. The sun was just glinting through the mist out her window. It took a moment, but it struck her that her back did not hurt in any debilitating way. She got up and dressed herself, choosing a waistcoat that fastened in the front, and leaving off stays for the day when her wounds were completely healed. At the door to the room, the stacked trunks and the crates of Jason's clothing and things were gone. How had she not heard them being moved in the night? She guessed that the bath had worn her out more than she'd imagined.

She sat for breakfast with Mary and Georgie Channing. It was wonderful to be up.

"Mary, Jason is gone. When will they sail, do you know?"

"A messenger came late last night. From what Michael told me they sail on the tide mid-afternoon, around three, I believe. The warm this past week inspired them to rush the goods on board and set off. Goodiel has been worried about the merchandise. Michael said they will be stowing goods all day. They will make the roads by this evening, and leave the bay at first light."

Oona realized that with the ship in harbor all day, she still had time to give Jason her gift. She urgently needed to get to the Goodiels's and back down to the harbor, so she excused herself and left the house, her first outing since that late night when she had arrived in such pain.

At first, she felt unsteady on her feet, but the ground was clear of ice. She moved slowly and did not have too much trouble staying upright. Someone had set up a rope banister to help during the long weeks of slippery sidewalks, and Oona used the rope for support until her balance improved. She climbed Oliver Street to the Goodiels's house, not at all sure what her welcome would be. She needed to get to her room, find Jason's gift, and bring it directly to the harbor. He was so kind and true, he would walk through fire and flood for her; she had to find the old box and put it in his stateroom.

"Oona, you sure are a sight for sore eyes – look at you, girl!" Mrs. Prince smiled her wonderful welcome as Oona walked into the kitchen.

"Mrs. Prince, it is great to see you." Oona hugged the kind cook and kissed her on her cheek. "I will be back soon, but I must get something from upstairs. The *Catherine* is sailing this afternoon." Mrs. Prince, who knew Oona better than anyone, nodded understanding that the *Catherine* sailing meant that Jason was leaving on the voyage. She grinned at her own unexpected joy at watching Oona in love, though, she guessed, the girl didn't know it yet – not really.

In her room at the top of the house, Oona slid the trunk from under her bed. Inside the divided trunk, she found what she sought, and sat at her little writing table to write a reply to Jason's note. On her way out of the house, she kissed Mrs. Prince on the cheek again, and fairly skipped down the hill to the harbor. Not only was it a warm winter day, warm enough to throw the hood off her hair, but it felt wonderful to be moving nearly painlessly on her two feet.

At the pier, she watched workmen carrying goods onto the *Catherine*. She matched her steps with two men carrying long board planks, lumber to be stowed for sale or used for repair. As the men carried the lumber toward the hold, she veered off to find the cabin Jason would occupy on the voyage.

It was not hard to find the chartroom, with its tall cabinets and wide, shallow drawers. She opened the doors off that room until she recognized Jason's gear in small, well-appointed quarters. She didn't want to be seen, so she left her note and small package where he was sure to find them. She was about to leave, but turned to lay her head on his pillow. She kissed the spot where he would lie for the next months, then rose and forced herself to leave the room and the ship.

She walked away from the *Catherine* through the crowd to Dock Square. There, she bought an apple and a pigeon pie from a street vendor. She sat on a stray barrel, ate and watched the ships for a while.

Oona was sad, but the work of the busy port came first in all of their lives. She understood that as well as anyone else. When there was no one looking in her direction, she walked boldly to the stairs and climbed into the tower. She saluted her old friend, the gold weathervane grasshopper who held court over the hall and the town. Then she put her well-trained eyes to the ships moving in the harbor. She spotted the *Catherine* and pulled a small telescope from her pocket. She sent a prayer to the heavens and the various gods who ruled the seas for a successful voyage, and a safe return. It was the same prayer muttered hundreds of times a day by hundreds of wives and the sons and daughters of sailors and fisherman the world over. Oona felt deep in her heart that she had learned that prayer in infancy, long before she came to Boston with the Goodiels. She added that to the long list of things she wondered about herself.

Jason walked the ship with Captain Powell, meeting their crew and seeing that they had everything they needed, that all goods were on board and were correctly stowed. The captain was responsible for all the men and goods on his ship, and Powell took his job seriously. He stood on the quarterdeck and gave the command to have the guide ships attach their ropes and help the large merchantman out of port.

Jason had nothing much to do, but as an officer, he was expected to be on deck and a part of the departure routine. He took a moment and turned to the golden grasshopper glinting in the late afternoon light of mid-winter. He couldn't see her, but he knew Oona had made it out of her sick bed and was standing in that small tower staring at the *Catherine*. He took off his hat and made an elegant bow to the shrinking town, pledging a quick return to both Boston and Oona. His body reacted in a way that he was sure would not make friends with his new neighbors. He cursed his needy self and vowed not to think of Oona while abovedeck, unless he was under cover of darkness.

In a few hours, the guide ships released the larger ship and sailed back to Boston, carrying with them Matthew Goodiel and the few guests Powell had entertained for the day. They anchored in Nantasket Road, the narrow and very deep channel that connected the harbor to the Massachusetts Bay. As night fell, they lit guide pots so they could be seen if anyone should sail by. It was a safe spot to spend the night. They would be on the open sea at first light. Jason would not be needed for watch this early in the voyage, so after dinner in the mess, he prepared to retire to his quarters.

Jason checked the night sky, as he always did before climbing the ladder down to the chart room and his small quarters. He opened the door, and was struck with the familiar scent of lemons and rosemary. He hadn't known it, but they had become his favorite smells. And as much as he loved them, they did not belong in this lonely cabin. He scanned the room, thinking for a second that Oona had stowed away. The idea gave him a certain glow and a now-familiar pulling of his breeches. Sadly, she was not in the room, but on his pillow he found a note and what looked like a small box wrapped in a piece of linen lace. He studied the note.

My love, Dearest Jason –

I cannot possibly express my appreciation for your care these past weeks. I am leaving you a small surprise. I confess that I had more memory of you than you knew, or that I was bold enough to reveal. That I would come to feel so strongly toward you – that has been unexpected.

Jason, Since the day we met, even through the years when we were hundreds of miles apart, your smile has lived in my heart. Memories of your good nature have cheered and warmed me during my darkest times. I will always be grateful for meeting you then.

I am sure you don't remember, but when you were a lad you told me that I would fly. And thanks to you and your faith in me, I find I can.

Know that, were I a bird, and could truly fly, I would soar high and find you again on the wide Atlantic Ocean, but since I cannot, I return this gift to you, so that you might find your way back to me. That I now might be to you what you have been to me – true north.

Thank you for coming back into my life, I remain ever yours –

– O

She signed the missive with a decorative O. Jason held the short letter to his nose, hunting for her soft smells. He felt the ship sway with the ocean current, reminding him that they were already far away. He adjusted the guarded candle in the cabin lantern, and held the small wrapped gift up to the light.

Jason untied the ribbon and carefully unfolded the linen handkerchief. Inside was a familiar object, something he had put out of his mind ten years before. He stared at the letters and dial of the mariner's compass his uncle had given him on his first voyage. The patina of the old wood and the smooth surface of the familiar object pulled him into a memory of the last time he had seen it.

The surprising memory was of a small girl with flashing, dark violet eyes. He remembered that they flashed defiance and energy, her face crowned by long, unruly black hair that escaped her prim white cap even when she was sitting still and behaving herself. His first image of her was of her sobs at being chastised because she could not pick up a trunk that was as big as herself. He groaned at his stupidity for not seeing what Oona must have realized days if not weeks ago. How like her to keep her secrets. Even this one.

Jason remembered watching as the small girl tried to pick up a case as big as she was. Frustrated, crying and clearly angry, she had dragged it up the ramp and onto the ship. There she stopped. It would not budge over the rough boards. It was clear that she was simply unable to carry it further onto the ship or down to her family's cabin.

"Oona! You lazy child, why don't you bring that case over here, it is not so very heavy!" the woman traveling with her scolded. Jason felt bad for the girl who was no older than his younger brother. He picked the case onto his shoulder and carried it down the ladder to the guest stateroom.

He looked inside the room. The girl had run ahead and sat huddled in the corner whimpering and trying not to cry. The woman ignored her, trying to speak to her husband over the noises of the ship and the crying girl. Finally, exasperated, she turned to her.

"Child, it can't be so bad to eat when you are hungry. Stop that whining. Why don't you go up to the deck and watch the seabirds or something."

Jason jumped out of the way and out of sight while the bedraggled waif climbed ahead of him up the ladder and into the sunshine. He couldn't imagine a little sun consoling what appeared to him to be unconsolable sorrow. He hoped he was wrong.

Later, when his chores were finished, he found the girl on the foredeck, sitting next to a coil of rope. She seemed to be trying to become invisible and almost succeeded.

"Hello, I'm Jason." He felt very adult now that he was fourteen and a member of the crew for the spring and summer.

"I'm Oona." The girl had been crying for so long her nose was stuffy and her eyes were red and swollen.

"Why are you crying?" he had demanded, not wanting to take too much time with a drippy girl, even if he did feel slightly sorry for her.

"I'm not supposed to tell." Oona rubbed a dirty hand across her face to wipe her nose, surprised that anyone would notice or care about her tears.

"Why not?"

"Mistress said not to."

Jason had assumed the older woman was a strict mother, but mistress? He'd grown up in a world of servants – one this age would be useless on a journey. "You're her servant?"

"That's what she said. She says I'm to live with her and her family 'til I am grown. She said that she will take care of me, and I will take care of them."

"Oh." Jason knew servants, but he'd never considered that mutual caretaking was part of it. He couldn't see this one taking take care of anyone.

The girl started crying again, sobbing something about her mother and father, brothers, sisters and home. Jason was not used to childhood emotions. His family were all coddled until they decided on their own to move on.

There were certain expectations of each of them, but no one would openly rebel or choose to cry about it.

He had made the decision to accompany his uncle to sea himself, his parents allowing it only for one chosen voyage at a time. His thoughts were interrupted by the girl's words.

"Daaaa! I didn't say good-bye to him."

He put an arm around her small shoulders until she calmed. Then he went to the mess to get some dinner. While he was in the hall, he explained to Mr. and Mrs. Goodiel that Oona was fine and would be back with them later.

Jason brought back only one plate. It was piled high with food, and he carried two cups of weak tea. They sat and ate and talked of simpler things. Jason told her about his family, and she told him how she came to leave her mother and siblings and live with Mrs. Goodiel.

She didn't know or understand much of it, but she'd watched the fancy lady hand her mother something in a pouch, and then her mother pushed her at the lady and had told her to be good.

Jason recognized a business transaction when it was described to him, but he didn't want to attempt to explain to the girl that she had been bought and sold. He'd found it hard to understand at the age of fourteen, and he remembered thinking that it was nothing he could explain to a ten year old.

He'd taken her under his wing for the voyage from Plymouth to Boston in the Massachusetts Colony. His uncle was the captain on this voyage, and gave his newest ship's boy permission to miss some duties as long as the important parts of his work were completed on time.

After weeks at sea, Oona got used to the Goodiels. As she became less afraid of them, she became less likely to burst into tears around them. One day, as land was spotted and the three hills of Boston came into view, Jason found Oona airing sheets before packing them in crates.

"Oona, I want to give you something, so you can always know where home is."

She folded the sheets over an arm, and turned her now-dry eyes, questioning to Jason. "Where home is? What do you mean?"

"Well, this is a compass, and you can find the direction with it." He'd held it out and showed her how to find north, and that just then they were heading west, into the harbor. Britain and Ireland, they were behind them, to the east. Oona was entranced by the shiny instrument and carefully put the chain over her neck and the compass beneath her jacket, tucked between the outer garment and her chemise. It was heavy, but instead of pulling her down, the extra weight seemed to give her strength. She held her shoulders a little bit straighter as she'd looked back at him.

She leaned into him and gave him a shy kiss on his cheek and smiled her thanks. Then, with her head held high, she carried the folded sheets down to her mistress.

Jason didn't see her or the Goodiels leave the ship that day. In fact, he hadn't seen her again until that night at the *Cromwell's Head Tavern*. He thought she might have recognized him immediately. He wasn't sure he really wanted to look like his fourteen-year-old self. But that kiss – that was worth anything.

Jason opened the small rosewood box. Inside was a compass with the familiar inscription from his uncle carved into the wood.

To Jason-

May the seas be calm and the stars lead the way and may you find true north.

Your uncle, S. Jason FitzSimmon.

Uncle Jason was now retired and living near his family. He would bring Oona home to him and tell him the tale, when there was a happy ending to tell. Feeling like such a meeting might be soon within reach, and too restless to sleep, he went up the ladder to take a turn at watch. The winter night was cold and the sky very clear. He found Orion the hunter, and Polaris, that fixed point in the northern sky. He found a small, bright unnamed star that hung near Polaris and named it for Oona, setting her in his firmament as firmly as the north star itself.

Much later, as sleep overtook him in his narrow bed, he thought that he was probably responsible for Oona's fascination with all thing nautical. Maybe, as well, she was to be credited for his.

Chapter 10

*A*fter watching the *Catherine* sail away in late January, Oona's life settled into a new pattern. She refocused on the one goal she had had all these years; to make sure the last months of her indenture were uneventful, so that the contract was fulfilled exactly on time. Before she moved back to Oliver Street, she spoke to Reverend Peirce about the anger she harbored toward Anne Goodiel, knowing that she could not be burdened by such rage and still do her job. He listened, and gave careful advice about forgiving and moving past the anger while needing to acknowledge her pain.

By the end of their conversation, she was able to say that she could live back at the house on Oliver Street without rage creeping into her heart. She understood that a mistress was not forbidden from beating a servant, but it wasn't until speaking with the minister that she could forgive Anne's anger. He told her that he believed that she was not obligated by God to forget, but as a servant she owed Anne her time, and God required she do her best to forgive. They agreed that if Anne Goodiel acted with such anger again, Reverend Peirce would help Oona in front of the magistrates. Knowing he was there to help her made moving back to the Goodiels's less frightening, and Oona moved back soon after.

Dear Jason, I am back at the Goodiels's. My bed feels strange after sleeping in your large and delightfully soft one for so many weeks. I am resigned and ready to resume my work in the household. I don't believe there will be any more trouble. Anne seems contrite and I am resolved to be quiet and pleasant for the next few months. Thanks to you she cannot force a marriage on me, so I have no reason to be nervous or angry.

She relayed the news of the town – which ships were in port, and which leaving – continuing in that vein for a page or two.

When she was done, she walked down the hill to Matthew Goodiel's warehouse to inquire about posting the letter to the *Catherine*. The clerk assured her that most letters did reach ships on this sort of voyage, and he would be pleased to post it for her. He gave her an understanding look. She felt obvious, but no longer worried about Matthew finding out about her friendship with Jason. It was not a problem, for he could not return before June. After May, the Goodiels would no longer have any say in her life, unless, of course, they wished to be friendly or even become family.

Nasty winter weather held on, and spring was late as usual. Oona threw herself into her work, hoping to make the time go faster and stay busy so she did not worry over much about Jason. Anne was as nice as she could be. Most days, she simply requested that Oona spend time with the girls, helping them with schoolwork and sewing pretty gowns for their dolls. Soon she did not jump at the sound of her name, and life moved along pretty much as it had.

Jason, you are not going to believe it! I am now the queen over at the Mount. Goody Brackett has hired two younger girls to train. She figures, correctly, that I won't be around much longer. Molly has been in a foul mood, so the men all want to flirt with me. I don't mind their foolishness anymore, so I go home with real tips at the end of the night. I hope to save enough to find a good place when I leave the Goodiels's house at the end of May.

In March, while Oona was working to please everyone around her, to calm waves of discord and accept the good will of others, the Parliament in London did the opposite. It was the decision the townsfolk of Boston had been worriedly expecting since the tea was thrown in the harbor in December. Most people expected a forfeiture or fine, or some sort of agreement to pay for the tea. Others expected the British to send troops to the Island, their headquarters just south of Long Wharf. It was possible they might quarter some of them in town, as they did after the Stamp Act riots in 1765, leading to the anger and the "Boston Massacre" of 1770.

But no such pallid consequences were imposed by the British government. King George and his government were angry at the unruly, ungrateful colonials. The King was specifically angry at the Province of Massachusetts for its continual disobedient behavior, much of which was codified law, written into the very parchment of its Charter. The Crown felt that document, which had been in place since 1689, gave too much power to elected representatives, and not enough respect or power to the King's appointees.

Rumor had it that George III frothed at the mouth when he was asked to deal with Massachusetts Bay.

Parliament would pass a series of laws pertaining to Massachusetts. The first was passed by that august body in March of 1774. News of the *Boston Port Act* arrived in Boston ten weeks later, in mid-May. Far worse than the news of the act was the man who brought it. The newly appointed Royal Governor, General Thomas Gage, arrived on the *Lively*, a Man 'o War, on May thirteenth. The last civilian governor, Thomas Hutchinson, was generally despised, but he was a known quantity and locally born. Gage was an absolute unknown, except that he was expected to impose martial law on the town as soon as he was able.

Accompanying the General was the Act itself, read to the citizens in front of the Town House on King Street. As per the Act, Admiral Montague arranged his ships throughout the harbor on May thirtieth, ready to blockade the port exactly two days later when it became law.

Oona needed to read the law for herself so she would know what to expect. She paid a penny for her own copy and read it carefully over her coffee. She rephrased it for her diary, trying to understand the complicated English. *Boston Harbor, and all bays, inlets, rivers and wharfs, quays, islands with landing places or tidal marshes that might be navigable, are closed to all boats and ships, except those sent from Salem with provisions for Boston, providing they have been inspected and are accompanied by a customs official and his officers.* When she was finished, she folded the cheap paper and put it with her writing in the pages of her diary. She found wry humor in her indenture ending just as her town became indentured to the British over the value of tea.

The Act imposed a punishment far worse than what

the chattering experts in the coffee houses had expected. The *Boston Port Act* would prevent all commerce in the town, and it would allow the British military to punish anyone who tried to continue working for his livelihood at the port. There could be no goods coming in to be sold. There would be no food of any variety or quantity. To Oona, what seemed most horrible was that the *Act*, and the Navy whose ships were already spread throughout the harbor to enforce it, would prevent the *Catherine* and all other ships now at sea from returning to their home port, to Boston. She wondered where the *Catherine* would go when she was prevented from docking in Boston. And she worried how and when Jason would find her. Finding him seemed daunting and out of the question.

The Act further demanded that the customs officers in Salem were to provision Boston. Even on paper that was an impossibility; in reality it would prove to be even worse. Everyone saw that the act was constructed to strangle the port and starve the town. If the East India Company wanted an apology and the money they lost into the murky waters of the harbor, she knew, as did everyone else, that the merchants would never reimburse them. It promised to be a long stand-off.

As Oona, and the town, came to grips with the new law, the first letter from Jason arrived. He had written it weeks before. It was so like him to solve some of her problems without even being asked.

My dearest Oona,
I am enclosing the keys to my rooms at Mary Channing's. The first is the house key for the kitchen door, the second is to the rooms on the backstairs at the rear of

the house. I'm sure you remember listening to the chickens and their happy rooster. My reasons for this are twofold. I would like you to keep an eye on my things. I trust Mary and her family, but I once leased rooms that were subleased by my landlord while I was away, and I have paid for these rooms through next Christmas.

Far more important than my belongings, I need to reassure myself of your safety after the final date of your indenture. Captain Powell got news that Matthew Goodiel will relocate with his family to London, perhaps by the time this letter reaches you. How many others will do the same, I wonder? Of course, this may all be old news to you.

I have convinced myself that you will not accompany them. Unfortunately, that will leave you even more alone. I cannot let you suffer because I am at sea, and since you and Mary Channing have developed a friendship, and I have paid for the continued use of the room, there should be no problem. Knowing that you are safe with Mary and little Georgie will ease my worries tremendously. I would give my life that you never feel that you are desperate or alone!

But, I have another, more selfish reason for giving you the keys. I'm sure you remember our beautiful, large, comfortable bed – you called it delightful in your letter to me. I am sure you recall hearing me groaning, quite unfairly, during the weeks of your healing. Enough of my drive – I am giving you the keys so that I can imagine you lying on that bed, healed, healthy and naked, your long dark hair spread loose on the white linen pillow, your body pale pink, and your violet eyes flashing with desire.

You believe I did not notice that look in your eyes our last afternoon together, but I did and I ache to see it again.

We are heading to Majorca on this voyage, and

there I intend to buy heady oils made for rubbing into the body. These oils smell dark and sensuous. They warm and soften the skin, causing it to tingle and generate a gentle burning sensation. At the same time, the smells, from a number of spices, blended into a complicated mixture known only to the apothecary, drift up to the head causing an alteration of reason, and allowing the senses to surpass the brain in importance . . . In my dream of you on that delightful bed, I rub these oils into your skin, beginning at your feet and not stopping till your ears and neck tingle with sensation and unresolved passion. Suffice it to say the resolution is at hand.

Before this letter goes where it shouldn't, let me tell you a little of our voyage. I will try not to bore you totally. As you know, we headed south at the beginning of February. The winds have been good, and except for some rain and a slick deck or two, the weather has been favorable.

We made stops in New York, Charleston and Savannah, buying indigo and yellow pine to augment our stores. Both are needed in the Caribbean as well as the Mediterranean, where we are headed. I already mentioned Majorca. It is a mountainous island with an ancient town, just off the coast of Spain. It has catered to voyagers for hundreds of years, since the time seamen began plying the coastal cities of the Mediterranean; before the era of the other Jason and his Argonauts.

After Savannah, where we acquired the yellow pine, a beautiful wood by the way, we headed southeast to the Caribbean. There we not only sold our cod, rum, sugar, barrel stays, dried meats and a portion of our lumber both northern and southern, but a group of men came with me to map a large section of the islands. This was the project that

Matthew Goodiel and I discussed when he took me on as mate. I think the charts will be good. We got many soundings, and sketched miles of coastline. Our new work already shows many errors in the existing charts. The work there took a large part of the month and we are now headed northeast toward Spain.

I am writing this letter over a few days. I will rush to send it as soon as we spot a vessel heading to England or New England.

We just met such a vessel. The captain is speaking to our captain, and the men are all rushing to finish up their letters home. I noticed Capt. Powell had his ready to go. I guess he writes with an end in mind.

During our short visit with the Staffordshire, we got news of the Boston Port Act passed by Parliament just last month. I am sure it comes as no surprise to you by now, but this will do irrevocable harm to the town. I will certainly send letters to my foolish brothers, letting them know that such an act will only incite further anger toward the Crown and Parliament itself. As for not arriving back in port as planned – Wherever and whenever we dock, I will get word to you.

I must seal and send this. With words too dear to write, I am yours – J.

Oona sighed with the pleasure of hearing good news and the image of herself that Jason had offered. There was so much to tell him about the worries in the town, and her own as well. But none of those changes had occurred, for all the town waited.

Dear Jason,
The Goodiels are relocating to London, just as you

predicted in your letter. I am staying with them to help them ready and pack. I don't believe they will get out before the port closes without my help. Part of me wants them to leave, and another is deathly afraid to live my life without the order that working for them had imposed. Currently ships are still allowed to leave, but none come in. Every day the harbor gets emptier. I have not had the chance to view the water from the tower, but I am sure it is very different.

Because they needed her help, Oona stayed with the Goodiels past the date of her freedom. It was her choice. She saw no reason to leave them and have their lives be made more difficult. Now that Jason's thoughtfulness assured her of a safe place to live, she was glad to stay and help the Goodiels. It felt good to be generous, something she had never been in a position to offer before. It was an indulgence to grant her skills and her time to the family she had lived with for so long.

In between the last-minute chores, Oona walked her few letters to Matthew's office at the wharf to see about posting them. The office was closed. The sign on the door merely said *Inquiries to Salem, office of Mr. Dexter*. Disappointed, Oona walked to Thomas Crowninshield's shop to buy a log to use as a letter book. If she could not send her letters, at least there would be some order and decorum involved.

Dear Jason,

It is May as I write. The Goodiels are sailing in the same party as Governor Hutchinson. I am not sure on which ship, but I assume one of Matthew's. I am still in Boston completing the packing that Anne left for the last minutes. The family visits Anne's sister in Milton. I received a most curious note from Mr. Elisha Appleton, Anne's brother-in-law the solicitor. He has invited me to spend some time with them after the Goodiels sail. He certainly knows that I will not be indentured by that time. I wonder why he wishes to speak with me. Of course I will go.

There is much packing still to do if the family is to be ready to leave. The law gives them till the fourteenth of June to depart. After that the Port will be closed to all ships except Naval vessels of the line.

It has been trying here, although Anne has not been cruel, not at all. In fact, she is quite meek. She runs all over the house telling the movers to pack this or that, then cries that she will need whatever it is before they go, and it cannot yet be packed. I am relieved they have gone to Milton and left the work to me. It is far less of a bother this way.

Matthew has removed many of his goods to another merchant's warehouse in Salem, but he will not stay to oversee his merchandise. I hope he has written Capt. Powell with instructions. I foresee chaos. But I believe that is what the Crown intends.

Most merchants have simply moved to Salem to the north, or Hingham to the south, hoping it will be only for a while. I heard that Mr. Rowe is too involved in his work and the town government, so cannot, or will not, move. He, like the others, has a relative seeing to his business at another port, I think his brother.

The little girls I will miss most of all. They alternate between excitement over their move and the adventure of the ocean voyage, and tears and deep sorrow over leaving their friends. Tomorrow they return to Boston. I have decided to stay with them and wave them off.

Of course theirs is not the only household changed

by the Act. Merchants are scrambling to get goods and ships to sea before the port is closed. No one has ever seen such frantic activity. My good friend Sukey Hubbard and her family have chosen to leave. Her betrothed is from Connecticut and they will remove there. I do not know when I will see her again. Her mother has been what Sukey calls my bossy aunt. (She has three of her own, so she knows the species.) I will miss them terribly.

Jason, I will try to smile and expect you by fall. I refuse to worry that I will not see you before frost.

With all my heart – Oona

The Goodiels arrived the next morning, just as Oona finished packing their trunks for the ship. "You'll come with us, yes Oona? I'll write and tell Elisha that you can't go to Milton." Anne Goodiel stood in her garden watching the roses, as if she expected them to erupt into glorious color any second in tribute. She seemed miffed that they were not quite in their glory. Their ferocious budding seemed to taunt rather than please.

Perhaps, Oona thought, poor Anne was annoyed because it was a perfect spring day, one of so very few, and something New Englanders pray for all year. It was all in all a terrible day to even think of leaving.

The last of the goods was brought down to the harbor and stowed. The Goodiels waved tearful good-byes to their friends on the dock and boarded. It was the first of June. Oona accompanied them onto the ship and talked briefly to the girl hired to help them in the crossing. She kissed the girls good-bye and turned to leave.

"Oona!" Matthew Goodiel caught her attention. "I wanted to say good-bye and good luck to you, girl. We have known each other a long time, no? I don't have the cash for your freedom dues, and I'm sorry." He spoke quietly so that no one else could hear. "But, I want you help yourself to anything left in the house, odds and ends of old clothes and bits of furniture. Knowing that the things were going to you makes it feel less like we are abandoning our life. Leaving it with a daughter, keeping things in the family – so to speak. Take what you will and then leave this under the potted rose near the garden door." He handed her the key ring with the keys for the house on Oliver Street. "Warrens from Brattle Street in Cambridge are renting. They take possession July 1. You have the month."

Oona nodded. She felt overcome and mute. What Matthew had just gifted her far exceeded the value of any freedom dues she could have expected. She knew very well what was left in the house. She had assumed the Appletons would come for the furniture, or perhaps those remnants were to be rented with the house. It was overwhelming to receive such bounty for her future, for her past work, and in spite of her anger over her plight and Anne's rage. It was nice to know that Matthew really had seen her as family, as a daughter. Letting her inner spirit show in an unusually bold way, she stood on her tiptoes and kissed him on the cheek. He grabbed her to him for a big bear hug. Then he wiped his eyes and blew his nose as he turned to his own little daughters.

Anne walked her out onto the deck. "Oona, I know what Matthew gave you and I agreed to it. There is a letter in Elisha's files. It explains a lot." Then Anne took Oona's hands in hers, kissed her quickly on the cheek, and turned back toward her cabin. The last Oona saw of her, she had pulled out her own handkerchief. Oona was sure it was having to leave her beautiful home, and her home town, that had caused her to cry. On the other hand, it was nice to have discovered that Anne and Matthew did care about her, and would miss more than her skill for making their furniture shine.

Oona slept that night alone in the house. She woke early and simply walked through the now nearly-empty house, hearing the echos of ten long years of her life.

On Monday morning, she packed clothes for an extended visit and caught the public coach to Milton, a town about ten miles south of Boston. With all the scheduled stops, she arrived late in the day and was ushered into the garden for tea. When it was served, she was slightly surprised to discover it was stewed from rose hips and lemon verbena. She had not known that the Appletons were supporters of independence.

After they had drunk the tea and eaten a good pie, Mr. Appleton asked Oona to come with him to his study. Oona had always trusted Elisha Appleton and his wife Martha in ways she had not trusted the Goodiels. When she was young, it was Elisha who had explained indenture to her, and had made himself available to answer any question. As she followed the thoughtful man, Oona wondered if maybe there were papers for her to sign related to that contract. She couldn't imagine what else it might be.

Appleton motioned for her to sit and handed her two files, bound in string. The first was fairly small, the other quite fat. "Oona, these are papers Anne and Matthew gave me to hold for you when you first came to live with them. The thin one is a letter from Anne to you, written about that time. The other was given to her by another woman.

"You may think it nosy of me to have done it; I am sorry if you do, but I felt it was necessary to read the files first. Oona, I want you to find a quiet place and study them carefully. I am aware of what the information means, but its importance in your life will exceed anything I might think. When you are ready to talk, and I believe you will be, both my wife and I are here to help you." Oona stood up, grasping the files to her chest, not knowing what to imagine.

"Oona?" Appleton interrupted her, "plan on staying a few days, perhaps a week. We would enjoy taking care of you for a few days." Oona smiled at the thought that someone would take care of her. She realized that until she met Jason, no one ever had – at least, not since she was old enough to remember.

Oona took the tied paper files and went back to the little table in a sheltered corner of the garden where she had eaten her pie. The day was warm. She stared sightlessly at some flowers, aware of the sounds around her. A bird chirped; bees in the flowers hummed. She put the two files on the table in front of her. She pulled the thin file closer, untied the string, and spread the papers. It was a letter from Anne Goodiel, written just over ten years ago.

Dear Oona,

You are reading this at the time of your freedom from the indenture we signed with your mother in 1764. So I suppose it is now spring of 1774. I hope your time with us was a good one. I want to explain how it was you came to live with Matthew and me.

I know you remember your father, mother and brothers and sisters in the little house in the town near the sea. However there is more to your story than that. Let me start with my part in the tale. I think that will help.

Ten years ago this spring, Matthew and I were traveling in England and Ireland. He was meeting with shipping agents and such, and I was visiting and viewing the countryside. One day on the west coast of Ireland, I was invited to lunch at the manor of a small town. It was the home of the McClouds. They were very gracious, the old stone manor was beautiful, especially to a girl from the brick town of Boston, and we had a lovely luncheon. The whole family happened to be at home that day, and I remember that we were a large and lively bunch.

The daughter of the house was Brigid, a famous beauty. She was just a few years older than me, about twenty six. She had striking violet eyes and thick, wavy black hair. She had just become engaged to the squire of the next county, so there was much talk of the wedding and great celebrations for both towns. "

After lunch, the young lady stopped me in the back hall. She pulled me into a small counting room, not then in use. She then asked me if I was to return to America soon, and when I said yes, she opened a drawer and pulled out a folder. She also gave me a leather purse of coin and notes. She told me that nearly eleven years before, she had foolishly given her heart and innocence to a man who had come to work on her parent's estate as a gardener. She had gotten pregnant, and given birth to a baby girl, in late May.

Oona pulled her eyes away from the paper. Her hand trembled. She put her hands firmly in her lap, and with the letter flat on the table in the shade, forced herself to stay calm enough to read.

The young women's parents had wanted to take the baby away, but she had refused them. In any case, she had been allowed only one month with her baby. Her parents kept them locked in her rooms. Only when the house was empty was she allowed to take her baby into the small enclosed garden at the back of the house. Then, one day at the end of that month, the baby was gone. She was never told what happened to her, or where she had been taken. Her parents never learned of it, but just one time during that month she had sneaked out from the house and taken her child to the church to have her Christened. She had chosen a name for the baby, but had no idea if that name was still used.

Over tea she told me that the week before my arrival in their town, she had been shopping, and because of a bridge having been washed away in some heavy rains, the carriage took a route down a side street she had never been on before. Playing in the dirt, in front of a small cottage was a group of red haired children and one very dark haired girl. The young women told her driver to stop. Miss McCloud left her carriage and went to talk to the children, and give them some sweets she had bought.

The children told her their names and ages, telling her that, yes, they were all brothers and sisters. While talking to the children, she was struck by the similarity in the ages, and difference in look, of the two oldest children, a boy and a girl. The boy, who shared a cookie cutter likeness with the younger children, and the dark-haired girl, both assured her that they were ten. That was precisely the age her daughter would have been.

She went home and asked her father about her child. It took some time and effort, but he admitted that he had given money to a woman in town with a newborn son to take and raise his granddaughter as her own. He also admitted that he continued to provide money each week for the care of the child. Of course Miss McCloud was very angry. At the same time, she did not want to tell her fiance about her child or confess that she had lost her innocence so foolishly in her youth.

Instead, she went to her family solicitor and had papers made up. She did not tell me what was in the packet she handed me. She made me promise never to look at them. She pleaded with me to hand them to a solicitor when we arrived in America.

She also had an indenture written. She had made up her mind that if she found someone willing, the child would be spirited away and her identity would be hidden from the world. Perhaps more important at that time was that her youthful indiscretion would be hidden from her fiancé/ husband for many more years. After she had made her plans, she waited, hoping to find someone who would take a young child and give her an opportunity she would never find in the dirt floor of a crofter's cottage.

Well, Oona, you know the terms of your indenture; that you would work for us until you reached your twentieth birthday, which was ten years and two months from the day that paper was signed in Ireland. The contract stipulated that you would be raised into a healthy young lady and trained for reasonable employment. Your mother also insisted that we were to be as strict as necessary to prevent you from making the "mistakes of your mother." I'm afraid that is why I have been so harsh with you where young men and your innocence were concerned.

The money to buy you from the woman you considered your mother was supplied by the woman who birthed you.

I want you to understand, that I agreed to the arrangement only because she begged me to get her child away from that cottage. It was not in my nature to separate a child from a parent, even an adopted one who was paid for the raising. It is also not in my nature to have a child as a servant, and I'm sure you noticed that neither Matthew nor I was very comfortable about your indenture.

Miss McCloud insisted that you be provided with skills that would provide for you if times were hard, and the only thing I knew to teach you under those terms were the ones you by now have learned. You can answer better than I can, if they will be helpful. I am sorry if the training was too long or too boring, those were your mother's terms.

Your schooling in arithmetic, reading, writing, Latin and history, those were my terms for my own conscience. As you know, here in America, all freemen and women need those skills, as well as the ones on which your mother insisted.

I am leaving these papers with Elisha Appleton. I will ask him to be your solicitor and advisor and friend – if you ever need one. I hope he is kind to you and helps you with this if, for whatever reason, I am not with you.

It was signed simply "Anne Goodiel." Oona recognized the person who wrote this letter. This was the Anne Goodiel she had known most of her life – the cool, but caring, mistress. It was good to remember her that way – the gentle woman who had taught her to knit and read, who waved good-bye from the ship, not the panicked harpy who flew into a rage as Oona's indenture neared its end.

Someone had put a lemon water on the table in front of her, with a few chunks of clear ice saved from the winter ponds. Oona took a long drink. She stared through the mottled shadows in the maple tree at the blue sky. She froze the moment in time, realizing that she was about to find out who she was. She already had the name Brigid McCloud – that was more than she had just three minutes before. A mother, Brigid McCloud.

Oona's hands trembled slightly as she untied the second string and cracked the seal on the thick folder. She stared out into the garden at the voluptuous roses that had chosen this afternoon to unfurl their glorious colors and scents. Her mind was so full of ideas and memories. All these years, the Goodiels had never broken their promise to keep Brigid McCloud's secrets. They had succeeded in preparing her for any number of professions. She could be a nursemaid in a household with young children and teach the youngsters their letters and numbers. She could mend and sew quite well, if she had to. She could make and remake ladies' clothes, and certainly she could organize and run a home for any but the most aristocratic household.

She ached at the thought of never seeing Jason again and needing to pursue one of those lines of work. Hopefully, she thought a little dreamily, she would not need her acquired skills to earn her own living, but would help Jason in his work, and raise her own children, their children, rather than care for someone else's. She pulled her mind back to the file in front of her.

The papers were in order. The first was her baptismal record, naming her Oona Brigid McCloud. It was odd actually, to have been nobody, and suddenly to have a real identity, a real name. Brigid was a pretty name, though by now she was used to Oona. She was also certain she had no use for 'McCloud' now that she had Jason's name. Even with the indenture over, she had gotten so used to keeping her marriage a secret that she still had not told anyone. She had never even written "FitzSimmon," or used it aloud. She guessed it was time.

The other papers in the file were stock certificates for small numbers of shares in various English companies. She did not understand what these had to do with her, or what she could do with them. It was certainly something to ask Elisha when she was finished with the file. Oona continued through the stack of papers. Next was a bank statement from an account. It showed that rents from various properties in Ireland and England would be going into it. The document did not have a record of who managed the property trust, but the account was in the name of Oona B. McCloud. Now that she had her baptismal record, she supposed she could legally access the money. The thought of having her own money made her giddy. She took a moment to let the feeling begin to sink in. She wondered how much there was and how to get at it. Those questions would be easy to answer, she was sure.

Under all the papers and parchments in the file was a raw muslin sac. Oona pulled it open carefully, letting the drawstrings reach their full length before reaching inside. Slowly, she pulled out objects long pressed flat. The first item was a wheat grass cross. It was a shape she had never seen before. There was a woven square in the center, and shafts of wheat extended from the square forming the cross. They were tied at each end. A small note was pinned to the cross. It said: *Oona tiny babe, this is Saint Brigid's Cross. She is the saint of babies and children in need of love and home. Sweet daughter, I hope you have found, or will find, both.*

With the cross was a baby's christening gown, and a tiny silver cross on a thin chain. Oona had been raised as a Puritan in Boston. She understood that these pagan symbols, and Catholic ritual, had no place in her life. She would carefully put these things away, out of sight. She would always hold them dear for what they had meant to the mother she had lost. Brigid McCloud was a woman forced by circumstance to lose her child – a child, for however brief a time, she had cherished and hoped would succeed.

Oona put the small items gently back into the linen bag. She breathed in the heavy sent of the roses, letting their beauty meld with new memories of the mother she would never meet. A peace settled on her as she let tears fall. She cried for herself as a lonely child far from home, and without a home; she cried for Jason, missing him terribly when she would like to share this with him; and she cried for what would become of her home and town under army rule. When she felt all cried-out, she went to find Elisha Appleton to discover what he could tell her about her accounts and investments.

Oona spent ten days with the Appletons. Elisha explained that normally there would be little difficulty getting the information she needed from London, although he wasn't sure what the situation was just then, with the port closed, but he would look into it. They agreed to stay in touch. Oona took her files back with her, but told the Appletons where to find her at the Channings's house on Beach Street. She promised she would visit again if it were possible. Feeling as if life was offering new friendships and possibilities, Oona took the coach back into town with a sense of peace and equivalent feeling of anxiety. The former was for herself; the latter was over what she might find back in the town.

Chapter 11

*O*ona went immediately to Mary Channing's on Beach Street to tell her that she would be taking Jason's room upstairs. The next morning she went to the Goodiels's and used her keys to get into the empty house. She found various bits of furniture she would like – side tables, mismatched chairs, a mirror, and a sketch of herself done by a portrait painter who hadn't noticed she did not belong with the Goodiel boys when their portraits were done. The sketch caught a proud defiance she had done her best to subdue. Maybe that painter had not made a mistake as he'd claimed, but wanted the chance to capture that spirit before she suppressed it, as he must have known she would. Maybe, she thought as she stared at her young self, she would try to find that spirit again.

In her hunting, she found the trunk of boys' clothes she had pushed into an attic corner when the Goodiel sons had moved away. She remembered those clothes. Anne had told her to pack things up for the church, but some of her stepson's things meant too much to Oona, so she had made one trunk of things to save. She pushed it back into the dark corner. Then she took her finds downstairs and set them near the door.

"George!" Oona called down Beach Street at the boy and his friends who were playing ball in the street. "Any of you fellows want to earn some coins and help me carry a few chairs from Oliver Street?"

In a short time, Georgie and the group of boys, with Oona as their leader, carried the trunks, tables, chairs and knick-knacks back to her rooms. They stacked them neatly along the wall.

"Miss Oona? Do you want us to help you set the things around the room?" Georgie looked hopefully around the small room, always liking an extra moment to linger where his hero lived.

"Just the few chairs, George, and thank you." Oona smiled to herself, understanding why Georgie didn't want to leave.

After a small dinner, she looked at the pieces she had brought. Most were unmatched things from Matthew's first marriage, things that Anne did not want cluttering her life. Oona had not cared for these pieces with lemon oil and careful cleaning, but they were lovely and she knew they would shine in her home someday. But now she needed to hide them. Already, with the soldiers moving into the town, there were shortages of things like – well, like firewood – and it was only going to get worse when autumn and winter came. She decided, during that first night in Jason's rooms, to have a false wall built to hide and protect the wooden furniture from the fireplaces of what was sure to become a cold and hungry town.

For weeks Oona had listened to Mary plead with her young son not to spend so much time with the redcoats. The boys marched on the sides of the regiments, imitating their drills. Most of the men did not mind, but to some, the occupation of a rebel town was distasteful. Such men's anger had left Mary worried about Georgie. The inevitable happened at the very end of the summer, when she left a letter for Michael in the back of the kitchen cupboard explaining that she and George had gone to his sister's in Brookline, and were safe.

"Oona, are you sure you will be all right, dear? I will worry so."

"Mrs. Channing, I will be fine." And she was. With so many teachers gone, she had no trouble attracting students to her new school, which she opened in Mary Channing's front parlor. She even found slates and horn books in the back of Mrs. Jennison's abandoned schoolroom. Oona also agreed to feed the chickens that the Channings would leave behind.

"It will be tough to find feed, if the state of the town continues down this path. Just feed them till you have to eat them. I'll understand. I'm bringing my best layers and the rooster with me. I can start again."

Oona noticed the glint of tears in Mary's kind eyes, but didn't say anything more. She pulled the kind lady and son close, hugged them good-bye, and wished them the best. She wanted to be sad, now that there were so many familiar faces among those leaving their nice homes. And now, unknown soldiers were replacing them and occupying the town. But the possibility of a new life was too exciting. Besides, Jason and the *Catherine* were due to dock somewhere nearby at the end of September. And so, scared as she was, she raised her chin like the impish girl in that sketch.

Dear Jason,

I have arrived back in town, having spent a pleasant ten days in the country. But even if the Appletons could feed and keep me, which they cannot, I would not desert my home. The town has changed considerably in the few days since the Act was put into place. Today, although it will be as hard for you to imagine as it is hard for me to believe my own eyes, there is not one top-sailed merchantman at the harbor. Missing also are the sounds of sails and clapping of dead eyes on masts. Of course there are sights and sounds of the Men 'O War in and around the harbor, but they are not comforting or pleasant.

Other things have changed as well. I believe people are quieter, perhaps more refined. This might be because they are afraid of the soldiers; might be because there is no longer any haggling over goods at the market or food stalls; maybe it's that the loyalists flocking into town from the countryside really are quieter and more refined than we Bostonians. Probably all those things.

They, the loyalists, have come from all over, but especially Brattle Street in Cambridge. The Goodiels's house has been rented to one such family, the Patrick Warrens. Their man sent a note to me before I left for Milton, asking if I would like to work for them as a maid. It seemed easy – an answer to questions I am afraid to ask. But I wrote him right back and said that no, I would not be interested in that position. I have decided, with Mary Channing's permission, to open a dame school for the youngest children. So many of the small schools have closed, and there will be a real loss if new ones are not opened. There are even slates and books left behind at one nearby school.

Something strange occurred to me yesterday as I walked out. The colors of the town have changed. You know how some Boston women wear a red cloak in winter, but mostly we match the sky, trees, brick and mud around us? Well, everywhere you walk now, you see red. It doesn't simply break the monotony of the sea of black and gray cloaks and greatcoats. No, now the monotony is red. It is most upsetting. By the time I returned from Milton, there were two regiments of foot encamped on the Common – the 4th and the 43rd, one by the frog pond, the other near the poor house. More arrive daily, and now Fort Hill, just by the Goodiels's house, is taken over by the 23rd Royal Fusiliers. I'm sure they and their staffs will soon outnumber whatever town folk are still here.

I remind myself that these are young boys, no older than myself, and far from home. I also have to think long and hard about how to protect myself from their flirtations, which I am afraid could become something frighteningly more. Perhaps I will dirty my hair and dress like a hag, or take to dressing like a young boy – though I have learned that that may lead to its own set of problems.

Jason – we recently had word of Parliament's next Act against the town. The news reached us on June second, but I confess I ignored the broadsides, feeling distracted with my own problems. Parliament informs us that our judges and sheriffs will now be appointed or confirmed by the Crown, either directly or through his appointed governor. It is now possible for the governor and the Crown to remove an elected officer without consent of the local councilmen. They have also changed the rules surrounding Town Meeting, so that Mr. Adams can no longer call a meeting whenever the selectmen deem an issue worthy. Town Meetings throughout the Province of Massachusetts can only be held once a year, unless approved by the Governor himself. They say that to someone who grew up in the Colony of Virginia or in Britain, these changes would not seem onerous, but our way of government has been in place since the Charter of 1630 and affirmed in the Charter of 1688, which has now been revoked by a stroke of the pen of George III. Whatever seething there is in reaction is done in whispers and closed meetings. The printing presses are not silent, but they don't have much new to say.

I know that none of this is good news and I am sorry. I have much to tell about my visit to the Appletons, but that will wait for another letter. I am, as always, yours – Oona.

Not all the changes brought to the town were bad. For Oona, teaching the small children pleased her and gave her a new sense of purpose. She addressed each day with a joyous optimism she had never felt before. She found the young scholars delightful, and their parents, glad for any school, did not mind her inexperience. She charged a small amount for each child, but often forgot to collect the money if she was sure the parents could not afford even the small payments.

There was little to buy. Merchants sold off older stock, but the prices were high and she had no reason to purchase new gloves, gowns or tea sets. What food there was she used her barmaid money to buy. The school day was necessarily short, and she wandered through the markets along with the rest of the townsfolk looking for enough food to feed a family. No one knew what would happen when the weather turned cold in the fall, if food was scarce and dear now.

Looking for a way to supplement the money she had stored, she went back to the *Mount* in July, but quickly realized that she was afraid of the soldiers' flirtations, so she said sad good-byes to her friends and promised to stop by once in awhile during mornings. Soon she found another source of specie.

Dear Jason,

It is now August and I am fine. I cannot say the same for the town, but I am sure that with enough care even she will recover. I am teaching my little charges every day. Right now I have eighteen students. They range in age from five to thirteen. The oldest read and cipher quite well, so I set them to reading books we've borrowed from the neighbors. The youngest I teach what I can, given that we have limited access to any sort of materials, even the outside is off limits to us for parts of the day. It's that a few of the little ones are truly afraid of the redcoats, and there simply is no way to avoid seeing marching and mustering. So we stay inside even on warmer days. Luckily the summer has not been extraordinarily hot.

The students each pay a small sum each week. I think it is traditional to bring firewood, but there is so little wood I do not know how that could possibly be accomplished. Right now what bits we have are all used for cooking. Of course, the humorists remind us in broadsides and in coffee shops that with so little food, there will be no need for a cookfire. I do not know how we will survive the winter. I hope to see you well before that.

You will find me resourceful and energetic. I had one of the children's fathers build me a false wall in the room. It is that same problem with firewood I mentioned before. You see, people have begun burning their furniture for heat. I felt the need to protect your bed and some bits and pieces the Goodiels gave me. I think that, come winter, people will be desperate enough to burn beautiful things. The bed is apart and hidden behind the wall, along with most of the furniture I brought back from the Goodiels's house.

But that is not the only mark of my resourcefulness. When I took apart the bed to move, I remembered the tea you had hidden under the floorboards. Well, with the town full of loyalists, I have been going door to door very quietly around the Oliver Street neighborhood, telling the wives and their cooks that I had good Souchong for sale. They give me more than I would ever dare charge. The tea is now completely gone, and the safe place under the rug now houses the specie.

I wish you could receive this on your voyage to know that I miss you and am thinking of you. I am Yours – Oona.

Oona chronicled the days in the occupied town in her letterbook to Jason. She wrote about the soldiers going out to raid Grape Island for hay and dry wood, only to be attacked by farmers who were now calling themselves Patriots. And how the supplies continued to dwindle, now aided by Patriots outside the town who were blocking the neck and other points of entry to try and starve the army. And it turned out that Oona was right about hiding the wooden furniture, as even the meeting houses were not immune to being raided for their wood. First the North Meeting House was taken down for fuel, then Old South's pews were burnt.

The Governor announced that he would give a pass to all those who wanted to leave Boston. But of course that was not precisely true. Not everyone who requested a pass to leave was given one, and not everyone who could have left did so. In one important instance, a merchant was not allowed to leave with his warehouse of goods. Of course he stayed, rather than abandon his entire wealth to thieves and marauders. Oona also chose not to leave. Her things were not priceless, but she couldn't help but remember that they were all she had. She would leave, she was sure, when there was a safe way to bring her things with her.

And she felt needed, part of the fabric of the town that waved as a silent flag under the bright red uniforms of the occupying army. The dame school was one necessity. And there were rumblings among some of the Sons of Liberty about finding a way to distribute the food and clothing that was slowly being smuggled in. Oona knew she would be a part of that effort as soon as they asked.

There is an expression known to people who live their lives by the edge of the sea: Slack Tide, the short, almost infinitesimal moment when the tide is neither coming in nor going out, neither rising nor falling. That was how Oona described those weeks during the summer and fall of 1774. The merchants who remained continued to refuse to pay the East India Company for the tea. It seems they preferred to declare a Fast Day, a day of reflection and prayer that would cost the merchants more than the total price of the tea. For some, the move was foolish. Others, who wanted Boston to be the tinderbox that set off a war, were pleased. For Oona, it was still too soon to worry about Jason's return, but nearly time to do so. And the British Army, Navy and military government, acting at the direction of Parliament, did nothing to create ease.

The only changes were that the flow of loyalists from outside the town relocating into the town increased and continued, as their country neighbors, Patriots, blamed them for the harbor closure and the fate of Boston, making flight from home their only choice.

Dear Jason,
Parliament has passed yet another act to punish the people of Boston. This one, the Quartering Act, makes it legal for soldiers to occupy any house whose residents have

left or have an extra room. We have no say where they will live. I think only the fact that there are fifteen or twenty small children here each morning has kept this house from being occupied. I do not relish the thought of strange men moving into my home.

I feel the need to explain why I have not left. There are the children, and I love feeling important to them, but there is more. I confess to be enjoying an adventure of sorts. I am still healthy and safe. I promise I will flee if I become unsafe or ill, I do promise. I have not considered how to tell you where I might be if I did leave, and that worries me enough so that as long as there is no compelling reason to leave, I will remain. When you send for me, I will need at least two wagons. The Goodiels gifted me various things, and there is your bed to consider.

I remain constantly yours – Oona.

By the end of September and beginning of October, Oona knew the *Catherine* must have docked in some port town, perhaps Portsmouth, Hingham or Salem, but she'd still had no word. She was frustrated, but there was no one she could ask without raising too many questions about her own business. She did not want that. She was sure that if there had been a disaster at sea she would have read it in the papers. She raised her chin and vowed to stay hopeful.

A letter from Jason, written earlier in the year, found its way to her in October. She loved hearing his voice speak to her through the letters, but they gave no clue as to where he was now.

Dearest Oona–
I will send this to Goodiel's agent, but I don't know where the man is. Maybe we will read each other's letters

together, sitting in front of a warming fire.

I hope you are well; you are resourceful enough to survive the most daunting circumstances. I am quite sure that a few redcoats parading down King Street won't confound you.

We are right now, April 28, off the coast of North Africa. The other morning I woke and went on deck before our breakfast, just to watch the sun rise over the Mediterranean Sea. The water is a beautiful color, very different from our Atlantic; a mix of blue shades that lack the gray we are used to. So there I was drinking in the morning, when a fellow with a cutlass in his teeth pops his head over the bow. He was a foul looking man with clear malice in his eyes. I think he was as surprised to see me, as I was to see him, and since we were the only men in the immediate area, I pulled my pistol and fired for help, hoping I might hit him in the cry. I did not, but I was able to rush him and push him overboard. He fell back onto his small boarding vessel.

Well, we had a perfectly jolly battle, guns blaring, swords clashing and all manner of mayhem. We came out with few scratches – they went limping home to their accursed Bey with their masts shattered and most of the scurvy crew injured or dead. The saddest part was that I missed my morning coffee and breakfast, and did not eat till nearly dinner time.

The Catherine will go nowhere near Tunisia again, even if we have to hug the French coast for an extra week. I'm afraid we will be looked for on our return. Their leaders love nothing more than to steal everything on a ship, imprison the sailors and hold them for ransom, which they call tribute. If it is not paid, they gladly cut off the heads of their prisoners with their sharp swords. The King would normally pay any ransom for a British ship, but I suspect we are no longer in his good graces. Perhaps in time someone will be brave enough to fight this war once and for all and end the cycle of theft and ransom.

I apologize for my graphic description, but you are a brave and worthy wife of a foolish seaman. Do know that if this gets to you, I am quite safe. So though a chill might pass through you, you will have no worries.

I am, as always yours – Jason.

I enclose your birthday note – celebrating the date for what it really means to you: the end of your indenture, your freedom, and our wondrous future. I may be presumptuous and assume that my Husbandly Attentions toward you will now be appropriate. Written for the day. Our part will be played when possible.

Dearest wonderful Oona,

If you are not home now, I think it would be good sense to head back to our rooms at Mrs. Channing's before opening and reading this missive. As you are aware today is your birthday, Happy Day! And it is also the day your indenture to the Goodiels has ended. It will be long in the past when you read this, but such time and distance cannot be helped.

I am aware that much has changed in Boston, but since I am far away, I don't know yet what those changes are. But promises are real and should be kept in time of peace and war, and that means the promise I made to you, and kept to my own satisfaction and enormous frustration, has been fulfilled and is over.

Oona shivered with anticipation for what would follow, if only in words. She sat on the edge of the mattress and kicked off her shoes.

Oh my delicious Oona, how I have waited for this moment. If only I were actually there to enjoy it with you and hold you in my arms, instead of far away, on the vast Atlantic Ocean.

But enough of my travelogue. Today is the day I plan to fulfill your deepest desires, even those you haven't yet recognized, if alas, only on paper.

Darling, there is no reason to skimp in the preparations for such an auspicious event, so I will serve you a glass of this fine Madeira I have recently purchased and ask you to sit with me a while. It is too warm for a fire here. I hope it is finally warm there, but with Boston one can never guess, I know.

The wine is good, but I do not want to get drunk, nor should you, so we will put our glasses down on the table near the bed. I will take time, all the time in the world, to undress you. You know I have seen you naked, and it is that image I keep in my head for very lonely nights. So here in your room, I will take you into my arms and kiss you. My hands will not have stayed still, and have already undone the buttons down the back of your gown.

Your thin linen shift with a fine edge of needlework – just where my fingers start to tease your soft skin – is still covered by stays and your gown. I need to taste you so much, my mouth will kiss and my tongue will taste and then join my hands in caressing the soft skin of your neck and shoulders.

I move behind you and enjoy your neck and back. My anxious fingers will untie your shift and I push it off your shoulders. It catches on your arms, almost revealing your lovely breasts. I gently kiss your neck again, my hands now slowly tracing your collar bone, working their way slowly and sweetly forward to the beautiful mounds. I touch you through your layers and feel your body quake gently and swoon against mine.

You shiver, and I imagine your breathing getting faster and just a bit beyond you. You start to get wobbly. I admit to loving your pleasure and watching you revel in my touch. Your thick long hair drop heavy from its pins with just a few tugs, and jumps into curls over your shoulders.

Oona read the rest with glee. Her toes curled and her heart beat a bit faster. The glorious details of how Jason would finally love her made her warm and swoon with arousal and delight. Even if this letter was months in getting back to Boston, she was glad it had found its way to her. It meant more to her now than it would have at the beginning of the summer. But as the weeks dragged on, she missed Jason with a terrible aching. And, as time dragged on, uncertainty and then worry set in. Taking a risk that it might get lost, she wrapped the letterbook, now full to bursting, in old broadsides and tied it up with string. She entrusted it to some neighbors who were moving in with their relatives on the Massachusetts north shore. They promised to deliver it right away to Mr. Davenport, Goodiel's agent in Salem.

By the time the *Catherine* was once again off North America, Captain Powell had gotten formal word of the blockade, and Jason set a course north to Salem instead of attempting Boston Harbor. They made good time, and had no trouble from American privateers or the British Navy. As soon as the *Catherine* docked, they were met by David Davenport, the man Goodiel had left in charge of his affairs. The men were pleasantly surprised that the embargo had raised the price of goods so high that what they had in the hold was worth far more than they expected. The man also had a large book addressed to Jason. It was wrapped in old broadsides and tied with a piece of string. The fellow did not know much about it, just that it had been delivered from Boston by some folks recently arrived in Essex County.

Jason took his payment for his role as navigator and first mate on the voyage. He was dismayed to find that Davenport had no knowledge of, or interest in, Goodiel's Caribbean mapping project. He suggested that Jason take full ownership, since Matthew Goodiel had not left any notes behind. The agent suggested that Jason talk to a chart printer whose shop was on the next block. Jason thanked him, took his odd package, stored his trunks, and went to find rooms.

The town of Salem was crowded. It was older and smaller than Boston, and now it housed its own people and many from the larger town to the south. Jason inquired at all the types of places a sailor might find rooms: warehouse message boards, pubs with attics or basements, and likely strangers sitting down for a pint. He slept in Goodiel's storeroom near the docks for three nights. Even this space was crowded, and he was fearful for his charts and instruments. He barely closed his eyes.

The next morning he met Oona's friend, Thomas Crowninshield, at the wharf.

"Mr. Crowninshield, what brings you to this crowded spot?" Jason asked as he stood by the older man after he had eaten breakfast and was once again reading the list of people with rooms to let.

"Jason, isn't it? Oona's friend. I recognize you. I am just posting this for my sister. Her house is nearly empty with only me, and she decided to rent the top floors. She will cook. She misses her big family."

"How many does she have room for?"

"There are three rooms up there on the third floor. Big enough for the five beds she had up there. You I remember – do you know four fellows who would be good guests?"

Jason assured Mr. Crowninshield that it would be no problem to find the tenants. Later that afternoon, five men moved themselves and their gear into Mrs. Holyoke's house. The beds did not sway with the movement of the ocean, and they were more comfortable than a ship's hammock, but barely wider. In any case, he was only sharing the room with one man, and as long as the fellow did not snore or talk in his sleep . . . He had slept in worse. Jason put thoughts of bringing Oona to Salem out of his mind for the present; it was not feasible.

Later, he found a minute to himself. He took off his boots and stockings and climbed onto his bed. He pulled himself back into the corner against the headboard and unwrapped the package he had been carrying around unopened. He did not know exactly why he knew, but he wanted to be alone, with time to enjoy whatever it was that was in this package.

Jason hadn't been sure if any of his letters had gotten to Oona. He wondered if any had gone awry and had been read by another. He hoped not. This wonderful package contained a ship's log full of her letters to him. He opened it slowly, savoring the feel and smell of paper and ink, knowing that it wouldn't be too long till he saw her again. The letters told him much of what life was like in Boston during these past months, but she had left much out of the narrative. He found he was relieved that she was still in his rooms on Channing Street, but was sad when he read that

Mary and her family had taken the governor's pass and moved to a relative's home.

He chuckled at Oona's description of the small house full of school children. And he had no trouble imagining Oona as an able teacher of those children. He pulled his wandering mind away from a vision of Oona surrounded by his dark-haired, violet-eyed children, and pulled it back to her book. Reading the letters, it quickly became clear that feeding and clothing the residents of the closed town had been, and was going to be, a continuing problem, especially when winter came.

He finished the book and went down to the *Rusty Anchor* to see if any plans had been formulated for getting materials into Boston. He found that some of the privateers were making an effort to divert goods from British ships to their own, which they sold to the Americans in Boston. Some goods were supplied to churches, and some foodstuffs had been delivered from Connecticut and as far away as South Carolina. He listened to the well-meaning, semi-drunken chatter and realized that it would be a long time till he could move Oona out of Boston. He might well get himself arrested or killed, but he knew he would have to act, to formulate a plan. What would be needed was something more organized than the haphazard efforts made so far. After a decent length of time, he excused himself and went back to his room.

Tugging at the corner of his mind was a memory of a sketch. He pulled his sea trunk at the foot of his bed, hoping he had not left the notebook with his things in Boston. There at the bottom, under a waistcoat he had worn only once on the voyage, was the small notebook he had carried for years tucked deep in his coat pocket. It was full of designs, equations, love letters and notes to himself. Pleased to have found it, Jason sat with a sharpened quill and fresh paper to see what could be constructed to help care for Bostontown.

By the time his roommate returned, he had sketches and the germ of an idea. He laid out the nascent plan to his friend.

"Jason, it seems as solid a bit of skullduggery as any. The problem will be money. Do you have any? I have what the last voyage paid. I'm afraid that's the way it is for all of us."

Jason knew Rob was right. He still had the charts he had done for Goodiel's publisher. He had felt odd moving on his own, but it now seemed like a necessity. The next morning, he went to the publisher the agent had recommended and showed him the charts.

Dear Oona,

I just returned from the publisher. He is very interested in my charts, and will begin the process of redrawing them for printing right away. He says there is always interest in the Caribbean, even among people who simply want to dream of warm waters and trade winds. He gave me a generous advance. Of course, this is a wonderful thing, but it is as good as spent.

I am designing, and having built, a flotilla of small maneuverable craft to bring goods into Boston under the noses of the Men 'o War. I have discussed the project with the ministers and the leading men of Salem. Though they all agree there is need, none has so far stepped forward to undertake the work. No one has been as adamant about the work as I. Perhaps I am crazy. I have enlisted the willing to help in any way possible. Even the busiest shipyards have found time and men to build these small fast ships.

I laugh when I think of them. They are far from

beautiful. The hulls are to be tarred, not varnished or painted. This method is fast and cheap, and the dull color will hide the little wasps, as I have termed them. They ride high in the water, their shallow hulls gliding over sand bars and rocky shoals. The tarred wood reflects no light, so that on the open water, they will be invisible in the ocean mist.

I am afraid this means a further delay in finding us suitable accommodations. I hope to remedy this as the royalties begin to come in from the charts. I do so want to hear about your life, but since this letter will now sit in my sea chest, joining with dozens of other letters and trinkets I am keeping for you, it is futile to ask.

I am yours as always –
Jason

By November, a small fleet had been assembled, and two dozen seamen who were not at sea for whatever reason agreed to take turns manning the boats. To Jason's delight and relief, the minister of the Brick Church and his wife agreed to take care of organizing their parishioners, and the others as well, to handle the gathering of food and clothing for the men to sneak into Boston.

Oona's letters had described how the harbor was blocked by the navy at eight points. It would be necessary for Jason's tiny flotilla to go where the large ships could not go. Also, they needed to move at times when no sane man would even think of attempting to maneuver a ship over rocky shoals into shallow inlets and marshes. In other words, they counted the sheer unlikeliness of the operation to keep them safe.

Each "wasp" was manned by two sailors. Six boats would sail each night. They were built with a single mast and mid-size triangular sails, designed for the coast and built for agility, but not for stability. The men understood that, and they knew small fishing vessels when they saw them. They were happy to accept orders never to travel during a storm, but to find a safe spot partway home and wait out the weather, and also to leave with their ships immediately if any group were caught, burning a ship if necessary. As a group, they planned that deliveries would be made often enough that it would be unnecessary to risk life, limb, or capture to sail such small, unstable ships in bad weather, or into danger.

The men sat in the *Rusty Anchor* one evening making plans for their first foray into Boston Harbor. They had taken delivery of the first wasps, and trial runs around Salem and Marblehead were successful. After a few drinks, his friends asked where Jason had gotten the idea for the shallow-hulled boats.

"When we were boys, my brother John and myself, we used to fish in the rocky coast near the house." Jason very carefully did not use the words "manor" or "estate." "Most summer days we left early, as boys do, and spent the day swimming and fishing. The coast there is similar to that just north of here, around Gloucester." The men nodded understanding. "My father's younger brother, Uncle Jason, was the seaman. He took me on as cabin boy when I was fourteen. He always seemed to prefer time with us to that spent with landlubbers, even if they were adults. So one time when Uncle Jason was visiting, he came with us on our adventure.

"We had rowed way out and left our lines in the water while we swam awhile. While we rested on some big rocks, Uncle Jason told us of his travels through southern Europe. It was that afternoon he told John and me about a flat-bottomed, single masted sailboat used by the fishermen of southern France. 'Course, we all understood that on the North Sea, those simple little boats would snap like twigs in a high breeze. But we boys were intrigued. And John, who fancied himself a draftsman of great ships, sketched one he adapted for use in colder, rockier seas. We never did have a chance to build one – but now, let us raise a glass to my younger brother, who has helped us all commit treason with his fine design."

It was just after dawn on a late November day. The first of the little wasps was sighted returning to Salem harbor. The men scheduled to take the trip the following night waited to hear how it had gone. Nothing much had happened, the sailors said; the stuff had been delivered where the Committee of Correspondence in Boston had designated. But the men cautioned that on the trip down, the supplies acted as ballast, and that the little ships rode higher in the water on the return than they'd expected. Silently the men added that bit to their list of cautions, every one of them understanding the dangers that heading north with a light ship would incur. The goal was to deliver the material into Boston safely. Speed on the return was not an option. Using fog and moonlight, they were to sail quietly and quickly around the islands, staying as close to the mainland as tides would allow. This was possible because of the extraordinarily shallow hull. Using all precautions, they agreed they would make the trips at least four evenings or mornings per week. At the instigation of one of the men – Jason did not know who – they named themselves the Argonauts, after the crew that sailed with Jason in the Greek tales. Jason hoped their voyages would not be as long and complicated as his namesake's.

And the town was hungry. As it became obvious that the small amounts of food the Navy let through its blockade were meant to go to the Army and its followers first, people began to get scared. But without knowing how or why, food slowly began to get into the town. In July, a shipment of rice arrived from a church in South Carolina that had heard of the privations in Boston. And, of course, New Englanders helped as well, with flour and apples coming in the autumn from the nearby countryside. But although some food and supplies were successfully smuggled into the town, it was only just before Christmas that deliveries became regular and could be counted on. At first, no one knew who was delivering the food and clothes. The Committee just seemed to find the packages and deliver them into church basements. It was after the New Year that the Committee asked the other groups if they would coordinate collecting and distributing the food, warm hats and mittens when they were delivered. A few weeks later, a method was created for people to contribute a few coins to help the rescuers purchase more goods.

With regular arrivals of food, some of the incessant worrying was relieved. No one was well fed, but just knowing that a group of men were braving the Men 'o War and delivering food to shallow coves all over the town made everyone feel better.

Oona bought a new book from Points East, even though Mr. Crowninshield had moved away. She had spent a pleasant few days with the Appletons in Milton around Christmas, but again preferred her own life to one spent hiding and waiting. Elisha Appleton had not yet heard about the rents on her properties, but as soon as his agent in London got back to him, he said, he would let her know.

She returned to Boston on the new year and finished

the letter she had started the week before in Milton.

Jason –

I sense you are nearby – why, I am not sure. I have great hopes this blockade will end soon, though I fear the governments are the real blockheads in this story. Our New Year's celebration was especially somber, as there was very little food and nothing much to be cheery about. It seems more regiments arrived weekly during the fall and now everyone around me chooses to feel sorry for themselves, even though there is now more food than there was a month ago. I retain my general optimism. I am sure there is no good reason for that.

The harbor is almost frozen. This is the time of year when people can walk across the river and even the deepest channels in the harbor freeze. The ink in my inkwell was frozen this morning, and worse, the tears were frozen in my eyes. But that has happened before. I have heard people tell of it, and I have lived it myself in my cold attic at the Goodiels's. So I, perhaps better than most, know that even the coldest weather will not last all winter long. And spring always arrives. Of course, we don't know what will arrive with the spring. Will it bring more regiments, or perhaps another act of Parliament?

It was during the first days of spring sunshine when Oona saw an angry broadside from the Committee of Correspondence proclaiming that the Occupying Army in Boston had announced a bounty for information on, or capture of, "a small and annoying group of sailors who are supplying the citizens of Boston with smuggled food." The writer called for all the good people of the town to ignore such temptation to betray the good people trying to help us.

He called anyone who would a traitor, and hinted that the Sons would having no trouble tarring and feathering such a fiend.

It was soon after reading the broadside that Oona was approached on a walk by Edward, a leader of the Sons of Liberty. Oona recognized him, since he lived in a house not far from the Goodiels on Fort Hill.

"Oona, I know this may not be something you are comfortable doing. But we have lost some numbers of people since the battles out in Concord and Lexington, and more leave each day now that the general's given permission to take household goods and go. If you can help, we meet at the corner of Cow Lane and Long Lane, at three this morning. The sailors make the delivery as near to low tide as they can, and sail as soon as it begins to rise again."

Oona understood what a small window they all must have to move the goods, and how desperate they must be for help, if they needed to ask a small woman like herself. The meeting place was nearby – she barely needed to leave her street. It would be petty to claim she needed her sleep any more than anyone else. Of course, she agreed to help. She began that night and every third night thereafter.

Most evenings the food was already there, the deliverers and their boats long gone by the time the group came to carry the goods to whichever church basement was designated for the delivery that night. Occasionally, as they approached, they heard a ship hoisting her sails, but both groups were cautious, and no one could claim to have seen a sailor, or even gotten a good look at one of the ships. The organizers kept their knowledge of where the goods would be dropped as secret as they did the sailors' identities. Every afternoon, after the children had left her school for home, a messenger would stop by to tell her which of the four drop-off points on the south side of the town would be used that night. Oona assumed similar actions were taking place in other neighborhoods, but knew better than to ask.

It had rained and drizzled for days on end during the first weeks of May. Hard rain meant the smugglers would not attempt the trip. There was never enough food delivered to create a steady supply, let alone any kind of surplus, so everyone was hoping that a night of light fog and drizzle would not keep them away. Oona got her message at four o'clock that there would be a drop-off at Wind Mill Point just before dawn. She had an early dinner and went to bed to grab as many hours of sleep as she could.

In the cold damp of the very early morning, a cold, slightly damp group huddled at Wind Mill Point waiting for the ship. The delivery had never been this late before, but someone reminded the group that sometimes the men had to wait for a lower tide to ensure their safety before they ventured close to town. Someone else thought it might be the weather. Everyone had an opinion. But that did not lessen the worry that the sailors could be caught by daylight, if they did not come soon.

It was still full dark when two small ships were sighted. Relieved, men and women ran down the steep embankment to the sand to help bring the crates of breads, meats, dried fruits and sacks of flour onto the muddy beachhead.

People worked in silence so as not to attract any sort of attention. In minutes, the crates were on dry land and were being handed one-by-one up the steep hill along a human chain. The people at the top loaded the goods onto handcarts, which were already being pushed to the cellar at New South, the closest church.

The group gathered together for a minute at the top of the rise, tired but proud of a job well done. They watched the first little ship push off, catch the wind and disappear into the fog. Oona turned to push her cart over a hillock and onto the road. She looked back to check the strand line and make sure they had left nothing behind. There, at the water line, she spotted a small barrel. The group had a strict rule about not leaving evidence. She told her partner that she would catch up as soon as she had the barrel, and ran down the steep hill to the rocky strand.

She grabbed the barrel, which proved not to be heavy, and hoisted it to her shoulder. As she did so, it was lifted out of her hands. One of the sailors who should have left was being a gentleman – a move which could very easily get them all arrested and sent to prison, to Britain for trial, and jailed or hanged.

Jason and his team were running late. The moon was high, and the fog had blown away to the south. The weather pattern had kept Boston shrouded, but there were clear seas further out, and conditions were perfect for getting caught. When the men realized how vulnerable they would be leaving the shore after the drop-off, they delayed at Marlboro until the moon was on its descent.

The trip turned out to be uneventful. The group of townsfolk were waiting, helped them unload the foodstuffs, and carted it all away. He stood at his ship and watched people move in their scripted roles. He watched a young man run back toward the water to collect one barrel that had been left behind.

It took only a second to realize that a wool cap and heavy sweater did not completely hide the curves of a young woman. It took less time to recognize the hat and sweater, items he had once given to a young maid, part of an extended Christmas present. He walked over and lifted the barrel from her shoulders, not sure what would happen next.

He had nothing planned. He had not expected to see Oona on this run or on any other. He wasn't ready to offer her the home she deserved, but just that afternoon something had happened, and he'd met a man who needed to sell his house, and sell it quickly. It was just too soon, too dangerous. His heart pounded in his chest as he put the barrel on the ground and turned Oona to face him.

Oona turned, ready to give the man a stern word. She inhaled in a surprised gasp. The next moment she was enclosed in powerful arms, and pulled against a lean strong body. She looked up into Jason's gold streaked eyes. The morning light was only a vague lightening of the sky over the water, but she felt, as well as saw, those wolf eyes bore into her's with a wild intensity. There was nothing to say that wouldn't take longer than the sun would take to rise. She lifted her mouth to his, and time stood still as her body curved to his, fitting like a lost puzzle piece.

"Come with me," Jason growled as he unwillingly pulled away. Even as he spoke, he knew it was not yet the right time. Where would she live? In his rooms, shared with four other sailors? He had nothing to offer her, not yet.

"I can't, not now," Oona whispered into Jason's lips. She thought immediately of her young charges, the documents proving her wealth and identity, and the nice furniture she had worked so hard to collect, and then to protect, through two cold, miserable winters.

"You're right. I admit I have nowhere for us to live. But soon I will send word."

"Yes." She put her arms around his body, and tucked her head under his chin, against his chest, seeking closeness and safety. Finally, she pushed him back toward his boat.

She heard the sail catch the wind. She turned away silently screaming "NO!" at the unfairness of life. She hoisted the barrel to her shoulder and, feeling a little relieved the little boat had caught the wind before dawn, she trudged up the bank to the handcarts, ignoring the tears that fell unbidden onto the damp ground.

Chapter 12

The name "Argonauts" had been used in Boston for the men from Salem, but no one had given a good explanation as to why. At least she now had the answer to that puzzle. And now, at last, she understood where her husband was, and why he had not come for her. It made her loneliness easier, and so much harder.

Oona waited for word from Jason that he was ready for her to move north. She continued to teach her small schoolroom of students, and help the Committee of Correspondence distribute the food the seamen brought. She never again glimpsed Jason and his boat, but she looked each time the sailors came close. She tried not to get discouraged, but as weeks, and then months, went by, it got harder and harder to believe that anything in her life would ever change.

There were changes to the town, though. The battles in the countryside on April 18, 1775, and then subsequent rumors of soldiers carrying out executions on the Common, brought thousands of countryfolk to the Neck, prepared to attack the British within the town. Their appearance, and the hint of violence, made the occupying troops, young, inexperienced and far from home, very nervous. Their unease and close proximity in every house and on every bit of open space made the townsfolk nervous in turn. Starting with general discomfort and unease, it peaked at barely-contained hostility and anger. Though no general rioting or violence erupted, rumors flew like gulls before a storm. And in the midst of this disquiet, the town heard that the appointed governor, General Thomas Gage, and his American wife, Margaret, were packing for London. Replacing the Governor was another general whose attitude toward the unruly town, they guessed, could only be more harsh. General Lord William Howe arrived in late May, and accompanying him on the warship Cerberus were two men who would alter the American situation in the coming years, Generals John Burgoyne and Henry Clinton.

It was early August when Jason sent word. It was a short note telling her to start packing in earnest. She found the note addressed to her among crates of dried peas. It was just as well, she wrote in her letterbook – the school was about closed, and they were down to four students. That afternoon, she dismissed the class and told the children that the school would be closed from that day on. She didn't imagine that either they or their parents would notice or care. She had done her best to teach, had done her best to stay, but now cannonballs were flying toward the town from Washington's American siege lines established at high ground around the town. It really was time to leave.

Jason had gathered his group around him. The Essex men, as the sailors from Marblehead to Newburyport referred to themselves, were a tough lot. They were as comfortable at sea as on land – as comfortable being merchant seamen, or privateers, sailing under letters of marque from the Continental Congress, paid with captured booty, as they were maneuvering miniature ships to avoid British warships and their smaller cutters. Now, he had asked them and their land-locked families help him find a house for Oona. And being men of the world, able to withstand forces of nature and wars of men, they asked their wives and sisters for help.

Jason had grown to like Salem, and thought that Oona would, too. It was older than Boston, but the two towns were near, and each was an important port. Each of them would surely grow with the new nation. Since he did not have the luxury of asking her opinion, or the luxury of choice or time, he decided that the bustling of the busy port would feel like home to her. They found his house on Turner Street only blocks from the harbor, newly vacated and ready for a buyer.

Oona requested, and was given, a pass for herself and a wagon full of her possessions for any day after August. She began packing the day a heat wave hit the town, limiting hard work to early morning and late evening. Stopping in the stuffy heat, she prowled the small space. Letting her mind wander back, she remembered the room with Jason's extraordinary bed stretching corner to corner, a fire in the hearth and strong hands in her hair. Excited to finally start a life with Jason, she began her preparations with the trunks of his clothes. One by one she pulled out his things, touching them to her face and breathing in his scent, faint and overpowered with fleabane, daisy and cedar, but still there. Her things were next. She wished she could burn the clothes that she had made over from Anne Goodiel's largesse, but that would be impractical. So she packed them carefully, planning to give it all away as soon as she could contract for new.

Next, she found all the winter things she had brought from Oliver Street and stowed haphazardly. She used Jason's trunks and placed her things carefully around them. Lastly, she crated anything from the kitchen that was light enough to move – pots, pans, small kettles, spoons, spiders, and fire lions. Some of the kitchen things were hers from the Goodiel house, and some were Mary Channing's. She would find the woman one day and pay her for everything she took.

Anticipating the men's arrival, she began to pull out the tables, chairs, cushions, rugs and draperies she had taken at Matthew Goodiel's direction. She knew the sheer volume would surprise her movers, but she wouldn't be surprised herself if Jason had nothing in that house. Working late into the night, she was finally finished and the small room, hidden behind the false wall, was empty, except for the ornately-carved bed from Jason's mother's family. She heated water, added cold from the spring, and gave herself a long soak after a hot day.

The only thing she did not let herself think about were her feelings for Jason. By now she was used to missing him, but the memories of the happy boy who had cheered her during a decade of dark nights had changed. Now she had grown used to the fact that love was a sort of aching desire, but little else. She had not allowed deeper feeling to take root, because there was always the fear that they would never be together, through one twist of fate or another. Now she wondered what she would feel for Jason when confronted with the realities of marriage and of daily life.

Jason and his friends sat in his new house sharing a bottle or two. They had been lucky in their find. Caleb Dawes, a rich Tory, had needed to sell fast or lose everything. He was willing to sell cheap, and Jason matched and raised his price as much as he could. Dawes was a decent man who had chosen to move to his inland estates, rather than live near angry neighbors. He simply chose to pack all of his belongings before his politics were made even more public. As soon as Jason handed him what specie he had on hand and a note for more, the man raced out of town to meet up with his wife and children.

The house was three blocks from the harbor. It had two stories, with a cellar, an attic, and a few outbuildings. The roof did not leak, and the pump worked. Other than that, Jason had not one bit of furniture, nor a pot or kettle, in his house.

His friends drank to their phenomenal luck at outrunning British gunboats and cutters. They cheered their ability to hide and run from danger, two concepts that they found reprehensible, so they got drunk and congratulated themselves for overcoming their natural bravery and manliness. In the morning, two of them took a pair of wagons and a few mules and drove down the post road to Boston. They found it surprisingly easy to get through the guards at the neck, once they showed that the wagons were so empty they'd been swept clean.

Peter Daggette knew where Beach Street was, and his friend Davy happily followed him to the little Channing house. Oona greeted them and offered them cold water, the one thing there was plenty of when the springs were running. By the time they were done, the wagons were full and Mrs. Channing's house was nearly empty. Oona would have liked to protect the house from being used by quartering soldiers, but that would be impossible. It was late at night when they finished loading the wagons. The men fell asleep outside to guard their loads, and Oona collapsed on the last large item in the house – her mattress on the floor.

The early morning was as hot as the previous day's late afternoon had been, and the men wanted to get over the neck and out of town before the animals were too hot to move. Being in Boston made them nervous, though neither said precisely why. Oona did not doubt that they were part of Jason's Argonauts.

She helped the men negotiate the narrow stairs with her last trunks: her good clothes and the bitticle containing her collection of nautical instruments. She kept only a carpet bag with a hairbrush and a few summer gowns to last her until the first packet on Monday morning. That would give Jason and his friends a day or two to unload the wagons and move things into the house. Peter and Davy checked the ties one last time on their loaded wagons and set off. They were stopped by two redcoats asking for their pass. Peter Daggette pulled it from his pocket; one of the soldiers read it and waved them on. The men slapped their reins on the animals and made as if to leave, but waited, watching the soldiers move toward Oona's house.

"Miss Goodiel?" Private Jones, a young soldier she had seen often in town addressed her formally.

"That is not my name, but I could understand why someone might think it was. What is wrong, officers?"

"Oona, Mistress Goodiel, we have a warrant for your arrest. I don't know why or who issued it." The first soldier spoke, buttoning his lips as if he was about to say more.

"Jimmy, who is gonna tell?" The second redcoat, Mickey Jones, turned from his friend to Oona, "Ma'am they have all these cases and no judges. So the magistrates, officers you see, are tryin' to decide whether to send cases to London or New York for trial, or to dismiss them. Your name came up. Something to do with Mrs. Morse swearing a warrant against you."

Oona shook her head, baffled. "Private Jones, please slow down – why are there no judges? I am confused. Who is Mrs. Morse?"

"Well firstly, there's no judges, cause they can't get nobody to sit. Every time somebody accepts the job, he gets threatened with tarring and feathering. So no one will do it."

Oona remembered the *Massachusetts Government Act* revoking the old charter and replacing it with one written by Parliament and George III. The act proclaimed that all councilors would be appointed by either the Governor or the King. No wonder no one would serve as a judge! It could be dangerous to be perceived as being a direct appointee of the King here in Massachusetts. There was another action by Parliament she had read about, she thought quickly as she washed her face and grabbed a clean shift and hair brush to bring with her – the *Administration of Justice Act*. That one stated that the King or his Governor could move any trial to London, or elsewhere, if it were deemed necessary. Those acts were usually invoked to save the hide of some Tory, or a crown official, but Oona considered they could be used the other way. She reentered her kitchen, ready to confront her imprisonment, willing herself not to show the fear that was creeping in. "Officer," she pushed the words out, wanting some information. "I understand that about moving trials and why there are no magistrates, but I still don't understand what I am accused of doing."

Jimmy – Private O'Hare – spoke first. "I'm real sorry, Miss. But somebody has accused you of murder. The General's aide says that he doesn't want to send twenty witnesses to a London trial only to discover that the fellow died in a barroom brawl. So they are bringing everybody in on Monday. The accused, they say, has to come 'when found'."

A cold chill swept down Oona's spine in spite of the

horrendous heat of the afternoon. She had known who Mrs. Morse was, but she had no idea why she would accuse her of murder. She hadn't even known Lawrence was dead. Not for sure, at least.

She tidied her hair, used the privy quickly and marched off in line with the young soldiers. Did the army know of her work with the Sons of Liberty? She hoped the case would not get to trial. Maybe she could convince a magistrate of her innocence. Could they try her before a jury of soldiers? Who would be acting as magistrate?

She could only imagine the answers to her own questions. There was no one to consult and no one to help her. She recognized that she was very scared. In spite of the heat, her teeth were beginning to chatter and her body felt strangely cold. The soldiers had allowed her to gather a clean shift, gown, stockings and hairbrush in a small package for her cell and the hearing on Monday. Now she clutched her small package as if it were a life preserver and she was adrift on the cold sea.

She stood between the two men, her hands in front and her head held high. She fell into step as they marched her toward *HMS Lively,* a 20-gun frigate commanded by Captain Thomas Bishop that was anchored at Long Wharf. She did not notice the two men from Salem, Peter Daggette and Davey Jones, as they stood to the side watching, listening and following the small procession as it marched toward the harbor. It was after Oona disappeared on board the Man 'o War, and they were sure they had learned all they could, that they drove their wagons out of town.

Oona was ferried the short distance to the ship and locked in a small room below deck, with a slop bucket and nothing else. She tried to ask when her case would be heard, but none of the jailers knew or were at liberty to tell her. The room was very hot and nearly completely dark. The day had been windless, and the ship, sitting in the hot sun, had retained the day's endless heat. She wryly appreciated the fact that at least on a day like this, the lack of a window would not alter the lack of cooling ocean breezes. She took off her gown, stays and stockings, leaving her clad in only her light shift. She reasoned that since there was no one there to see her in the dark, there was no reason not to be as comfortable as she could be. She draped her clean clothes in a corner, and folded her gown into a pillow for what promised to be a few long nights.

Oona paced the small room. She wrote imaginary letters to Jason asking him to come and rescue her. She wrote paperless treatises on the acts of Parliament and how they affected the people of Boston. Anxious, she walked around the small cell and counted her steps from wall to wall and then from corner to corner. She recited prayers – Latin ones she remembered from long ago, and English ones she knew in her heart and soul. She spoke aloud her own recipes for lemon oil furniture polish and rosemary hair oil. She remembered the children she knew when she was young and recited their names. She sang every song she knew. She recalled the street names in Boston and recited them north to south, then south to north, east to west and west to east. She wished she had something to mend, read or make. At times she slept fitfully.

Jason spent the weekend pacing the floors of his empty house. Peter and Davey had come roaring back the thirty miles from Boston, screaming that Oona had been arrested. They argued about what the charges were. Peter heard it was a charge for murder, but Davey insisted it had to be something to do with the deliveries and that it was a trap for Jason. He said he refused to let Jason go into the town.

Jason wanted no part of their theories and just told them to move the furniture into the front rooms and leave him alone. Then he left his new house and went off to find a tailor and a wig. He had such hopes for seeing Oona walk through the door in the next day or two, it was hard to formulate a plan to find out what was going on. Whatever the reasons for her arrest, there was no way he was leaving her to face the charges alone. "Enough of that!" he growled in the street, causing more than one dog to growl back in sympathy.

If anyone hazarded thoughts that a ship docked in the harbor might be cooler than the land, caught as the entire region was in a hazy, uncomfortable, heat wave, the weekend Oona spent locked in a small room on the *Lively* would have proven them thoroughly false. If the heat was nearly unbearable on land, it was worse in the tiny, dark, room. They fed her when someone remembered, but she stayed hungry, and very thirsty. She did not have the sense that they were punishing her so much as no one had any idea she was shipboard, and no facilities had been arranged for her internment. The room she was in was not the brig, but a storage closet put into quick service. Oona thought for a while that she might be the only female on the ship. But that was proven wrong when, late at night, she heard the sound of female visitors coming onto the ship to entertain the sailors while the Admiral was at the Castle. She wondered, in a passing thought, if she knew any of the ladies, but decided that it would not help her case to ask. Monday morning could not come soon enough.

Tickling her mind was the thought that she could become despondent, and Oona wondered why she wasn't. In her life there had been so many rooms with her locked inside. But tossed and turned by fate as she had been, she flatly refused to give into that feeling that she was not in control of her own destiny. She had discovered, since the end of her indenture, that she was as strong as Jan Hubbard had predicted. She would survive this with her feet firmly planted on the ground and her head held high. Monday morning she would look the magistrate, and her false accusers, right in their faces. She would listen to every word, be fully engaged in understanding the false accusations, so she could counteract them with the truth. She would answer every question in a firm, steady voice. She would not show how utterly frightened she was. This was, after all, an English courtroom, she told herself over and over during her imprisonment on the ship, and her innocence would outweigh anyone's accusations.

She spent the long hours thinking about her life, about life's hardest lesson. That was to accept that good things could happen even in tiny ways. It might seem that it was fate that had sent her on life's path. She understood that she could not change any of what had happened to her, and she was beginning to accept that none of it was her fault. But much of her life had been good. Now, again locked in a dark room, she would not be a leaf tossed by the winds and trampled in the storm. She would do what she had decided she would do and keep her feet firmly planted on the deck against the storms. She did not really understand all the arguments about liberty, but she was sure it must have to do with being free to make one's own choices, mistakes and all.

She wished she had Jason's company in this dark, cramped room, so warm while the first, the closet under the stairs, had been so cold, but she had a goal. To get out of this cell, she would overcome this trial and go home to

Jason. She would not let whoever wanted her convicted of a murder she had not committed succeed. She concentrated on that for a while, and then finally, in spite of the heat and the hard floor, fell into a real sleep.

On Monday morning, Jason was dressed in silk and fine linen. He had considered borrowing a snuffbox, but stopped at that pretension. However, the wig the wigmaker had sold him – the one sitting in the window, looking elegant and attracting no buyers in the oldest, most Puritan town in the Province – added just the affect he wanted. His father, who inherited his title and the duchy in his early twenties, could not have looked more elegant. No, he wanted to be more than simply elegant, he needed to become the duke in manner and attitude. He needed to sail into Boston unannounced, board a 20-gun British Navy frigate without an invitation, and find the court that was holding the hearing to decide Oona's fate. He needed to do those things without getting stopped or slowed by ensigns or privates asking his direction or seeking his credentials. Once he found her – well, he would play that by ear.

Monday morning finally arrived. Oona's one thought was for a cool bath. At last, the door was opened and she was escorted down the hall into a room with porthole windows. She felt bedraggled and filthy. She had the thought that if she could wash, brush her hair and change her clothes, she would be better able to hide the fear that was creeping from her belly to her fingers.

Happily, she recognized the soldiers who were sent to escort her to the magistrate. "Private, do you think I might have a bit of wash water? I have my clean clothes, but I can't put them on – well – me. Please?" She whined just enough to encourage the men.

Jimmy looked baffled, but Mickey laughed. "I have four sisters and a mother. Jimmy, find the girl some water and tell the lieutenant she'll just be a minute." As though given an order by Howe himself, the man marched off to find water and relay the message.

Oona sat on a bench in the room and kicked off her wooden shoes, glad she had worn the comfortable things. He was a lieutenant, she almost mused out loud; her magistrate was really going to be a military man. She tried to force the fear down, suddenly too scared of what was about to happen even to care about being clean. It would not do, to let fear rule her actions. She forced herself to get ready.

Jimmy nudged her. She turned and watched through the doorway as General Howe's staff walked toward their offices down the corridor. "I'll just tell the Lieutenant that you need a minute to preen, then, shall I?"

"Yes, please," Oona squeaked. She chided herself that such a noise would be the last foolish sound she made that day. Preening indeed – if they had not kept her hot and filthy all weekend, she would not need the minute to bathe.

In a few minutes, a young sailor in a red vest and white pantaloons came in carrying a bucket of warm wash water. He put it down and left. Oona looked around the well-appointed room, finding what she was seeking on the dresser. She moved swiftly to soap and rinse her face and as much of her body as she could reach, concentrating on her face, arms, neck and feet. Once she was soaped as well as she could be, she stood in the bucket and rinsed. The cool water felt heavenly. She allowed only one second of pleasure, and called out that she was about finished.

She was as clean as she could manage, and dressed in a clean shift and gown, her teeth rinsed and her shoes on, when Mickey came back. She brushed her hair, braided it and pinned it up quickly as the men stood waiting to escort their prisoner to the dock. They might have insisted that it was a hearing before a magistrate, but to Oona it was a trial before a hanging judge, the only witnesses Lawrence Morse's family – out to see her hanged.

Jason counted the minutes the packet took to sail from Salem to Boston. Luckily, Parliament had not seen fit to close off the connection between the two towns. He knew as well as anyone that he was free to travel as long as no trade or goods were involved. Finally, he caught the familiar site of church spires, and the weathervane he considered Oona's grasshopper.

He tipped his hat to the large gold insect, and told him to bestow luck on his friend. Then he disembarked at the front of the line, pulling full aristocratic rank. It was for a good cause, but he felt the perfect cad for doing it. He glared at the naval ensign assigned to the *Lively*, and the man rowed him over to the ship without thinking of asking for his identification. She was flying full colors, proclaiming that the admiral was on board. Such display would have been festive had she been in London; here, it proclaimed her country's dominance over a land Jason was coming strongly to believe she did not own.

Since his youth, Jason had always been as comfortable on ships as he was walking down the streets of a familiar town. This ship made him uncomfortable. It was not only the worry he brought on board. There was more to it, as any merchant seaman in the English world well knew, and he tried to move through the ship clumsily. He hoped to look like he had not more than a passing knowledge of how ships were built and moved at sea and at anchor. He walked down the corridors where official business took place, looking for the office where a hearing was being held, holding onto the walls on either side. It was important to find Oona. It was also important that he be seen as a landed landlubber. After all, if he jumped too agilely over a coil of rope, or climbed the ladder with noticeable skill, he could be pressed into service in the Royal Navy. He had never had any interest in naval life, and certainly had no desire to join against his will.

Oona counted every step as she followed her guards down the corridor. Her hands were loosely tied in front of her. She assumed this was standard procedure. She was relieved they had not thought to use shackles. Her feet were unbound, and she took small steps hoping they would not think to remedy that.

They climbed a ladder to a higher deck. She blinked at day light. This deck was light, brighter than where she had been imprisoned. Not only did a dull light sneak through doorways, but she thought she sensed a cool moistness in the air. The change in the weather was confirmed when she was ushered into the room and looked out the windows. The clear blue sky and the unbearable summer's heat had been replaced with dark gray clouds. The half-closed windows were being pelted with a cold, driving rain. Oona hoped no one thought to close them. She breathed in the cool sea air, pleased at least that she was dry, while Lawrence Morse's mother and brothers were soaked to the bone from their walk to the dock, and from the ferry ride from dock to ship.

She looked them over and thought they looked like dead cod in the market. Their eyes gazed outwards; looking but dead, they seemed to see nothing. Their mouths were set in the sort of frowning grimace one expected to see on fish. She stifled a nervous laugh, nodded politely at them, and stood next to the soldier who had walked her into the room, her hands demurely in front.

Oona looked. Her impression was of red, and it was not a comforting sight. The magistrate sitting behind his desk wore an impeccable uniform. The color and cut of his jacket was so much finer than those of the other soldiers in the room that he seemed to be wearing a different uniform altogether. The pewter buttons on the red jacket shined like silver, polished as they were. And his wig – it might be the same style and color as the others, but it screamed perfection in a way theirs did not. No, this man would not let a single thread fall out of place, or a fact slip away unnoticed. If there was guilt to be found, the Lieutenant here would find it. Oona gulped, hoping there truly was no guilt to be found.

Oona knew the first question he would ask would be about her name. She had never used a last name, since she had always been just "the Goodiels's girl." There had been no reason for more. For the past year she'd had two choices, and for her safety she had chosen McCloud.

A single woman alone might be presumed to be a virgin, something most of the soldiers, with plenty of whores available, had no interest in pursuing. An abandoned married woman, on the other hand, might be ripe fruit ready for the picking, so Oona had chosen her mother's name even though it had never really been hers.

Finally, the magistrate looked up coolly from his desk. He looked the room over. Oona could see that he noticed everything, taking in all of them, one at a time and as a group.

He spoke. "You are Oona? Goodiel? Of Beach Street?" he asked politely, stating the question simply, as he had to. Oona looked into his eyes hoping for a hint of humanity as she gulped air. His eyes were cold, the iciest blue she had ever seen. She must have stared a moment too long, because she heard him repeat the question as if she were daft or deaf.

Finally she answered. "Yes, sir, I am Oona. I was a servant, and my master's name is Goodiel. Some might think that is my name. Currently, I live on Beach Street."

He turned to his clerk, who seemed to correct something on the papers stacked in front of him, and then look up and nodded. "Miss Goodiel, is that the name you prefer?"

"It will do." She knew she could have corrected him, offered McCloud or even FitzSimmon, but the occasion really didn't call for such precision.

"Miss, do you understand why you are here? This is not a trial. We need to discover which cases should go to trial. This is a preliminary hearing. There is a backlog since all the judges of Boston have resigned their commissions and fled.

"And since I and . . ." – his eyes moved over the room to include his colleagues – "are the staff of the Governor, General William Howe, I alone will decide whether or not this case will be moved for trial. Someone else will determine where and when the trial will be held." They all understood that such a trial would be held in London or elsewhere in the Colonies, but not in Boston. "Does everyone understand?" Everyone in the room nodded and murmured their assent. He glared at the Morse family, maybe for wasting his time. He made a careful note of their nods, noting that they understood that no finding of guilt would occur at this hearing.

"Then let us proceed." He looked over his papers. He looked again at Mrs. Morse and her two sons.

"Miss Goodiel, do you know the missing man,

Lawrence Morse?"

"Yes, I did know Lawrence. I knew him since we were children. I have not been friendly with him since we were fifteen or sixteen years old."

"That would be five, six years ago?"

"Yes, sir." She remembered to hold her head up and speak as clearly as she could. She also remembered to breathe.

"Miss Goodiel, have you seen Mr. Morse recently?"

"No sir, I have not."

"And when did you last see Mr. Lawrence Morse?"

"I believe it was in January of 1774. It was after that terrible ice storm that damaged half the ships in the harbor. I was helping to serve chowder and coffee to the workingmen who were moving damaged ships to dry dock. The storm was on the twenty-sixth of December. They moved the ships soon after the new year."

"You have a very clear memory for something that happened over a year and a half ago."

"Yes, sir. It was an important storm and cleanup for everyone. I expect anyone could tell you stories about that week."

The magistrate nodded his understanding, and went on. "Was Mr. Morse among the men moving the ships?"

She shrugged, "Lawrence was at the harbor that night. I don't know if he was working. He was a butcher, not a seaman."

"You said you were serving chowder and coffee? Why were you there doing that?"

"My master, Matthew Goodiel, was an important merchant in the town. One of his ships, the *Catherine,* was badly damaged and was being moved. Many of the workers were his men. He asked me to help."

"Was Leonard Morse one of those workers?"

"I'm sorry, I don't know. He might have been. He did not work for Mr. Goodiel, but he may have been hired by one of the others."

Oona did not know what the Morse family thought they knew about that night, but she remembered it in horrible detail. Luckily, it had not stopped her life, but it might have, as surely as Lawrence's seemed to have been stopped by someone.

The lieutenant looked over his paperwork again, and consulted with one of his staff.

Oona let her mind consider the motivation for the Morses' sudden interest in the case. Why would the Morses think she had anything to do with Lawrence's disappearance and death? She watched the magistrate, but let her mind consider the Morses for a moment.

Glad of a good night's sleep, in a flash she saw the connection between those horrible minutes more than a year and a half ago and today. Of course, the Morses had seen the handbills looking for the smuggler. They must have decided the reward was worth more than their healthy fear of the Sons of Liberty. Maybe now, with so many of the Sons having left town, they felt emboldened. Someone must think she knew the name and whereabouts of that smuggler.

They had always been shrewd and greedy. If they believed there was a connection between the man who rescued her and the smuggler, then they might try to trick her into revealing his identity to save herself from a trial and the noose. And, it would be all legal, right here in front of the magistrate. It would give them a reward for the smuggler's capture and revenge for Lawrence's death.

She stilled her fear, realizing that she must be very careful not to reveal anything that would expose Jason to arrest, even if meant enduring a trial in New York or London. "Lieutenant, I last saw Lawrence Morse in a small shed, near where I was serving hot soup. I was putting out the fire and sitting for a moment when he grabbed me, pulled me into the shed, and forced me . . ." – Oona's voice got very tight and quiet – "forced me to – forced himself on me. I last saw him was as I was running away after someone heard me cry out and stopped him from raping me again. I caught up my things and fled. I do not know who it was who came to help."

The Morse family started shouting that she was lying about Lawrence. The men stood up and ran to Oona to shout in her face. Before the soldiers in the room could react, Mrs. Morse ran over and slapped Oona and started to pull at her hair.

"Oona Goodiel, you are a whore and a murderer. I would see you hanged for killing my Lawrence." The woman was spitting mad, her gray hair falling out of her cap while she shrieked and clawed at Oona.

Oona held up her tied hands to protect her face. She stepped back from the screaming woman. The soldier who was standing by her was too stunned to move quickly. Mrs. Morse pushed at Oona and they both fell to the floor. Shrieking even louder, she stood up. Oona would have liked to cover her ears with her hands, but the ropes did not allow it.

The magistrate motioned for his aides to contain the Morses. He motioned to the young soldier to help Oona stand. Then he stared the Morse clan down and they subsided, moving back onto their chairs. His voice was even more icy as he addressed them. "Mrs. Morse, you and your sons seem not to be able to control yourselves and let others speak. Something happened on the night in question. If you won't let Miss Goodiel speak and tell us what she knows, would you rather accuse her of sneaking into your son's rooms and strangling him to death? You said he was a butcher – was he not stronger than this small woman here?"

"Naa, she's not strong. Lawrence could 'a stopped her. He always said he knew just what to do with her." Lawrence's younger brother spoke. Oona had forgotten his name.

The Lieutenant sighed and rolled his eyes. The boy had just confirmed what the pretty defendant had said. He motioned with his hand as he addressed the guards in the room. "Clear them out of the room We are not going to get this story told if they insist on insulting and beating my witness." He nodded at the door with his chin. The soldiers who had been in the room left to guard the corridor, leaving one soldier and the Lieutenant's clerk behind.

"I presume this was more than an *attempted* rape?" He emphasized the word. Oona nodded. He turned to the clerk, "Please note that we are now charging the missing man with a capital crime.

"All right, Miss Goodiel, tell me the story and in greater detail. But first, did you see Lawrence killed?"

"No sir. He was alive when J . . ." She stopped herself. My rescuer told me to leave. I never saw Lawrence Morse again."

Simm looked over the pretty girl. She did not look like she killed Lawrence Morse. She did not look like she could kill anyone. She was too kind, too slight. He sighed silently. But she had the looks men would kill for. He could imagine killing for her, and then letting her thank him with soft curves molding to his body, his hands running through that thick dark hair. Those eyes – a man could get lost in those lovely amethyst eyes. A servant for ten years? How old was she now, twenty, twenty-one? She was a goddess; he expected she knew it.

"How well did you know Lawrence?"

"Fairly well, sir. I met Lawrence when I was a child. I was brought to Boston from Ireland when I was ten. I knew no one. Lawrence was a year or so older. He was apprenticed to a butcher near the Goodiels's house on Fort Hill. We got to know each other along with some other children, servants and apprentices and such. Lawrence always insisted that I would marry him, that no one else would want me, a poor orphan servant like me. He said other things, too, but I think you understand."

Simm certainly understood how a crude butcher's boy might try to convince this beauty to cleave to him. It wouldn't take a brain to see that, orphan or not, servant or not, there would be many other men would want her, men who were far less obnoxious and grasping than Lawrence Morse. He was disliking the dead man enormously. That was not what an impartial hearing officer did.

What did the Morse family want from her? Why were they bringing this up now? The man had been scum and was found dead over a year ago.

Simm looked over at his prisoner, wondering what had really happened. This Oona Goodiel, or whatever her name was, was extraordinary. Her eyes alone could cause men to do things they shouldn't. It was no wonder Lawrence wanted her, but the man had been an idiot to think rape would make a woman chose him. A woman this lovely should never settle for less than her prince. Too bad it wasn't going to be him. Too bad, indeed. He motioned for her to continue.

"Lawrence had gotten angry with me. I had moved

away from our crowd. Some had married and a few had gone back to their parents' homes or moved away. I started spending time with a man Lawrence did not know, someone from away. He is a sailor. He was first mate on one of the injured ships, the *Catherine*."

"So this man, is he the fellow who heard you scream?"

Oona did not reply. She thought hard about what would happen if she refused to identify Jason, and what would happen to Jason if she identified him. She looked at the magistrate. He looked familiar, and yet not. She wondered if he had been in Boston long.

"Lieutenant, I would like to say I wasn't sure, or to tell you he was not the man who saved me from Lawrence." Oona wanted to cry; this was so close to revealing Jason's identity. She would rather die than put him in danger. But she knew he would be very, very angry if she fought his battles for him and put herself in danger instead. He would just howl with laughter and dare the truth to catch him.

"The same man, yes."

"And what did Lawrence say to you seeing this other man?"

"He said that he 'would fix it so the fancy man would not want me anymore.'"

Simm wanted to vomit – anything but make this young woman tell this story. He could see exactly what happened. He wished he could let her stop. But he couldn't. A record needed to be made. "And by that he meant?"

Oona looked around desperately, hoping there was some respite from telling her most intimate secrets to this hard man. His eyes were like ice, but something in him put her at ease. He was understanding in his way. She looked at the lieutenant as he waited for her to speak. There was that thing again, something familiar about his voice and the shape of his jaw and cheeks. It tickled at the back of her mind. Maybe from before, at the *King's Mount*? "I believe that Lawrence meant, that if I was not a virgin I would be rejected by my beau, the sailor. He thought that I would be forced by my ruined state to marry him." Part of her wanted to whisper the last words. But she didn't. She spoke softly, but as clearly as she could. Of course, she wanted to collapse onto the floor in embarrassment.

Simm would have loved to offer this pretty girl a seat. It was cruel to have her stand. It was cruel and stupid that her hands were tied. She was clearly exhausted. She probably had not slept at all, what with the heat building up in that little closet they had locked her in. Damn the Morses for swearing the warrant at the end of the week. Unfortunately there was no way he could break tradition and protocol and have the prisoner sit. It simply wasn't done. The best he could do was to finish this as quickly as possible.

"Miss Goodiel," he spoke as softly as he could under the circumstances, "could you give me some detail about the events the night the ships were moved?"

"Yes sir. As you know, I was cooking. We were heating the food over a fire in large kettles. The other girls and I broke up the fire as the men finished their work and started to go home. Because the coals were very hot, we didn't want to leave until it was cool enough to stamp on. Fire is a big problem, I am sure you understand. Anyway, I was among the last to leave the area.

When we were satisfied that the fire was out, I started for Oliver Street, and the Goodiels's house. I had gone only a step or two when I was grabbed. I screamed as loudly as I could. I think I screamed my friend's name, hoping that if he were nearby, he would hear.

"Had you seen this friend in the area? Might he have already planned to hurt Lawrence Morse?"

"I saw him earlier in the day, but not at that time, I don't believe he knew very much about Lawrence. He was new in town, and I had not even seen Lawrence for weeks."

"The attack, the man who grabbed you – are you sure it was Mr. Morse?"

"It was Lawrence. He made sure I knew who he was. He said that now was the time he 'was gonna make it so no one else would want me'. He pushed me down. He pulled up my skirts quickly. I fought a bit, then I bit my lip and stared into the darkness. During, the . . ." – Oona stared into Simm's blue eyes hoping he could save her; he nodded encouragement, but said nothing – ". . . event, I heard someone else in the shed.

"The other man shouted something. I believe I screamed again. Yes, I must have because Lawrence hit me then. I don't remember it, but I do know that he finished, I heard him grunt, and he pulled up his pants. Didn't slow down, even though someone else was there.

"Then he got up to look for the person who interrupted him. It was dark, really dark. I could see the light at the open door, but not much else. I heard a voice yelling at me, telling me to leave. I grabbed my things and ran out the door. I never saw Lawrence again. I assumed he was killed, but I never asked. I didn't want to know."

"Did you see your rescuer again?"

"Yes I did. He came to the Goodiels's house to ask after me the next day."

Well, at least someone cared about what happened to this girl. If necessary, he was prepared to horsewhip the Morses for putting her through this. He pulled himself back to the matter at hand. "And where is this friend now?" He bent his head with his clerk for a minute or two. "I believe the *Catherine* has been back, and shipped out again a number of times since winter a year ago."

"I don't know. I am sorry." Oona did know, and had a sudden anger that she was not at this very moment on her way to Salem to see him. At least remembering what happened that horrible night was reminding her of why she loved Jason so much. She must have looked lost in thought, because the Lieutenant looked at her strangely.

Simm thought the girl looked sad. It didn't seem to have anything to do with the rape and Lawrence's death. Something told him that she had moved past that and figured out the Morses' motivation before he did, and it upset her. Earlier, she had looked only a bit frightened and very stoic. But now something had her looking worried, and she was near tears. This fellow, whoever he was, was a lucky man. He was also a scoundrel, leaving this prize alone with an occupying army at her doorstep. If he found the man, he would thrash him for that. For the murder, well – for that, he would buy him an ale.

"Oona, Miss Goodiel, if you could, please tell me his name. I think we need to create a record and ask him, if we can find the fellow, if and how he happened to kill Mr. Morse." Simm was feeling a little lost in all this. He did not want to officiate over anything this personal. There were no witnesses, and the accused had not done a thing. It was clear to any thinking man that Lawrence would have hanged for his crime anyway. Simm needed to clear his head. "Miss, do you know if the Morses have other reasons to want to place the blame on you? I don't believe you have any guilt in this. They might want something else from you. That happens occasionally, and I would see you safe."

"Thank you." Oona spoke more sharply than she meant to. She looked out at the driving rain and wondered when, during her captivity, the weather had shifted from the southwest to the northeast. She moved her eyes over the young man in front of her. Her imagination changed his eyes from icy blue to brown with warm gold streaks. She made him very slightly shorter and more muscular, and tanned his skin. The face – it *was* the same! "I believe they do. Not me, you see, but my friend."

"Fine, explain it to me. But could we have a name, Miss Goodiel?"

Oona said nothing. Suddenly, there was shouting and other noises coming from the corridor. The noise got closer until the actual shouts and bellows disrupted the talk in the room.

The damn Morses! Simm had had enough. Here was an innocent woman, too beautiful to be ignored, in his courtroom, trying not to answer the questions that would save her but throw suspicion on her paramour. Now all hell seemed to be breaking loose out in the blasted hallway, or whatever they called the thing on a ship. He rose from behind his desk and went to the door, pulled it open and looked out.

He was shocked to see a well-dressed man, of obvious high birth, swinging a walking stick and shouting at his staff as the fellow came down the narrow corridor. Simm groaned as he realized what was about to happen. Just what he needed – more interruptions in this farce of a murder investigation. He listened to what the man was bellowing at the top of his lungs. He recognized a word: "Wife." Did the man say "wife?" The Goodiel girl had said nothing of being someone's wife. Did he mean her?

Jason had humphed and harrumphed with all the gusto he could muster until he found the corridor lined with redcoats instead of bluejackets. Then he started bellowing *"Where is my wife? Where in the Lord's name have you scoundrels put my wife?"* with greater gusto and increasing volume. Finally, a door opened. An officer in a red uniform peered out and down the corridor. The young man looked harried. It had obviously been a frustrating morning, and the look on the young officer's face said that he was ready to eviscerate anyone who further interrupted his work.

There were people on the other side of the door, behind the young officer. They all turned and stared at the noise and at the aristocratic man so out of place in the Boston of 1775. In any case, Jason was relieved, the crowd did not recognize him, either as Lawrence Morse's attacker or as the smuggler. That would give him the minute he needed to talk to the officer in charge. He pushed his way through.

Jason walked toward the door with the man leaning out of it. The light was from the room, and Jason could make out the man's height and the scowl on his face, but not his other features. The crowd hovering outside the hearing room door looked hot and miserably damp. He saw the officer step back into the room, throwing the door open for his intruder. The door slammed as Jason stepped into the room.

"Excuse me, Miss Goodiel." He said as he stepped back into the room. "We have an interesting intruder."

The familiarity that had been tickling the edges of her mind clicked into place. John FitzSimmon had gotten a promotion. When Jason described his little brother he had been a sergeant. So this was the younger brother, and best friend! He was just older than Oona, but she would not have guessed it. The wigs blurred their ages so. The man already had responsibilities ahead of his age or rank, if they wanted him to hear all the cases of mayhem in Boston.

Instinct said she could trust him with his brother's name, but what if she were wrong? She spoke as clearly as she could before she dared to turn and see the newcomer. "Lieutenant? I do know why the Morses have accused me of the murder."

The Lieutenant whipped his head to look at the man who had just stepped into the room. At the same time Oona craned her neck to see, but Simm, standing near the door stood in her way and completely blocked her view. It didn't matter. In seconds the men were in each other's arms laughing and crying.

Oona could not see the other man's face. His white wig was as grand as the Lieutenant's – no, grander. She did not know who would come and disrupt such a hearing, but now that the tension was at least temporarily gone, she realized that she was really very hungry. Her feet hurt, and she was tired of standing. The chaos in the room was making her head swim, and she barely registered what was happening. It was possible that she had fainted from heat and exhaustion, and this was an odd dream. She really shouldn't move from the spot where she was standing. Decorum seemed to have broken down completely. She turned to the one guard in the room; she raised an eyebrow and shoulder to ask him silently if he knew what was going on. The man shrugged back. She moved from her spot to get a better look at the second man. If it was strange finding him at the edge of the ocean near dawn in the smuggler's boat, it was stranger seeing him on the *Lively* dressed in aristocratic elegance. Her jaw dropped.

Jason FitzSimmon had been the man bellowing in the hallway. And he was wearing the most ridiculous and beautiful clothes she had ever seen. He held himself with such presence she just knew it was true that he was the son of a duke. Suddenly, she felt dirty and clumsy in her plain gown and dirty feet. What had he been bellowing in the hall? The Lieutenant – John, she should think of him as John – backed away from his brother.

"Wife? Jason, did I hear you bellow 'wife'? Oona, sister-in-law?" He might have been laughing or sneering; she was too confused to tell. "You could have saved a lot of time if you had told me your real name."

Jason moved to Oona. He pulled a knife from his boot and carelessly cut the binding on her wrists. The ropes fell to the floor. He put his arm around her and pulled her to him. They faced the magistrate together.

John went back to his desk and looked over his documents. He addressed Oona directly, now wanting to finish this as quickly as possible and visit with his family. "Mrs. FitzSimmon," he started pointedly. He turned to glare at his clerk, daring him to utter a word. "You were about to tell me why the Morse family accuses you of murder. Please continue."

Oona looked at Jason. He smiled and shrugged. "If I may?"

"Someone, any one of you, tell me what is going on. Jason, you didn't disrupt the work of this office – hell, the entire ship – merely to make a social visit to your brother in the middle of a work day, did you? Or had you suddenly noticed your wife was missing?" Simm wanted to take his anger at this lovely girl's rape, and her loneliness, out on somebody. His brother, the beauty's blasted husband, was the clear target. Why had the man left her alone for over a year? How could he?

"The smuggler's reward." Jason's words interrupted John's thoughts. Oona lifted her hand to her mouth and stifled a nervous giggle. Jason caught her hand on its way back to her skirts and brought it to his lips. Reluctantly, he let it go.

Simm looked up at the couple in front of them, and then down at his desk again.

"We will discuss this smuggler over lunch. Jason?"

"Yes, sir."

"Did you beat Lawrence Morse after and during the rape of Oona, previously known as Goodiel?

"McCloud."

"McCloud?"

"Yes," Oona broke in, "I was given a letter and some things from my real mother. I was christened Oona McCloud."

"All right. Well, then, Jason, did you beat Lawrence Morse after and during the rape of Oona McCloud?"

"Yes, I only wish I had been sooner."

"Yes. Jason FitzSimmon, did you kill Lawrence Morse and dump his body?"

"No, sir, I left him alive in the small shed. He was drunk but alive."

"Not according to the record. He died by the harbor, under a pier."

"Not me, then, I left him in the dark shed. Either he ran into someone else, or froze down there later. Either way, Oona had nothing to do with it, and now it looks as though I didn't, either."

John went back to his papers. He motioned to the

clerk to come over They spoke quietly for a minute, and the man left the room.

Jason spoke to Oona so that John was included. "Oona? How, pray, were you going to tell the lieutenant about your smuggler? Did you guess who he is?"

"He walks, talks and looks like you. I was going to show him the earring."

"You weren't!" Jason gulped down a laugh. He looked at his brother who was staring at his ears.

"Jay, where is that wanton ruby, by the way? I see only a very virginal diamond and pearl confection." He turned to look at Oona, who turned a deep red from the roots of her hair to well below a pretty neckline. She instinctively folded her arms, protecting her breasts.

"Jason, my brother," Simm's eyes opened very wide. "You sir, are a very lucky man." He stood and walked Jason to the door, He spoke softly. "Jay, leave here before I let the Morses back in. Go to Oona's rooms. I will escort Oona there when the hearing is done. Then, I might beat you for being a scoundrel and abandoning your wife. Wife! Wait till mother hears." There was a touch of delighted alarm in that statement.

Jason loudy harumphed and left the room without a backward glance. As soon as he left, the door opened and the Morses were led in.

"Mrs. Morse," Simm went on looking the very model of a British Lieutenant, "let me say how sorry I am that you lost a son. Let me also say that Miss Goodiel's recollection of that night is very clear, and she had nothing to do with Lawrence's death. She last saw him alive, and in the shed. The report clearly states that he was found at the harbor, under a pier. Someone else, or simply the cold, seems to have caused his death."

Simm looked at the Morse brothers. "Gentlemen, I am convinced that Lawrence committed a capital crime, and if I had been the magistrate in *that* case, he would have hanged. English law on both sides of the Atlantic is clear on that. Is it clear to you?" He fairly roared the warning. In return, the boys looked very young and scared. They nodded in understanding and agreement.

"I intend to dismiss this case and put in the notice that there is no need for any further hearing or a trial. Are there any disagreements?" John scanned the room, making it clear he would like to would run through anyone who would dare to object or disagree with him.

Jason walked the familiar streets in a cold downpour. The fancy wig was going to be ruined, but he couldn't take it off. A man in his garb would not be seen without it. Besides, he needed the disguise. It simply wouldn't do to be identified as the head of a ring of smugglers with a bounty on his head. He let himself into the little house and set a fire with the little dry wood at hand. In a short time, he set water on to boil. Lulled by the fire, he put his feet on the stool and fell asleep.

Simm escorted Oona through the town in the drenching rain. He held his cape over her head, and lifted her over puddles. He imagined the least he could do was play the gallant to his brother's bride, since he had arrested her. Of course, it was easy to be a charming gentleman to such a sweet and beautiful lady. He wondered again why Jason had been away from her so long. By the time they arrived at Beach Street, they were drenched and laughing.

Jason woke to the unexpected sounds of joviality. He pulled himself upright and out of the daze of his nap. A knot of jealousy turned in his stomach; he was not sure if he should be pleased at the comradery between his wife and his brother, or call the man out. He decided quickly that it was too wet for a duel, and found some plates for the food and cups for the dark ale they had brought. Jason flung open the door as they appeared in the yard. They brought the cold and wet with them, so Jason made room at the fire. Soon, they all sat to eat. After a while, John stood as if to take his leave.

"Oona, it has been a true pleasure meeting you. Jason, I wish I could stay and discover more about your affairs, but that would probably put me in a position of committing treason. I'd rather not be shot."

Jason interrupted his brother mid-speech. "Well Johnny, I'm sure all you really need to know is that the bane of your existence was designed by a twelve year old – you! We're using a modified version of the 'wasp' you designed that summer when Uncle Jason fished with us."

Simm mockingly put his head in his hands and feinted horror. "Such is the life of a brilliant man. Jason, do me a favor and don't get caught. Please. I really would hate to have to explain you away.

Simm turned to his sister-in-law. "Oona, you mentioned you had some papers you wanted me to deal with in London?"

She left the table and went upstairs to her room. Jason looked quizzically at his brother, but he shook his head. "She told me it was to be a surprise for you. I suspect she will explain when I leave."

Oona came back with a folder and handed it to John. He put it carefully inside his coat to protect it from rain and mud. "Thank you, John. As I said, the others are being dealt with by Mr. Appleton's agent in London. He said he would tell me soon what it amounts to." Simm kissed Oona's cheek, and pulled her close for a brotherly hug. He clasped Jason to him – hard. He turned with military precision and left the house.

Oona looked over at her husband, truly the last person she ever again expected to see in this kitchen. She felt sweaty and filthy, not fit to be in the same room as this peacock, and oddly shy. They had been through so much, but now it had been so long. How did they start again? Where did they leave off? She decided to speak the truth, and say what she truly desired above anything else. "Jason, I need a bath."

Chapter 13

"You do?" He smiled and started taking off his wig, waistcoat, and shirt, thrilled as he watched her blush.

She nodded, smiling a little shyly as she filled the wooden bucket with warm water, and started for the stairs. "And did you want my help?" She responded by swishing her hips as she climbed the stairs. Jason quickly filled the second bucket, caught up to her, and took the first bucket from her. He carried both water buckets into his old room and looked around. It was nearly empty. There was nothing left but a wooden tub, a mattress with a thin sheet, a small carpet bag and a hand mirror. The bed, most of which he'd seen in his parlor before he left Salem, was only a feather mattress on the floor. He made a note to order a new one the minute they got home.

Oona had poured water into the large tub. She stripped off her clothes and climbed into the lukewarm water. She grabbed her soap and started on her shoulders and arms. She was glad Jason seemed distracted by something. She felt so sticky from the weekend locked in that small cell that she needed to get clean before she could even think of doing what she knew Jason was thinking of doing.

It had been nineteen months and three days since she

had last seen him, and those last hours were not especially romantic, with her badly injured back, and Jason practically growling in frustration. She had to admit he was very lovely to look at. She washed one leg to the top and started on the other foot.

"Mr. Gardiner."

"Who? What did you say? Mr. Gardiner?"

"Just a man who makes mattresses. We will need a new one."

"Oh, of course. That makes sense then."

She started on her hair while Jason prowled the room, taking in the false wall and difference in size it created. He looked inside the little room and came out with a small chest. He put it down and opened it.

He looked at Oona. "May I?"

"Yes, please do. It will be better if you read it all before we talk. That's what Elisha Appleton said to me." She worked suds in her long hair, adding water from the second bucket, a cupful at time. Jason read through some of the documents, reading the letter from Anne Goodiel and the notes from Brigid. He looked at the Baptismal record and Oona's full name.

He put the folders down and came over to her, lifting the cup and pouring rinsewater over her hair as she worked the clean water through. She stood, and he used the last of the water to rinse away the last of the soap and dirt. He handed her a clean towel he found.

"Jason," Oona dried quickly and wrapped the towel around her hair. "Is there anything you want to ask me about the papers, like what Mr. Appleton said about the investments?"

"Later. I have more important things to do now than ask you what you are worth. Here I thought I had married a penniless servant and she turns out to be an heiress." He reached for her and pulled her to his for a kiss. "I don't care, you know. I would be happy with a penniless wife, so long as she is you."

She was wearing nothing but the towel. Jason pulled that off her hair and tossed it over the windowsill. Oona thought it felt luxurious to be clean, on clean sheets with cool moist air blowing in through the open windows. "Oona, you are the goddess of my dreams." Jason sat next to her. He kicked off his elegant boots and pulled off his elegant linen breeches, then let his finger slowly follow the line of her collar bone as he gazed into her fabulous eyes.

"No, not a goddess. Please."

Jason understood. Not an untouchable goddess, but a human lover, someone fully involved in her life, and now in the act of love, not something on a pedestal to be worshipped. He felt the enormity of this moment, not sure how to proceed.

Jason turned away from the mattress and looked at the pouring rain. "The 'wasps' won't sail down in this weather. We'll have to take the packet tomorrow afternoon. I'm sorry." He dropped his hands to his side and knelt next to Oona as she lay on her side. "I'm always planning, but I'll stop." Oona reached for him. She traced his jawline with her finger, following the shape of his lips with her finger, until he smiled into her eyes. Then she pulled him down to her for the kiss she had dreamed of for months.

Jason deepened the kiss as Oona's hands ran through his hair, undoing the queue and spreading it over his shoulders as she touched his head. It occurred to him, as they pulled away for a split second to gather breath and balance, that this was his wedding night, and that Oona, for all her worldliness and experiences was a virgin in all ways that mattered. He kissed her again, his fingers combing her long damp hair, letting the scent of her fill him in ways he had been too long without.

"Oona, my darling." he spread long gentle kisses over her neck while his hands ran over her body from shoulder to hip, touching places and reveling in her soft skin and gentle moans. He kissed her breasts, pulling one into his mouth and noticing that the earring made the left more sensitive than the right, but suckling them both and loving how Oona's breath shortened and her hips moved beneath him.

He touched the sensitive spot between her legs to make sure she was truly ready for him. She was perfectly warm and as moist as the summer rain that still ran down the windows. He rose above her and filled her. It was heaven. Jason had no thought except for Oona. To love her. He wanted to stay slow and gentle, but his own need outweighed that wish, as did her thrusting her hips and screaming his name as she moved into him.

They finished in a tangle of legs, hair and naked, sweaty skin, all thoughts of gentlemanly behavior lost in raw need, desire and love. He couldn't say he was sorry.

Oona lay back, satisfied in places and ways she could not have imagined. Jason's leg lay over hers and one hand was in her hair. She thought she might have wished for pillows and bed curtains, or at least sheets and blankets, but the naked honesty of the bed matched the raw passion they had just shared.

She woke late. Oona was glad for the deep sleep she had fallen into once the morning sun glinted at the horizon. It had been quite a night. Another storm had come in, battered at the house with thunder, and lit the sky with bright lightening, but nothing had matched what had happened in that small room. After dozing and waking together throughout the night, each time awakening wrapped tightly in Jason's arms, she turned to him to find him gone. She heard someone downstairs in the kitchen knocking on the door. She dressed quickly and went down.

"Hi Oona," it was one of the older boys from her little school. "Jason said to dress for a day in the country, meet him down Windmill Point in an hour." The lad tipped his hat and left.

So Sammy is a runner for the Sons now, is he? Oona thought as she pulled out the only gown she had not yet worn these last days. She looked at, and considered, a box of her old clothes that she had carried to Beach Street from the Goodiels's but had not worn. Oona pulled the out a skirt and bodice she wore when she beat the rugs. In minutes she was dressed in the old skirt and jacket, pinned closed with a hawthorne from the tree in the lane. She grabbed a boy's coat from the box, and pushed Matty's old leather tricorn onto her head. Feeling free and ready for anything, she left the house and went down to the point to watch for Jason.

The day had been completely scrubbed clean. The rain and drizzle that had enveloped the town all day the day before had brought lowered temperatures. It was a comfortable late summer day. Now, a brisk wind was chasing away the last of the wet on the grasses and drying the mud.

It took a few minutes for the silhouette on the horizon to turn into a small boat with Jason at the helm. As she watched, she took the time to take stock of herself, since she sensed she was about to leave her old life completely behind. Her arrest and trial had put a strange topping on the year. She had found an unexpected strength in herself. And though it had turned out to be barely necessary, the whole thing had turned into a Shakespearean farce with two capital crimes, a smuggler king, and a magistrate who turned out to be the smuggler's brother. She still thought she could have withstood it.

She took off the hat and let the wind unwind her hair. She let the year's worries fly away on it. She plopped the hat back on her head just as a gust of wind grabbed it. She chased it over the sand as she watched the little 'wasp' pull closer.

Jason maneuvered the craft as close to Windmill Point as was safe. He looked to shore, hoping to see the familiar black hair playing in the brisk wind. The day would be perfect for a picnic as soon as the sun was high enough to burn off the mist and chill. He had left Oona's side by moonlight, hoping to catch one of his crew, if any had made the trip south in the rain. They had. He would have to talk to them about taking unnecessary risks. He'd arranged for a team to double up on the trip home so he could take Oona out in one of the little vessels.

He could think of no better way to stay away from trouble than to spend a few hours on a deserted island in the harbor. By trouble he meant the Morse family. The men this morning had gotten word from the Sons at the drop-off. It would be to Jason's advantage if, from now on, he left the Boston smuggling to other men. The Morse family and their friends wanted his skin for tricking them and getting away. Oona had been a means to an end. They were convinced to their souls that he had killed Lawrence. Jason would be glad to leave, but not without Oona. Too many things had gone wrong: ice storms, brutal attacks, even an occupation by a foreign army. They had spent too long apart.

Even a peaceful day like this was not without its

problems. The harbor was well-patrolled. British regulars and their navy counterparts were always on the lookout for raiders. They would not take the time to differentiate between picnickers and anyone out to destroy the forage the occupiers needed for their horses. In recent months there had been fires on the islands, with hay and grassland destroyed by the patriot farmers, and skirmishes occurred with some frequency.

Jason worked his way over the flats and pulled near the point, using his oars to get to shore. The nice thing about sailing in a small craft at full light was that not one of the patrol boat or cutter crews would think anything of it. He was sure he looked completely innocent, a lone man in a boat, ready to pick up a pretty young woman for a picnic.

The island was covered with vines, not grassland, and he hoped it was of little interest to either side. There had been enough confrontation, and he just wanted to spend time with Oona, alone and uninterrupted. He intended to leave the 'wasp' at the point and take Oona openly on the packet this afternoon. He might rather spend the day in their safe little room, but he did not relish listening to marching boots while they waited for their ship.

He pushed his basket of meat pastries and fruit aside to make room so that Oona could climb in. She looked happy and as fascinating as she had that winter day he had met her at the top of Faneuil Hall. Today she wore a man's summer linen coat and the leather tricorn he remembered. He also remembered a blue hat with a jaunty feather, which was probably already in Salem. He felt a familiar tightening in his breeches at the joy and energy that Oona brought to any day. He felt blessed by fate.

"Oona, I have breakfast from the *Milk Maid* – they

didn't have much, but what they had they sold me. And I borrowed a wool blanket from Mary Channing's attic. You, I see, have brought bright sunshine and a following sea."

"Thank you Jason, you make me smile." And other things she was still to shy to say. She leaned into him and gave the captain of the little "wasp" a kiss.

He had shed his finery of the day before and changed back into the Jason she recognized. That other man, the one who had bullied the Royal Navy and General Howe's army regiments, had awed her, as had his brother in his bright red uniform. She knew that without them, she would probably be on her way to a British prison awaiting trial. Now that she had time to consider it, the finery Jason had worn was better than even those Matthew Goodiel owned. Oona hoped that when the money from the rents finally arrived, she could purchase the equivalent. If she lived in Philadelphia, New York or London she might want to. But John Hancock, the richest man in Massachusetts and now with other patriots in Philadelphia, didn't dress that way most days. That suit had announced to all that he was English and an aristocrat. And that wig - what pomp!

He had shed those trappings last night, when they had been as honest and naked as the empty room. Today, he wore the leather, wool and thick linen of a working sailor. She didn't know where he had gotten these clothes either. Had he sent one of his men homeward in a silk waistcoat and powdered wig?

She sat and watched him work the ropes of the ship, steering the small craft through the narrow channels. His tricorn was brown leather, weatherbeaten and soft. It clung to his head as though the two of them had been together through seas, stormy and calm. She supposed they had. His jacket was wool, a burnt red; his breeches, shirt and boots, all shades of brown and softened by salt and sun. He looked competent and strong. She sighed. He was beautiful. A perfect man, perfectly in control of his ship. Perfectly hers. She had a wicked desire to climb into his lap and distract him from his work; he was so at one with the vessel, she felt foolishly jealous. She knew better than to be petulant, so she put that emotion away and watched him, deep in pleasure with the movement of the ship.

Jason maneuvered over the flats and around the Castle, the island fort where General Howe had his headquarters. From there, it was a short distance over open water to a protected and hidden harbor on Moon Island, a small bit of land off the Squantum section of Dorchester. There, safely hidden on the backside of the island, they anchored the ship and climbed ashore, stepping out onto sand and smooth gray-blue pebbles.

They climbed around the island, over rocks and under blueberry bushes, looking for dry wood to use for a fire. When they had collected enough for a small cookfire, they settled back on the beach to heat water.

"Jason, is there water? I didn't see a spring on the island." Oona settled on her heels, setting the kindling to light.

"We keep a barrel filled below deck on the ship. Never know when the need will arise. He made light of it, but Oona knew that even on short trips, many emergencies existed that might require clean water. He carried the small iron kettle to the ship, and brought the water.

Oona had arranged the wood and was using tow to get the fire started. She blew in her hand to start the sparks in the strands of fiber, carefully putting the glowing fiber in the center of the twigs they had collected. Puffing gently, she soon had a healthy fire burning on the beach.

Jason put water on to boil, adding coffee as it started to heat. He opened the basket of food and pulled out meat pies and apples for breakfast, while Oona opened the blanket he had brought. He lay propped on his elbow and ate an apple. He handed the other one to Oona.

"How did you put together such a meal – and a blanket?

"The blanket is Mary's from a back closet, and the food – well, you slept late." Oona was sure there was more to it – how did he happen to get one of his little "wasps"? – but it was not the right time to talk about it. They were still in Boston, there was still danger.

Oona put the serious thoughts away and stared at her new-found husband. "You bring to mind a certain serpent with an apple," she said, moving onto the blanket facing him. She took a bite of the apple, handing him one of the small pies and putting the other in front of herself. The day was fresh, the sky was blue, and Oona felt luckier and freer than she ever had before. When they finished drinking their coffee, Oona tidied their little camp. Jason stored the leftovers on the ship; putting rocks on top of the basket to discourage, or at least slow down, the various four-footed thieves.

"Oona, I want to hear all the things you left out of the first letterbook. It was handed to me when we docked last year, but I had no safe way to tell you I had read it. I am especially curious about the Goodiels leaving. I know only that he didn't tell anyone about the project to map the section of the Caribbean before he left. And since he arrived in London, he has sent no word to me or his agent about the project.

"The charts have sold well. In fact, they bought us a house." He pulled her onto his lap as he spoke. "Did he say anything to you about that, or anything at all before he left?"

She snuggled against him, feeling his strength and warmth. "Jason, there was one thing. They wanted me to see them off, and he spoke to me on the deck just before they left. He said he had discussed this with Anne. He explained that he did not have specie enough to give me the money owed to an indentured servant at the end of the contracted time. So he gave me keys, told me where to leave them for the new owners, and told me to take what I wanted from the house. Do you suppose he knew about our marriage, and considered the charts part of the gift? I don't suppose we will ever know.

"As for when they left, it was right after Governor Hutchinson and his household left on the *Minerva*, in May. The Goodiels left the same week. I don't know remember the day, but it was only a day or so before the deadline, when the harbor closed. Matthew had a hold full of things to sell. They will thrive, I'm sure. Anne begged for me to accompany them. She knew I was to go to Milton to talk to Elisha Appleton about the documents, but she pleaded with me to ignore that and come with her. I hugged her good-bye, but going with them, that was impossible.

"And then the next week when I went to the Appletons, I learned that I have a mother, a name, and money. Amazing, isn't it? My middle name is Brigid. She was the Irish saint of lost, illegitimate or hurt children. I wonder if she knew the meaning when she gave it to me, or was it because it was her name? Did you read the note she included in the sac? She had me Christened, with a tiny gold cross. She must not have realized that she was sending me where little gold crosses were symbols of Papist idolatry." Oona smiled, and Jason roared with laughter at the image of a little amethyst-eyed baby girl, his wonderful Oona, being an instrument of the devil.

"I've done all the talking, Jason. Tell me about your journey."

"No. Nothing happened after that letter you already received. I'll tell you all the rest about that pirate attack another day, but not now." He sighed. "Generally, it was a successful voyage. You already know about the charts. And of course you know all about the smuggling. There is one thing my men told me this morning. Things have changed – the Morses wanting my skin, and John finding out that I'm his smuggler, and that he designed the little 'wasps.' I am finished with sailing the little ships. You won't even have to nag me. I have no interest in being butchered, press-ganged, tried or hanged. So I promise, dear wife, to stay on dry land and keep you warm until Howe and his army have evacuated Boston." He looked into her eyes, his own glowing with that wolfish glow Oona adored, and thought how lovely it would be to stay home. Jason did not speak, but gently traced a finger over her arm as he held those beautiful amethyst pools. *Home with my luscious dark-haired beauty – it sounded too good to be true.* Jason was beginning to believe that a bit of his fantasy might just come true, though.

He looked over the deep channel toward the mainland in time to see the crew of a British Naval Cutter notice them on the beach. The last thing he wanted was to have their day disturbed or to have to explain to the patrol who he was. To show the men that they were harmless, he waved at the ship and pulled Oona into his arms, bending her back into a blistering kiss – one that was noticeable by all the sailors on the cutter, who showed their appreciation by whistling and calling out. As they sailed off, Jason showed his appreciation by kissing Oona gently on the lips. He lifted her hand from his cheek and drew it to his lips. He blew gently into her hand, and placed a slow deliberate kiss on her palm.

She inhaled audibly enough for him to hear, and jumped away, running down a narrow trail away from the beach. She called "catch me!" and Jason ran after her, feeling carefree and uncaged, after feeling pent up from his sense of duty and the deep fear that he was doing the wrong thing, for Oona and maybe even for Boston as well.

He chased her, but though he could hear her, he could not find the right path. He laughed as he sat in a protected copse and waited for her. In a minute Oona walked into the clearing with their blanket and bunches of ripe purple grapes that were growing over the island's stunted trees. She put one in her teeth, bit into it and let the juices run down her chin. Jason felt like he understood the pull of Eve as Adam had watched her eat the apple.

She took another grape into her teeth and leaned over to offer the half to Jason. He let out a small growl and leaned toward Oona. He took the grape from her with his teeth and bit down. He let the sweet juices fill his mouth. He traced her lips with his finger, letting her kiss and nip at his hand. Then he pulled her to him for a kiss, filling her mouth with the sweet juice of the grape in turn, as his tongue found her and they drank each other and the sweet, sticky fruit.

Jason kissed Oona's chin, following the juice trails with his tongue. Oona leaned back, giving Jason access to her neck, and breasts. Jason unbuttoned her coat, realizing that this was the first time he had undone a man's coat that he was not wearing. He slid the damask off her shoulders and unpinned the short jacket, the only layer she wore over her shift. *No stays, no stockings and bare feet. Wonderful savage – how could a man get so lucky?*

He continued to kiss her neck and shoulders, only

teasing with his thumbs at the mounds of her breasts, loose now without the tight jacket to hold them. He untied the drawstrings of her skirt and let it fall to the beach. He sat back on his knees, breathless and silent on the blanket staring at her, letting her shadow fall over him, watching the sun and wind play with her hair and create little goosebumps, either from the chill wind or anticipation.

Oona felt a small smile play on her lips. She sensed her power as she watched Jason looking at her. He moved off his knees and lay down on the gray blanket, on his side, his head leaning on his hand. He motioned for her to join him. She felt drawn by his glowing wolf eyes and the intense desire they displayed. Like a beacon, she followed the glow and sat on the blanket. She leaned into him.

Oona picked up the bunch of grapes, pulled one of the round ripe fruits from the others, and making sure that Jason was as involved in the observing as she was in the acting, she very carefully and very slowly peeled the skin from the grape. When it was fully peeled, she put it in her mouth. She licked the juice from her lips letting her tongue play on her lips catching every drop, then very slowly she devoured it and swallowed.

Jason felt himself swallow as Oona did, he had a look of pure enchantment on his face. Oona leaned over the dazed man, and fed him one perfect grape, holding the bunch over his mouth and making him reach just slightly with his neck and lips before he could grasp the fruit. She repeated this, eating one and feeding Jason the next. Then she moved closer, her breasts just brushing against his chest, and fed him grapes she peeled for him, deliberately, one juicy orb at a time.

Jason gave up the notion that this had anything to do with the lost innocence of Adam and Eve. By now, he had the image of Bacchus, the debauched and happy god of wine, being fed grapes by a beautiful concubine in a thin toga. He had seen such in a mural on a café wall in southern Italy on one of his journeys. He chewed and swallowed, savoring the sweet fruit as well as the moment. It was amazing – the pretty girl on in the mural could not compare with Oona. And this beautiful woman now leaning over him, making him think of all the deliciously wicked things they could do in their legally sanctioned marriage, was his wife. Oona leaned close and again brushed her breasts against his chest, and he hardened in response, but he did nothing to interrupt; he stopped thinking.

He did not remain passive for long. He turned on his side, propped on one elbow, and reached out with his other hand to begin soft tracings over Oona's neck, down her shoulders and over her waist and hips over the thin linen shift. Keeping a small distance, she leaned into him and put her lips firmly on his. The kiss was deep and telling. Oona lost herself in the kiss. This, she thought, was as much as a kiss could be. She was wrong. Jason lifted her onto him as he rolled onto his back. Jason held her to him and deepened the kiss.

There had hardly been time for slow kissing last night, but now she remembered that a kiss could be an act of love all by itself. She opened to him further, her tongue responded to his searching, and she found a way to tease his lips, teeth and tongue, remembering those fleeting moments from so many months before.

But this touching and kissing was different. Now she could indulge in all the touching and feeling she had denied herself and Jason. Even when she had been weak, Jason had not. His pledge not to violate her chastity or break the law had not been something he would let her wish away. How she had wanted to make him moan and cry as he had done to her! Now was her chance. She pulled her shift over her knees and straddled his hips. Jason had put his hands behind his head. His wolfish eyes were in a full hunt, but there was a tender, daring smile just teasing his lips.

She leaned into him and unbuttoned his vest and shirt. He wore no cravat, just a simple working man's neckcloth, which she untied. She pulled him to sitting and pulled his shirt over his head.

Jason nearly reached for her as she pulled at his shirt and vest. He could feel her loose breasts through the thin linen, but he let her push him back, and he lay still to enjoy her sweet touches. He looked up; the sky was a soft summer blue, and he realized he had seen very little daylight since they had started their smuggling. He breathed in the familiar sea breeze and lost himself in the sun, the wind and the strong, yet exquisitely delicate, hands exploring his chest.

Oona ran her hands over Jason, as she had dreamed of doing even while her back was raw and bruised. She indulged herself, pushing into his muscles and rubbing his soft skin. It was covered in an intriguing pattern of fine brown hair. She traced the lines of that hair with her eyes and hands from his flat nipples down his torso and trailing into his breeches, already showing strain.

Hungry to taste as well as touch, she used her mouth and lips to retrace the trails her fingers had taken. She returned to his hard, flat breasts, so different from her own. She took one nipple in her teeth and bit, pulling it into her mouth and letting her tongue swirl and play as he had done to her. She teased and touched his chest with her mouth and fingers, till her lips and tongue began to follow the thin line of hair down over his torso. She put her hand on the bulge in his breeches.

"It can't be good for the leather to stretch so." Oona forced herself to keep her voice light. She wanted to moan with the pleasure of touching him, so long denied her. She would never forget the frustration as she'd felt as she healed from her wounds; how much worse it must have been for Jason! She untied the laces at the waist of his heavy leather breeches. Then she undid the one button that held them closed. She climbed off of him and pulled the breeches over his strong lean legs. She ran her fingers from ankles to knees, noting that he would never need false calf muscles to make his legs beautiful. She sat on her haunches looking over the naked and very aroused Jason.

His hands still rested comfortably behind his head, yet he looked alert, as if he were the wolf waiting to pounce and devour his prey. She ignored that look, and stared instead at the length of him. It was as if she had never seen him before. Last night it had been evening and then full dark as they lay together, and this morning he had dressed and left before she woke. Last year she had peeked, but those glimpses had been brief, far too brief.

Oona was not innocent as to what men looked like. She lived in a busy town with a harbor operated by men of all sorts, shapes and sizes. She had grown up as a servant in a household of men and boys turning into men. She had gone swimming, and had spent a childhood playing with boys and girls of all types. She also knew perfection and beauty when she saw it.

Jason was beautiful. She had been held by him and loved by him, but Oona realized that she had never had a chance to look at him in full light. Every inch of his chest, stomach, legs and hips was taut and muscled. His color struck her as it had when she first spotted him. Nearly all of his chest was a uniform light tan color. His legs were paler to just below the knees. His forearms were a shade darker than the rest of him, the hair on them a shade lighter. His shoulders were broad and his arms were thick, proving that although he was a navigator and ship's mate, he spent his days and nights at sea, his breeches rolled up and his shirt off, doing the hard work of pulling ropes and hauling goods.

Her fingers gently played along his legs as she considered them. Then she ran her hands over his hips and turned to look into his eyes. She smiled at his curious expression. He seemed to be asking what she had planned. She moved her eyes again and stared openly at his erection, feeling better acquainted with it after one long, heavenly night. That he was so obviously anxious for her only made her heart beat faster, and started a now familiar and wondrous clenching deep within her body. She ran her hands over his chest, leaning over him to put her lips to his.

In seconds Jason's hands were on her. Her shift was lifted over her head. She felt the cool sea air catch her body, caressing her just as Jason put his lips and teeth to her breasts. Oona gulped for air and moved her hips searching for release. She moved lower until she found his shaft and impaled herself, finding a new kind of pleasure.

Jason let the sensations roll over him. Oona was a dream realized in so many ways. And now she was so hot and wet moving over him and pulling him deeper into her body. His passion nearly overwhelmed him, but he slowed their movements until she screamed with the ecstacy of it – and he filled her with his essence.

"Oona, I love you and I love everything about you." He pulled her close, his hands in her long, thick hair. He breathed her in, pulling her scent, her very being deep into his body. He spoke again, murmuring into her ear. "I don't believe I ever told you before, I'm sorry." He gently ran a hand over her hips and buttock, luxuriating in having her near.

"Mmmm, Jason," Oona reacted to being so thoroughly touched. "I know that you do. I've known for a very long time. You know" – she turned and nuzzled his neck, finally resting her head on the curve of neck and shoulder – "I always thought I was in love with you, all the years in Boston. This is better." She caught his hand and pulled it to her mouth. She rested her cheek against his palm.

Jason took a quick breath and spoke. "Oona, I think you should take out the earring." He turned them, so he was on top, staring down into her sparkling eyes. He kissed her breast and his tongue found the jewel, turning it in his mouth. Oona gasped with a sudden intense yearning, deep in her belly. Jason spoke between gently suckling at her nipple and the ruby ring. "I put some replacements under your pillow for you to find. They are not to be hidden, mind you. They're for your neck and ears. I never did give you a wedding gift."

"Oh – I will explore the bedding as soon as I get home. I will miss this one, though." She showed him that his play at her breasts was creating the desired reaction. She put her legs around his waist as they again found the rhythm that brought them to new heights. Oona understood now that an earring or brand paled in comparison to real possession, real connection. She would have no trouble giving it up if she had Jason in her bed, a ring on her finger and a child growing in her womb. The thought brought new desire and she shattered and reappeared in his arms.

The afternoon hung still as they loved and dozed. It was a timeless afternoon, moments together without the world intruding. Maybe it would mark the beginning of their life together. It was obvious that both lovers wished it, yet each felt the moment was too fragile to speak of it. The fates had not been kind or on their side.

Jason woke and stretched. He was glad that they had spent the day in their cocoon, with only the salt air and sounds of the sea for company. Such pleasure had been a long time coming. He dressed quickly and sat back down on the blanket next to Oona. Gently, he kissed her awake. She looked up into his eyes and smiled. He watched, still enjoying the wonderful daze of sunshine on Oona's lovely body, seeing the soft wind teasing at her hair, and the pleasant after-effects of hours spent in Oona's arms. He allowed himself the luxury of watching her dress. She pulled on her shift and tied the neck and arms, pulled up her skirt and retied the drawstrings. Lastly, she pushed her arms into the tight jacket and pinned it back into place. He sighed as her full breasts were once again hidden and corseted. She did not put on the gaudy man's damask coat she had worn earlier, but pushed it into the basket.

Jason shifted his weight and held out a hand to her, never taking his eyes from hers as she helped him to standing. Facing into the wind, she shook out the sand, twigs and pebbles before she folded the soft, thick blanket. She took a moment, breathing in the memories of the day, as if they were air and she could hold them inside herself forever. Oona and Jason walked hand in hand to the little boat that would carry them back to reality. Neither spoke; the moment hung heavy with their silence.

Jason helped Oona onto the boat and got her settled among the few items they were carrying back. He pushed off and let the currents push them as close to the mainland as was safe, before he started to row.

"Its good we don't have to hoist the sail and draw attention to ourselves." Jason talked just to reassure himself that what they had shared would continue into the uncertain future.

"Yes," Oona spoke slowly, not wanting to break the mood. "It's lucky we timed the tides just right. You'd think we woke up just to get back." She rolled her eyes and Jason laughed, willing himself to relax and believe they would be in time for the afternoon packet, and that they would be unnoticed and allowed to leave the closed town. He jumped out and pulled the small ship up on the sand. Oona climbed out as Jason handed her the basket of food. In shadow now, she put on the damask to block the west wind, and scrambled up the bank while Jason tied the "wasp" under a nearby dock. He checked to see if any part of the little boat showed from the land. Satisfied, he followed Oona.

From down below she was barely recognizable with her man's coat and hat and her hair all tucked up. Jason smiled at her excellent disguise, reflecting that it would be fun to unravel another of Oona's little mysteries. He looked up the steep hill at her. The last thing he remembered was shouting at her to run.

Jason heard footsteps before he saw the men. Moments after, he felt the heavy bag pulled over his head. It smelled of fish and rotting sea weed. Helplessly he lashed out, hoping to break a nose or two. Then they tied his arms to his body and threw him into the bottom of a boat. He hoped Oona had taken his screaming as a sign to run far and fast, not as a sign to come after him. In a moment of clarity, he assumed that these were the Morse family or their good friends. That was the last clear thought he had. Something hit his head. He stopped thinking completely.

Jason heard voices. He was aware that men were arguing about something, but he couldn't get his mind to focus, and besides it was too much work – better to sleep and forget trying to figure out where he was being taken. Finally, they stopped their yelling, and then there was the unmistakable sensation of being rowed. He lay very still. Pretending to be out cold was easier and much more pleasant than getting hit again. It seemed like forever, though it was only a short time later when the boat was tied and he was carried – no, hoisted over some enormous man's shoulder, and dumped rather unceremoniously onto a hard, cold floor.

He woke with a headache and opened his eye. His wrists and ankles were tied, but not very tightly. He ignored that for the time being, and sat still for what seemed like an eternity, trying to focus in the almost pitch-black room. Finally, from his far right, he saw a small ray of light coming through a crack high in the wall. As his vision adjusted, he could tell he was in a basement or storeroom of some sort. He looked for stairs, a door or some way of escape, and decided that there must be a trap door in the low ceiling. There was no stair or door that he could see.

He must have slept again, because he woke a second time when someone came in with a bit of food and water, and a third time when someone else, with better ropes to bind his wrists and ankles tighter, came and made better knots. No one spoke to give him information, and he did not offer any of his own. He hoped they would get the stupid reward before the Sons of Liberty found them and killed them for their stupidity. If that happened, he would probably end up abandoned in this hole forever, and likely starve to death.

Oona heard Jason scream. She finished climbing the bank and hid behind a bolder to see what was happening. The men were shouting at one another. It took her a minute to get used to their speech, but soon she was understanding their argument.

"They said to bring the sailor and the girl. Do you see a girl? She was spotted with him this morning."

"I only saw a boy, he was on the hill over there. Not anywheres near 'im. We'll check on the girl at her place after we get him stowed." It took only another minute to realize they had no interest in following her. The men had their quarry in hand. And they wanted her, Oona, a woman, not the boy they had spotted from down below. She thought about how to continue the charade, protect herself and find Jason. All the while, she watched them carry Jason's motionless body back to the water, throw him into a dinghy, and push off from the shore.

Oona crouched in the shadows. Later, she realized she had no idea how long she had stayed there shivering, even though the heat of the day had lingered. Finally, at full dark, she made herself walk the short mile back to Beach Street. Checking the yard to see if there was anyone awaiting her, and finally secure that no one was, she let herself into the dark house. She went upstairs to her room and collapsed on the mattress, bursting into tears. Sobbing, she undressed and carefully removed Jason's ruby earring from her breast. She had worn it for so long that she felt the thing was a part of her. But she couldn't be sad to remove the weight.

Then, as instructed, she pulled at the bedding until she found a black velvet pouch. Inside were two earrings, much larger and gaudier than the ruby, each with small diamonds and larger rubies and blue stones she did not recognize, suspended in gold filigree. Also in the pouch was a matching necklace. The set would look tremendous with the soft blue wool he had given her for their first Christmas. She packed all the jewels together into the pouch, and wondered where to put them where such valuables would be safely hidden. She took her silver hairbrush and pried off the face that held the bristles. She put the pouch inside and put it back together, making sure it was tight. Remembering to bring a pretty hairbrush should be easy. Certainly no one would think that it was odd. Content with her effort, she lay on the mattress to rest.

Hours later she woke, hungry and scared. She did not know where to turn, or who could help, or even who would want to help. She found the basket of food, and ate the leftovers of their picnic in the dark room. She was afraid to light a candle lest the kidnappers be watching her house. As the food calmed her, she began to plan. The first thing was to avoid her own detection. The men who had grabbed Jason had given her the clue to her own safety. None of the men had recognized her in Matty's clothes, so she needed the rest of the boys' clothes stored in the Goodiels's attic, not just the hat and coat she had been wearing. According to Matthew and Anne Goodiel, they were hers if she wanted them.

Resting lightly, she left the house before dawn. She did not want to be seen in a skirt or gown again until she and Jason were safely in Salem. She let herself in at the kitchen door of the Goodiels's old house, finding strange solace in knowing every creaky floorboard, and every squeaky door. She climbed to the top floor and tiptoed past her old bedroom and the other occupied rooms. Some of these had never been used while she lived there, but seemed to be now. At the end of the hall were the storage rooms. The keys were just where Anne always hid them, on the hook at the top of the molding, out of her daughters' reach.

The rooms nearest were full of cases and boxes belonging to the current residents. Oona had no interest in them. It took searching through all three storage rooms before Oona found the old trunk with outgrown boys' clothes. She was pulling the overlarge trunk out from under the eaves into the faint light, now beginning to show at the windows, when she heard footsteps coming her way. She abandoned her find in the hall, and ducked into a small side room. It was being used as a bedroom, but right at the moment the inhabitant was missing. The footfalls came closer to her down the corridor, and stopped right at the door. It was probably the room's owner, ready to return to bed from the privy. She sincerely hoped not.

She held her breath, trying not to exhale, and hoping that whoever was out there, on the other side of the door, would ignore the old trunk that had suddenly and unexpectedly appeared outside his bedroom. She prayed that he move away so she could finish her simple errand, change into breeches, grab a few extra articles of clothing and leave. He – she was sure it was a he – did not move on, away from the door.

Simm had indeed woken with the birdsong, and gone down and outside to use the privy. He decided another hour of sleep on the pretty, late summer morning was a tempting indulgence. He had gone back upstairs to indulge. At the top of the stairs, he noticed an old trunk in the hall outside his door. It had not been there before. He stopped to explore, and heard his door click.

He stood outside his room, waiting for whoever had invaded his space to reveal himself and vacate, so he could grab a nap. It had been a long night in conference with the Generals. Each man had had his own idea of how to end this impasse with the colonists. Unfortunately, no two of them agreed.

On the other side of the door, Oona wanted to stamp

her foot like little Willie Goodiel did when she was angry with an unfair world. And it did seem completely unfair that she be trapped in a room that was very nearly her old bedroom, in her old house, simply for taking a trunk that was technically hers. Of course, she did understand that though the trunk was hers, being in the house at this hour, uninvited, might put her in an uncomfortable position.

Deciding that the best approach would be to claim that she had used to live here, and that the box of clothes was hers, Oona fixed her hair, hoping she looked like a girl and an innocent and charming one at that. She pasted a sweet smile on her face and opened the door.

Staring back in surprise were somewhat familiar ice-blue eyes. They lit with laughter as soon as he recognized the woman on the other side of the doorway.

"Oona!"

"John!" They spoke at once.

"What are you doing here?'

"I live here."

"You do? I thought the Warrens rented the place from Matthew Goodiel."

"I guess they had, but they need the money the rents bring."

"Times are rough, even for Tories." Oona tried not to speak too loudly or brashly, not wanting to insult her brother-in-law. "I suppose you know that I lived her until recently. I came back for a few of my things."

John went over to the old dusty trunk, blew a cloud of dust off the lid, brushed away some cobwebs, and, with great drama, lifted the lid. Oona cringed as he held up a boy's white linen shirt, a few dark linsey-woolsey work shirts, two pair dark colored breeches, and various stockings, garters and shoes.

"You left behind these clothes?" He spoke with a bit of levity, since the clothes could never have been her's.

"Well, they were Matthew's sons' clothes." She moved as if to grab the handle and move the trunk down the hall.

"And you need then now, why?"

"I just want them. You know we are leaving Boston. I just don't want to leave them behind."

"I don't believe you. Something is wrong."

"You have to believe me." Oona stamped her foot, not very hard. She considered that she might need practice.

John sat on the floor and motioned for her to sit next to him. She spread her skirts and sat. "Oona," his voice was firm but she understood he was being kind, "something is wrong, I know it. I also know that you are not involved with things of which I am officially unaware. You told me so only a day ago. I know who Jason is, and all about his little armada. So, I insist you tell me. It's my job as Howe's aide, and your brother, to help you."

"My brother?" Tears started to well up in Oona's eyes. She had put all her crying behind and vowed to find and save Jason. But she had not slept well, and yesterday had been so wonderful and full of the most wonderful feelings, and then so draining and horrible. John pulled her into a friendly hug and let her cry against his chest.

Oona hardly knew what this new safety could be. She rubbed her eyes and looked at the imperfect replica of Jason. "John, I have a family? You w-want to be my brother?" she looked into John's clear blue eyes to see the truth.

"Oona, yes I want to be your brother. That's what happens when you marry my brother. You get me, and then much more family than you will ever know what to do with. Now we start over – tell me what is wrong!"

"John, it's Jason. He was seized by the harbor, yesterday afternoon. We'd had a picnic on Moon Island, and were coming in to get ready to take the packet north." She told him with as much detail as she could remember, and then more as he asked good questions. When he finished, he asked one more.

"So why the boys clothes?"

"Yes, that." Oona fidgeted. It was not the thing for girls to dress as boys, and she knew it. "The men who took Jason thought they were looking at a boy and ignored me. They are looking for Oona, so I thought I should be Oliver."

"Okay, Ollie, I'll turn my back, and you put on some of these clothes. I will help you cart the rest back to Beach Street. Then we go and figure out where Jason's being hidden." Oona looked up at John, deeply grateful for family and the friendship he offered.

John went off to his regimental headquarters for a day's work after he carried Oona's trunk back to Beach Street. He left strict orders that she not do anything foolish or dangerous. He would be back when he could. She wasn't sure what foolish or dangerous meant, coming from a redcoat, but she took it as kindly as it was offered. However, his well-meant warning did not cause her to alter her plans.

Chapter 14

A short while later, Oona looked at herself. She was wearing men's clothing; shoes, stockings, breeches, waistcoat, shirt and coat. Her breasts were flattened under the waistcoat and her hair was hidden under a hat. She looked nearly boyish, if not actually manly. But that unruly hair would have to behave if it were to stay hidden, and she knew it wouldn't. There were no scissors at hand, so she went to the kitchen to find Mary Channing's good carving knife.

Oona made a queue and braided the rest. Allowing herself to think only of finding Jason, she took the sharp knife and cut her long dark hair right at the end of a longish queue. It was the length of hair of a young man who badly needed a barber. She tied the braid with a ribbon at each end and carelessly threw it in the trunk with the extra boys' clothes. Then she went to a place where she would be recognized – to see if the disguise were any good, and to begin her search for Jason.

No one was hiding in the yard or garden. Oona walked up Fort Hill, past the soldiers' encampment, to the *Cromwell's Head* on School Street. The sign showing Lord Cromwell's likeness under his wigged head had been broken down and burned by the occupying redcoats, but the tavern was still a place frequented by those who worked in nearby print shops. The place was quieter now, but it amazed Oona how many printers were still working in Boston. She would have guessed that the Crown, or one or the other governor, would have ordered the shops shuttered, or worse, but there they were, still printing fairly incendiary diatribes against the King and Parliament, as they had before the troops took over the town. Of course, there were just as many printers writing in defense of the King and his armies, but their owners did not drink here.

Oona scanned the crowd for Ben Edes and John Gill, the printers of the *Boston Gazette* and members of the Sons of Liberty. She asked the man at the tap where Ben Edes was, speaking as softly as she could among the clatter of tankards and loud talk.

"Edes moved his press and family out to Watertown. Says he won't be back till the Redcoats pack up and leave us. Gill is still here." He pointed with his chin to a man sitting among a small group. The men all wore the leather aprons of their profession; as if further evidence of their authenticity were needed, their aprons and fingers were splotched with black ink.

Oona climbed onto the stool next to John Gill. He looked up, not too happy to be interrupted, but curious.

"Mr. Gill, I was wondering if you had heard news of a smuggler being captured?" Oona waited till the man took a long draw on his ale.

"I ain't heard. Nothing the lobsters want printed and nothing in the gossip." He looked around to see if anyone in the tavern might be someone who would know. "Do I know you, boy? You look familiar."

"Mr. Gill, you do know me, but I am glad you don't recognize me. It's Oona." She let him take in the shorter hair and the boy's clothes. He looked a question at her. "Yah –

the smuggler was grabbed at the harbor yesterday evening. They were also looking for a girl." She motioned to herself and her clothing. "I need to find him." Gill nodded and went back to his tankard, making room for the newcomer heading in their direction.

Edward came over and sat at Gill's table. "Oona, that you?" He did not wait for a response. "I couldn't help but overhear. FitzSimmon was grabbed at the harbor? Not by one of us. I'd skin anyone of my men alive if he got in the way of the boats. Boy," he grinned at Oona, "that man has done good work for the townsfolk who can't leave. He probably helps the Brits from looking like the murderous bastards they are" – he laughed – "but that's a small price to pay for fresh food and dry firewood.

"I don't think there is a reward any more, but no one has made any declarations. Now that General Howe has been giving passes to almost anyone who wants to leave, I think he is happy to let the food and goods into the town. One less thing he has to worry over.

"The reward was Gage's order from last winter. Don't know what he was thinking, but Howe has no interest in such close management. There is no reward. So whoever grabbed the fellow" – he looked at Oona, gauging her reaction – "will get no money for his work. That might make it worse."

He pulled a stool up to Oona and spoke quietly to her. "And it won't make it easier to find him. The Brits may be bent on destroying our liberties, but they're hellish particular to protect our right to open trials. If they had him you'd hear, especially since you are known to them."

Oona looked up, surprised that the man knew about her trial, and her release.

He nodded understanding. "The Sons have eyes – we

can't always help, but at least we try to know what is going on."

"I see. So what do I do now?" She carefully did not mention John FitzSimmon's connection to General Howe, and the real reason for the revocation of the reward.

"I don't believe the men who grabbed your smuggler are from this end of town. I'd guess this is related to the Morse family. Could be one of their cousins, even a friend. So it's a North End problem. I'd check at the *Salutation*. Revere has left, so the North End Caucus are in a bit of disarray, but you should be able to hear something up there. Oh, and the disguise is pretty good. Dirty your chin, and be sure to wear long coats so the lack won't show." His eyes wandered to her lap, to illustrate his point.

Oona felt her face turn red. Two days as a married woman had not toughened her sensibilities, but she was glad for the compliment and the advice. She thanked the men and left.

Oona walked up School Street to Tremont and walked through the heart of the town to her other home, the *King's Mount*. She didn't expect her old friends to know anything about Jason's abduction, but the *Mount* was as good a place as any to go next, and the girls who worked the back side of the hill often had more information than anyone else in town.

The clientele had changed since Oona had spent her evenings working there. The *Mount*, whose sign still hung from its pole over the door, was now frequented by soldiers and a wide variety of reds, yellows, and plaids were distributed throughout the room. Oona peeked in, caught Belle's eye, and went round to the kitchen.

"Young man, you are darling, but I am too tired to

take a young'un like you to my bed."

"Belle, I wouldn't think of asking. It's me, Oona."

"Well, well. Trying to get the othah trade? Might work, there are many want a change from the ordinary."

Oona groaned. "Belle, I was just wondering if you'd heard of anyone bragging about capturing one of the smugglers who bring the goods in?"

"No, these fellahs don't tahk to me about thaht. I don't suppose any of them did it?"

"No, I don't suppose it could be soldiers. I was thinking North Enders."

"Mor'in likely. But you'll have to check the *Salutation*. Careful over there. Don't let 'em figga you out to be a girl. They don't behave like gents in that place." Belle's eyes looked stern, and a little bit sad. Oona did not have time for Belle to tell one of her stories. She took her hand and held it briefly, tempted to shock the woman and kiss her, but she stuffed the temptation for another day and went off into the dark.

"Thanks, Belle, I'll be careful." Oona tossed the words over her shoulder, knowing that she would not be careful, but she would try not to do anything stupid, or get caught.

She returned to Beach Street, walking unnoticed by the watchers who had placed themselves in front of the house. She let herself in the back, ate a small lunch, and went upstairs to lay down for a nap. Her plans involved staying up all night, for as many nights as it would take, and occasional short naps seemed like a good idea.

Oona woke to the sound of footsteps walking through the house. She stayed very still until she was fully awake. Then she went into the false room that had hidden the wooden furniture until just a few days ago. She stayed very still, hoping whoever it was would be satisfied that no woman was living in the house and go away.

The intruder came closer. She heard him check to see if there was anything in the other rooms on her floor. Finally, he came into hers. She watched him look at the bare windows and the simple mattress on the floor. He opened the trunk and pulled out a pile of socks that Oona had stuffed into the corner. Then he began to empty the trunk, one item of clothing at a time. Oona watched, horrified, as the long braid of hair fell off the clothes and into the empty space between the trunk and the man's random pile. Eventually, he seemed satisfied with what he found or did not find, and left. Oona ran quietly to the door to try to follow him by sound.

"Joey, there's only boy's stuff up there, the others must have left. The house is real empty."

A second voice responded. Oona was sick with the realization that two men were in the house even though both doors had been locked. "Yeah, it does seem empty. Guess that means some lobstah's gonna move in. All uninhabited houses immediately go to quartering the troops." He spoke with a sneering disdain. Oona knew how he felt, but right then she wanted nothing more than for a particular "lobstah" to appear at the back door. She needed a little rescuing. Also it was time to make plans for the night.

It was at that moment she heard that very soldier open the back door. The two intruders spoke at the same time. "Sorry officer, we was just leaving." "Yes, sir, we will get right out of your way." "No, sir, there is no one here, I guess you can move in, of course you can, I mean." Oona heard the men open the kitchen door. It slammed behind them. She watched through the window as they ran down the hill, back to the harbor and the shortest way back to their neighborhood.

Oona listened to Simm checking the windows and doors for broken locks. She dressed for the evening, putting on a clean shirt, and a long waistcoat. She grabbed a handful of soot from the fireplace and created the illusion of whiskers; as long as no one looked too hard. She pulled her hair back into a queue and went down stairs to meet her unexpected ally.

Simm pulled admiringly at her queue, but did not say another word about her shortened hair. Jason really was a lucky man, but he was going to miss that hair. He noticed she had dirtied her chin and wore a disguise that did a good job of hiding the fact she was female. She hoped she looked like a small, dark man. She knew her size would make her seem like no more than a boy, but that might help her fade into corners as an observer.

They walked quickly over the hay market, neither having much to say and each worried into a separate silence. Simm wore the uniform he had put on that morning. The cuffs were dirty and his wig needed powder and a good combing. He looked like a soldier out for an ale after a long hot day of administrative duties. He hoped that his being in uniform would make whoever was keeping Jason uneasy enough to do something conspicuous. The plan was then to follow the perpetrators to wherever they were keeping his brother.

To a casual observer they did look like two disconnected men simply strolling down Fish Street. At a dark corner, Oona turned left into Salutation Alley, a street so narrow it barely deserved a name. The *Salutation Tavern* was not crowded when she entered, but more patrons were moving in than were going out. It was going to be a busy night.

So close to the harbor, the mist had turned the evening cool, and there was a fire in the corner stove. The room was dark, the only light supplied by filthy lanthorns on the tables that emitted only half the light the flames produced. Simm had stopped at the harbor to stare at a Man 'o War, and he entered the tavern a few minutes later. By his presence, he intentionally drew attention to himself and raised the tension in the pub. Oona drifted deep into the shadows.

Sitting at opposite ends of the small room they nursed their tankards slowly, watching other tables and listening to the multiple conversations that swirled around them. Oona's years serving at the *Mount,* and Simm's various life experiences, allowed them to listen for pertinent information or unlikely behavior, anything out of place that might lead them to Jason.

They sat there until there were streaks of light in the east. Then, disappointed and tired, they separately left the tavern. Once they passed the Town House on King Street, Simm spoke for the first time. "Oona, walk with me to the house on Oliver Street. I'll grab my kit and come with you."

" John, you don't need to do that. Those men didn't find Oona; they won't be back."

"I can't take that risk. If anything happened to you, Jay will kill me. That is, if I haven't killed myself first. I will be staying on Beach Street."

"There is only the one mattress."

"With that beard coming in so nicely, I don't think you have anything to worry about."

Oona heard the smile in his voice and returned a weary one. It would be no problem, letting Lieutenant John FitzSimmon into her house. And it would be good to have a comrade for her late night vigils at the *Salutation Tavern*. It took two more long nights before anyone made a move.

Jason hurt. His ropes had been retied sometime in the last day, he thought. He wasn't sure of anything but that his head and belly hurt – hurt more than he could remember having hurt. One man had returned, saying something about there being no reward. He had kicked him repeatedly, even though his bound hands and legs had made it impossible for him to run, or even turn away from the hard kicks. From then on, Jason hadn't been sure of time or anything except the pain.

He thought he sometimes saw daylight, but he blacked out so often that he was not sure. He knew he was not aboard a boat as the floor didn't move, although sometimes he could smell the brine and the tar of the ropewalks, so he knew they had not taken him far inland. But the cold salt air was not going to cure him, and he knew that he was not going to get any better lying on the damp floor, in the dark room, caked in his own vomit and excrement. He had no hopes of getting found. He hoped to be out-cold when he died.

As usual they got back late, discouraged by their lack of success or temporary failure, as Simm called it. Oona was becoming discouraged, but Simm was undaunted, or tried hard to seem that way. He cheered her up and insisted they would go the next night and the night after that. He told her if it went on three more days he would bring the in army to clean out and search the whole neighborhood.

"John, your can't just bring the whole army into the North End for one. It would start enormous mayhem; the country folk would storm the town."

"Oona," Simm put his head in his hands. He had

taken off his boots and wore nothing but a shirt and linen breeches. "I am Howe's right hand, charged with keeping the peace. But Jason FitzSimmon is my brother and best friend in the world. I don't care about mayhem or a bloody war – I am going to find my brother."

Oona thought she was learning a lot about love, spending these few days with John. She had been in love with Jason so long it had become a habit. More recently, she had meshed that love with deep sexual desire, but she had never told Jason that she loved him, and could not, because she did not know. It was all such a jumble of emotions. Was love this constant worry and the fear that she would never see him again? There were too many hours to think, and far more questions than answers. Rather than thinking, the days had been spent sleeping while Simm went to his office. He returned each evening in time to accompany her down Middle Street to the *Salutation,* and stay there with her until dawn.

Mornings, before she slept, she washed the smoke and sweat from the few boy's clothes she wore. In the middle of preparing to go out on the third evening, she asked, "John, I was thinking how strange it is for me to play the boy. Has anyone noticed that you are staying with a very feminine young man? I'd hate to be responsible for destroying your reputation as a rake."

"Well," he laughed at her question, "there are very few men here who know me well enough to notice. Don't worry, Ollie, I'm sure it won't take long to set my reputation back on the right track."

"Ooooo!" she tried to laugh, "I would throw a pillow at you and start one of those fights we had back when I was a very young child, but we haven't got any pillows here.

FitzSimmon, I owe you!"

"As long as Jason is there to join in. He loves a good, all-out pillow fight."

Oona bit back her tears as she tied her hair in its queue so they could go back to the *Salutation*.

It was now Friday. The tavern was crowded, which raised Oona's hopes that they might learn something. She spied Edward, the south end leader of the Sons. He was sitting alone, but looked up and nodded slightly at Simm, recognizing him and that he was with Oona. They had given up sitting apart, and after Simm found a table, the other man came over and introduced himself. Edward jumped right in and challenged Simm to defend the British position on the blockade and occupation of the colonies and the Crown's taxation policies. Simm, understanding that this was a ploy to distract the crowd from the attention they might draw if they were friendly, joined in and enjoyed himself. In no time, the two men found interesting diversion discussing the works of Voltaire and Benjamin Franklin and Adam Smith. Oona left them to their conversation, and watched the crowd.

She had not realized how much she had learned from her hours working at the *King's Mount*. She was able to read the crowd. She could tell by the way people moved who the regulars were, and, by the crowd's reaction, if anything or anyone was new or different. For hours the crowd moved in what Oona considered a normal pace, eating, drinking, talking, with occasional laughter, and entering and leaving in a natural order. It was well after midnight when a man walked in, caught a barmaid's eye, and motioned for her to follow him outside.

Oona accepted there was nothing unusual about that.

Barmaids had lovers and messages from mothers and friends as often as anyone else. But this felt different. The girl did not go out immediately. Instead, she prepared a plate of food and then left. Oona watched her set the tray. Most meals from taverns consisted of a bottle or jug of ale, some meat, and bread or pastry. The barmaid put none of those things on her tray. Oona watched as the barmaid pulled fresh water from a barrel, and ladled soup into a trencher, straining out the meat and vegetables. Unless someone's toothless grandmother needed dinner at one o'clock in the morning, something was very unusual.

As the barmaid finished the tray, Oona grabbed a candle from the dirty glass, snuffed it and pushed it far into her pocket. She waited near the door the second it took for Edward to look up and glance in her direction. She nodded at the men and slipped outside. She moved silently and hid in the shadows at the corner of the old wooden building. The man who had motioned to the barmaid stood in the alley, smoking a pipe. Oona did not recognize him, but she was sure he looked enough like a Morse, even in the dim lamplight, to be one of that family.

It was only a minute before the barmaid came out with the water and clear soup. She handed the tray to the man. Oona stayed where she was until the barmaid turned and went back into the tavern. There was no time to tell the men she was leaving to follow this man. She knew in her very soul that he would lead her to Jason. She would simply memorize his route, in case she had to bring the men back.

The *Salutation* was at the corner of North Street, the spine of the North End. The man turned down the dark alley toward the water, and took a left to the North Battery. Oona stayed as far behind as she dared, monitoring his direction until he was nearly at the harbor. Luckily, he moved slowly, not wanting to spill the soup on himself. As it was, he cursed regularly as the hot liquid tipped and splashed onto his fingers. At the harbor, he let himself in through a broken gate and onto the property of Grant's and Greenwood's shipyard and wharf. It was a large facility with many buildings. Oona stayed just behind him as he moved through the shipyard, watching desperately to make sure she did not lose him in the maze of wharf and out-buildings.

Even on the darkest night there are reflections from the moon and stars over the water. On the other hand, if you are in a strange place in the dark, there are few signposts to help you find your way. Oona watched the man go into what looked like a storage building. There had been no shipbuilding since the Port of Boston was closed by decree. The shipyard and wharf had seen better times. Even in the dark of the middle of the night, Oona could see doors crooked on their hinges, and broken boards on wharves and shutters. It was the perfect location to hide someone you didn't want found.

Oona waited until the man left. He walked right by her, anxious to get back to the tavern, no doubt. He did not notice the small man standing in the dark corner of a building. The fellow had not brought food for a guard, so the prisoner must be alone. Oona checked for the knife in her boot, as she had checked for it fifty times that night. She hoped not to use it against a person, but she knew she would. More than likely, knowing the knotting skills of the out-of-work sailors in this port town, she would use it on ropes.

Oona walked into the dark building. The man had left a small lantern burning on the table. It was nearly out of oil and dark. Chances were he had not even noticed the dim light it produced, and walked by it on his way out. She used the small flame of the lantern to light her candle, and moved down the long, empty passage.

The building was built into the hill. From the street this big, empty room was on the first floor. But there was a ladder that led down to a lower floor on the harbor side. She put the candle just out of reach, so she wouldn't knock it over. If John and Edward had followed, the light would act as a beacon and show them where she went.

Now, in total darkness, and not really sure what she would find, she used both hands to feel her way down the ladder and into the lower room. The smell of human waste was almost overwhelming, but she forced herself on.

"Jason, Jason FitzSimmon! Jason, are you here?" Oona called into the dark.

She heard a grunt, as though someone were deeply asleep and trying to answer. She ran toward the noise, and stumbled. She caught herself with her hands and felt around to see if she had, in fact, tripped over Jason.

She had. He barely grunted as she felt for his hair and ran her hands down his arms. As she touched his body he flinched and moaned in pain. Oona swallowed anger and fear. She felt tears start to pour down her face. She willed herself to act, to remedy this, and not simply give over to emotion.

Through her tears, she spoke very calmly, with as strong a voice as she could muster. "Jason, this is Oona. Sweetheart, don't move, I am going to cut the ropes on your wrists. Stay still, I can only feel, I can't see. Do you understand?"

Not a sound escaped but the moans of pain.

Oona's fear for Jason was nearly unbearable. She wasn't sure she would be able to catch her breath. She'd expected to find him tied, tired and hungry, but this was so much worse. And she could barely see. She summoned whatever strength she had, felt her way, and cut through the ropes that bound Jason's hands and legs. She kneeled next to him and gently rubbed his wrists, instinctively trying to relieve the raw skin and get the blood to flow into his cold hands. Oona checked his arms and legs for broken bones, as well as she could given the filth and the dark. She was relieved that she found none.

She couldn't move him alone. She could only hope John and Edward had followed and would come soon. She moved him to a clean spot as well as she could, and sat near, to wait for the men or one of Jason's jailers. Oona cradled Jason's head in her lap, letting her hands comb through his matted hair, and kissing his forehead. She let herself relax, acknowledging that at least she had found him, and he was no longer alone.

Jason understood that he was no longer a captive. His head hurt; he could not move, talk, or even open his eyes. But he relaxed, knowing only that someone kind was running soft fingers in his hair and singing a sweet lullaby. Oona was with him. He smelled her as she cradled his head in her lap, murmuring into his ears. He was also aware of men. He heard voices, then footsteps, then silence. Oona stayed. Her warm body next to his began to warm him, and the pleasantly sharp scent of rosemary reminded him of good things. He had been cold – it seemed that it must have been for days now – so cold. The warmth of Oona so close began to thaw him. It seemed like a miracle.

The voices were back, and Oona gently put his head on something soft, and moved away. He thought he recognized the voices, but he could not place them. Fear rose and he tried to fight, as he felt himself tied to a board, picked up and carried. But Oona's voice came back and told him he was safe, and he calmed. His mind drifted back into dreamland, as it had so often during the past days.

The dream this time was not of dark seas and death. This dream was of Oona, long dark hair flowing over her naked body as she cradled his weary head against her soft, full breasts. He turned to her and took a breast into his mouth. As she moaned with desire he rose above her, strong, healthy and manly. He took her mouth, and in moments, finding that he was naked too, he was in her and coming into her in ecstatic release. Then the dream flowed in and out of focus. He was on a ship, it was docked, but he had no idea where they were going or who the crew was. He was aware that he was supposed to make an important statement, to set the voyage in motion, but he could say nothing, and no one saw or heard him shout. He looked around for a familiar face, but saw no one he knew. Jason shook his head trying the clear the dream. The blurry images would not go away; there was only the pain that howled every time he moved his head.

Oona walked beside the fir plank the men carried as though they bore an important monarch. She considered Jason's injuries. His captors had clearly brutalized him, probably because he was no longer worth the reward money. She uttered an oath she was sure would shock the men. John said something in agreement. Edward laughed. Jason muttered something in response, but she did not understand. She just gripped his hand harder, walking beside him as he was carried along the edge of the dark harbor.

"Oona," Simm spoke easily, as though his burden

was a light one. "Edward and I want to find one of the dinghies and row him over. But we'll need to wait until it is at least a little light."

"That's fine. I'll run from here over to Beach Street and pack up the last of it. I'll see you at Long Wharf by full light." She kissed Jason on a sunken cheek, and swallowed her tears. She waved a quick farewell to the men, and ran off past the unused piers and docks, hoping she looked like a boy running an early morning errand.

She headed inland and up Cornhill, before she reached the barracks in Faneuil Hall, but stopped just west of the building to salute the weathervane, giving her grasshopper the courtesy he deserved. She said a hurried good-bye to the hall, the gold grasshopper, and the town that had been her home more than half her life.

Then, ready to start a new day and a new life, she kicked up her heels and ran, glad to be in breeches, just another unworried young man. The streets were empty of redcoats, and at this hour the town appeared nearly unchanged, if one did not look too carefully at streets that needed rolling, or lamps that should have been lit. And though she would not have chosen it, her walk through the streets took on the significance of a long good-bye to the town she had worked for, come to love, and would always hold dear.

She entered the yard and house on Beach Street carefully, but both were empty. By then, there was enough light in the September dawn to reveal her way through the house. She made a bundle of clothes – hers and those of the Goodiel boy – threw in her silver hair brush, and wrapped it all in a single sheet. Then, she picked up Jason's blanket to wrap around him on the boat. She left everything else for John. He might as well quarter here as anywhere. Oona considered that at least it would be warmer in Mary Channing's best bedroom than it would be in the servants' rooms at the Goodiel mansion next winter.

It was one hour later, as sunrise and full light announced the new morning, that Oona stood on Long Wharf with a bundle of clothes, a gray wool blanket and a bucket of warm water. She scanned the few people walking along the shore and the boats heading in from the North. These few things were her only worldly possessions at the moment. She dearly hoped that everything else had been moved successfully and delivered to Jason's house on Turner Street in Salem. If not, well – she would beg and borrow until John or Elisha Appleton's London agent found her money. *Or Jason recovered. Please, Lord, let Jason recover.* She uttered what would be the first of many prayers, spoken aloud and thought in quiet desperation, that she would pray over the next few weeks.

Oona heard oars slapping the water, and looked down to see John, Edward and Jason arriving in one of the small craft used to row sailors and visitors to the ships in the harbor. Jason was still carefully tied to the board. Edward moved the craft skillfully next to the pier and threw the rope to Oona. She pulled it taut as Simm hopped out and tied it to the mooring cleat. Some workmen noticed the invalid in the boat, and came over to hold the little craft still, so that Jason could be moved. John knelt to lift the board. As he did, he leaned down and kissed her cheek. The act was spontaneous and comforting. Oona turned – surprised at the simple act of affection. It would take some getting used to, this friendship and easy familiarity. She smiled, thanks to her new brother.

John and Edward carried Jason to a small shed on the wharf. The men lay the board on the ground. John left without a word. He returned not long after. "Oona, Dr. Hay, the Admiral's surgeon, will be here as soon as he finishes his breakfast. He is going to take a look at Jason."

Oona, ignoring the weariness that nearly had her keening, nodded her gratitude. She stepped forward with her canvas bucket. "John, you will give me a minute. I brought some warm water and want to clean up the patient before the doctor comes."

She went into the little shed. Not sure if he could understand a word, she spoke in what she hoped was a soothing and comforting tone. "Jason, I need to wash you. A doctor is coming from the Admiral's ship and frankly, well, you reek, you need a bath." While she spoke, she pulled off Jason's boots, stockings and breeches. She put the boots aside, but rolled up the breeches and stockings for burning. She dipped a clean rag into the warm water. She sensed John next to her as he took the rag from her fingers. "Oona, go sit in the sun, and close your eyes. You must be exhausted." Oona could not disagree.

She sat nearby and leaned back against the wall of the shed, facing the open water. She listened to John carrying on a cheery, one way conversation with his older brother as he washed days' worth of filth from him. She marveled at his energy. She was near total collapse, and she had slept during the days while John had gone to work.

Jason moved in and out of consciousness. He would have liked to respond and say that John was an ass blaming himself, but all he could do was relish the clean water smell and move in and out of his dream. He heard the doctor speak to him and ask him questions. He knew which were questions and he willed his eyes open, and his mouth to try to answer, but he wasn't sure if he succeeded. He felt the cold, slimy bite of leeches as they were placed on the wounds of his belly. Then he fell back into sleep, this time dreamless.

"Who is going to be in charge of this patient?" The doctor came out of the small shed an hour later, his jar of bloated leeches under his arm.

Oona knew she looked more like a vagabond than a competent adult, either man or woman. Her hair was loose in a messy queue, too long for a man's and ridiculous for a woman of means or sense. Her clothes were those of a boy, but without her concealing long coat, which was under Jason's head, she was clearly a female. Feeling that this was as much of a test as anything she had yet endured, she stepped forward. "I will be, sir."

The older man looker her over and sniffed, but having been with the navy for as many years as he had, he had seen too much to judge. "Young lady, I can't tell you for sure what the future holds. I've seen cases like this go for days unchanged, and then the patient ups and dies. I've seen patients like this worsen, sometimes for weeks, or even months if you can get them to eat something – and then suddenly get better. So, as I said, I don't know.

"But let me tell you what I do know. He has two major and separate injuries, probably caused by the same foot. The first is to his head. When you get him settled, try not to let him sleep too much. When I was talking to him just now he woke and he tried to answer me. Those are good things.

"The other injury is to the organs in his abdomen. I've bled him to release some of the heat. Keep him in bed and resting. You're going to have to figure out how to get him to rest and keep him awake at the same time. At the end of one week, you will have a good idea if he is going to live or die. Even if he lives, he might not know who he is, recognize you, or speak again."

The man shook his head sadly at her. "Good luck, young lady. I recommend prayer." He reached for her hand, shook it, turned, and left.

Oona felt lost and very alone. She looked around on the dock and saw her brother-in-law coming toward her. He stepped close and pulled her against him and into an encompassing hug. Together they turned and watched the packet arrive from Salem.

"Oona, I wish we could go with you. Please know, I would." She nodded. Of course he couldn't go. He could not leave Boston without permission, or on such short notice. Also, it remained unsaid, but obvious to them all, that Edward could not leave Boston and expect to return unmolested. This was her battle and she would fight it – alone if necessary. She did not think it would be necessary. She had seen Jason's Argonauts. He had friends in Salem. He would not be alone there, she would not be alone there, it would work out – it had to.

"John," she pulled away and drew herself up to her full height, pushing exhaustion away as she pushed back her shoulders, "we will be fine. I will write tomorrow. There will be only good news." She wiped tears away with her sleeve, all smiles for Jason's brother. He had already helped so much, but she must do the rest herself. "Thank you." She reached up to kiss his cheek, then it was her turn to turn away and follow the litter holding the sleeping Jason onto the ship.

The sea was choppy during the nearly three-hour trip, and Oona would have worried over any other invalid tied with cinch ropes to a board, on an unsteady deck. Glad of her breeches, she sat with Jason to make sure he was not uncomfortable, but as the storm moved closer and the deck heaved in the large waves, it was her stomach that churned. Of course, he barely noticed. He would have grinned at her, she was sure, if he had been up to it.

In spite of the intense hunger she had felt earlier, she was now glad that she had not eaten very much in the last few days, glad that she did not need to lean over the rail and embarrass herself in front of her sailor husband, even in his daze. She had not been with Jason on a ship since they were children. She stared at his sleeping form. They had spent so much time apart. There was so much that she did not know about him. Yet, she thought, she knew him better than anyone she had ever met. She gripped his hand and watched clouds pile up over head.

She must have slept a little, because she woke just as the ship and her stomach lurched. She opened her eyes to a building storm and rocking ship. Jason was unperturbed. Either he slept too deeply or he really was at home on the sea in all her forms. Oona considered the life of a sailor's wife and wondered if she could ever compete with such a mistress. Would he always leave her for the sea? Right now, she harshly reminded herself, the only thing to wish was that he recover enough to first come back to her, and then go back to the sea.

The weather had slowly but steadily worsened since dawn. Now, it was oppressively warm and damp, and the south-westerlies were blowing stronger. With so much else on her mind, Oona stopped worrying about the hurricane, though she knew it was coming. She had hopes that they would dock before it became dangerous.

A drizzle started as they spotted Salem Harbor, and by the time they made the town, the wind had picked up.

Soon it was raining steadily, and threatening to turn into a real deluge. The dock workers helped her carry Jason off the ship and into a dry warehouse at the dock. She noticed that although she was dressed as a man, the rain had left little to anyone's imagination as Matty's shirt was now clinging to her. She pulled it away from her wet skin, and went looking for someone who could help.

Workers ran through the open door with their coats pulled over their heads as the downpour broke. They grouped together, talking and smoking, waiting for the rain to let up. A few left and returned with oilskin coats. Those few went back outside to attend to their work. Oona left Jason's litter and walked up to the men who were still inside. She felt undressed, as though the men could see her exhaustion and filth, as well as the fact she was a girl dressed as a boy. She felt awkward and very shy, but she spoke up anyway.

Wracking her brain for a name, she blurted out, "Excuse me, does anyone know Peter Daggette?" She was relieved to be able to pull the name of Jason's friend out of her memory. He was the man who had moved her things. She barely knew how she accessed it, what with her exhaustion and the worry. She only hoped she had his name right. Worry increased as she considered what she would do if no one knew the Daggettes or Jason FitzSimmon.

A boy she had not noticed before pushed his way to the front of the group. "That's my pa. I'm Petey. You must be Mrs. FitzSimmon. Ma sent me. I been here for three days keeping an eye out for you at every packet. Come this way; I'll show you to your house and get my Ma."

"Petey, wait, slow down. Mr. FitzSimmon is hurt. I need help getting him home." The word "home" hit her hard. She had never had a home, and now she was going to her first. She looked over at Jason, still asleep, tied to a fir board. She was about ready to cry.

The boy looked over at the man asleep on the small litter in the shadow. "Wait here, I'll be back." And without a care for the rain, his clothes or his shoes, the boy ran out the door and toward the houses on a nearby street.

Oona took a minute to look around her at her surroundings. Salem Harbor was nearly as busy as Boston's had been before the port closed, but even from this vantage point, she could tell that the town was smaller, maybe even older. The houses were mostly wood, with small gardens between and behind. As in Boston, they bore symmetrical faces, with upstairs windows as eyes and cheeks and front doors their mouths. Most had a central chimney with a second stack in the kitchen, behind the main rooms. It was barely different from the world she knew. She knew she could trust that, in time, this new place would feel like home.

Chapter 15

*I*n what seemed like only minutes, a woman just a few years older than herself, and a big man who looked so much like young Petey he had to be his father, walked out of the rain and into the open warehouse. Their little procession was led by Petey, who had put on an oiled jacket and hat. Oona watched their approach. The boy was probably eleven or twelve, still young and short, but clearly on the verge of growing to his father's size. His mother was dressed for work. She had not taken off her cap or apron when summoned by her son, and Pete senior was dressed in leather breeches and vest. Perhaps he'd been planning a day of chopping wood for the coming winter.

Oona walked forward to introduce herself. She was stopped by Claire Daggette, who took her elbow, put a cloak over her shoulders, and pulled up the hood as she led her away from the warehouse. Oona looked behind. Peter Senior, another man, and young Petey were carrying Jason between them. A fourth man held a tarpaulin over the injured man.

The sad, drippy procession walked a quarter mile or so in the heavy rain along the harbor to Turner Street. There, Claire took a key from her pocket neatly stored under her apron and opened the front door. She handed Oona the key and motioned for the men to carry Jason into the house.

Oona walked back outside to stare at her new house.

It was white with dark red trim on the windows. The eight-over-eight panes might need cleaning, but they were not broken and the windows looked strong and well maintained. She watched smoke begin to come from the two chimneys. She hurried in to thank her new friends for their welcome and help. She found the group in a small storage room behind the kitchen. The men set Jason's litter down and looked around for direction. Oona went upstairs to search for clean clothes and blankets for him. Claire followed.

"I didn't know where you wanted anything. Once you were obviously delayed, I brought the boys over here to move the furniture around. I hope you don't mind."

"Mind? Why would I? Mrs. Daggette, I'm just so grateful that things are spread out and easy to find." She lifted a dry nightshirt and warm socks out of Jason's trunk.

"Call me Claire, please, and you are? Jason didn't tell us your name."

"Oona. It's Irish."

"And pretty, isn't it? Claire is French; my father wandered down from Acadia and stayed. Oona, let's get you warm and fed, while I set Pete on getting Jason comfortable. I don't suppose you know of another bed, one that might fit in that little room?" She looked over at the antique four poster with its elegant carving and massive size.

"I think there might be one in the furniture included with the Goodiels's gift. I remember a child's bed. Maybe someone put it in one of the other bedrooms."

Oona walked down the hall exploring the house. "Claire, it is down here. It's not set up yet, so we can carry it right down. I don't think there is any sort of mattress."

"Let's bring the clothes and bed parts down. I have to go and see to dinner, or nobody will eat. I'll bring Pete with me and send him back with bedding. I guess we'll have to get a new one for that bed."

"True, I'm afraid I had to leave it in Boston. Jason mentioned a Mr. Gardiner." Oona saw no way to explain that she *wanted* the quartering soldier to be comfortable in her house. It seemed as though that would be too complicated a story for right now.

"Before I leave, I'll show you the tub Jason put up here. Too bad you still have to carry up the water. But, Sir Isaac Newton's gravity brings it back down." Claire pointed out the window at a pipe leading down the side of the house.

"Oh my, and it drains into the down spout? I've never seen anything like it."

"I hadn't either, but I've got Pete planning one just like it. No more bathing in the kitchen."

The water was already hot in the kitchen, so Oona brought it in buckets upstairs, bathed quickly, and found her trunks and clothes. It surprised her how much she liked dressing in skirts, as herself again. She was almost tempted to put on full stays and an old fashioned stomacher, just to declare herself, but that was foolish. This was to be an afternoon of nursing and cleaning.

Oona descended to a calm kitchen and a clean, comfortable patient. The bed had been set up and a mattress found. Jason moaned and tossed as he slept. Claire had left Petey behind to run errands and carry messages between the houses. He sat waiting in the kitchen. "Ma says for you to tell me what you want to eat, so she can fix it. She says she'll have a nice beef-bone and a stew in the pot.

"Oh, thank you!" Oona was so relieved to have help this first day. "Petey, could you tell her that Jason can only have clear broth for now? I'll strain the stew, and I would be most grateful. And Petey, could you point me in the direction of the market?" She had no intention of leaving today, even if the rain stopped, but she was also sure that her going out for a while now and then wouldn't alter the course of Jason's recovery in any way.

The boy walked her to the door and pointed, while giving specific directions from Turner Street to the main streets. Then he ran off. Oona walked through the kitchen. She went immediately into the little storage room to see how Jason fared.

She sat in the chair left at his bedside, and took his hand in hers. He had been washed again, this time with hot water and soap. He smelled good, so much better than he had, though she loathed admitting that, even to herself. He wore the clean nightshirt she had found, and lay comfortably on a small bed made with fresh, clean sheets. She uttered words of thanks, so grateful for her new friends. Then she leaned over and kissed Jason's pale cheek. He moaned in his sleep, weakly acknowledging her. She knew that she should wake him, but she hated to do that until there was food. He must be gnawingly hungry.

In a short while, Petey arrived with a pot of stew. Oona strained some for Jason and a large bowl for herself. After Claire's good stew was eaten, Oona felt much better. Even some of Jason's disquiet eased after she fed him the warming soup. Oona was relieved that some of his discomfort was from hunger. At least that was something she, with the help of her new friends, could fix. After his dinner, Jason fell into a lighter sleep, one that Oona interrupted with one-sided conversation, and then later by letting Peter Daggette into the house to help him to the privy.

"Oona." Peter was clearly shy about offering help. "I know young women – I married one, and have more than one sister. I know you young ladies want to do it all yourself. But the boys and I, Jason's Argonauts we call ourselves, we're going to want to come and do the heavy stuff, like your woodcutting, and helping to move Jason off the bed. We figured two fellows will come by in the morning and two others at night. We won't disturb you, and don't need food or nuthin. So I'll be seein' you in the mornin'." The announcement seemed to wear the taciturn fellow out, and he left without another word.

The sun had not quite set, but Oona realized she was bone-tired. Strangely, there was nothing else she needed to do on this extraordinary, and long, day. If she stayed awake another minute she would probably fall apart – tempting, but she really didn't have the energy. So she fixed bedding on the floor near Jason, kissed his cheek, and climbed onto her own little bed right next to his, where she could hear him if he needed her. Then, for the first time in days, Oona fell asleep.

She awoke a few hours later. At first she was panicked and unsure of where she was. She stared around, not moving until she remembered the night before and the long day behind her. She found she was still dressed in her gown. Jason was quiet in the bed next to her, the kitchen fire was nearly cold, and the sun had not yet set. She stood and shook off her nap. She was determined not to spend this time in worry and tears. She decided to explore the house.

First, she looked into the gardens out the window. It was too dark to see much, so she promised herself that, first thing tomorrow, she would start exploring the gardens. It would be a good idea to get some planting done now, and note what was growing before the plants died back for the winter. She had never done more than hoe Anne Goodiel's small kitchen garden, but like so much else, she was ready to try and learn what she needed to. She pulled her gaze indoors. The first room past the kitchen was a formal dining room. She imagined a big table with lots of happy people sitting around it – maybe even children reaching over each other, and getting glared at by an indulgent Jason. Yes, he probably would be a ridiculously indulgent parent. A too-familiar wave of yearning came over her. She pushed it firmly away and continued her explorations.

From the dining room, she walked through the front hall. An empty parlor was on the other side. All the rooms needed furniture and rugs, but the wallpaper was of real quality, and the trim had been painted recently. There were cobwebs, however, and every step left a trail of footprints in the dust. That kind of problem Oona knew how to fix – in fact, she looked forward to making curtains, covering pillows, and cleaning the house almost as much as she relished the thought of buying new furniture and fabric for her projects.

Up the stairs were the bedrooms, a few of which she had already seen. As she walked into the room that would be Jason's, she wondered if he had given any thought to their sharing the room, and the bed. She ignored the emotions that brought up. She knew that many aristocrats had separate rooms. The Goodiels had shared their bedroom, and to her that seemed normal. She would have to ask Jason, though.

Suddenly, the house was dark. They really had reached the end of summer. Now, the still-long days ended abruptly – no more summer's long twilight. She had slept dusk away these past days, and had not noticed that the year had shifted. She stood in the center of the room and realized that in the morning, after she walked in her own garden, the very first thing she needed to buy were candles and lanterns. There was absolutely nothing to use to light her way. That put an end to her explorations, so she found her room, washed, and pulled a clean nightrail from her things.

Clearly they needed candles. The mattress maker was to be the second merchant visited in the morning. There was so much to do, and she knew that worry over Jason should not stop her from getting it all done. In a few days, or even weeks, when he woke up – and he *would* wake up – she needed him to see that she had succeeded in making his home. Contemplating the tasks ahead of her, Oona made her way back down the stairs and into the little room off the kitchen. The one small candle in the house was burning there in a glass chimney.

"Jason!" she shook him gently. " You need to wake. Just for a minute." He turned his head a tiny bit and grunted in pain. "Jason, darling I saw that. Oh, I also saw . . ." She shushed, not sure if she wanted him to know that she'd seen the pain pass over his face. The tension was obvious, as was the pull back into himself.

Jason tried to turn his head, to tell Oona that he was awake and had heard her clearly. But it hurt so much to move. It hurt almost as much to stay still, but even through the daze he knew that was unavoidable. Moving was something he could avoid.

Oona hated that such a small movement brought such pain, but at the same time, she was relieved to find that he heard her. The surgeon had told her to wake him regularly, but if being awakened caused so much pain, she would let him sleep, and not wake him as often as the surgeon had recommended. If this was to be her life, she would have to make her own decisions.

She leaned over her sleeping patient and kissed him goodnight. She savored the taste of his lips as he instinctively returned her kiss. She let her fingers gently comb his hair, and breathed in his smell. Even now the familiar essence was comforting. "Jason, my love," she whispered, "however long it takes you to recover, I promise you, I will be here." Then she blew out the candle stub, and climbed into her blankets on the floor. Thoughts of love, and what it meant, played in the corners of her mind. She thought that she might finally feel free enough to choose to love. The thought that it was choice, a part of free will, something that brought people together, was enlivening. So as much as the fates might push people together, or tear them apart, it was choice that allowed them to act on what the fates offered. Choosing to love, it seemed to her, strengthened the feelings she had harbored for so long. And now the strength of that feeling overwhelmed her for a minute. She climbed out of her blankets and stood over Jason. She sat, took his hand in hers, and talked to him for a while, telling him all about her theories of free will and choosing to love, even though it had never really been a choice.

Morning brought more rain, and Claire and Petey, their bright smiles lightening up Oona's kitchen.

"Hi, Claire. Petey, are you coming with us on our great adventure?" Oona looked up from stirring some barley into a broth for Jason.

"No, I'm to be Jason's helper. I'll be here if he wakes, and I can run and find Ma in no time. I have your eye-tin-er-ary." He pointed to his head and smiled. "No school today." He answered Oona's next question before she asked it. "Too many of the kids need to help with harvests. Teacher said to come back Monday, 'ready to learn.'"

The women laughed. "Well, Petey, your Dad and one

of the other fellows was here and took care of the big stuff, clean sheets, privy, and bathing Jason. So just keep him company and talk loud to him once in a while to wake him."

"Jason and me are great friends. No problem."

"Oona, really, he can handle it. Let me show you our town." Claire put down her basket of fresh rolls and a pound of coffee beans. Oona made the coffee while Claire laid out their plans for the morning. She outlined the pros and cons of each of the shops, the honesty of the merchants, and the speed with which certain goods could be acquired.

Jason smelled coffee and felt he would die if he could not have a cup, but on second thought it would be too hot and strong. He decided he would try again tomorrow. He could hear the women working on the strategy of shopping, like generals planning an attack. He wanted to tell Oona where he had hidden his share of the smuggling pay, but he could not make his lips or voice form words.

Oona looked into the darkened room off the kitchen. She saw a look of frustration move over Jason's face. She stood to say "bye" to Jason and young Petey. She spoke quietly, hoping Jason could hear and understand. "Jason, don't worry about the amount. Claire promises I can get credit, and when I straighten out my inheritance, I will cover it. You needn't worry."

Jason started to shake his head, but the pounding of drums against his brain stopped him. He withdrew into himself, to a place where the pounding subsided, at least a small bit.

Oona forced herself to look cheerful. She pulled on her cloak and hat. They waved to Petey and heard him lock the door behind them. "I think Jason is worried about me spending money we don't have. But you see, soon I will have quite a bit from an inheritance, and I don't want him to worry." Oona confided in her friend as they walked from the quiet side street toward the busy town center.

"I think men always worry about money. It shouldn't mean we can't buy what we want. I find that simply being frugal helps it work out the way I want." The women laughed at the contradiction between frugality and desire.

Oona had spent her life poor, first sharing a crofter's hut with two brothers and two parents, as well as a bed with three sisters. Then, there had been little that was hers in the mean attic room at the top of a mansion. Now, at the cusp of her new life, she had no intention of buying the cheapest goods. Being frugal would only mean getting the best for what she was willing to pay. Even if it shocked Claire, she had no intention of holding back.

Boston had lately been closed to all things interesting or fine, but during the ten years she had lived in the attic in the Goodiels's mansion, she had lived among the finest American, British and European-made goods. Now Salem overflowed with everything its southern cousin might desire. Oona was willing to sew the curtains herself, but she was not willing to scrimp on damask or chintz. And so, she bought plenty for each window and extra for bed coverings and cushions. The same was true for furniture, floor coverings, their new mattress, and the pots and pans.

Claire was nearly speechless at the extravagance, and the change between the shy, weary Oona of yesterday and today's savvy shopper, who clearly knew quality goods and how to bargain for them. Before they returned home, she introduced Oona to the grocer and butcher. At each, Oona ordered staples and perishables to be delivered to the house. The only things she carried after a day of shopping were one small oil lantern and a package of candles, the finest ones from the shop.

"You see, where I worked, we never used smoky tallow, and Claire, I just can't start now." Oona felt a bit sheepish showing such extravagance in front of a new friend. She knew that neither she nor Jason would live lavishly, but he had never been needy or gone without, and she wanted to be surrounded by the quality goods she enjoyed.

Claire nodded. She understood the habits of others. It was not her way to judge. Oona would have a difficult time before her these next weeks. Claire felt it was everyone's duty to help this young couple through the hard times. If Oona had money to spend, then good for her, and good, too, for the merchants who had seen too few of their better goods sold since the redcoats closed Boston and troubles in the Colony began.

"Oona, if you have the strength for one more, I would like to introduce you to my second favorite store."

"Fine, Claire," Oona felt delightfully full of purpose and slightly conspiratorial. "But only if you first tell me, what is your first favorite?"

"That would be a mantua maker with the most charming laces and fribbles. All smuggled from France, I suspect."

"Sounds like we'll need another day of shopping. Promise me we will go as soon as Jason is well enough for me to go missing for a full day. And when we do, I want to buy you something, so think hard about what that is to be. A silk shawl or length of damask?" The talk, even briefly, of Jason had made her want desperately to shorten the rest of the trip and hurry home, but that would not be fair. "But not now. So, Claire, what is your second favorite?"

"This one." And Claire opened a door and ushered

Oona into a little shop stocked from floor to ceiling with herbs and spices, dried fruits, and nuts of all sorts. There was coffee roasting in the back, its smell wafting over the other luscious scents.

"Jason loved, I mean loves, the coffee from here." Claire caught herself and was immediately sorry when she saw the stricken look on Oona's face.

"Claire, I barely know his likes and dislikes. Is he much of a coffee drinker?"

"Yes, and this is his favorite roast. He always brings me some when he visits, just as he always brings Petey dried figs."

Oona bought coffee, a few figs for her helper, and a few spices for the house, but only what the few coins in her bag would cover. She also made mental notes for the future. This was indeed a fabulous shop, and one that, unknown to the proprietor or the ladies, was a forecaster for what Salem and all of the other Essex County harbor towns would soon become – the maritime capitals of the spice and China trades.

Petey was an excellent companion. He did not sit and fret, but opened the back door and ran into the small fruit orchard and explored, as little boys will do. His laughter as he slaughtered invisible enemies entertained Jason as he drifted in and out of the half-sleep he was getting used to. One time, when he was more awake than asleep, he decided to wake and assess his wounds.

He started with his sore abdomen. He touched his belly and jumped with the pain, but it did not seem to go too deep. No one had ordered a coffin or been heard sobbing, so there probably were no signs of internal injury. He'd heard Pete Senior say that his piss was yellow and not blood red.

That was good. His belly probably looked as purple and red as Oona's poor back had. But those wounds would not lead to death. Healing would take some time, but the wounds would heal.

He knew he could not open his eyes. He didn't know why, and he hadn't tried to ask because he could not use his voice. Lying absolutely still so as not to start the pounding in his head, he tried to use his voice. His first attempts were little more than croaks, but after what felt like hundreds of frog-like noises he was able to call softly for Petey. At first, the boy was too far away, so Jason waited till his play brought him closer to the house.

"Petey!"

"Hey Mr. FitzSim. You can talk?"

Jason had to hold his body very still. "Pete, why don't my eyes open? No one has said anything."

Petey came over and looked very carefully. Jason heard him moving in the room to look at him from new angles.

"I think they are swollen shut. That happened to one of the boys at school after a fight when one of the big fellows busted his face. He got better, though. I guess you will too."

Jason appreciated the child's honesty. He remembered that first afternoon, fighting back as the men pulled the dark bag over his head. He'd passed out then – maybe someone punched his face in that fight. Well, like his belly, that would heal too.

That made two bruised areas that were sure to heal if he did not die from whatever made his head hurt so damned badly. "Pete, could our chat be our secret? I don't want to fool anyone into thinking I can't talk, but I don't know if I will heal, and I don't want to give false hope."

"Sure, Mr. FitzSim. I can keep a secret." Petey moved to close and lock the storeroom door, ready to keep his adventures in the yard, and Jason's speech a secret.

Over the next days, things were delivered. Jason heard men scraping boxes and walking into the two front rooms and up the stairs. These bursts of activity occurred with some frequency. He supposed being disturbed by delivery men was almost as good as when Oona woke him, but not quite.

He had kept his promise to himself, and spoke only to young Petey when the boy came to keep him company. Most of the day Oona sat with him. She woke him gently, often kissing his lips and running cool fingers over his hair and face. She sponge-bathed him each morning before the men came by to help. He looked forward to Oona's bathing him. It was the highlight of each day. At first, he could not open his eyes and made no effort to talk. He just lay there enjoying her stories about her outings, and sometimes about her brothers and sisters in Ireland, or her early days in Boston. So not only did he discover that he was still very much alive and easily aroused by Oona's touch, he learned things about her he might never have learned.

After what must have been a week but felt like a lifetime, when Jason tried to open his eyes he saw his backroom. It was blurry. Even the dim light that came through the new curtains hurt his eyes. He closed them quickly. They might still be sore, but they worked. Over days, bit by bit, the blurriness went away. So did the pain in his belly, but the pounding in his head barely lessened.

Oona sat by the little window in Jason's sick room, hemming her new curtains. It was a bright October day, three weeks since they had brought the injured Jason home. He still had not spoken, opened his eyes, or moved in the bed on his own. But she could tell he was getting better. The pain that lived just behind his closed eyes had lessened, and he did not moan during the night the way he had. The purple bruises on his abdomen had faded, not festered.

She looked up from her work, as she often did, to rest her gaze on the sleeping Jason. As she watched, she saw his eyelids flutter and then open wide open for just a second. He did not see her, but seemed to stare briefly at the ceiling. Then they closed again, and he seemed to fall into a contented rest.

She tiptoed out of the room. She closed the door behind her and paced the floor in the shiny front hall. It was so like Jason not to burden her with his healing. She did not know if she should prod him to tell her what had healed and what had not. She would probably have to beg. If she begged, she was sure he would tell her. She also knew that Jason needed her to let him heal in his own way. But either way, she found the movement of his eyelids, and a momentary glance at his wonderful brown eyes, tremendously exciting.

She had twice written his brother John since their arrival in Salem. He knew that Jason had made it through the first week without worsening, and that Oona remained optimistic. She had also told him about her shopping for furniture and other domestic tidbits. She did not want the general's staff to know that the lieutenant had helped locals, even if they were family, so she drenched the letters in eau de violette. That way they would be presumed to be from a lover – not a sister-in-law. She knew he was going to tease her unmercifully for the cloying scent, but she could conceive of no other way to be sure the letters would get past a censor.

Listening to Oona's nervous pacing in the hall left Jason wondering what she had seen. He slowly turned his head to see what she had been doing by the window all afternoon. It was unlike her to be idle, and he had been curious since he'd started to awaken more often. This was the first time she had left her work behind. What he saw was yards of fabric being turned into curtains, like the ones that now hung at the window. So Oona had used this time, sitting here talking to him, to transform the house. He was sure he would be more than delighted with whatever she'd chosen.

He had dozed off again before Oona returned to her sewing. She sat and calmly finished her running hem. Then she went upstairs to get ready. It was one of the afternoons when Petey came by so she could go out for an hour. She came into the little storeroom as soon as she was dressed. Jason woke, strongly aware of Oona sitting close to him on the bed. The motion had not made his head pound, but he did not move.

"Jason," Oona spoke softly as she always did. "I have decided to host a dinner party. A letter has arrived from Elisha Appleton. He and his wife Martha are coming on the packet from Boston. They will be here next Thursday, October the nineteenth. They arrive in the morning, stay at the White Bird, and leave on the following morning. Elisha wrote that he understands how ill you have been, and they would not think to impose on us. He seemed to know all about your infirmities. His agent I suppose.

"The dinner party – I will invite the Daggettes, of course, and I will ask Claire whom else. I think Pete knows your friends. I wanted you to know, not to pressure you to get better suddenly, well I would if I could – I think. Well, silly of me, I guess." She kissed him, perhaps with more energy than she had before. Jason nearly reached for her, but he turned his head just too fast and was immediately punished with drumming that reminded him not to try. Oona left humming, full of plans, and Jason wanted to pound his own head into the wall in frustration.

The day after Oona took Jason on the packet home to Salem, Lieutenant Lord John FitzSimmon, wearing his red uniform, but with his own hair and without a hat, walked into the *Cromwell's Head Tavern*. Immediately conversation ceased, and all eyes turned toward him. He hated wearing the damn red coat when he went out for an evening, but he didn't want anyone to think he was spying. It was only fair to tell the locals what sort of fellow had just invaded their space.

He walked up to the tavern keeper, "Sir, I am not here in any official capacity. I would like a pint of your best ale," he put a crown on the table, "and I was wondering if you could help me find a man named Edward? I repeat, sir, this is not in any official capacity. When you see him" – he now spoke loudly enough to address the whole room – " tell him John FitzSimmon needs to speak to him. He knows who I am." A young man slid out of the small tavern room and ran down School Street. Pleased, John took a swallow of his draught.

"He'd rather not come into the *Head* just now. Follow me." The young man was at Simm's elbow. He'd reappeared while Simm was on his second pint, having nursed the first one very slowly. He followed the man down Milk Street to a dark alley, not far from the water. He opened a door in a wall that John was sure had no door, and ushered the lieutenant inside.

"John! Welcome, I hope finding out about this place

will not put you in danger."

"Thanks for your welcome, Edward. I trust all here know about the abduction and rescue?"

"As much as they need, but why are you interested, now that the man is safe, and healing, with God's help?"

"I want to find the men who hurt him. I have some plans for a sort of revenge."

"Interesting. Does the General know his staff has such ideas? Lieutenant, we will take care of the Morses – they crossed the line and put the town in danger. The Committee will see they are punished.

"Jason is my brother."

"And you were reunited here. Didn't know you'd find him in Boston, did you? Yes, I can see that in your face. And I thought my Mama raised interesting boys. What did you have in mind?"

"Friends of mine in the Navy find themselves in need of some strong young arms and backs. I was thinking your Morse boys might make good Navy men."

"Press gang, interesting form of punishment. And it gets them out of my hair." Edward stood and turned to another man who had been sitting very still, but paying close attention. The men spoke for a few minutes, then Edward turned back to John. "FitzSimmon, let me tell you how to find those boys. A few years in the British Navy will certainly teach them some manners. Maybe we'll get lucky and one of our privateers will blow them out of the water."

The men all laughed wryly at Edward's joke. The British Navy was still one of the most formidable forces on earth. American privateers were just beginning to get their sea legs, so to speak.

"Petey, we have to get me up and walking."

"Of course, Mr. FitzSim, is your head all better?"

Jason cringed with pain as he pushed his weak legs over the side of the bed. He put his feet on the floor. "No, Pete, I wish it were." He spoke through clenched teeth. "But I want you to help me stand; maybe being upright on my own will help my head." It can't make it much worse, he thought to himself.

Although it was barely successful that first day, Petey and Jason worked on Jason's balance until he could stand, walk, and finally join Petey for a stroll around the orchard. The pounding lessened, not immediately, but by the day of Oona's dinner party he'd be damned if he wasn't ready to surprise her.

"I won't move him upstairs and out of my way." Jason was awakened by an impassioned speech coming from the kitchen. He had meant to wake and dress in the clothes Oona placed in the corner for him each day, but after his walk with the men down to the harbor to view a new three-master that had just been launched, he had needed a nap. Now, he realized he'd completely missed Oona's dinner. It would be more polite, and safer from the sounds of it, to lie here with the door cautiously closed, than to appear like some sort of cheaply-timed resurrection. So he lay back; he couldn't help but overhear. It was clear that dinner was over, and the only people in the house were Oona and her solicitor, Elisha Appleton, perhaps his wife also. He heard only two voices.

"You should get some more help. Especially now that you have your money. There is no reason to be tied to a husband you barely know. For who knows how long."

"I know how it looks, but I know he is getting better. I can make this decision any time. For now, I must continue the way I am."

"Sleeping on the floor? Oona this is ridiculous."

"We need the space during the day, so there is no room for another bed. I am leaving that room the way it is."

"Then do as I say, and move the man upstairs."

Oona did not want, or feel the need to explain to Mr. Appleton that the men who came to care for Jason carried him into the sun on nice days, or that Petey ran in and out of that back door. Yes, she knew, and she thought it was fine. She also thought she heard Jason, or someone, go to use the privy when he was sure she was asleep or out. Jason had not spoken to her, but she was convinced the month had brought healing. She was not going to move him into a small room upstairs and away from her kitchen, the heartbeat of any house.

"Mr. Appleton, thank you so much for looking into my affairs and getting my rents. I truly thank you for your time. I will take what you suggest under advisement, though I don't see myself becoming one of those wives who take lovers because her husband is away or incapacitated, like someone suggested tonight."

"Well, Oona, my dear – you know I have always wanted the best for you. Your life has not been easy. Do what you must, and stay in touch please, will you?" he took her hand and kissed the back of it. "Good night, Oona dear. I will go back to the inn and join Martha."

"Good night, Mr. Appleton, thank you again." She walked him to the front door and closed it behind her, collapsing against it with weariness. She had her money. It had all been taken care of. A shipping agent with offices in Salem and London had been chosen to get the money to her in whatever form was possible, whenever they could. She would spend tomorrow seeing to all her debts at the various merchants. Then, she would seriously consider the rest of her life, but she would not move Jason upstairs and into a closet.

Jason heard Oona in the kitchen, and the sound of water buckets being brought upstairs. When it got quiet downstairs, he left his room to explore the house. It was interesting that he had not done so in the days he'd spent regaining his strength, preferring to wander the garden and feel the sun and wind. Also, he had not wanted to spy on Oona's work, but more than that he was not yet convinced he wouldn't collapse. He would rather be found dead in the orchard or herb garden than in the parlor. He felt strongly that this house was his gift to Oona, and he did not want her rooms to contain an echo of his death.

Convinced finally that he would not die, he wandered the dining room, front hall and parlors. Each was clean; polished with lemon oil, if his nose was working. There were heavy damask curtains on every window. And he would guess the glass was as clean and as dust free as the floors and the highest corners of the ceilings. It was a fine way for her to have worked out her nervous energy, but he would insist that she hire at least day help in the future.

The kitchen was a hungry man's dream. He had not yet eaten much solid food, so he did not want to overdo it, hungry as he was. He made a plate of the roast turkey with cranberries and corn cakes, and saved space in his shrunken stomach for the apple pie that was teasing him from under a plate. As he ate, he gauged the time it would take Oona to bathe. He did not want to startle her while she was relaxing after a difficult dinner, one she had needed to spend defending her life's choices. He understood very clearly what she had done, and he was awed by her love and caring.

Thought he was not surprised, he thought she might be.

Jason straightened the kitchen, washed down his dinner with cold, sweet cider, and steeled himself to go upstairs. He stopped at the foot of the stair, then chastised himself for lacking his usual energy and spontaneity. Not wanting to sneak, he did not take off his shoes or tiptoe as he climbed the stairs and approached the door to the biggest bedroom. It had been a warm evening, and the window was open, the wind blowing through Oona's hair as she brushed it dry. He had not noticed how short it was, and wondered when and why she had cut it. It did not matter. He wanted to be that brush, and be pulled through that thick, dark hair, no matter its length.

Oona felt, more than she saw, Jason standing at the door. She thought she had heard footfalls in the parlor, but it might have been one of the fellows who came to care for Jason. For the most part, she had tried not to interfere with them. It had been only fair, since they were kind and asked for nothing in return.

But now, Jason had climbed the stairs. He was standing so near. She took a deep breath, filling her lungs with the tangy autumn air and the scent of Jason. Then he was behind her, and taking the brush out of her hand. He finished her one hundred strokes. Then he reached around her and took the small jar of rosemary oil from the armoire. He poured a few drops onto his hands and lifted them to his own face. Then he rubbed his hands through her hair and deep into her scalp, releasing the fragrant herb into the room.

She turned and started to ask when, how, why – her mind was full of questions that didn't need answers. She looked at him in wonder. He had simply stopped looking ill. When had that happened? She had willed herself to look past his injuries, caring for him so completely that his death had remained an impossibility. In so doing, she must have blinded herself to his healing. Well, she told herself, she was indeed happily surprised. She didn't see how he had gotten the sun and wind in his cheeks. He had accused her of holding her secrets tight; perhaps they were more similar than she thought.

Jason sat on the rug in front of her chair. "Oona, my head hurt like there were drums pounding from the inside. I really thought I would die. I didn't mind if the men, or even if little Petey, thought I was improving but I died instead. Oona my love, I couldn't do that to you. I just couldn't. So I made them promise not to tell you I could stand, walk or even talk. Petey helped me the most – that youngster is a good man." He smiled at the thought of Petey, then he smiled at Oona, opening his arms to her.

Oona slid off her boudoir chair and down into Jason's arms. She curled into him. His smile was the most welcoming she had ever seen. There was a look of pure joy on his face, and his eyes had that wonderful wolfish glow. His joy at being alive was clear, but more clear was the sheer joy he showed as he looked into her clear, violet eyes. She closed them as he covered her mouth with his and she melted into his kiss.

"Only Jason kisses Oona," he murmured as he picked her up and carried her over to the elaborately carved bed with the new mattress and crisp linen sheets.

Afterward

"Johnny, come and sit, we've got your plate ready," Jason called upstairs to his brother. It was New Years, a Roman bacchanalia ignored and despised in traditional New England households. Simm had arrived directly from London on a merchant vessel. Dressed as a civilian, he was wearing the studiously unrefined clothing of an American merchant. He had sent his clerk off to Boston with their official correspondence, and had gone directly to Turner Street to see how his brother fared.

He had gotten many of Oona's lavender-scented notes before he left for Britain. At that point she was optimistic, but Jason had not yet opened his eyes or spoken. He assumed she had sent happier missives to his Boston address, but he had not been there to receive them. Now he was tremendously relieved to see his older brother in such good health and spirits.

"First, I want to toast you both for making it through 1775!" They raised their cups of good local ale. "Secondly, I want to toast the New Year and hope 1776 brings peace and prosperity to both Britain and America. And thirdly, I want to toast the new owners of FitzSimmon Shipping." He turned to his sister-in-law.

"Oona, the stock purchases went without a hitch. The brothers have no idea Jason and I have gained controlling interests in the company." He went over to his valise and returned with certificates showing that Oona McCloud now owned 40 percent of the shipping company, and Jason and John each owned 6 percent. "Oona, I want to thank you for lending me the money to buy my shares. I will repay you when I can."

Jason looked from his wife to his brother. "John, you just arrived. I know it has been a long trip, and not to be rude, but what are you talking about?"

"Oona and I discussed it last summer." John motioned for Oona to continue.

"Jason, when I discovered that I inherited stock in various companies, I wanted to make some changes, but not through Elisha Appleton. He wanted to get my rents and dividends, but disapproved of having his man sell and buy shares in British companies for me. So when I met John, I authorized him to use whatever legal means were necessary to get the controlling interest in FitzSimmon Shipping away from your brothers. From what you told me, they have no clear notion of how the world works. At least, not nearly as keenly as you and John.

"Nor you." Jason chimed in beginning to see what had gone on. He fairly glowed with pride in his wife.

"I'm afraid we tricked them. And I hope they don't hate us when they sort it out. You see, as far as they know, an angel investor showed up and gave them lots of money. A stranger named Oona McCloud, a friend of John's, bought shares, but not a controlling interest. And while he was there with a bit of cash, he bought six percent for each of you. What your brothers and brother-in-law don't know is that Oona McCloud is Mrs. Jason FitzSimmon, and that means their little brothers, John and Jason, now make a majority bloc."

Jason looked surprised, then his dark wolf streaks began to glow with delight, and he started to laugh. He grabbed the bottle and filled the three glasses. "A toast, to the new American-run FitzSimmon Shipping Company, and my own toast to 1776 – let it bring true liberty, and a healthy Oona, and a healthy, happy baby." He smiled at his wife, while it was John's chance to look surprised. "And Johnny, leave the hat when you leave in the morning – much as it looks great on you, I've missed that tricorn."

Oona, put down her glass. She was feeling safe and warm with John back safely, and Jason up and healthy again. Her plan had worked. Jason no longer needed to sail for others, and they would make Salem their home. She felt happier and stronger than she could have imagined. She turned to Jason, put her hands on the either side of his smiling face. His eyes pulled her to him and silently spoke his love. She leaned to him, put her lips on his, and kissed him for the New Year, and forever.

Dear Reader:

*W*hat has come to be called "the Boston Tea Party" was known at the time simply as "the destruction of the tea." In the small town of Boston, this was an event most people had hopes would blow over, or that Parliament would send a bill. No one expected the closure of the port or the other laws passed to punish the colony and town that have come to be called the Intolerable Acts. For more on the Tea Party itself, I recommend *The Defiance of the Patriots*, by Benjamin L. Carp, Yale University Press, 2010. Professor Carp explores everything there is to know about the tea trade and the destructors, and the aftermath. To understand the people who fled America, like Thomas Hutchinson and my fictional Goodiels, I recommend *Liberty's Exiles* by Maya Jasanoff, Alfred A. Knopf, 2011.

Oona and Jason, of course, were invented by me, but the terms of her indenture are based in real law. Most terms of indenture were for seven years, but in the case of children without parents, the term was longer. There were two reasons for this. The first was that the work done by a young child was not valued highly enough to pay off the indenture, and the second was that the indentured servant was not deemed mature enough to survive on his/her own if released from the indenture before adulthood. By the eighteenth century, the courts oversaw indenture very closely, especially in the New England colonies.

For day to day life in Boston, even the date of the big ice storm, I relied on the *Letters and Diary of John Rowe: Boston Merchant, 1759-1762, 1764-1779*, by Edward Lillie Pierce and John Rowe, edited by Anne Rowe Cunningham, W.B. Clarke Company, Boston, 1903 (reprinted on demand). Mr. Rowe was a well-known man of his time; today's Rowe's Wharf at Boston Harbor gives a good idea where his warehouse and ships were. As a man of considerable means, he was not allowed to take his goods out of Boston, and so, like Oona, he and his household stayed in the town for the entire occupation, and happily for me wrote daily in his diary.

I am sorry to say that I have no confirmation on the existence of a smuggling operation into Boston from Salem. But historians do know that there were outside efforts to get the people in the town fed, and as one major historian of the era said to me, "there is no reason to think there weren't smugglers."

And so, dear reader, I hope you have enjoyed reading Oona and Jason's story as much as I have enjoyed writing it. Please visit me at www. doryshistoricals. com for tidbits of real history and fictional romance.

*D*ory Codington is a student and teacher of history and sometime guide on Boston's historical Freedom Trail. Her primary interests lie in using historical references and her imagination to understand the daily lives of those who lived during significant periods in history. Dory currently lives in Massachusetts with a husband, a daughter, a son and a tortoise.

Edge of Empire books take place during America's Colonial, Provincial, and Revolutionary Periods. The *World Turned Upside Down* is the way many people in America, and Britain, felt about the outcome of the American Revolution. At the Yorktown surrender, Lord Cornwallis's troops stacked their muskets to a song by this name.

Books in the series are:
Cardinal Points
Beside Turning Water
Fate and Fair Winds

Other books by Dory:
Through the Eyes of a Poet: The Life and Writings of KateFort Codington

Visit **DorysHistoricals.com** for the latest news and historical tidbits.

Turn the page for an excerpt from
Beside Turning Water,
the second in the
Edge of Empire Series.

Beside Turning Water

Breed's Hill, Charlestown, Massachusetts, June 17, 1775

"Retreat!" The command was given and repeated as men moved back and out of the redoubts. Cool rain might have been welcome on this implausabily hot day, but the order was not. Most of the Continentals couldn't hear the command through the cannon fire and chaos, the blood-red haze of battle. It had been a day of heat, of successfully repelling two British assaults on the Americans dug in on Breed's Hill. That was before reality hit – they were simply out of everything – powder, musket shot, and really out of cannon balls. It was the third assault that was successful for the redcoats, causing chaos among the Americans and forcing their retreat.

The Continentals had, over the course of the long hot day, inflicted more damage than they themselves had suffered. The American riflemen, skilled at shooting vermin from afar, could see no reason not to aim at the bright red coats of the staff officers. So technically, the British won the Battle of Bunker's Hill, but it would go down in history as one of the worst single days for the British Army at war. In short, General William Howe's staff was decimated by what some had promised would be a ragtag bunch of farmers with old muskets and pitchforks, but instead had turned out to be local militias of undisciplined but skilled marksmen committed to a cause.

The General was not well-pleased, but he was not surprised. He had fought with these militias against the

356

French in the American wilderness. His brother George had died there, and was buried near Albany, New York. George Howe had been honored by the General Court of Massachusetts with a plaque in Westminster. The General gave up all notions of sympathy and called for his troops to charge the Americans, to work around them to the top of the hill – this was successful when the Americans' ammunition ran out.

Alex Peele moved backwards in the hastily constructed earthen redoubt. He had been in this spot since just after sunset the evening before. It had been a long night spent digging this hole with walls into Breed's Hill. The heat had struck with dawn, before the British Army had made their clumsy way across the bay, making June 17, 1775 the hottest day anyone could remember. Certainly it was damn hot on the open land of the cow pasture where they had chosen to take a stand.

The spring had been like that, cold in the morning of the famous ride to Concord and Lexington, and brutally hot during the British retreat. That had been just two months before, when the town militias had come out that April morning to defend their lands and liberties. Now militia groups from all over New England had come to help, to defend Boston from British efforts to control the countryside.

Alex was one of those who had come to help. He left his schoolroom and students as soon as he heard, and arrived at Cambridge in late April. The commander had taken one look at Thorne, his magnificent gray, and decided that horseflesh like that should not be left moldering in the stable. So Alex had been sent straight out as a messenger to the Congress in Philadelphia.

He'd gotten back to camp just in time to have been

357

handed his musket and told to join the New Hampshire regiment, the reinforcement for the Massachusetts regulars. They had held their position, shooting at every advancing contingent, succeeding in holding off attempt after attempt, until after their third attempt the British pushed through and the retreat order was given.

He had probably killed a dozen redcoats as they held their line before the ball found his leg. Now he was bleeding, and barely half aware of being dragged behind a dirt wall. He could hear the low wail of the cannons, he smelled gun powder, and other more disgusting things, that stuck to his sweat-soaked clothing and skin. Like every man on that hill, he was hot and he was thirsty. He was keenly aware of this discomfort, more than of the wound in his leg. He hadn't felt the musket ball tear into him, ripping his pant-leg and pushing the filthy linen deep into the wound. Later, the misshapen ball would be placed in a wooden box and locked away with the other souvenirs from his travels. Gathering his wits, he crawled forward with the retreat and collapsed into the man in front of him, finally losing consciousness.

So Alex, and the rest of General Artemis Ward's small army, lost the hills in Charlestown, a glacially-formed peninsula facing the Town of Boston. It had no real value other than for its clear spring and grazing cows. But the two hills rose over the larger town, making Bunker's or Breed's Hill strategically important. Charlestown was directly between American headquarters in Cambridge, and the British – blockading, occupying, and now suffering, in the water-locked Town of Boston.

The Americans' attempts to grab the high ground over Boston was the idea of Joseph Warren, head of the Committee of Safety and the Province's great leader. Now he lay dead, the most famous casualty of the afternoon.

Alex regained consciousness on the way back to Cambridge. He looked straight up into the bright blue of the June afternoon, and though it took a minute to realize that shouting men and hoofbeats did not belong in heaven, he understood that he was not dead. He was being moved away from the battlefield, but the man next to him on the wagon had a foul odor and most likely was. He dozed again, and woke in the field hospital set up near the college, the students having been removed west. He had a moment of sheer panic that they would take the leg, but someone pushed a bottle toward his lips, and after a swallow or two he found retreating to his own memories more pleasant.

He regained consciousness hours later on a dormitory cot. His head felt woolly and his leg throbbed. He touched it gingerly, hoping to feel flesh. The leg was there, swollen and aching miserably, but it was not ghost pain.

"Disgusting mess your breeches made of the wound. Sometimes well-made clothing is the very devil. We got all the damn threads out of there. Probably would have been faster to take the leg, but the ball missed the bone." The doctor sounded disappointed as he loomed over him, checking his forehead for fever. "I'll change the bandage in the morning. In a few days, barring fever, you can go recover in your own tent." True to his word, Alex was back to his own quarters by the end of the week.

For Alex, being infirm was nearly insufferable, but to be a Yale man immobile in a Harvard dormitory had its own indignities. He wished himself well, and by the second week in July, he was able to tag along as a passenger on a supply run to Braintree Harbor, to the south. The doctor, a Connecticut man, had recommended ocean swimming as a way to heal both the wound and the muscles.

359

Shipyard at Braintree Harbor, July 14, 1775

A lex climbed out of the water, shook himself off, and lazily dressed. Nothing would have been so nice as a nap on the warm sand. That was not going to happen, but the ocean swim had been good for both the weak muscles and the ragged scar. He vowed to swim in the river, given a chance in his schedule. It wouldn't have the healing properties of ocean water, but his leg would benefit from the swimming.

It had been a favor, this coming here early enough to get in a swim. His new friends had agreed to leave camp before dawn to give him time before the shipment arrived. He rubbed at his sore leg, a new habit that brought no pride. Above the strand he found a rock and sat. The wharf was busy now that it was full day. He watched as businesses and warehouses along the docks pulled back their shutters to the morning. The sandy beach on the side of the wharf was full of children running in and out of the cold water.

Lost in the warm sun and the lazy sounds of the ocean, Alex looked up as a horse whinnied. The fellow stood in the traces of a substantial wagon being loaded with heavy barrels, each one needing two workmen, who were carrying them from a small ship docked not far away. The men had been at it for a while, and they were building a sweat, though the early morning was not yet hot.

Alex moved onto an empty crate so he could put his

leg up onto a granite block. He was absently grateful for the perfect height between crate and rock. The wind blew off the harbor. Alex noted that it snatched some bits of conversation away, and amplified others. He took off his hat and let the wind dry his still-wet hair. Watching the men and their horse was a pleasant enough diversion, a way to pass the hour he and his colleagues would spend waiting for their ship. The *Cardinal* was late, so he would no doubt endure some ribbing that he had made them wake too early.

Alex had been happy to leave camp, and not just for the chance to swim. Prior to his wounding, he had not minded the disorder of the American camp at Cambridge. He accepted it as normal, and knew that chaos was what he could expect as an enlisted soldier, but since the injury he'd become less tolerant. He hoped the anxiety would pass with healing.

His fellows had chosen not to join him in the water and had gone into a small tavern for breakfast. Coats and musket balls, that was what was expected on the *Cardinal*. Considering the shape of the quartermaster's records, they would be lucky if it was a half shipment.

He was hungry. They had left camp before the ovens were warm. Smells from the tavern were good, but even the thought of hobbling the short distance was unpleasant. Sitting on this crate in the silence of sun and sea breezes was not. He enjoyed the bustle of shipyard activity, as he had when he first encountered it in New Haven. That young man, just arrived from the mountains of New Hampshire, seemed so alien to him now, but the fascination for the ordered chaos remained, no matter where he was. He had seen the same on his travels to London, Naples, Greece and Istanbul. But now, just beyond his hearing, another scene unfolded. He watched it with pleasure, since it involved a rather pretty young blonde.

361

The blonde's face, from what he could see under a pleasing straw bonnet, was tightly drawn, showing frustration as she tried to explain something to the local cooper. Alex could not hear the words, so he allowed himself the luxury of silent eavesdropping. They seemed to be having an argument. The blonde gestured again and again, pointing to the man's barrels. Alex heard a squawk of anger. He wondered if he would go over to help if his leg were stronger. It was none of his business, but the maiden did seem to be in distress. His instinct was to rescue such a fairy-tale blonde. Unfortunately, the aching leg telegraphed that he remain where he was. The sun had moved, and he now sat in the shade of the chestnut that grew upland of the beach. There was no reason now to leave his perch. Yes, it was rude to watch so closely, but since he'd been shot, he had had so little fun, and the blonde was so very nice to look at. Besides, he knew he would help if the man moved to hurt her.

***

Nina Bigelow was not shaded by anything more than a flat straw bonnet that was trying to fly off like one of those screaming sea gulls. It had not been an easy few months, and she was tired of Mr. Jones' excuses for not supplying new barrels or coming to the *Wheel and Hammer* to fix old ones.

"Mr. Jones, the *Wheel* has been buying your barrels for years, decades even. My father-in-law these past thirty and probably the Bigelows before that. I think it very wrong of you to ignore my needs." Nina bit her tongue, holding back her words. She was already known as "the alewife," and she didn't want to vent all her frustrations on this one older man.

It was not his fault if the maltster she had known since she had come to work at the *Wheel* patently refused to sell to

362

anyone in the countryside, preferring to stay in town and supply the British. It was not Mr. Jones's fault that she wanted new gowns and her modiste was trapped at her shop with her goods. Marianne wrote that she could get a pass to leave, but her fabrics and notions had to stay behind. So she had remained in Boston, taking care of the wives and mistresses of the officers who had moved in over the past year.

Nor was it his fault that Newton, along with every other town in the Province, had agreed four years ago not to import or wear British-made goods, so everything felt old and tired, even before the British blockaded Boston. Nina could brew good ale from apples and pumpkins, maybe even rocks, but she could not make window glass, plates or mugs. It was also true that she could not sew, or make or remake, anything more than an apron, and the most utilitarian one at that.

If times were normal, she would find another cooper. But times were not normal. Too many local shipyards had closed, and the coopering with them. Mr. Jones had relocated from Boston months ago, and she had only yesterday uncovered his new location.

"Please, Mr. Jones?"

It was her brother David who discovered that Mr. Jones had set up shop at Braintree. David, the owner of a sawmill used by the shipyard for some of their lumber, found out only in casual conversation, and passed the information on to his sister. Nina had come to the shipyard as soon as she could, bringing David's son Davy, and her own young Jack. The boys had considered the short journey south a fine adventure, and were spending the warm, sunny morning, exploring the tidepools that flourished beyond the yard, but not quite out of sight. Though they both swam well

363

and would stay together, she had made that one demand.

It took one more footstamp, but at last Mr. Jones, of Jones's Coopering, agreed to whatever the forceful lady was requesting. He lifted his chin and retreated back into his small shop. Alex nodded his approval. The removal of the gruff old man had improved the scenery nicely. He watched as gusts off the ocean pulled at her hat, revealing a mop cap and pale blond hair that looked too fine and silky not to jump and fly out of pins and ribbons.

The blonde was dressed in a plain blue vest, pinned in front, and a striped skirt of the same color – the plainest of clothing. No doubt she was a servant and these were her best clothes. But the tilt of her chin and her forceful behavior with the cooper said that was not so. Perhaps she dressed plainly as a uniform of sorts. She did seem to have a relationship with the cooper. She might be a maid, or the wife of the local fish monger putting pickled herring into barrels.

Alex felt he had almost puzzled it out, and then chided himself to stop this fancy. It was a bad habit of his, filling in make-believe stories with facts he had no business collecting. It had been a hobby of his since childhood. He did it rarely now, or it had been rare until that musket ball had forced him to sit still. As a boy, his family had become used to it and left him alone, always aware that he might piece together their private dealings and learn more than he ought. He had learned early not to let on what he'd learned. Often it was false, but too often it was true.

It was mostly innocent, and he liked to see how close he could come to the truth through observation alone. He had vowed, as a boy, that he would never read letters or diaries. Such activities did not amuse him, even if reading private things had been moral by any standard. No, Alex got

364

his information by simple watching.

After the cooper went back into his shop, the pretty blonde, as he had named her, waved at the two boys at the water's edge jumping in the waves. They hollered back acknowledging her, but made no effort to join her. Alex was surprised when she laughed at their antics, seeming to enjoy their fun instead of insisting they return. Clearly she was not in charge of their welfare. Maybe they were all servants in the same household.

She went to her small cart to put her hat and cap under the seat, out of the wind, walking the cart horse to the trough to let her drink. She spoke to the horse and petted her neck, but he couldn't catch the one-sided conversation. Alex pulled out a piece of wood he had been carving and contemplated the work. He looked up again as she turned back toward the water to watch the boys. Without cap or hat, the strands of her hair caught the light and danced in the wind. He sighed at the sight.

Alex considered himself an expert on women's hair and its color. It wasn't a topic that came up in ordinary conversation. Still, he marveled at the dark richness and airy lightness of different women's hair and how each styled it. Occasionally, he'd had the opportunity to remove ribbons and pins, and feel the various textures as well. The pretty blonde's hair, now floating out of her reach, was unusually pale. It would be false to call it colorless – it was, in fact, pale honey streaked with dark, rich hues. The effect was stunning.

Alex turned to see if the *Cardinal* had arrived. His cohorts were still not on the dock. There was no reason to leave the shade or his comfortable crate. He forced himself not to look back at the blonde. She was bound to feel eyes on her and he'd hate to make false excuses; he'd been having such a pleasant morning.

365

She moved toward the big tree, almost sharing his shade. She turned again to watch the boys, clearly not yet anxious to leave. She leaned back against a boulder. Alex knew something about boys, having been one and taught more than a few. The older boy was thirteen, maybe fourteen. The younger one was smaller, no more than ten, maybe even a tall nine. The three had a remote family resemblance, a few features in common. The younger boy had her hair, pulled at this instant into an untidy queue, but he was too old to be hers. They might all be cousins, at the harbor for their errand, much like he was.

The blonde could be no more than twenty-six; he thought closer to twenty-five. He supposed a woman that age might have a child the age of the younger boy. But in his experience, if that were the case, there would be others, probably many others, all playing in the waves. He imagined the blonde, the mother of a happy family, babes in arms playing at the ocean's edge. He felt a tightening in his breeches and his leg wound pulled uncomfortably, reminding him that thoughts of pretty women and children were painful, and could not be his.

Nina felt appreciative eyes on her. It wasn't a new feeling; in fact there were times when it seemed like that was all she felt. At the *Wheel and Hammer*, a tavern at the Lower Falls of the Charles River, she expected it. She had always supposed it came with being a young woman working in a busy taproom. Most times she ignored the looker, and he'd become interested in something or someone else, usually one of the young tavern maids. He would turn away, and the feeling would stop. But the sense of being watched by the man under that spreading chestnut, sitting on the wooden crate with that interested look on his face and his longish, dark, ash-brown hair, didn't go away even when he turned. It

366

was as though his concentration never wavered, even when he looked elsewhere. Mostly he hadn't tried to hide that he was following her with his eyes. At least he hadn't come over to say something ridiculous.

To acknowledge that she knew he had been watching her, she turned, nodded and smiled at him, thinking as she did that she would have tipped her hat if she had been wearing it. She had expected him to turn away embarrassed, but instead he grinned back at her, bright humor glowing in soft gray eyes as he returned her look. She giggled, happy that the wind whisked the sound away.

Alex wasn't surprised that his pretty blonde lady had a lovely smile. He appreciated that she hadn't come over to slap him across the face for being impertinent. She seemed to take being stared at in stride. He gave her credit for having a sense of humor. Most women, he knew, didn't.

Her smile was lovely, and the accompanying laugh chased away all the tension from those thoughtful blue-green eyes. It was one of those smiles and laughs that seemed conjured up solely for the recipient. Alex sensed he'd been extraordinarily lucky enough to have that smile bestowed on him just then, as though he had been granted a rare gift.

The pleasant reverie of the sunny morning broke when a barrel, falling from its precipitous perch on the end of the workmen's cart, made a loud, jarring sound. The men had gone into the tavern, and when their horse shied at a far away cry and stepped backward, a barrel shifted and fell. Alex jumped at the noise and watched it begin to roll down the slight incline. At that angle it was sure to roll harmlessly past the tree and down the hill toward the flat beach.

The small barrel gathered speed, which was not really

a concern, but it changed course when it ran over a ditch and hit a small rock. Alex registered that it was very heavy, probably filled with nails from the nearby pig iron mill in Weymouth. The blonde, for whom he had no other name, stood in the trajectory of the barrel. She had turned back to the boys, and she strained to hear what the older one had shouted. It only took seconds, but Alex wasn't going to wait to see if the blonde noticed the damn barrel. It would break her legs when it hit. It was that heavy.

Nina started at the sound of the heavy barrel rolling directly at her. It rolled unevenly as its heavy load shifted inside. She knew she ought to jump, to move, but there was nowhere to go.

Terror struck. She could not move back into a granite boulder, could not have even if the rock had opened a magical door right next to her. Her feet were frozen to the spot. She shook her head "no" when the man shouted at her to move. She closed her eyes, hoping the horrible pain would be brief and praying that someone would bring the boys back to her brother.

The last thing Alex saw before he launched was the blonde shake her head and close her eyes. He propelled himself from his spot, stepping onto his good leg. He winced as he pushed, putting his weight on his injured right leg. He grabbed her around the waist and pushed off back to his original spot, keeping his weight on his left leg. He tried to balance, but the trajectory and extra weight of the blonde was too much. He put his right foot down to get his balance, but it crumpled beneath him as he knew it would. He fell backward onto a pile of leftover sail parts and bits of wood, pulling her on top of him, and knocking the wind out of him. A part of his mind acknowledged that the stitches in his leg had opened and he was probably bleeding.

368

Nina waited for the agony of the barrel hitting and crushing her legs, for the noise of bones snapping. She heard the barrel crash, and the sound of loose metal scattering over stone. She wiggled her toes, but pain did not come. Her breathing eased, and as she became aware of where she was, she realized she was lying in a pile of broken floorboards and sailcloth. She didn't know if it was better or worse, but she was on top of the man who had been watching her, and had grinned that silly grin at her – the man with the thick brown hair and laughing gray eyes. He had pulled her away from the rolling barrel, and it seemed she was lying on him, his arms holding her tightly.

She took a deep breath, taking a moment to let her head stop swimming, her heart stop pounding, and the taste of fear in her mouth go away. She closed her eyes and forced her breathing to slow. The man had not moved. Maybe he had injured himself saving her. She hoped not. Most likely he was in shock, and would get up in a moment.

Nina could not be found lying on top of a strange man, any man for that matter, no matter the circumstance of their meeting. She needed to stand, curtsy, and say a gracious "thank you." She needed to get the boys and rush away. She needed to open her eyes. She could not be seen lying on a man in a shipyard!

The gray-eyed man didn't seem to notice he was holding her in place. He hadn't yet moved or spoken. Pressed against him, she could feel every inch of him. It was most disturbing. He had not yet loosened his grasp – in fact, he was holding her very tightly in strong arms. She tried to lift herself up, but his grip was too strong. She wanted to get up and move away, but that would require opening her eyes. She was not ready for that. Really, it felt very safe here under these sails.

Nina wiggled her hips, finally trying to squirm away or

369

get him to relax his arms. It did not work. She heard him moan in pain. She might have hurt him further. She stopped concentrating on her escape and sought to discover where he was hurt. "Have you hurt your head?" He didn't answer. She put her hands into his hair to feel his scalp, to hunt for a bump or a wound. Running her hands slowly through his hair and over his scalp, Nina was relieved to find there was no wet blood, and no large bump on his head, but he did moan again.

The leg was a low dull ache that Alex chose to ignore. He was dreaming that he was holding the pretty blonde in his arms, her body stretched over his, her firm breasts pushed against him while she moved her hips over his, her hands seductively in his hair. He moaned with pleasure. He breathed in her scent. It was unusual, and he didn't think that was because he had not been with a woman recently. If he was right, it was the smell of hops and ale. He knew he was dreaming. He'd had a good life, but a luscious body pressed against his, who smelled flowery clean, and of good ale? He must have hit his head, or died and gone to heaven.

He was proven alive when she spoke. It was barely understandable, and then she pushed strong fingers against his scalp and through his hair. He felt his heartbeat quicken and his body warm.

Slowly, awareness increased. The memory of what had happened hit him in a flash. He was mildly embarrassed to find that he was almost fully aroused – only mildly, as it had been a delicious few minutes, a wonderful dream. He shifted his hips away from the woman lying fully over him. He opened his eyes. Hers were staring back at him, pools of blues and greens, so much like the joint colors of sky and sea. A perfect way to remember this unusual day.

Her eyes showed concern. It felt unique to have anyone

worry about him, sweet but unwanted. So, as much as he would have loved to hold her in his arms for a few minutes longer, he forced them apart. In seconds she was up, turning away from him, pushing down her skirts and fixing her short bodice. She looked up and smiled that magic smile at him. "Thank you for your quick thinking. You are unhurt?"

"Thank you, Mistress. Yes, I am fine, and you are very welcome. I am happy that you are unhurt." His voice was as lovely as the rest of him.

"Well," she pulled herself out of the reverie, "thank you again, goodbye." She gave a sort of desperate look in his direction, as if she wasn't sure what was supposed to happen next. Then she turned and ran down the beach to the boys. The little group of pale heads walked up the little hill to their wagon. The boys hitched the giant horse to the trace, and the three climbed onto the bench and, with the crack of her whip, they were gone.

Alex watched the little group drive away. He was relieved to have saved her, and honestly could not regret his leg collapsing or having her lounged for a moment on top of him. She truly had been a delightful armful.

He turned to wave at the wagon as they rode off. The pretty blonde – he would always remember her by that name – actually lifted her foolish bonnet in his direction. Then, just as suddenly, she plopped it back onto her head. The boy next to her took the reins, while she tied the ribbon and pinned it securely in place.

Nina had felt a deep blush from her eyebrows to her toes. It began that moment when the brown haired man's arms relaxed, and she had opened her eyes and gazed into the deepest, most lovely soft-gray eyes she had ever seen. Not finding any wounds on the back of his head, she'd insisted to herself that she had to keep checking. The truth

371

was, she found his thick, wavy hair irresistible. It smelled like fire and horse and some faint cologne he might occasionally use. It was shiny brown, like the sun glinting off winter trees. It was the same color as a nut ale her father-in-law had brewed, that time someone had brought Italian walnuts as a gift.

Nina was not naive. She knew what her thrashing, and running her hands through his hair, had accidentally done to his body. She was embarrassed to have made him uncomfortable, when he had been so kind as to save her from certain death. It would have been rude to point it out to him by apologizing. She had simply thanked him. She had been in the same uncomfortable state, being trapped in his strong arms, his firm body beneath hers. She understood how uncomfortable and unpleasant such reactions could be. Nina pushed these thoughts out of her head, yet the memory of his scent, the feel of that thick hair, and his small moans, stubbornly would not leave.

During the two hours in the wagon, she told herself that she had wanted that grey-eyed man to loosen his arms and let her go. She scolded herself that she could not possibly have enjoyed feeling a man's hard body under hers, that she felt sorry about his arousal, and had not been aroused herself in response. She let the boys chatter about everything they had seen and heard at the beach, not hearing a word.

She knew that later, alone in her bed, these tingly feelings would come back. She didn't like them. They made her uncomfortable, and she didn't want to be uncomfortable like that, not ever again. She had been married once. She didn't want to marry again. She would let the incident fade in her memory until she could forget it. In time, she would forget the man with the gray eyes – forget how strong he'd felt, how safe she'd felt in his arms. Even if that were not the case, she would never see that man again.

Near her own home, they stopped at her brother's sawmill to drop Davy. A large man appeared out of the workshop. He was followed by two little girls and a dark-haired lady with a big basket.

Nina waved hello while the boys jumped out of the wagon and ran toward their fort in the dark hemlock forest. After exchanging pleasantries, she had a private word with her brother.

"David, you should come with us to the wedding tomorrow. It won't take but the middle of the day. You know that Natalie would love to see everyone. Father should have at least a glimpse of Davy and the girls." By then, they had walked up the hill for a basket lunch under a giant oak. The little girls raced off after their brother with their mother following, a hawk's eye on her twins.

David Tyrie had the muscles of the sawmill owner, operator, and carpenter. He was a darker version of his little sister, having the same dark blond hair without the nearly white streaks, his eyes a dark brown where hers were sea green and the blue of a summer sky.

"I'm surprised you want to see the old fool, let alone let him at Jackie." David huffed away, feigning to leave the picnic and go back to his work.

"David, he is old. Should we stay angry at him for the rest of his life?" Nina's raised voice followed David. She looked to Natalie, who shrugged.

"Maybe not at anything so public as a wedding, Nina. I will try to get over there soon." Natalie got up and ran after her daughters, who were pretending to cry that their brother and cousin would not let them into the fort.

373

Later, as she mounted the wagon for the short drive along the river, her brother came out of his workshop. He leaned into her. "Nina, I love you. How often has it been that you and I are all we have? If you want to put yourself in direct fire by going to that wedding, you'll have to do it yourself. Natalie supports my decision – she doesn't want Davy and the babies hurt by their grandfather. You say he has changed, but I don't believe it, and I won't find out I'm right at someone's wedding. You know as well as I, he's as likely to pronounce the lot of us as 'lost beyond redemption' as he ever was."

"He can't be that bad. He can't." Nina mumbled the words under her breath. She was tired, it had been a long morning, and it would be a busy night at the *Wheel*. "Dave, tell Jackie to come home by dinner. I need to go." She got back into her small wagon, *ghe'ed* at the horse and drove the two miles down to the Lower Falls.

The *Wheel* was already busy though the sun was still high in the sky. Sukey and Dodi were serving the men from the forge across the road who wandered in as they finished their work, and those travelers who stopped to eat and rest their horses. Those were the regulars – easily identified workers and travelers. There was also a new group that had begun to come to the tavern in increasing numbers and regularity. They were the mounted troops from Washington's army at Cambridge. It had started when a horseman noticed that the distance from camp to the Lower Falls was just long enough to give the horses a good workout, but not so far as to tire them. So while the men ate and drank their fill, their horses grazed on grass kept soft and green by the spray from the falls.

Nina surveyed the taproom. It was well under control. Going to her house for a change of clothes, she took a

374

minute to wash before reappearing to take her place as proprietress and chief brewer at the little tavern and inn. She laughed that what she called her work-clothes were so much finer than her day wear. The reverse was more common, but she'd found that evenings moved more smoothly if she dressed as a woman of substance.